An Einstein-Chaplin Thriller

MIDNIGHT BURNING

PAUL LEVINE

ALSO BY PAUL LEVINE

JAKE LASSITER SERIES
To Speak for the Dead
Night Vision
False Dawn
Mortal Sin
Riptide
Fool Me Twice
Flesh & Bones
Lassiter
Last Chance Lassiter
State vs. Lassiter
Cheater's Game
Early Grave

SOLOMON vs. LORD SERIES
Solomon vs. Lord
The Deep Blue Alibi
Kill All the Lawyers
Habeas Porpoise

LASSITER, SOLOMON & LORD SERIES
Bum Rap
Bum Luck
Bum Deal

STAND-ALONE THRILLERS
Illegal
Ballistic
Paydirt
Impact

PRAISE FOR PAUL LEVINE

"Take one part John Grisham, two parts Carl Hiaasen, throw in a dash of John D. MacDonald, and voilà, you've got Jake Lassiter."
—*Tulsa World*

"Jake Lassiter is great fun." - New York Times Book Review

"Lively entertainment. Lassiter is attractive, funny, savvy, and brave."—*Chicago Tribune*

"Mystery writing at its very, very best."—*USA Today*

"Jake Lassiter is the lawyer we all want on our side, and on the page." —*Lee Child*

"Remarkably fresh and original with characters you can't help loving and sparkling dialogue that echoes the Hepburn-Tracy screwball comedies. A hilarious, touching and entertaining twist on the legal thriller." – Chicago Sun-Times

"Breathlessly exciting."—*Cleveland Plain Dealer*

"A thriller as fast as the wind…a bracing rush, as breathtaking as hitting the Gulf waters on a chill December morning."
—*Tampa Tribune*

"A lively and skilled caper…one of the best mysteries of the year."
—*Los Angeles Times*

"Clever, funny and seriously on point. Top-notch stuff from Paul Levine. His Jake Lassiter is my kind of lawyer."
—Michael Connelly

"One of the best legal thrillers of the 21st Century."
—BestThrillers.com

"Levine's writing sparkles."—*The (London) Times*

"Cracking good action mystery…funny, sardonic, and fast paced."
—Detroit Free Press

"A blend of raucous humor and high adventure…wildly entertaining."—*St. Louis Post Dispatch*

"Paul Levine is one of Florida's great writers, and Lassiter is his greatest creation. Funny, smart, and compelling."—Dave Barry

"Filled with smart writing and smart remarks…Jake is well on his way to becoming a star in the field of detective fiction."
—Dallas Morning News

"The most dangerous detective liaison since Sam Spade and Brigid O'Shaughnessy tangoed in The Maltese Falcon."
—Charlotte News & Observer

"The legal excellence of a Grisham thriller with the highwire antics of Carl Hiaasen."—David Morrell

"Levine's prose gets leaner, meaner, better with every book… And Jake Lassiter has a lot more charisma than Perry Mason ever did."—*Miami Herald*

"Another enjoyable, breathless thriller."
—*Oline Cogdill, South Florida Sun-Sentinel*

"Filled with smart writing and smart remarks."
—*Dallas Morning News*

"A sexy, wacky, wonderful thriller with humor and heart."
—*Harlan Coben*

"The writing makes me think of Janet Evanovich out to dinner with John Grisham." —*MysteryLovers.com*

"Since Robert Parker is no longer with us, I'm nominating Levine for an award as best writer of dialogue in the grit-lit genre." —*San Jose Mercury News*

"Bum Deal is the real deal. Jake Lassiter at his smart-talking, fast-thinking best. A funny, compelling and canny courtroom thriller, seasoned with a little melancholy and a lot of inside knowledge." —*Scott Turow*

"Hiaasen meets Grisham in the court of last retort. A sexy, wacky, wonderful thriller with humor and heart." —*Harlan Coben*

"Solomon vs. Lord is a comic romp, a romance, a legal thriller, and a mystery, all written with heart and warmth and wit, razor-sharp dialogue, colorful memorable characters and a more than generous amount of genuine emotion." —*Oakland (MI) Press*

"Some of the juiciest and funniest lingo I've read in a thriller in a long time." —*Connecticut Post*

An Einstein-Chaplin Thriller

MIDNIGHT BURNING

PAUL LEVINE

Blank Slate Press | Harrisonville, Missouri

Blank Slate Press
Harrisonville, MO 64701

Copyright © 2025 Paul J. Levine
All rights reserved.

Publisher's Note: This book is a work of the imagination. Names, characters, places, and incidents either are products of the author's imagination or are used fictitiously. While some of the characters and incidents portrayed here can be found in historical or contemporary accounts, they have been altered and rearranged by the author to suit the strict purposes of storytelling. The book should be read solely as a work of fiction.

Without in any way limiting the author's and publisher's exclusive rights under copyright, any use of this publication to "train" generative artificial intelligence (AI) technologies to generate text is expressly prohibited. The author reserves all rights to license uses of this work for generative AI training and development of machine learning language models.

For information, contact:
Blank Slate Press
www.amphoraepublishing.com
Blank Slate Press is an imprint of
Amphorae Publishing Group, LLC
www.amphoraepublishing.com

Manufactured in the United States of America
Cover Illustration by Stephen Blue | Cover Design by Asya Blue Design
Set in Adobe Caslon Pro, TT Modernoir, and Amandine

Library of Congress Control Number: 2025932440
ISBN: 9781943075966

For Kimberley Cameron—
fierce advocate, steadfast friend, and agent extraordinaire.

"I'm a citizen of the world and a patriot to humanity."
—Charlie Chaplin, when asked why he hadn't become an American citizen

"The world is a dangerous place, not because of the people who are evil, but because of the people who don't do anything about it."
—Albert Einstein

"The victor will never be asked if he told the truth."
—Adolf Hitler

1

I CAN SEE NOW

January 30, 1931
Sixth and Broadway, Downtown Los Angeles

Stylishly clad in tailored tuxedos, the two most famous men in the world stepped out of a Rolls-Royce limousine and waved to a joyous crowd. The throng surged forward, a tidal wave of twenty-five thousand souls crashing toward the overwhelmed police lines.

"Smile, Albert," Charlie Chaplin said. "You look terrified."

"No more so than the Hebrews pursued by Pharaoh to the sea," Albert Einstein said.

Flashbulbs popped. Women screamed. Men shouted "Huzzah!" Klieg lights swept across the Corinthian columns that towered above the theater marquee, which read: WORLD PREMIERE CHARLIE CHAPLIN IN "CITY LIGHTS." Policemen escorted the two men into the opulent movie palace, past the three-tiered fountain in the lobby, beneath an ornate chandelier, up the grand staircase to the mezzanine to their seats in a cantilevered box close to the stage and screen.

With the lights not yet dimmed, the orchestra struck up the musical score. On its feet, the audience turned toward the mezzanine and applauded. Once again, both men waved, Chaplin smiling broadly. At forty-one, with a chiseled jaw and silver-streaked hair, he was movie-star handsome, looking nothing like the bedraggled Tramp of his films.

Einstein's face flushed with embarrassment. The applause was not for him, and basking in its glow he felt like an imposter. At fifty-one, he sported a bushy mustache and wild, wiry, white hair that looked as if he'd jammed a finger into an electrical outlet. Though he still lived in Berlin, he was wintering in California while he lectured at Caltech, enjoying the celebrity that accompanied his theories of relativity, which had turned the world upside down. A few weeks earlier, when asked who he wanted to meet in Los Angeles, he mentioned only one name: Charlie Chaplin.

"What I most admire about your art," Einstein said over the applause, "is its universality. You don't say a word, yet the world understands you!"

"But your achievements are greater," Chaplin replied. "The whole world admires you, even though nobody understands a word of what you say."

Einstein laughed, the lights dimmed, and the projector rolled. Einstein sat transfixed, emotions churning, as the Tramp, smitten with a blind flower girl, endured derision, beatings, and prison to pay for the operation that would restore her sight. Believing all along that a wealthy man had been her benefactor, she finally realized in the last scene that the Tramp was her angel.

"You can see now?" the Tramp asks, via title cards on the screen.

"Yes, I can see now," she replies, wistfully.

A line steeped in deeper meanings, Einstein thought.

She sees the goodness in a man others scorned as downtrodden and undeserving of respect. She sees the power of his love and sacrifice for her. His compassion has enlightened her even more than the surgery.

Einstein wiped away tears as the screen faded to black. "Oh, Charlie, the humanity of your art," he whispered. "I've never cried at a comedy before."

"If you hadn't cried," Chaplin said, "I'm not sure we could be friends."

As the audience applauded and cheered yet again, Einstein clasped a hand on Chaplin's shoulder. "Charlie, we shall be friends for a very long time."

☞ ☜

William Dudley Pelley, a screenwriter who had penned two Lon Chaney pictures but whose career had stalled like traffic at Hollywood and Vine, had neither laughed nor cried. From his perch in the second balcony, he scratched his graying mustache and silently fumed. *City Lights* was sappy—typical Chaplin pablum for the masses—and as for that rumpus in the street, slavish hero worship.

Chaplin's a lucky duck, and life ain't fair.

Both Pelley and Chaplin were born storytellers who had been raised in poverty. But Chaplin was a millionaire, and Pelley ate beans from a can. As the audience filed out of the theater, still buzzing with excitement, Pelley analyzed the picture.

So what's your theme, Chaplin? That self-sacrifice is admirable, and good deeds are their own reward? Poppycock!

Pelley imagined himself a man of power and fortitude, so at odds with the Tramp's empathy and tenderness. He believed he was destined for greatness but, at forty, knew that time was running short.

I ain't bellyaching. I just need a cause.

He pictured mobs in the street, not enthralled by maudlin sentimentality but by righteous convictions. His followers would chant his name in reverence, would march under his banner.

He made a vow.

I will be a leader of men, and my glory will exceed Chaplin's wildest dreams.

2
WHO WE GONNA KILL?

May 4, 1937
Santa Monica Mountains

The sign on the sheriff's office read, DUSTY CREEK, ARIZONA. True, there was plenty of dust but no creek, and Arizona was three hundred miles away.

The saloon, hotel, and general store were flimsy wood facades. The town was as phony as a politician's promise, a gigolo's smile, a mortician's sympathy.

Welcome to the Paramount Movie Ranch in the Santa Monica Mountains north of Malibu, California. A forlorn and forgotten donkey stood in the street outside the make-believe assayer's office, as if waiting to be loaded with saddlebags of gold. Otherwise, the mythical town was empty and as silent as the films shot there.

Half a mile up a gentle slope, a dozen men huddled in a clearing behind a stand of laurel bay trees. In the center of the group was William Dudley Pelley, who appraised them like an auctioneer at a cattle sale. The men were tall and short, fit and fat, smart and *dummkopfs*. All were Caucasian and untrained as soldiers, except for a few of the older ones who'd fought in the Great War. No obvious losers, misfits, or poseurs.

Or FBI agents, not that J. Edgar Hoover gave a hoot, as long as Pelley's troops targeted communists and not Republicans.

"Welcome to the new world order," Pelley said to the group. "Not the world of Franklin Delano Rosen-*stein*. Or the Wall Street bankers or the Brits, or the scum-of-the-earth immigrants who infest our cities, despoil our daughters, and steal our jobs."

The men mumbled their agreement. They wore corduroy trousers, blue ties, and silver shirts with epaulets. Sewn over the heart on each shirt was a large, embroidered *L*, the color of blood, signifying the Silver Legion of America, Pelley's homegrown paramilitary. "Silver Shirts," the newspapers called them.

Two men stood out among today's recruits: Skowron and Zorn.

Skowron was in his late thirties. Thick neck. Hands like grappling hooks. A scarred face, as if he'd escaped prison headfirst through barbed wire. A prizefighter's smashed nose and the tattoo of an anchor on his neck.

About forty, Zorn was a husky, scowling fellow with one cauliflower ear, two missing front teeth, and the neck of a Brahman bull.

Pelley sensed that both men had moxie to spare.

A thousand like Skowron and Zorn. Oh, the torches I could light!

At forty-seven, Pelley had a gunmetal gray mustache and Vandyke beard that was trimmed to a sharp point, giving him an unfortunate resemblance to popular images of Satan. In his white jodhpurs tucked into knee-high black leather boots with a riding crop in one hand, he might be taken for an English gent, readying the hounds for a jolly good fox hunt.

"Some call you the 'American Hitler,'" a newspaper reporter had baited him several weeks earlier. "Are you comfortable with that?"

"I stand deep in the Führer's shadow," Pelley answered, "but if others should say it, I shall not tell them nay."

The *Los Angeles Times* headline had read, AMERICAN FASCIST RECRUITS WHITE CHRISTIANS FOR HIS CAUSE. Other than the phrase "Nazi copycats," which Pelley found insulting, the story was dandy and brought several hundred new men to the meeting hall at Alt Heidelberg.

Now Pelley jabbed his riding crop into the chest of a pudgy man in his late twenties with a receding blond hairline. "Eckart!"

"Yes, sir!"

"Eckart, can you kill?"

Theatrics, a tactic of the Führer himself.

"I…I can kill," Eckart squeaked.

"Have you killed?"

Eckart grabbed the seat of his pants and pulled his undershorts out of his butt crack, nervous as a schoolboy facing a bully. "I've shot rabbits, sir."

"Rabbits, eh? You'll find that Jews aren't as quick."

So much work to do, but Pelley was undeterred. The strength of his will, unyielding as a slab of granite, could shape this butterball into a fighting machine. He believed that a man with unbridled self-confidence could leap any boulders that life had strewn in his path. Hadn't he risen from deprivation to become a Hollywood screenwriter and now the leader of a movement that would revolutionize the country?

Revolution! The ultimate goal.

It would take years, of course. But as he liked to say, Rome wasn't sacked in a day. Now, he smacked his thigh with his riding crop like Charlie Kurtsinger whipping War Admiral at the clubhouse turn.

"You wanna be Silver Shirts?" he yelled to the group.

"Yes, Mr. Pelley, sir!" came the robust replies.

"Can you kill?"

"Yes, Mr. Pelley, sir!" Louder this time.

"As the Führer has instructed, 'The first essential for success is a constant and regular employment of violence!'"

Oh, the strength of the Führer! No feeble notions of the brotherhood of man.

Three years earlier, Pelley had attended the Nuremberg rally where Adolf Hitler preached the gospel of fascism to three-quarters of a million followers. Pelley could still feel the electricity coursing through him, could hear the staccato *clip-clop* of goose-stepping soldiers, the music of victory.

"Who we gonna kill?" Pelley sing-songed to his men.

"Com-mu-nists!" the men sang back.

"Who we gonna kill?"

"Jews!"

"Who are we?"

"Pa-tri-ots!"

Pelley noticed that Skowron hadn't joined in the chant and was about to call him on it.

But before he did, the man said, "Talk's cheap."

"How's that?" Pelley asked.

Skowron scratched at his chin stubble, which ran jagged thanks to his scar, the wound apparently stitched by a blind doctor or a drunk sadist. "How 'bout some shootin'?"

Pelley didn't regard this as insubordination but rather an eagerness to engage the enemy. "Grab your weapons!" he shouted.

The men scrambled for their 1903 Springfield rifles. Hurrying faster than his fingers could manage, Eckart stabbed himself trying to attach his bayonet. He yelped and stuck his bleeding thumb into his mouth.

"Eckart, jam that thumb up your ass!" Pelley waggled his riding crop. "Hit the dirt, men! Low crawl to the perimeter."

The men belly flopped to the ground and wriggled up an incline toward a ridge, where they jammed together, as close as peanuts in a Baby Ruth.

"Spread out, dammit!" Pelley ordered, and the men repositioned themselves into a prone firing line.

Twenty yards away were half-a-dozen makeshift targets, sheets of plywood nailed to trees. Each sheet had a crudely drawn body in black paint with a large photo of a man's face on top. Six targets, six different men.

"I wanna shoot FDR," Eckart said. "Knock him out of his wheelchair."

"I got Joe Stalin," another man said. "Commie scum."

"What's Groucho Marx doing up there?" a third man asked.

Pelley did not say that the target was supposed to be Karl Marx, but the lad gathering the photos did not know the difference between the revolutionary socialist and the mustachioed comedian.

"Why are we shooting King George?" asked another. It didn't take an Anglophile to recognize the monarch, as he wore a crown.

"Pipe down!" Pelley demanded. "Two men to a target. Sort it out."

The men debated distances, traded targets, shifted around and—other than Skowron and Zorn—took so long to get ready that a Civil War cavalry officer on horseback could have slaughtered them.

"Hell's bells," Pelley whispered to himself. He drew a silver flask from a pocket and took a long pull, a warm cascade of Old Quaker whiskey sliding down his throat. He knew that Hitler suffered many failures before spending a full year preparing for the Night of the Long Knives.

"Fire when ready!" Pelley ordered. "Kill them all!"

In a moment, the hills were alive with the sounds of gunfire. Stalin and FDR took several flesh wounds in the plywood, but nothing near their heads. Pelley grabbed his flask and knocked back another two slugs of the whiskey.

"Scope's cloudy," complained one man.

"Don't worry, fellow," Pelley said. "New weapons are on the horizon. Browning Automatics."

"US Army rifles?" He sounded skeptical. "How's that possible?"

Pelley gave him a crooked smile. "You'd be surprised how many friends we have in the American military."

As the firing continued, Groucho took one in the mustache and His Royal Highness one in his diamond-studded crown. Eckart missed Roosevelt with his first two shots but then nailed his forehead with his last three.

"Attaboy, Eckart! I knew you had it in you."

A body like a bowl of pudding but a steady hand.

Skowron was teamed with Zorn, the two bruisers even more fearsome with rifles in their meaty paws. They fired ten rapid blasts at the sixth target, a square-jawed, handsome, silver-haired man with a cocky smile. Every shot true, shredding the photo.

"Great work, men," Pelley said.

My squad leaders.

Maybe it was the warmth of the whiskey in his belly or the sweet smell of cordite in the air, but Pelley's mood became positively buoyant.

I have found my cause. A fascist America.

"Who's that guy we just plugged?" Skowron asked.

"That bastard's Charlie Chaplin," Pelley said, spitting out the words.

"Didn't recognize him without the mustache and stupid hat," Zorn said.

It had been more than six years since Pelley had watched the masses slobber all over the pint-sized actor at the premiere of *City Lights*. If anything, Pelley's distaste for the man had only grown.

"Chaplin's got more money than God and gives a lot of it to a commie front called the International Relief Association." Pelley hawked up a wad of phlegm and spat onto the ground.

"Never heard of it," Zorn said.

"It was started by that so-called genius Albert Einstein. They're bringing Jews and gypsies and what-not into the States to replace white Christians. I've got my eyes on them, and one fine day I may reward you boys with the chance of putting bullets in both their heads."

3
TWO MEN, TWO SECRETS

Chaplin Estate, Summit Drive, Beverly Hills

Twenty miles to the southeast, at the same moment that his photo was being blistered into confetti, Charlie Chaplin—garbed in white linen trousers and a matching long-sleeve cotton shirt—bounced a tennis ball several times, preparing to serve. The tennis court was located on Chaplin's ritzy estate, as befitted a multimillionaire. His opponent was Albert Einstein, two geniuses, one of the arts, one of the universe. With thunderclouds of war gathering across the globe, the newspapers had stopped calling them "the two most famous men in the world." The burden of fame now rested on the shoulders of men named Hitler and Stalin, Chamberlain and Roosevelt.

After traveling from England as part of a vaudeville troupe at age twenty-one, Chaplin knew, early on, that he'd be more than a comedian playing music halls in the red-light districts of midwestern America. He spent those days polishing his visual comedy and bedding down a legion of young women who sprouted like wildflowers on the prairie.

Now, at forty-eight, as writer, actor, director, and producer of his films and co-owner of the studio that distributed them, he was at the pinnacle of the world's most glamorous industry. He was still an accomplished athlete, still a master at physical comedy, still heartthrob handsome and well aware of it.

Chaplin never forgot his impoverished childhood. An alcoholic father who died in his thirties, a desperately poor mother in and out of mental asylums, suffering from venereal disease and dementia.

Oh, the things me Mum had to do to put scraps of food on the table for her two boys.

When his mother was hospitalized, seven-year-old Charlie was sent to a decrepit British workhouse where lessons were meted out with birch canes.

How far I have traveled!

Chaplin looked across the net at Einstein, a man he admired for his intellect, his charm, his passion for social justice…for everything other than his lousy tennis game. Something was bothering Chaplin, a conversation he needed to have with Einstein but didn't know quite how to approach. Without consulting his friend, Chaplin had accepted an invitation for tomorrow night in both their names.

Albert, you're gonna be peeved. Maybe even furious.

Chaplin decided to wait until they'd finished playing tennis to bring it up. Now he tossed the tennis ball over his head and hit a graceful serve.

☞ ☜

Albert Einstein loved the time spent with his friend. Today was California bright, neither warm nor chilly, Chaplin's estate dotted with rose bushes of a dozen hues, while overhead gray mourning doves and red-headed finches perched in the palms.

Having fled Germany when Hitler came to power, Einstein, now fifty-eight, lived in Princeton, New Jersey, where he pursued his research at the Institute for Advanced Study. On his first trip to California, he had infuriated faculty members at Caltech by giving a lecture they considered an endorsement of socialism. "Instead of being a liberating force," Einstein said, "science has enslaved men to machines and to work long, wearisome hours mostly without joy in their labor."

Chaplin had been in the audience, and five years later released *Modern Times*, portraying a harried factory worker who was a slave to a relentless conveyor belt that would carry him into the maw of a brutal, unforgiving machine. *We march to the same drummer*, Einstein had thought on more than one occasion.

Now, he watched the fuzzy white ball cross the net and bounce, taking an elongated hop that reminded him of the puzzling elliptical orbit of Mercury. Remembering how general relativity solved that little cosmological puzzle might have caused Einstein to slap the ball into the net. More likely, it was his herky-jerky swing, as if he were swatting pesky houseflies.

"Thirty love, mate!" Chaplin called out, cranking up the Cockney accent he'd lost long ago.

Virty luv, mate!

"Fifteen, thirty, forty," Einstein said in his German accent, which was quite real.

Feefteen, Sairtee, Foortee.

"What *mishegoss!* What's wrong with one, two, three?"

"It's tradition, Albert."

"Five thousand years ago, the Sumerians invented the base-ten system. That's tradition!"

Chaplin did not fire back with one of his usual quips, and Einstein sensed something off-kilter. *Maybe I should just say, "Charlie, so tell me already! What's on your mind?"*

Einstein also had a secret to share with Chaplin, something that perhaps he should tell the War Department or even President Roosevelt himself. Charlie, who had been in the States for twenty years, would know what to do, he thought.

Chaplin hit a powder-puff serve, and Einstein's return sailed six feet beyond the baseline. "Forty love, Albert."

"Love? So, what happened to zero?" Einstein asked in the lilting rhythm common to Yiddish speakers.

"Try hitting with topspin to keep the ball in."

"Who knew that gravity needed my assistance?"

The two men could banter and razz each other. Equals, not dumbstruck in each other's presence.

Chaplin's next serve was soft as a kiss, but Einstein smacked the ball into the net. "That's game, mate," Chaplin said. "Your serve."

Instead of serving, Einstein twirled around three-hundred-sixty degrees.

"What's this, some experiment, Albert?" Chaplin asked. "A new way to measure gravity?"

"I'm taking in the sweet solitude of the wondrous place you've built."

Chaplin, too, looked around as if he weren't quite familiar with his own Beverly Hills estate. The red clay tennis court, the lushly landscaped grounds with dozens of olive, palm, and citrus trees. The Spanish Revival mansion with its stucco walls, red tile roof, and wrought-iron railings sat on a high point of Summit Drive, an appropriate name both for the street and the owner's career.

"You bet, Albert," Chaplin said. "It's a swell place. Now, let's play."

Preparing to serve, Einstein tossed the ball over his head but didn't swing. He caught the ball, tossed it again, five feet higher, and yet again, higher still.

"Albert, what the hell? Serve!"

"If I could throw the ball at eleven-point-two kilometers per second," Einstein mused, "it would achieve exit velocity and escape Earth's atmosphere."

Chaplin plucked a ball from his pocket, took a ferocious upward swing, and walloped it as hard as he could. Still thinking about their untold secrets, the two friends watched the ball soar over the backcourt fence, continue on an upward path, clear a line of olive trees, and disappear.

4
ROBIN HOOD

Pickfair Estate, Summit Drive, Beverly Hills

The tennis ball bounced three times on the pool deck and landed, soft as a dove, on Douglas Fairbanks's stomach. Fairbanks coughed himself awake from a booze nap, his barrel chest heaving, his puffy eyes blinking against the Southern California sun. Unaware of the tennis ball cradled in his navel like a poached egg in a ramekin, he took inventory of his surroundings. He was stretched out on a cushioned chaise.

Fine, I'm poolside.

Swim trunks, dry.

Excellent. I haven't been pulled from the bottom of the pool, moments from death.

He shaded his eyes. Above him loomed his four-story Tudor-style mansion, Pickfair, the centerpiece of the eighteen-acre estate, which included horse stables, a pair of tennis courts, an Old West saloon, servants' quarters, and a pool so large he sometimes paddled a canoe across it. He had built the mansion for his third wife, Mary Pickford, the charming, delectable actress the trades called "America's Sweetheart."

He was relieved not to be lounging poolside at some chorus girl's apartment building in the Valley. He was on his own property or what had been his until his marriage took a torpedo like the *Lusitania* off the coast of Ireland. This torpedo was a Brit named Sylvia Ashley, the latest of a long line of his indiscretions, and for Mary the last straw in a bale large enough to thatch a roof. Under terms of the divorce, he had to vacate Pickfair, which had been the scene of legendary parties that would make Caligula blush.

That unhappy thought made him realize he was parched.

"Reg-i-nald!" he called out.

Magically, as if in a movie, his valet was there. "Sir?"

A tall, gray-haired uniformed English gent with the posture of a Buckingham Palace foot guard, Reginald manned a cocktail cart six feet away in the shade of an umbrella. As discreet as a locked vault, Reginald did not mention the tennis ball on his master's stomach.

"A martini, sir?"

"Have I ever said no?"

"Black Friday 1929. You said, 'Leave out the vermouth.'"

Reginald poured several glugs of Beefeater gin into a silver cocktail shaker, added a wisp of dry vermouth and several ice cubes and affixed the top. He handed the shaker—emblazoned with the Pickfair crest—to Fairbanks, who made short thrusts like feinted punches in a boxing scene. As the ice *click-clacked,* Fairbanks looked at his reflection in the shaker, his mustache graying, the pouches under his eyes as creased as an ancient love letter.

He would turn fifty-four in three weeks. No longer as rakishly handsome as a Hollywood prince. Or a pirate. Or Zorro. Or Robin Hood. All of whom he had played in motion pictures.

Once dubbed the "King of Hollywood" by *Variety*, his career had nosedived with the advent of talkies. In *The Private Life of Don Juan*, his last role, he played the title character, an aging, broken-down lover.

Ouch. Sometimes life imitates art so closely, it's like shaving with a guillotine.

He didn't foresee any more leading roles unless DeMille wanted to make a biblical epic about Methuselah.

Life waited to reveal her cruelties until you could least endure them, did it not?

Fairbanks was one of Chaplin's dearest friends and a business partner in United Artists, and both shared the unfortunate trait of sleeping with women who were not necessarily their wives.

Fairbanks poured his own martini and drained it, an icy river of steel down his throat. He poured a second and gulped that one, too. He felt a blowtorch searing his gut. The doctors had ordered him to cut back on his drinking, which was like telling a fish to cut back on its swimming.

"The parties we had," Fairbanks mumbled.

"Sir?"

Fairbanks missed cracking wise with Gable and Lombard, missed a hundred friends dancing slow and easy to an orchestra playing "Three O'Clock in the Morning"—at three o'clock in the morning.

"Reginald, do you remember the night I fenced with that Australian kid, what's his name?"

"Errol Flynn, sir. Warner is remaking *Robin Hood* with him. In color."

"What! He's not yet thirty."

How disheartening. Fairbanks had been thirty-nine and at the peak of his powers when he took on the role. Passing the torch—or the bow and arrow—did not come naturally or gracefully. He desperately wanted to get out of the doldrums. Thankfully, there were festivities planned.

"Reginald, is everything prepared for tomorrow night's luau?"

"Yes, sir. But Mr. Chaplin sent his regrets."

"What! We're supposed to do our parody of Edgar Bergen and Charlie McCarthy, Chap perched on my knee just like the ventriloquist's cheeky dummy."

"He has a prior engagement with Professor Einstein."

"Without me! Is Einstein angry about my asking what's so special about relativity?"

"Mr. Chaplin said they have an important function. Rather mysterious, I thought."

Fairbanks felt adrift, like Captain Bligh after Fletcher Christian tossed him off the Bounty.

Did Charlie heave-ho me, too? It's one thing for my wife to leave me. But my best friend!

"Perhaps you can ask Mr. Chaplin this evening at the studio," Reginald suggested.

"It's embarrassing. Auditioning at this point in my life. And for Charlie!"

"I'm sure it will go well, sir."

Chaplin had mentioned that he was working on a secret project that was going to be controversial and perhaps even dangerous for the actors. There might be a part for Fairbanks, who sheepishly agreed to audition, grateful for the chance, even though it felt a bit like charity.

Fairbanks picked up the tennis ball and staring at it he said, "Good news, Reginald! Charlie hasn't forgotten me. Shall we return the little white ball the usual way?"

"With haste, sir."

Without further instructions, Reginald reached into a poolside storage bin and withdrew a sturdy bow and several arrows that had been props in *Robin Hood*. Taking the tennis ball in hand, he jammed an arrow cleanly through, making something which now resembled a chunk of chicken on a skewer of shish kebab. He then grabbed the bottle of Beefeater and doused the ball with enough gin for a dozen first-rate martinis. Finished, he handed the arrow to Fairbanks who placed the nock on the bowstring and flexed his fingers, stiffened with arthritis.

"Ready, sir?" Reginald asked.

"In the name of King Richard the Lionhearted and the Holy Crusades, yes!"

It was a line from *Robin Hood,* delivered with heroic panache. Reginald flicked a cigarette lighter and set the ball ablaze, yellow-blue flames flickering in the breeze. Fairbanks pulled back on the bowstring, veins rippling in his arms. He took aim, intending to clear the line of live oak trees that separated Pickfair from Chaplin's estate.

Is something moving there?

While Fairbanks's brain was occasionally blurry, neither cirrhosis of the liver nor misfiring neurons had affected his eyesight. He tossed the arrow and flaming ball into the pool.

"Reginald, fetch the spyglass and take a gander at the trees on the property line."

The valet opened a wooden storage bin that contained pool equipment plus a grab bag of items Fairbanks might request without warning. Picking up a small telescope that had been a prop in *The Black Pirate,* Reginald focused the lens and took the requested gander.

"Looks like a man with a camera, sir."

"A scalawag from *Hollywood Secrets!* Another damn exposé! 'Who's Fairbanks Sleeping With Now?'"

☞ ☜

The man in the tree did, indeed, have a camera, but he had no interest in Fairbanks's bedmates. Aimed over the boundary fence, his Leica 35 millimeter with a telephoto lens was focused on Chaplin's property.

Wearing forest camouflage gear of greens and browns, the photographer, a pencil-thin man in his thirties named Klaus Spengler, was born in Bonn. These days, Spengler made his living photographing weddings and graduations in the German American community of Los Angeles. Then there was the occasional special assignment from the Reich's Ministry of Public Enlightenment. Today's target was Charlie Chaplin, though Spengler had no idea why the propaganda branch gave a tinker's damn about the actor.

Albert Einstein's appearance in the viewfinder surprised Spengler. Any number of magazines would pay top dollar to have candid photos of those two celebrities, but Spengler would not risk losing a client and perhaps his ability to walk upright should he be caught double-dipping.

With the naked eye, Spengler could see Chaplin and Einstein sitting at a table adjacent to the tennis court. Through the viewfinder, he focused the crosshairs first on Chaplin, then on Einstein. It occurred to him that it was the same view he'd have if he were looking through the G98 sniper scope his father, a German Army sniper, had used in the Great War.

Spengler watched as Einstein pulled a paper from his pocket and placed it on the table.

No, not a paper. A photograph!

At this distance, Spengler couldn't make out the photo.

"*Verdammter!*" he said aloud. Dammit! Frustrated, he reached into his camera bag for a longer lens.

5
NUCLEAR FISSION

Chaplin Estate, Tennis Court

Chaplin and Einstein sat at the courtside table, where a uniformed footman had placed a pitcher of lemonade and a silver platter of cucumber and egg salad sandwiches, their crusts surgically removed by Chef Maurice in the kitchen.

The world was a powder keg, insurrections were brewing, American fascists were arming, but life was tennis, lemonade, and finger sandwiches in Beverly Hills…for now.

Chaplin sipped his lemonade and studied a photograph Einstein had placed on the table.

It showed two men in lab coats, their backs to the camera, staring at a blackboard with a mathematical equation partially visible:

"So, who are they and what are they doing?" Chaplin asked.

$$^{238}_{92}U + n \rightarrow$$

"Chemists who've been working with radioactive isotopes," Einstein said. "Otto Hahn and Fritz Strassmann."

"Germans?"

"Very much so. They're at the Kaiser Wilhelm Institute in Berlin."

"And those numbers…"

"The beginning of an unfinished equation related to the alpha decay of uranium."

"That would've been my guess," Chaplin cracked.

"They're bombarding uranium with neutrons, attempting nuclear fission."

Chaplin popped a cucumber finger sandwich into his mouth. "Okay, I'm stumped. Nuclear fiction?"

"Fission! In theory, a nuclear chain reaction would result, unleashing a staggering amount of energy."

Chaplin offered the sandwich tray to Einstein, who declined. "Energy to do what, Albert?"

"Run turbines, produce electricity…or create bombs the likes of which the world has never seen."

"Bombs for the Nazis?"

"No, for the Swiss. Of course, for the Nazis."

"Sodding hell!" Chaplin shouted, reverting to his British roots. "I'm going to need something stronger than lemonade. How far along are these Kraut chemists?"

Einstein shrugged. "No way to tell. There's no date on the photo, no accompanying letter."

"So where'd it come from?"

"It was sent from Sweden to my office at Princeton, then forwarded to me here. My guess is that Lise Meitner took the photo without Hahn and Strassmann realizing it. She's a brilliant physicist who discovered protactinium-231."

"My favorite of all the tiniums."

"It's a radioactive isotope. She worked with Hahn and Strassmann in Berlin, but Lise is Jewish, and last I heard, she was heading to Sweden."

Chaplin grabbed a piece of celery filled with cream cheese and took a bite. "So, are these chain reaction bombs even possible?"

"Some think not. Others say they could set the sky on fire and destroy the world."

"There goes our tennis game. What do you say, Albert?"

"In theory, the bomb is possible." Einstein tamped a wad of Turkish tobacco into the white clay bowl of his meerschaum pipe, struck a match, and puffed. "But going from the equations to a working nuclear device, well, it would be the most complex scientific and engineering achievement in history. And I use the word 'achievement' reluctantly, as you know my feelings about war."

Reading the troubled look on his friend's face, Chaplin said, "And you want my advice on what to do with the photograph?"

"Precisely. What is my duty to America, the country that took me in and has treated me with such kindness and generosity?"

"Well, old friend, you should drop a note to FDR and tell him to get off the dime. Offer to run a program that'll catch up with the Krauts."

"Charlie, I'm a committed pacifist. Informing FDR about the German program is one thing, but I cannot be part of a war machine, and I would never build a bomb."

They were quiet a moment before Chaplin said, "Albert, as you might have heard, 'No man is an island.' Hitler has changed the rules, and so too your moral obligations."

"If that is true, I wonder if my obligation is to work harder for peace, rather than to make war even more deadly."

6
ARSCHLOCH!

Pickfair Estate

In the tree, Spengler focused his long lens on the photograph on Chaplin's courtside table.

"*Was ist das?*" The men in the photo in lab attire? Do they even know they're being photographed? No.

He moved the camera to Einstein, whose face filled the viewfinder.

Professor, you do not look happy. Not happy at all.

His Leica *click-click-clicked* as he snapped photos.

"Heyyyyy, youuuuuu!"

The echoing voice startled Spengler, who nearly lost his footing on the tree limb.

☞ ☜

Still in his chaise on the pool patio, Fairbanks clutched a director's megaphone in one hand, his trusty *Robin Hood* bow in the other. He had a quiver of two dozen arrows with goose-feather fletchings.

"You ink-stained wretches frost my butt!" he yelled through the megaphone.

Spengler glanced his way, then turned back toward the Chaplin estate and resumed snapping photos. Reginald, looking through the spyglass, said, "I believe he's photographing Mr. Chaplin, sir."

"Ah, of course," Fairbanks said dejectedly. "That blue-eyed, silver-haired rascal is a bigger star. Wasn't always that way, was it, Reginald?"

"Certainly not, sir."

"No matter. We protect our friends, whether attacked by Captain Ramon or the Sheriff of Nottingham," Fairbanks said, covering the villains of both *Zorro* and *Robin Hood*. Adrenalized, he loaded an arrow, pulled back the bowstring, then smoothly released it, hearing that delicious *thwip*.

The arrow soared long and true and struck with a *twang* into the tree trunk a foot above the photographer's head. Startled, he turned toward Fairbanks and yelled, *"Arschloch!"*

"A Saxon assassin, Reginald?" Fairbanks asked.

"German, sir." Reginald handed Fairbanks another arrow. "He called you an 'asshole.'"

"Ribald dialogue. It'll never get past the Legion of Decency."

The next arrow pierced Spengler's camera bag and stuck there, throbbing and *humming*.

Needing no further inducement, Spengler scurried down from the tree and ran full tilt toward Pickfair's front gate.

7
THE WORLD IS A DANGEROUS PLACE

Chaplin Estate

Sitting at the courtside table, Einstein reached for a finger sandwich, then stopped. He had no appetite. His mind was swirling around the dilemma. He had spent his life trying to understand the universe. To expand human knowledge, to grasp our place in the cosmos, and to advance science for the good of humanity.

But what is a pacifist and humanist to do in today's world?

"Charlie, if the Nazis create this chain reaction bomb…" He couldn't go on.

Chaplin finished the thought. "They'll hold the entire world hostage."

Einstein relit his pipe.

"Or simply drop it on London or Paris."

Chaplin considered that horrific thought.

"I feel a tremendous sense of guilt," Einstein said. "Special relativity is the foundation of their work."

"Snap out of it, pal. You theorized that a small bit of matter could produce an astounding amount of energy. That's not the same as building a bomb, much less using it. And by the way, that Nobel Prize you won was created by the guy who invented dynamite. You think he felt guilty about blowing things up?"

Einstein raised his eyebrows, deepening the furrows in his forehead. "Actually, Charlie, Alfred Nobel's guilt was part of the reason he created the prize."

"Well, that's crackers!"

Chaplin grabbed an egg salad finger sandwich, chomped it in one bite, and said, "If the Nazis really are building a big bomb, you have no choice. You gotta help the Americans build a bigger one."

"Even ignoring my moral reservations, I'm a theoretical physicist. I can't make an omelet."

"Not buying it, pal. You're the world's greatest genius."

"Ach, Charlie! I stood on Isaac Newton's shoulders, and he stood on Galileo's."

"Then you're pretty damn tall. As for your pacifism, you've changed your position over the years. When we met, you said that young men should refuse military service, even if it meant going to prison."

Einstein relit his pipe, which had gone cold.

"At the time, I did not foresee the evil lurking in the shadows of Berlin. Now I recognize the naïveté of my position."

"It speaks well of you, Albert, that you can admit you're not infallible."

Einstein coughed a laugh and exhaled a plume of smoke.

"Infallible! From my little office in Pasadena, I can see the San Gabriel Mountains. Barely ten miles from the campus, as the bird flies, is Mount Wilson Observatory. It's where Edwin Hubble demonstrated the universe is expanding, proving me wrong. The biggest blunder of my life."

"My biggest blunders all involve women."

"Charlie, you're incorrigible."

"Let's get it sorted out and decide what to do with the photograph."

"I will give it to my boss."

"You have a boss?"

"Abraham Flexner. He hired me and runs the Institute. He has friends in the Roosevelt administration and will know who to talk to."

"Ha! Keeping your hands clean. But tell me this, Albert. What if FDR personally called you to the White House and pleaded with you."

Chaplin did his best impression of the president. "Professah Ayn-steen, we need yah help because that bah-stad Adolf Hitler has his bloody hands on a big new bomb."

"Charlie, that is a dilemma I hope never to face."

☞ ☜

Five minutes later, the two friends walked through the estate's lush gardens toward the house. As they passed wooden trellises threaded with red bougainvillea, Chaplin said, "Albert, I need to tell you something, so please keep an open mind."

They stopped in front of a bed of pink peonies. Puzzled, Einstein tried to read the look on his friend's face. Chaplin's lips were drawn tight.

"Charlie, what are you trying to say?"

"Only that I accepted an invitation for us for tomorrow night."

"The baseball game? That's fine."

"It's a day game. At night…"

His voice trailed off, and Einstein became impatient. Why was his friend behaving like a shy graduate student, afraid to report a lab finding that contradicted the professor's convictions?

"So, what then, Charlie? Dinner with friends at Musso and Frank? A party at Mr. Fairbanks's house? I'm amenable to anything you plan."

"Actually, it's more formal. We'll have to wear our glad rags."

"That's what you were reluctant to tell me?" Einstein laughed. "Tuxedos? I may need help with the bow tie, but that's fine."

"It's a reception. The dedication of a new building. A rather grand building. Champagne and cake, many celebrities, that sort of thing."

"Sounds boring, but whatever you want. What grand building are you talking about?"

"Konsulat von Deutschland."

"The German consulate? Next you'll tell me that Adolf Hitler will be there."

Chaplin shook his head. "No, but Joseph Goebbels will."

"The Nazi Liar-in-Chief? Ha, good one!"

"And his jackbooted bully boys."

Realizing his friend wasn't joking, Einstein pictured thugs in black leather coats, SS pins on their collars, men who used truncheons to shatter skulls, who inflicted pain as easily as they breathed air.

An evening in hell.

"Partying with Nazis, Charlie? You should be ashamed to show your face."

"I could go in disguise as a butler, like William Powell in *My Man Godfrey*."

"Is all life a movie to you?" Einstein asked, sharply.

"Only the best parts. C'mon, Albert. Let's go to their clambake and take their measure."

But Einstein wasn't having it. "The last time I was in Berlin, they spat on me in the street. They ransacked my house, stole my sailboat, and burned my writings. They fired every Jew at every university. More than a dozen Nobel laureates, half of all physicists in the country."

"The idiots will live to regret that."

"And things have only gotten worse. The book burnings, the beatings, the murders."

"I'm sorry, Albert. I should have asked you first. And I should have told you my reasons for accepting the invitation."

"Spare me your reasons. Please leave me home and take your wife."

Chaplin smiled ruefully. "Paulette Goddard was born 'Marion Levy.' She won't go."

"Then one of your hat-check girls," Einstein said, an edge to his voice.

"When Goebbels speaks, it's like reading Hitler's mind. I want to know what he's thinking."

"And you want to go into that chamber of horrors why?"

"Research."

Einstein walked toward the rose beds. "You're not writing a movie about Nazis, are you?"

"About one."

"*Meshuggener!* It's too dangerous."

"Hitler and I were born four days apart in April of eighty-nine. Doug Fairbanks says that with my Tramp mustache, I look a lot like him."

"Some compliment, that."

"Hear me out, Albert. I'll play a poor Jewish barber who's a doppelgänger for a vicious dictator. Plus, I'll play the dictator. I'll make the big bully look ridiculous, a laughingstock."

Einstein doubted that making a movie about Hitler—a mistaken identity satire, so it seemed—would change people's minds. Hatemongers would continue to hate, and civilized society already knew Hitler's depravity.

And what about the danger of tickling the nose of a rabid dog?

"Albert, I'd like to do as much as you do for the good of the world," Chaplin said.

"Excellent. Perhaps you can reconcile general relativity with quantum mechanics."

"I'm serious. You're not just a scientist. You *do* things. Your relief group gets refugees out of Europe before God knows what befalls them."

"And you write us very generous checks."

Chaplin laughed, a scoffing sound. "Is there anything easier for a wealthy man than to write checks?"

Einstein felt he owed it to his friend to listen. He also wondered whether it was morally right to dissuade Chaplin from taking a stand against such evil forces. Would it not contradict his own widely quoted sentiment, "The world is a dangerous place, not because of the people who are evil, but because of the people who don't do anything about it."

Keeping his eyes on a bed of pink and white roses, a beautiful sight so at odds with the perilous state of the world, Einstein said, "Tell me more about this movie."

"I'm going to end the picture with a speech, something you've influenced."

"Me? How?"

"Your compassion. Your empathy. Your humility. Albert, your very being." Embarrassed by the praise and tongue-tied, Einstein stayed quiet.

"The speech will be about turning our backs on hate, about treating each other with respect and kindness."

"You can do that in a movie, Charlie? Make a speech?"

"It's my money, my movie, and my studio. I can do what I want, which is to make Hitler look like a pretentious tyrant, a ludicrous fool."

"Then perhaps this is a movie I would not mind seeing," Einstein said.

"So, you'll go to the German consulate with me?"

"Give me time to think, Charlie. I feel like I'm free falling in an elevator."

"Hah! The illusion of weightlessness in your general theory of relativity. Just let me know before you hit the ground."

8
THE RALLY

Alt Heidelberg, Westlake Neighborhood, Los Angeles

Once a privately owned mansion on South Alvarado Street, Alt Heidelberg was now a Reich-friendly social hall housing a biergarten, a German restaurant, an Aryan bookstore, an auditorium, and mysterious rooms on the upper floors that were off-limits to all but a precious few.

In the alley behind the restaurant, Jimmy Mitchell, a short, slender Black man, picked up an empty trash bin and carried it into the kitchen. He wore rubber boots, a heavy apron, and dark brown trousers. With his close-cropped hair and neatly trimmed mustache, the twenty-four-year-old was indistinguishable from the dishwashers and pot scrubbers who toiled in the plate-clattering, pan-rattling kitchen that belched steam like a locomotive. Mitchell, however, did not intend to scrape platters of schnitzel into the garbage. He was a reporter for the *Los Angeles Sentinel*, an African-American newspaper, and he had a loftier goal. He intended to spy on a rally where hundreds of German Americans gathered to hear the hateful dogma preached by their favorite rabble-rousing fascists.

No journalists allowed! And a Black journalist? If caught, he would likely have his skull fractured by an oak blackjack wrapped in leather, a "kike killer," though the goons did not use it exclusively on Jews. The event was billed as a "True Americanism Rally," which was accurate, Mitchell thought, only if America stood for hatred and violence toward ethnic minorities.

Mitchell had spent the last thirteen months investigating the Silver Shirts, the German American Bund, the Ku Klux Klan, the American White Guard, the American Nationalist Federation, the Black Legion, and other crackpot cults chummy with the Nazis.

So many fascists! How can they operate so openly and go unnoticed by so many?

Less than a week earlier, a kitchen worker at Alt Heidelberg named Roscoe told Mitchell's editor he had overheard two waiters chatting happily about *"der tag"* and *"maschinengewehre."* Roscoe had picked up a little German in the Great War and knew the men were talking about "the day" and "machine guns." Disquieted by what he heard, Roscoe felt as if he were eavesdropping on John Wilkes Booth discussing his plans for Ford's Theatre.

Once in the kitchen, Mitchell ditched the trash bin, hurried through the scullery where workers chopped vegetables, and entered a long, narrow pantry where canned foods were stored. A Black man of about sixty with a salt-and-pepper mustache waited for him in the recessed corner of one wall.

"Are you Roscoe?" Mitchell said.

"Ain't got no name, and you never saw me." The man pushed a button on the wall.

Mitchell watched a sliding door open, revealing the tray of a dumbwaiter. The man with no name removed a stack of dirty dishes and said, "Git on in, little fellow."

At five feet seven and one hundred forty pounds, Mitchell hoped he was little enough. He crawled into the tray, which sank a few inches, the metal cable whining. Mitchell drew his knees up under his chin.

"When the door opens, hop out," the man said, "and run like hell to the end of the corridor, where you'll see a utility door in the wall. That'll put you onto the catwalk. Keep your head down, and don't let the Krauts see you. They're the meanest bastards this side of the Klan."

"How do I get out of the building?" Mitchell asked.

As the dumbwaiter door closed, the man made a scoffing sound. "On the wings of angels."

☞ ☜

Five minutes later, Jimmy Mitchell crawled across a catwalk thirty feet above the floor of the auditorium while a band heavy on brass and drums played a rousing version of "Horst-Wessel-Lied," the Nazi anthem. Mitchell kept his head below a spotlight mounted on the catwalk and peered down into the crowd, which he estimated at three hundred. Nearly all men, most in dark suits, many wearing swastika armbands. They belted out the anthem's lyrics in German.

On the stage, a portly executive of Alt Heidelberg introduced Reverend A. Earl Lee of the Immanuel Gospel Church. In a brief invocation, the reverend beseeched God to "annihilate the killers of Christ, the most satanic people on Earth."

The crowd hooted and hollered. Their stomping feet made the catwalk tremble, reminding Mitchell of a recent earthquake that had rattled dishes at home.

The might of hate, powerful enough to move the mantle of the earth.

Reverend Lee ranted for ten minutes, then gave way to Fritz Kuhn, leader of the German American Bund, who railed against Jewish control of Hollywood and demanded that America be ruled by white gentiles. "If George Washington were alive today," Kuhn said, "he'd be friends with Adolf Hitler."

Jimmy Mitchell thought he had been transported to another country. No! Another world where up was down and right was left.

The next speaker was William Dudley Pelley, who urged the crowd to join his Silver Legion of America and wear the silver shirts of its paramilitary. "We have thousands of stormtroopers who stand ready to take back America!" he boomed.

"Take back America!" the crowd responded.

Mitchell scooted to his knees to get a look at Pelley, a short man with a gray goatee who cocked his head to one side and soaked up the admiration of the audience.

"We will rescue our country from the God-hating Bolsheviks, and we will do it by any means necessary," Pelley continued, "and that includes at the end of a noose, the blade of a bayonet, the barrel of a gun. I will now meet with my commanders, and I can tell you, *der tag!* The day is near!"

"Der tag" caught Mitchell's attention, just as it had for Roscoe. When Pelley was finished, the crowd chanted "Heil Hitler" with arms raised in the Nazi salute.

Mitchell watched as four men in suits and ties hurried from the audience to the steps at the side of the stage and greeted Pelley as he descended. All five men disappeared through a side door. As the door closed, Mitchell could see a stairwell. They were heading upstairs.

The real meeting! Pelley and his commanders behind closed doors.

Mitchell scrambled on all fours across the catwalk to the far side of the stage and stopped at the utility door that opened onto the second-floor corridor. If he scrambled out and five bloodthirsty fascists were there, well, he would need more than the wings of angels to escape.

He cracked the door an inch and looked out. An empty corridor. Then the sound of men's voices. He couldn't make out the words, but they sounded enthused, happy even. The voices grew louder, and through the small opening Mitchell could see the group, Pelley in the lead.

"The Bund has more men and more weapons than we have," Pelley said. "We need to strike quickly to make our mark while Fritz Kuhn is still blathering."

"Machine guns strike damn quick," one of his commanders said, chuckling, and the other men murmured their agreement. Their voices grew dim, and Mitchell opened the door wider.

Figuring the men had gone around the corner of an intersecting corridor, he dropped to the floor.

Machine guns! Just as Roscoe had heard.

Mitchell gathered his courage. He was motivated, not by a journalistic scoop, but by the certainty that, at this precise moment, he was the only person in the world who could uncover just what horrific deeds these men were planning and, with help, could stop them.

Mitchell paused to get his bearings. There was a stairwell. If spotted, he would hightail it that way. Foot speed was not a problem. As a boy, he often fled bullies, leaving them cursing and winded behind him. Now he stopped at the intersecting corridor and peeked around the corner.

Nobody. No sounds. No nothing.

Pelley and his men must have entered one of the rooms. There were perhaps a dozen on each side of the corridor, every door closed.

Shouts startled him. Two voices yelling in German. Footsteps hammered the floor, but where? He couldn't tell the direction of the sounds. Then came a gunshot, and a man stumbled around the corner of the intersecting corridor and collapsed at Jimmy's feet, blood pouring from his chest. The man was husky and swarthy, but the color was draining from his face, and he wheezed, trying to breathe. He looked up at Jimmy with brown eyes that were beginning to glaze over, his mouth moving but no words forming.

Shouts from the intersecting corridor grew louder, footsteps heavier.

"Op-er-a-tion." His voice gurgled, and blood seeped from his lips.

"What?" Mitchell said.

"Op-er-a-tion Hollywood," the man whispered, his eyes closing.

Mitchell turned and ran for the stairwell. Three steps before he reached the door, two gunshots echoed down the corridor, and he heard wood splintering on the wall just above his head. Over his shoulder he caught sight of two men, running after him, pistols drawn.

Mitchell entered the stairwell, determined not to run down the steps, which would drop him into the meeting surrounded by hundreds of Negro-hating fascists. Hoping his pursuers would think he went down the stairs, he kicked off his rubber boots and tossed them down to the next landing. Then he headed up the stairs to the third floor and ran to the nook in the corridor that housed the dumbwaiter. He punched the button and waited. Ten seconds, fifteen seconds…an eternity.

The door opened, Mitchell jumped into the tray and reached out of the open door to hit the button.

☞ ☜

When the dumbwaiter door opened in the kitchen, the man with no name pulled Mitchell out of the tray, put his fingers to his lips in a *shush* gesture, and motioned toward a trash bin on wheels. Mitchell climbed into the bin, and the man poured two cans of garbage over his head.

Potato peels, goulash, and detritus of sauerbraten and bratwurst covered him.

Mitchell heard angry shouts in German as the man wheeled the bin through the kitchen and out the back door. "Taking my break now," the man said to someone.

Mitchell heard a match being struck, and in a moment, he smelled cigarette smoke. The man with no name, his rescuer, was still there. After a few moments, the lid opened, and the man said, "Now! Go."

Mitchell climbed out of the bin, shook off the garbage, and ran down the alley in his stockinged feet. He didn't stop until he reached the Red Car trolley station on Flower Street. Sweating and his feet bleeding through his socks, he climbed aboard and handed the conductor a nickel, ignoring the stares and whispers of the other passengers.

"Operation Hollywood," he said under his breath.

9
THE MOST POWERFUL MAN IN HOLLYWOOD

Metro-Goldwyn-Mayer Studios, Culver City

Riding in the passenger compartment of his Mercedes-Benz 770 limousine, swastika flags waving in the breeze, Georg Gyssling was headed to MGM Studios for an unpleasant afternoon of bowdlerizing scripts that might offend the tender sensibilities of Adolf Hitler.

I love movies, Gyssling thought, and hate what I must do to them!

Today, Gyssling, the Reich's consul to the City of Los Angeles, would perform surgery on *Three Comrades*, which portrayed Germany as a shattered country after the Great War. True, of course, but Gyssling's job was to warp reality into myth. When the Hollywood studios refused Gyssling's demands, which was rare, their films would be banned from Germany's lucrative market. That prompted *Variety* to call Gyssling "the most powerful man in Hollywood." It was not intended as a compliment.

Three Comrades was based on a novel by Erich Maria Remarque, who had infuriated the Führer with his earlier books, *All Quiet on the Western Front* and *The Road Back*. Less than a year earlier, Gyssling had wielded his red pencil as a saber, slashing the most provocative scenes from *The Road Back*, which described

German soldiers at the end of the Great War as humiliated and traumatized.

Well, weren't all defeated armies?

That script in tatters, Gyssling reported to propaganda chief Joseph Goebbels that he had made the movie "un-remarque-able." Goebbels laughed heartily, though he likely chuckled when a Panzer tank ran over a dachshund.

One week ago, Goebbels had cabled, somewhat mysteriously, that he had exciting new responsibilities for Gyssling, who took "exciting" to mean "perilous." Goebbels and wife Magda were due to arrive at the consulate today and, to Gyssling's dismay, planned to meet with leaders of American fascist groups. Many of those true believers were clearly unhinged, believing that God had delivered Hitler to Earth to save mankind. Gyssling hoped he wasn't being assigned to babysit those mobs of halfwits.

From the dashboard in the passenger compartment, Gyssling turned on the Autosuper—the world's best motor car wireless—then fiddled with the dial. The voice of a baritone announcer filled the limousine:

"From the Shrine of the Little Flower in Royal Oak, Michigan…Father Charles Coughlin!"

Oh, here we go. The Reich's best friend in America, the lunatic radio priest.

"Greetings, friends, and here's the truth," Father Coughlin began. "Our democracy is doomed! It is fascism or communism, and I, for one, take the road to fascism. Now, we're forming the Christian Front. It won't be a debating society. No, sir. It will be a well-armed militia. We'll fight, and rest assured, we'll win!"

One of the wonders of America. Geniuses and madmen are equally free to speak their minds.

Gyssling switched off the radio. The limousine turned into the front gate of the studio, passed the twelve-foot high statue of the MGM lion, then skirted the backlot and eased into a slot marked

CONSUL. They'd left off the word "German," but once the shiny, Nazi-flagged Mercedes was parked, could there be any doubt?

☞ ☜

"Bullshit! A steaming pile of bullshit!" shouted the young man, spittle flying across the desk of MGM's vice president for international sales. The shouter and spitter was Joe Mankiewicz, the producer of *Three Comrades*. A dark-haired, handsome man who exuded self-confidence, he waved a cold pipe like a hammer at Wilbur Walters, whose job it was to sell the studio's motion pictures abroad. Gyssling sat placidly on a sofa, out of spitting range, his fingers steepled in front of his face.

"What the hell, Wilbur!" Mankiewicz boomed. "He killed *The Mad Dog of Europe* and *It Can't Happen Here*. He cut the heart out of *The Road Back*, and now you're gonna let the bastard do the same to *Three Comrades*."

Gyssling knew he was the "bastard."

There was a fourth man in the room, F. Scott Fitzgerald, his features already dissipated by alcohol at age forty. MGM had hired the famed novelist to adapt Remarque's novel for the screen. Appearing either woozy or bored, Fitzgerald hadn't said a word.

"You gonna let the Krauts fuck us again, Wilbur?" Mankiewicz said.

"Please, Joe," Walters pleaded. "Kindly show some respect.".

"How about respect for Remarque's novel and Scott's script?"

"Why, thank you, Joey." Fitzgerald slurred *thank* into *shank*.

Gyssling spoke up. "Mr. Fitzgerald, I so admire *The Great Gatsby*. A devastating indictment of the decadence of American capitalism."

"Not my point at all, old chap," Fitzgerald said.

Old shap.

"Who are you, again?

"He's the Nazi who carved up your script with Hermann Göring's sword," Mankiewicz said.

"Is this a sword-and-sandals picture?" Fitzgerald asked, sleepily. "I enjoyed Ramon Novarro in *Ben-Hur*."

Gyssling cleared his throat and gave Mankiewicz his most sincere look, one he routinely practiced in the mirror.

"Mr. Mankiewicz, you are a brilliant producer and an accomplished writer for a man of your age. I cannot wait for you to begin directing your own pictures."

"Aw, save the grease job for your Mercedes," Mankiewicz said.

"My point is you have a wonderful career ahead of you."

Mankiewicz laughed, but there was no humor in it. "Why does that sound like a threat? Oh, I know. Because you're the bastard who got Warner Brothers tossed out of Germany, and now you're threatening me. I'll have a great career…unless I cross you."

"Returning to the case at hand, Mr. Mankiewicz," Gyssling said, his voice as placid as a summer pond, "your anti-German sentiments are unacceptable."

"Correction. Anti-*Nazi*."

"One and the same. You dare not portray Germany as economically crippled or spiritually traumatized."

"Have you forgotten those days, Gyssling? It's when your merry band of thugs planned their *putsch*."

Gyssling turned to Walters. "Let's get down to it then, Wilbur." He thumbed through the script and found the page he sought. "Ah yes. The old Jewish man who lost two sons in the war and says he still loves Germany. Wilbur, you shall remove that character from the film and all other dialogue I have marked."

"I understand, Herr Gyssling," Walters said.

"Oh, kiss the Kraut's *tuchis*, why doncha?" Mankiewicz turned to Fitzgerald.

"Scott, you got anything to say?"

"How much will I be paid for the rewrite?"

"Aw, jeez, Scott. Go to the commissary and drink your lunch."

In a tone that was equal parts concern and menace, Gyssling said, "Wilbur, so that we are clear, without the changes, *Three Comrades* will not play in Germany. That goes for MGM's entire slate."

"Now, now, Herr Gyssling. I'm sure we can satisfy your requests."

"Requests!" boomed Mankiewicz. "Like the lion requesting dinner from the lamb?"

Unperturbed, Gyssling continued. "And I'll also see to it that Italy and Spain are closed to you."

"I'm sure that won't be necessary," Walters said.

Red-faced, Mankiewicz increased his volume. "Oh, kiss Mussolini's and Franco's asses while you're at it, Walters, you spineless jellyfish!"

Gyssling considered telling Mankiewicz that he was too good a writer to use the redundant "spineless jellyfish," but why fan the flames? Smiling to himself, Gyssling couldn't help but admire the producer, all of twenty-eight years old. What would the Americans say?

"You got some brass balls, kid."

Oh, the Yanks! So different from Europeans. So individualistic, so free to express themselves.

"So we're in agreement, Wilbur?" Gyssling pressed.

"Down to the last letter of the last word," Walters replied.

"Excellent, my friend," Gyssling said. "I look forward to our dinner at Trocadero next week." He turned to Mankiewicz. "Now, Joey…"

"Only my friends call me that."

Gyssling could not resist a parting shot. "*Herr* Mankiewicz, I hear Sam Goldwyn wants to do a remake of *The Passionate Plumber*. Perhaps if you're looking for work…" He let his voice trail off, and Mankiewicz stormed out of the office.

Rolfe, the uniformed chauffeur, opened the rear door of the limousine, and Gyssling settled into the plush passenger compartment, all hand-stitched golden leather and burled walnut paneling. He pulled a Gitane from a gold cigarette case, ignited it, and exhaled a victory plume. Gyssling disliked the French—who didn't?—but he enjoyed their wines, their women, and their cigarettes.

In a moment, the chauffeur was back behind the polished mahogany steering wheel, firing up the powerful engine, which whispered like a cat despite its supercharger. The limo exited the front gate and slipped onto Washington Boulevard. Gyssling turned on the wireless and stretched his legs in the spacious compartment. A newscast was on.

"The world's most luxurious airship, the *Hindenburg*, took to the skies last night from Germany, and is on its way to the States," the announcer said in stentorian tones. "After passing over New York City, the *Hindenburg* will touch down, soft as a feather, at the Naval Air Station in Lakehurst, New Jersey, on Thursday."

Gyssling turned the volume down. "News from the consulate, Rolfe?"

"Herr Goebbels and Frau Goebbels have arrived, sir."

Gyssling sighed. "I suppose no day can be perfect."

10
THE BUTCHER BROTHERS

Long Beach Armory, 251st Coast Artillery Regiment

William Dudley Pelley scanned the armory grounds with binoculars from outside the chain-link fence topped with barbed wire. He wore a mixture of uniforms: wool doughboy breeches from the Great War, the new M1937 lightweight army jacket with four pockets and epaulets, and a black navy watch cap. He looked ready for a battle but had no intention of being here the following night for what he called the "armory assault."

The sign on the front of the building read: LONG BEACH ARMORY 2ND BATTALION-251ST COAST ARTILLERY. The armory was a solid, L-shaped structure that commanded a 270-degree view of its surroundings. There were rifle ports under the windows and additional firing positions in a tower that joined the two sections of the *L*. Thus far, no foreign hordes had attacked the little fortress, though drunks had been known to toss empty beer bottles at the building.

Pelley was hidden from view by the trees and shrubs that grew, untended, just outside of the armory fence. With him were Kurt and Max Diekmann, two of the promising new members of the Silver Shirts. To Pelley, what made them most promising was that they owned a truck. The three men were squeezed together on the bench seat of the Ford model TT panel truck, Pelley between the broad-shouldered brothers.

Through the binoculars, Pelley saw two uniformed National Guardsmen approach the forty-foot-tall flagpole, preparing to lower the colors, and a third, carrying a bugle. Two of the men had potbellies, and the third's shirt was untucked.

Pelley handed the binoculars to Max Diekmann, older of the two brothers. "Take a look."

Max peered at the guardsmen and snorted. "They look soft as *kätzchen,*" using the German word for kittens. Both brothers, owners of a wholesale butcher business, spoke with German accents, having emigrated to the States after the Great War, surviving Kaiser Wilhelm's military with all their limbs intact but a deep-seated distrust of government. Husky, broad-shouldered men who could manhandle sides of beef. Both men wore stained buffalo plaid flannel shirts, malodorous with the stench of dead meat.

"C'mon, let me see, Max," Kurt said, elbowing his brother.

Two of the guardsmen began lowering the American flag, and the bugler played "Retreat," the end-of-the-day ritual.

Not yielding the binoculars, Max said, "From here, I could cut 'em in half with an MG34. Pop-pop-pop."

"Not necessary, Max," Pelley said. "The American military is with us or will be soon."

"How's that, Mr. Pelley?" Kurt said, wanting details and forgetting about the binoculars.

"Our movement is growing in all the armed forces. As for tomorrow night, I have a sergeant who's set everything up."

The setup being that the armory would be empty from eight o'clock the next night until six the following morning. The crates of Browning Automatics, grenades, and ammo would be stacked just inside the sliding metal door that opened onto the loading dock. All that secured the door was a simple padlock that could be crushed with a sledgehammer wielded by a reasonably strong man.

Kinderspiel. Child's play, Pelley thought.

When the butcher brothers would be smashing their way into the armory, Pelley would be wining and dining at the German consulate reception, a perfect alibi should the LAPD start sniffing around for suspects.

Why do they knock on my door every time tombstones are overturned in a Jewish cemetery?

The Diekmann brothers weren't on any law enforcement lists, and as combat veterans they wouldn't crack under pressure. Plus, of course, they had that truck.

"And you're sure we're not being tricked, Mr. Pelley?" Kurt asked.

"Tricked?"

"G-men with tommy guns just waiting for us."

Pelley showed his most reassuring smile. "Kurt, you've seen too many James Cagney movies."

He knew that Kurt had a wife and children and had become an American citizen. He had a stake in the community that Max, a bachelor with dried pig's blood under his fingernails, did not. Still a German citizen, Max's heart remained in the *Vaterland*. Like rowing a double scull, both men had to be in synchronization for the mission.

"I just need to know we'll be safe and we're on the right side of things is all," Kurt said. "For the USA, I mean."

Pelley had not anticipated this reluctance. A bit of fear, a hint of misplaced patriotism, but he considered himself a master of psychology and could deal with it.

"Insurrection is not treason," he said. "Who said it was?" Max broke in.

Kurt poked his brother in the chest. "Pipe down, Max. Mr. Pelley's talking to me."

"When justified, insurrection is the highest form of patriotism," Pelley continued.

"I suppose that's right," Kurt said, not sounding convinced.

"The Yanks say, 'It can't happen here.' But it already has. America was born out of insurrection against the British."

"Killed my share of Tommies in the mud at Passchendaele," Max volunteered.

"America's democracy is riddled with moral decay," Pelley said. "Its end is near."

"And we'll just goose it a bit, is that it?" Kurt asked, catching on.

"Excellent way of putting it," Pelley said.

Kurt nodded, "*We're* the patriots."

"Indeed. Now let's look at that truck."

The Diekmanns had parked their rusty, ten-year-old panel truck behind a patch of olive trees. It was a dull gray, boxy vehicle with sagging suspension, and Pelley hoped it could carry eleven hundred pounds of cargo. His second concern was the lettering two feet high on each side of the truck: DIEKMANN BROTHERS FINE WHOLESALE MEATS. WE4-7826

Generally speaking, robbers don't stamp their names and phone numbers on their getaway vehicles. But Pelley knew there was no time to change plans…or trucks. The sergeant had told him the armaments were scheduled to be transported to the Presidio Army Post in San Francisco the day after tomorrow. That was the only reason they'd be waiting just inside the sliding metal door, ready to be plucked the following night.

There was another reason to use the Diekmanns and their truck. It was less than three miles from the armory to their cold storage warehouse near the harbor in San Pedro. No danger of roadblocks or breakdowns fouling up the mission.

"Let's take a look in the back," he said to the brothers.

Max opened the truck's double doors, and Pelley peered inside. Two sides of beef hung on hooks on one side and three skinned carcasses of hogs on the other. While there were plenty of refrigerated trucks on the market, this wasn't one of them. What had been a large block of ice in a metal tray had mostly melted, and now bloodstained water meandered across the cargo bed and dripped onto the ground.

Pelley took a fancy sidestep and saved his two-toned shoes from being doused. But the smell had already hit him.

"Jesus, guys," Pelley said. "Clean up the truck bed and get rid of the smell."

"What smell?" the brothers asked in unison.

11
FLANNEL CAKES

Chaplin Estate, Gardens

At sunset, holding aperitifs, Chaplin and Einstein strolled through the estate's gardens toward the koi pond on their way to the house for dinner. Einstein was thinking about nuclear fission, and it occurred to him that his dilemma—his pacifist dilemma—was intertwined with Charlie's desire to make a movie ridiculing Hitler.

Everything fell into the same category.

What is best for America and the world? Would going to the German consulate help Charlie shine a light on fascism...even if only a few photons?

From his first visit, he loved America and the warmth of its people. He remembered the standing ovation he received at the Metropolitan Opera in New York...when they should have been applauding the performers of *Carmen*. Then there were the parishioners of Riverside Church in Manhattan erecting a statue of him, and the Hopi Indians in Arizona initiating him into their tribe as the "Great Relative." He recalled his joy at joining thousands of his *lantzmen* at a Hanukkah service at Madison Square Garden.

Try that at Deutsches Sportforum in Berlin! America! What's not to like?

While it felt presumptuous to think he could affect the cause of freedom across the globe, he nonetheless felt a duty to try. Some days he felt guilty that he enjoyed such peace and contentment while so many in Europe lived in daily fear.

"If you think it will help you make the movie about Hitler, Charlie, I'll go to the German consulate with you."

Chaplin beamed. "Thank you, my friend. Damned happy we got that sorted out."

"But I vow to have a lousy time."

"Ha! You might enjoy it. I'm old news. But you're the shiny new object in town. Georg Gyssling, the consul, is dying to meet you, and he'll introduce us to Joseph Goebbels."

"What an honor. Remind me to bathe."

"We'll never encounter anyone who's closer to Hitler. Don't you see? It's a great opportunity."

"All right, *boychik*. I'm going. I'm going. You remind me of Max Planck, prattling on about quantum mechanics. Quantum this, quantum that. Enough already!"

"Spot on, Albert."

"With those Nazi *momzers* everywhere," Einstein said, "are you taking precautions with this movie?"

"You bet. The script won't be circulated. The shoot will be in secret, and the set protected by armed guards."

Einstein shook his head sadly. "Such is our world, where comedy can get you killed."

"That's what we're fighting against, my friend. We'll sound the alarm to an oblivious world."

"Which reminds me….Princeton recently took a poll of its freshman class. The question was, 'who is the greatest living person in the world?' I came in second."

"That makes sense as long as I was first," Chaplin said.

"Adolf Hitler was first."

"That's bollocks! And ignorant. We're fighting that, too."

They passed a flower bed where a uniformed gardener was watering orange peonies. "Flowers are looking swell, Manuel," Chaplin said.

"Gracias, Señor Chaplin," the gardener replied.

They approached a large bed of roses, finely tended, carefully pruned, clearly defined rows. Chaplin pointed out his favorite flowers, chattering away.

"Those red ones are a hybrid called American Beauty, the little pink ones are Dainty Bess, which reminds me of a chorus girl at a music hall in Kansas City."

Einstein's gaze settled on an adjacent rose bed, and he walked that way. "What happened here?" He pointed to a zigzag pattern of blackened branches and fallen petals.

Chaplin came alongside. "A blight of some kind. I'll ask Manuel."

"Is it my imagination, or do those blighted ones form a swastika?"

"Albert, you've got Nazis on the brain. I don't see it."

"You're at the wrong angle. Come over here."

Chaplin moved a few paces and studied the rose bed.

"You're seeing things, Albert."

"*Gottenyu!* I feel like Dr. Semmelweis, who was mocked for telling doctors to wash their hands. Two more steps this way."

Chaplin moved again. "Nah. The lines aren't straight enough to form a swastika. It's an optical illusion, like looking at a cloud and seeing a buffalo."

"I hope you're right."

Chimes sounded, the playful tune of "La Cucaracha" coming from the house.

"Dinner's ready," Chaplin said. "Let's see if Maurice remembers how to make lamb kidneys the way Musso's does it. Did I tell you? Flannel cakes for dessert followed by a good strong cuppa."

Meaning a high ratio of tea leaves to hot water, Einstein knew. "Flannel cakes, Charlie?" *Are we eating old shirts?*

☞ ☜

An hour later, Chaplin and Einstein sat at a banquette in the kitchen, rather than the cavernous formal dining room. They'd finished their roast lamb kidneys, fried eggplant, and lima beans and were just starting on the fluffy buttermilk pancakes with raspberries and vanilla ice cream, their flannel cakes.

☞ ☜

Outside, it was dark, and just outside the iron gate, a Chevrolet sedan was parked alongside a sixteen-foot-high hedge that surrounded the property. A man in his forties with a graying brush cut and wearing a wrinkled, baggy gray suit got out of the car and walked to Chaplin's ornamental mailbox adjacent to the gate. Holding a flashlight, he extracted a handful of envelopes from the mailbox and examined each one. He slipped two envelopes into a jacket pocket, returned the others, and walked back to his car.

The sedan slowly pulled away from the hedge. No neighbors saw the car as it descended the slope of Summit Drive. If they had, they might have thought little of it, except for the license plate: "US Government."

12
THE FÜHRER'S ALTERNATIVE PLAN

Konsulat von Deutschland, Los Angeles

The six-story building was quite lovely, Gyssling thought, in the same way a concrete pillbox is lovely. Sturdy, strong, utilitarian. Narrow firing slits for machine guns in the pillbox, small windows of bulletproof glass in the building. With a final coat of paint not yet applied, the building was surrounded from ground to roof by an orange metal scaffold.

Fastened with bolts to the front wall was a sign: KONSULAT VON DEUTSCHLAND-CONSULATE OF GERMANY. The double doors—wood reinforced with steel slats—were wide enough to accommodate a pair of dancing elephants. Perched above the doors: a four-foot-high brass eagle clutching a swastika.

Consul Georg Gyssling and Minister of Public Enlightenment Joseph Goebbels sat in deep leather chairs in the consulate's study, holding tumblers of Glenlivet Black & White Scotch over ice. Looming above them was a life-size portrait of Adolf Hitler, steely-eyed and stern in his military uniform.

Gyssling vowed not to drink excessively.

I must be aware, not just of what Goebbels says, but what he leaves unsaid. When dealing with a smiling Brutus, never forget that he carries a knife.

"I hear congratulations are in order," Goebbels said. "MGM today."

"You barely set foot off the ship. How did you know?"

"As Sherlock Holmes said to Dr. Watson, 'I have my methods.'"

With a PhD in literature, Goebbels was well-read in a variety of genres. Popular fiction, Gyssling figured, relieved the tedium of reading anguished confessions painfully extracted from political prisoners at Sachsenhausen.

"*Danke,* Joseph," Gyssling said, pronouncing it, *Yo-seph.*

Goebbels saluted him with his whiskey tumbler, ice cubes rattling. "No ruffled feathers?"

"A producer named Joe Mankiewicz squawked like a plucked chicken."

The propaganda chief chuckled. "Did you put him in fear for his job or his life?"

Fear for his life? Does the little weasel imagine I'm an SS thug?

Gyssling wondered how many others in the Foreign Service were appalled at the Reich's rapid descent toward inhumanity. Surely there were some, but no one he knew had the courage to speak up.

And I'm the biggest coward of them all, stowing my conscience in a footlocker for the sake of my career.

"With the bravado of the young," Gyssling said, "Mankiewicz held his ground like the Brits on the banks of the Somme."

"And then?"

"I scraped him off my shoe like a smear of *hundescheisse.*"

Pandering to Goebbels like a pusillanimous lackey. Dear God, who am I to call the young producer "dog shit."

"Well done, Georg," Goebbels said. "Well done, indeed."

Over the years, Gyssling believed he had learned what made Goebbels tick.

The tick-tick-tick of a time bomb.

Is there anyone more dangerous, Gyssling wondered, than a puny, scrawny, ferret-faced man with a chip on his shoulder and vast power over others? Throw in a clubfoot that gave Goebbels a painful limp, and you have a boiling vat of jealousies, a rage against the world. How unjust, Goebbels must have felt, that a man with such a superior intellect should limp through life, looking up at inferior men. How many times on the playground had little Joseph been called a runt or *der zwerg*, the dwarf? How many brutish boys imitated his limp?

Barely nine months earlier, Goebbels sat in Hitler's box at Olympiastadion, watching Jesse Owens, the American Negro, win four gold medals and humiliate the furious Führer. How must Goebbels have felt, watching that modern-day Mercury, the Roman god of athletes, run as gracefully as a leopard, leap so effortlessly that he seemed to be flying?

Gyssling pictured the three discontented Nazis at the stadium. The shrimpy Goebbels and the corpulent Göring flanking Hitler with his stooped shoulders, his flaccid body, and his bowels chronically plagued by intestinal gas.

Now what was Goebbels saying?

"In his genius, the Führer believes that film is the greatest tool of persuasion the world has ever known."

"Well, it hardly takes a genius."

"Careful, Georg," Goebbels said in a cautionary tone.

Ignoring his vow, Gyssling drained his Scotch and poured himself another. "I'm sorry, Joseph. Please go on."

"Would you agree that Americans are gullible and malleable?"

"I would add naive," Gyssling said. "Waifs in the ways of the world." Of course, innocence was part of their allure, Gyssling thought, but could not say.

"Precisely why the Führer believes that motion pictures can lead America in any direction we dictate," Goebbels said. "Adopt any politics we prescribe."

"Joseph, the only politics in Hollywood is making money."

"What you're missing, Georg, is that entertainment and politics are connected like notes in a symphony."

"In Germany perhaps, but only because the Reich demands that entertainment serve the state."

"Ach! You fail to realize that Americans are just like Germans. They crave a strong leader whose orders are not to be questioned."

Gyssling stood his ground. "An authoritarian government? Not in their makeup."

"*Falsch!*" Goebbels's eyes flicked to the portrait of Hitler looming above them like a hawk over field mice.

"When fed a diet of our propaganda, Americans will cleanse their schools of Jewish books and teachers. They'll quash free speech as the mistress of anarchy. They'll purge dissidents from radio and newspapers and motion pictures. And before long, America will choose fascism without even knowing it."

The scotch having loosened his tongue, Gyssling said, "Joseph, if you give political lectures at the movies, Americans will throw their shoes at the screen."

"Not lectures, Georg. Dramas, comedies, love stories. All with the subtlety of telegrams slipped softly under the door."

Gyssling shook his head. "It's one thing to get RKO to kill *The Mad Dog of Europe*. But quite another to convince them to make…say, *Hitler's Europe: A Love Story*."

"Who wrote this *Mad Dog*?"

"Herman Mankiewicz. Joe's older brother."

"Jews, these Mankiewiczes?" Goebbels asked.

"Of course."

"And who runs RKO?"

"David Selznick and Pandro Berman."

Goebbels nodded knowingly.

"Yes, Joseph. Jews. Same with MGM, Warner, and Paramount. Pretty much everyone in town."

"So isn't the solution as obvious as the noses on their faces?"

"Surely Berlin knows that I don't have the power to get rid of the Jewish moguls."

Goebbels finished his scotch and seemed to process his thoughts, this time without looking to Hitler's portrait for divine inspiration.

"Georg, if you cannot change Hollywood from the inside, the Führer has devised an alternative plan."

In his genius, Gyssling thought, but chose not to say.

"The Reich has the capital to purchase the major studios," Goebbels said, refilling their glasses. "Quietly through American middlemen. And you will handle the transactions."

"I know the moguls, Joseph. They won't sell their toys at any price."

"Perhaps not today." Goebbels twirled the scotch in its tumbler. "But after fires on their backlots and fatalities on their sets, after insurance policies are canceled and loans called, they will beg for buyers. And we don't need them all. Two or three will do."

"Joseph, I'm a diplomat, not an arsonist."

"Of course. Rest assured we have American friends with paramilitary forces."

Good Lord! Is Goebbels listening to the fringe elements who preach insurrection?

"Not the Silver Shirts and that crackpot William Pelley," Gyssling said.

"Pelley's men have infiltrated the unions at every studio," Goebbels replied. "Teamsters, electricians, carpenters, plasterers, cement masons. The men will do his bidding."

Gyssling knew that Pelley had drawn police scrutiny, and there were rumors about undercover operatives attempting to infiltrate his group. One slipup, and he'd have a one-way ticket to Alcatraz. "Pelley tells anyone who'll listen that he wants to kidnap congressmen, hang Roosevelt, and start a second Civil War."

"Rhetorical flourishes."
"Joseph, he's what the Americans call a 'loose cannon.'"
"Then, Georg, I suggest you aim him in the right direction."

13
THE AUDITION

Chaplin Studios, Hollywood

"Where's my makeup girl?" Douglas Fairbanks demanded, sounding like the movie star he once was.

"You don't need makeup," Chaplin said.

"What about the lighting technician?" Fairbanks shielded his eyes and squinted at the overhead grid lights. "I'll look like a ghost in this glare."

"You're fine, Doug. And I'm the only one who's going to see the film."

Fairbanks looked around, perhaps to make certain they were alone. There was no crew, and the set was bare, other than a desk and a chair. They were on Sound Stage Three on the Chaplin Studios lot at La Brea Avenue and Sunset Boulevard. It was after 8:00 p.m., and outside, the lot was as quiet as a prayer.

"When you say a closed set, you mean like a bank vault."

"You don't need the wisenheimers at *Variety* saying you're auditioning," Chaplin said.

"And you don't want the Krauts reading your dialogue, pal."

True enough, Chaplin thought. The still-unnamed Hitler parody was at least a year from filming, and its existence was as tightly guarded as troop movements in times of war.

"Any directions you want to give to this old thespian?" Fairbanks asked.

"Doug, you're one of the greatest movie stars who ever lived."

"Thank you, chum."

"Now, forget that! Just have fun with the material. The script is a first draft, so feel free to sail off in any direction that seems right. Mug it up. You're Benzino Napaloni, Dictator of Bacteria. Your name alone sets the tone. Broad physical comedy, not sophisticated banter."

"Got it, Chap."

Chaplin adjusted a boom stand so that the microphone hung over the desk and chair. He was reluctant to audition his friend, but Doug needed the work and insisted he could play a buffoonish character based on Benito Mussolini. Chaplin was skeptical but hoped to be proven wrong.

Under the lights, the spider veins on Fairbanks's nose formed a road map of the best watering holes in Hollywood. Notwithstanding dissipation and aging, the actor still resembled a broad-shouldered swashbuckler. He wore an oversize military tunic with a pillow stuffed underneath to give him a barrel belly and more closely resemble *Il Duce*. A bandolier ran diagonally across his chest, and a Shriner's hat with a gold tassel was on his head.

You certainly look ludicrous, Chaplin thought, but can you play ludicrous?

A door opened at the side of the sound stage, and in walked a fiftyish man with yellowish hair the shade of nicotine stains. He wore work boots, corduroy trousers, and a denim shirt and said, "Evening, Mr. Chaplin."

"Thanks for coming, Oswald. Doug, this is our camera operator and the only other person on the set. Oswald, say hello to Doug Fairbanks."

Oswald nodded and said, "Which is your good side, Mr. Fairbanks?"

"These days, my ass."

"Let's get on with it," Chaplin said. "Oswald, no director's commands. Just focus, roll film, and keep it rolling."

"Yes, sir. And thank you for the privilege of working with you both. Someday I'll tell my grandchildren about this night."

Chaplin took the seat at the desk on the stage and affixed a toothbrush mustache to his upper lip so that Fairbanks would regard Chaplin's Adenoid Hynkel as the satirical version of Adolf Hitler.

With film rolling, Fairbanks crossed the stage. He was supposed to be strutting, arms swinging, a rolling doughnut of a man approaching the desk. Instead, Chaplin thought that the athletic Fairbanks looked like boxer Joe Louis stalking his prey.

Moving behind the chair, Fairbanks clopped Chaplin on the back so hard he flew face-first across the desk.

"My friend Hinky!" Fairbanks boomed in a faux Italian accent, effortlessly hoisting his friend off the floor. "How you feel, my brother dictator?"

Chaplin, in character as Hynkel, was speechless, overwhelmed by his boisterous guest. In a matter of seconds, Chaplin's facial expressions changed from befuddlement to nervousness to outright terror when he became purposely tongue-tied with a line of dialogue.

Fairbanks moved to the side of the desk where an actor playing Garbitsch, the Joseph Goebbels character, would be standing during a real shoot.

"Ach! My friend the Garbage!" Fairbanks shouted, smacking the imaginary character in his imaginary midsection. "I am simply crazy about this palace, all the ivory and gold!"

At the desk, Chaplin delicately picked up a carnation with his fingertips and held it to his nose as a lady might do when choosing a corsage at the florist shop. Watching him, Fairbanks guffawed and fell out of character.

"Sorry, Charlie, but I just love what you do without saying a word. Your Hitler is hilariously effete and neurotic."

"Not to mention a narcissistic blowhard who, underneath the bluster, is whiny, petty, and weak," Chaplin said.

"How do you like my Mussolini?" Fairbanks asked, hopefulness in his voice.

Chaplin ripped off his mustache. "Doug, you grinned through the scene. Mussolini scowls." He tightened his lips and turned them downward into a sneer. "And I say this as a dear friend. You're not funny."

"The hell, you say! All my early stage roles were comedies. I'm hilarious."

"Your natural humor is droll and sophisticated. Cary Grant in *Topper*. William Powell in *The Thin Man*. But this role demands tomfoolery and farce. Laurel and Hardy. The Marx Brothers. We're lampooning with a harpoon, not witty chatter."

"But that's how I'm playing it, Chap."

"Problem is, I can catch you acting. You're trying too hard. I'm sorry, Doug."

Fairbanks tore open his tunic and pulled out the pillow. He looked downcast, as sad as a fading sunset. "Aw, dammit all. You're right, Chap. I don't know what I was thinking."

From behind the camera, Oswald said, "Should I cut, Mr. Chaplin?"

"Yes, of course, Oswald. Thanks for coming in."

Oswald shut down the camera and headed for the door, and Chaplin crossed the stage toward his friend. "Doug, it's not over for you."

"I don't know, Chap. The phone doesn't ring."

"All you need is the right vehicle for your considerable talents. I'll keep my eyes open."

"You're aces, Chap. And I admire your guts, taking on the fascists. Just be careful, pal."

At home in Silver Lake, William Dudley Pelley was in his boxer shorts and undershirt, elastic garters on his calves holding up his socks. He reclined in an easy chair, his feet on an ottoman, a tumbler of Old Quaker whiskey in his hand. He was reading page proofs of *Liberation*, his Silver Legion magazine, correcting typos in a story urging the United States not to spend a penny helping England or France in the event of war with Germany.

The phone rang, and Pelley picked it up but said nothing.

Always let the other fellow show his cards first.

After a moment, Pelley said, "Yes, Oswald, I have a pencil. Go ahead." Pelley listened a moment while scribbling in red pencil on the edge of his page proofs.

"Oswald, let me read that back to you. 'Effete and neurotic. A narcissistic blowhard who, underneath the bluster, is whiny, petty, and weak.'"

Pelley listened a few more moments, then said, "Thank you, Oswald, and good night. Heil Hitler!"

So many possibilities, Pelley thought. With Joseph and Magda Goebbels in town, he could burnish his own image by sharing this nugget of priceless information. The news of Chaplin's planned movie would reach the highest levels.

The Führer might want to meet me!

The thought sent a pleasant musical sensation akin to "The Blue Danube" waltzing up Pelley's spine. But conveying the straight dope to Berlin only goes so far. Action must be taken to stop this calamitous affront. Chaplin did not submit his motion pictures to the German consul and couldn't care less if his work was banned in Germany, Italy, and Spain.

You can't silence Chaplin by slicing up his movies. So, how do you stop the bastard?

Taking his cue from the Führer's Night of the Long Knives, Pelley thought the answer was clear.
You slit his throat.

14
THE TEMPLE

B'nai Israel Temple, Wilshire Boulevard

The temple was a huge structure of white limestone with arches, towers, and tile work in the Moorish Revival style. The towers supported a huge gilded dome, glowing at night with two dozen spotlights. The sanctuary sat under the dome, its primary feature a three-hundred-foot-long circular mural depicting the history of the Jewish people, from Moses fleeing Egypt to America welcoming European refugees. A museum, meeting rooms, and a theater were located in various corners of the building.

On this night, laughter came from the theater where about two hundred congregants watched Chaplin's *Modern Times*. On the screen, in a sweatshop factory, a mean-spirited foreman shouts, albeit silently, at Chaplin, who can't keep up with the speedy conveyor belt. Exhausted, Chaplin falls onto the belt and is swallowed by the machine, like Jonah and the whale. As the congregants laughed and stomped their feet, Chaplin twisted like a pretzel through the machine's giant gears.

In the fifth row, a man in his seventies leaned close to his granddaughter and *shushed* her.

"Please stop laughing, Sarah," he said.

"Why?"

"It's not a comedy."

"But it's funny, *Zeyde*."

"It's about rampant capitalism and the subjugation of workers."

"What's sub-jug-a-lation?"

On the screen, Chaplin innocently gets caught up in a communist street rally and is arrested.

"Police state hoodlums!" the old-lefty grandfather said.

There were two other men in the audience who weren't laughing. In the last row sat Skowron and Zorn, the sharpshooting thugs from the Silver Shirts' firing range. No one paid any attention to them.

15
ROUND UP SOME PHYSICISTS

Oakland Avenue, Pasadena

The bungalow in the Oak Knoll neighborhood of Pasadena had a pitched roof of wood shingles and pepper trees in the front yard. During the day, hummingbirds helicoptered over the bright orange bracts of birds-of-paradise. After sundown, the neighborhood was quiet and dark, but for the dim streetlights.

The town so peaceful, the people so friendly, Einstein thought, as he conjured Berlin where thugs menaced Jews on the streets and in their shops. In this tranquil suburb of Los Angeles thirty miles east of Chaplin's mansion, Einstein enjoyed riding his bicycle to the nearby CalTech campus where he lectured to eager and awestruck students. In the silky dark evenings, however, the bungalow felt forlorn, Einstein still mourning the loss of his wife Elsa, who had died five months earlier.

Now, he sat at his kitchen table, sipping tea, the mysterious photograph of Otto Hahn and Fritz Strassmann in front of him. He could not get the German scientists out of his mind, equations coming to him in his sleep, interrupted by nightmares of massive bomb blasts.

The radio was turned on, and he listened absent-mindedly until the newscast turned to world affairs.

"In news from Asia," the announcer said solemnly, "Chinese nationalist Chiang Kai-Shek vows a united front with Chinese communists to oppose Japanese aggression."

Can there be any doubt that the worst is ahead?

"In Europe," the announcer said, even more grimly, "just three months after Chancellor Adolf Hitler called the Treaty of Versailles dead and buried, Germany's production of weapons of war has kicked into high gear."

Einstein sighed and said aloud, "The world prepares for war… again." He picked up the photo and studied it.

Hahn and Strassmann. Just how far along are you?

The only reason they would bombard uranium with neutrons would be to create the nuclear chain reaction that his friend Leo Szilard had theorized would release enormous amounts of energy, in other words, bombs of astounding destructive force.

On the radio, the announcer's tone became almost playful, as if announcing the winner of a cow-milking contest at a county fair. "In other news, Germany's giant airship, the *Hindenburg*, has encountered strong headwinds on its journey across the Atlantic. Still, officials insist the pride of the Reich will arrive on schedule at Lakehurst, New Jersey, on Thursday."

Einstein turned off the radio and walked into the living room. On a large chalkboard was written the partial equation from the photo plus what Einstein had added.

$$^{238}_{92}U + n \rightarrow \,^{239}_{92}U \text{ (40 seconds)} \rightarrow \,^{239}_{93}ekaRe \text{ (16 minutes)} \rightarrow$$

"Uranium 238. Uranium 239. What have we here?" Einstein said aloud. He picked up his chalk and put it down. He grabbed his briar pipe from a table, tapped out the tobacco residue, tamped in a fresh charge of the sweet Turkish, lighted up, and puffed away.

Chaplin's words came back to him. What if FDR asked him to help design a chain reaction bomb?

No! A pacifist could never work on such a project. But could I encourage others if their weapon would be used for a just cause?

A "just cause?" A rationalization, to be sure. Yet would that be worse than allowing the Nazis alone to possess such a weapon?

Another thought occurred to him.

Would they even need me, an alter kocker of 58, for a nuclear program?

He could think of several brilliant physicists who could work with engineers to convert mathematical predictions into machinery. Enrico Fermi came to mind. He did groundbreaking work with radioactivity and was trying to flee Italy. Then there was Szilard, who had patented the design for a nuclear chain reaction without creating one. He was in Switzerland with a position awaiting him at Columbia University in New York. Niels Bohr, the Danish physicist who had become a Nobel Laureate at thirty-six, would doubtless pack his bags for the States the moment Germany marched into Copenhagen. Then there was J. Robert Oppenheimer, a brilliant young physicist who became a full professor at Berkeley at age thirty-two. He was the lucky one of the group, born in the United States after his parents emigrated from Germany.

So, FDR, have at it! Round up some physicists.

Einstein turned his attention back to the blackboard, picked up the chalk, and began furiously scrawling numbers and letters that perhaps a dozen people in the world could comprehend.

16
HISTORY REPEATS ITSELF

B'nai Israel Temple, Wilshire Boulevard

The temple was quiet. *Modern Times* had been over for an hour, and the congregants had dispersed, happily chatting, discussing the movie many had seen multiple times. Skowron and Zorn, the Silver Shirts who had sat in the last row of the theater, were not among those who left the synagogue.

The lights were turned low when Henry Singleton, the sixty-six-year-old chief custodian, entered the rotunda of the sanctuary to straighten up. A Black man who attended the Trinity Baptist Church on Jefferson Boulevard, he had worked at the synagogue for two decades, cleaning, occasionally cooking, and even teaching some of the younger children how to ride bicycles in the parking lot. After work, he sometimes sat in the back row of Hebrew school classes, and he could belt out a decent version of "Hine Ma Tov," a traditional song about brotherhood among peoples. He also was a frequent guest at Purim and Chanukah celebrations at congregants' Beverly Hills homes.

Then there was Thursday-night poker in a meeting room, a Men's Club tradition. Singleton was the dealer, both because he was the only one the men fully trusted and because his nimble fingers kept the game running smoothly. Singleton made a quarter from each pot, and it added up over a four-hour game. But that was nothing compared to the tips the winners bestowed on him. If Irving Thalberg gave him a sawbuck, a ten-dollar bill, the next week Jack Warner might leave a double sawbuck, and Louis B. Mayer, not to be outdone, might even lay out a fifty. Between the poker and the Chanukah bonuses, Singleton put three children through college, and his daughter Irene—named after Mayer's daughter—was one of the few Black students at USC Medical School.

When he entered the sanctuary, Singleton wore a yarmulke out of respect, even when no one else was around. His routine never varied. After slipping on the yarmulke, he bowed slightly toward the ark that held the Torahs, then slowly turned in a circle, taking in the mural that ran three hundred feet around the circumference of the great room. The mural told the three-millennia story of the Jewish people, and it struck a chord with Singleton because of the similarities with the lives of his African ancestors. History, it seemed, merged among oppressed peoples.

The mural begins with Moses and the Israelites having just crossed the parted Red Sea while the unfortunate Egyptians in their chariots are hurled into the waters. In the second panel, Samson pulls down the pillars of the Temple of Dagon. Then in rapid succession comes King David, King Solomon, the destruction of the temples, life under the yoke of Rome, and onward through the centuries.

The panel that struck home was called *Inquisition and Exile*. A fearsome warrior on a flying beast aims his spear at defenseless Jews while fire from the beast's mouth burns down their homes. In a corner of the panel, weary refugees carry all their possessions on their backs as they flee the carnage.

Singleton, who grew up in Mississippi, remembered as a child the Ku Klux Klan burning down his family's church. When he first saw the mural's portrayal of the Spanish Inquisition, he could smell the burning timbers, could see the ashes floating like snowflakes from hell across a country road toward his home.

The final panel showed European Jews arriving in America. A female figure, not unlike the Statue of Liberty, holds out a welcoming torch toward a ship packed with refugees huddled on a lower deck. Though Jews and Negroes shared much in common, Singleton thought, no one welcomed his ancestors ashore, except at the end of a whip.

Walking toward the bimah, he noticed the door to the ark was ajar. He climbed the three steps to the ark and saw one of the Torahs on the floor, unscrolled, its blue and gold mantle discarded. Suddenly, the door of the ark burst open, and a burly man leapt out.

What the hell!

His scarred face contorted with anger, Skowron pummeled Singleton with furious punches, knocking him to the floor. Singleton tried to get to his knees, but Skowron, wearing steel-tipped boots, kicked him hard in the ribs. Singleton cried out and collapsed.

☞ ☜

At the rear of the synagogue, Skowron's pal Zorn opened a door, and half a dozen men poured in, carrying sledgehammers, cans of red paint, and a burlap bag filled with baseball-size rocks. They hustled into the sanctuary shouting "Heil Hitler!"

Singleton's hands and feet were bound, like a turkey trussed with twine for roasting. He could identify the thugs. Would they let him live to see the morning?

Maybe they don't care about an old colored man. Maybe they think I'm too timid to face them in a police station or courtroom.

Singleton felt as if his own home were being ransacked by the Klan and wished he had his daddy's old 12-gauge to defend it. He lay on the floor of the bimah, his cracked ribs aching, but the far greater pain came from what he saw and heard.

The men hammered the ark to smithereens, splinters flying, the smell of sawdust in the air. They competed to see who could inflict the most damage with one swing of the sledgehammer, like the strongman game at a carnival.

It's all a game to these ignorant hoodlums.

Winding up like baseball pitchers—*Hey, I'm Dizzy Dean!*—the men hurled rocks at stained-glass windows which depicted the twelve tribes of Israel. The mosaics had taken thousands of hours to construct and shattered in seconds, spraying shards like a waterfall, dousing the sanctuary in fragments of blues and browns, greens and purples. The fragments were so small that the stories disappeared, not unlike the Jewish tribes themselves. Singleton felt as if each shard pierced his own skin. Destroying temples, Singleton knew, had been a devil's festival for more than two millennia.

"Whadaya doin' in a Jew church, Uncle Tom?" Zorn taunted him.

Do these cowardly punks, these devils-in-training, attend any church?

"C'mon, guys! Let's go," Skowron ordered.

The men hoofed it out of the sanctuary, hooting and hollering, leaving Singleton bound and bruised. Red paint had spilled next to him, and the acrid smell was overpowering. But after a few moments, what he smelled were the timbers of his family's Mississippi church ablaze. Then he squeezed his eyes shut, and tears streamed down his face.

17
THE DESK SERGEANT

LAPD, Central Division

The desk sergeant, a man in his fifties named Riley, had a beer belly and small, suspicious eyes that had seen it all and not liked much of it. Jimmy Mitchell, freshly bathed and wearing a beige lightweight suit with a patterned silk tie, approached the desk. He had witnessed a murder and had run for his life and was trying to figure out how to tell his tale.

It had been several hours since his trash bin escape, but his nerves were still jumpy. Or maybe it was the venue. Most young Black men did not willingly walk into the LAPD's Central Division.

Mitchell stood silently while the sergeant filled out a form, taking his sweet time. Finally, he looked up, ran a hand through his thinning gray hair, and said, "Smelled you when you came in."

"What!" Mitchell rocked back a step.

"Your cologne. Bay Rum, yeah?"

Mitchell felt his shoulders relax. "My fiancée bought it for me."

Sergeant Riley barked a laugh. "My wife won't let me use it. Says it makes me smell like a glazed ham, chock-full of cloves." He lit a Chesterfield, took a puff, and sing-songed through a smoky haze, "What can-I-do-you-for?"

"Did anyone report a murder at Alt Heidelberg, the German place on Alvarado?"

Riley's eyes got narrower. "Why, you wanna confess?"

"No! I…I…just wondered…"

"Don't you dare go to the police!"

That was Luisa Moreno, his furious fiancée unloading on him an hour earlier, first in English, then in Spanish. She had told him to stay away from the Germans. So had his editor, but in a tussle between the cautious wisdom of others and his own rigid obstinance, Mitchell seldom chose prudence.

The sergeant laughed again. "Relax, kid. This ain't the movies. No one walks in and confesses, at least not in my twenty-seven years. And the only homicide tonight is a knifing in Echo Park. So, what's eating you?"

"I guess you'd say I was a witness," Mitchell said, his voice quavering.

"You guess?"

There was a commotion at the front door, where three young Mexican American men in baggy, high-waisted trousers, broad-shouldered jackets, and wide-brimmed hats were shoved toward the bullpen by two uniformed officers.

Nodding to the officers, Sergeant Riley said, "Pachucos in cell three." He turned back to Mitchell. "Now, what are you trying to tell me, son?"

"On the second floor, in a corridor at Alt Heidelberg, two men with guns shot a man in the back. I'm pretty sure he's dead. They shot at me, too, but missed." The words came pouring out and stopped just as abruptly.

The sergeant lifted a fountain pen from its stand and slid a printed form in front of him but made no move to write anything. "Name of the victim?"

Mitchell shook his head. "I'd never seen him before."

"And the two gunsels…they have names?"

"I never really saw their faces, but they spoke German."

"At Alt Heidelberg, that really narrows it down," Sergeant Riley said, his voice tinged with sarcasm. "You got a description of the victim?"

"A man in his thirties. Average height and stocky. White guy but dark complected. Looked Jewish, maybe."

"A Jew and a Negro on the second floor of Alt Heidelberg. What in the name of sweet Jesus were you doing there?"

"I'm a reporter for the *Sentinel*, and I'm working on a story. The victim…I think he might have been spying on a fascist group called the Silver Shirts."

The sergeant put the pen back in its stand. "What's your name, son?"

"James Mitchell, sir. My friends call me Jimmy."

When questioned by a copper, always answer respectfully but proudly. You ain't got nothing to hide. That's what Jimmy's father, Coziah Mitchell a Pullman porter on the Santa Fe Railway, drilled into him, and he'd said, "Yes, sir," clearly and distinctly, thousands of times over the decades.

"Now, Jimmy, are you saying that both you and this Jewish fellow were trespassing at Alt Heidelberg?" Sergeant Riley asked.

"That's not a capital offense, is it?"

Riley pointed an ink-stained index finger at Mitchell's chest. "Don't get smart-mouthed with me, Jimmy boy. Your story sounds like horse feathers and filing a false police report is damn sure a crime."

"I heard his last words!" Mitchell blurted out. He hadn't intended to say it, but in a moment of panic thought this detail might add credibility to his account. "'Operation Hollywood.' That's what he said to me."

"And then he croaked?"

"Yes, sir. I believe so."

Riley's brow furrowed as he chewed on a thought. "I get it! I seen the picture." Confused, Mitchell stayed quiet.

"Where's my movie expert?" The sergeant swiveled a hundred eighty degrees in his chair. "Ay, Detective Cooper! Got one for you."

A crew-cut, paunchy, middle-aged man in a wrinkled brown suit walked toward the front desk, a cigarette hanging from the corner of his mouth. He eyed Mitchell sideways, a vulture examining roadkill. Like many Black men, Mitchell had developed a sixth sense about white cops. Sergeant Riley seemed better than most. Detective Cooper—Mitchell would bet his bottom dollar—was a bone-deep racist, though he had yet to say a word.

"Coop, what's the movie where the guy gets shot at dinner," Riley asked, "and as he's dying, he whispers that there's a secret message hidden inside his shaving brush?"

"*The Man Who Knew Too Much*. Alfred Hitchcock. Why you asking?"

Riley cracked a smile. "Jimmy here claims he was at the German rally over at Alt Heidelberg."

"Not the rally," Mitchell said. "Upstairs."

Exhaling smoke at Mitchell, Detective Cooper said, "Must have loosened their membership rules."

"Any-who," Riley said, "Jimmy claims he saw a couple Krauts shoot a Jew who says 'Operation Hollywood' just before he kicks the bucket."

"That's rich," Cooper said, glaring at Mitchell. "Boy, how many times you been arrested?"

"Never, sir."

Not even once, you bigoted muttonhead.

Sergeant Riley's expression hardened, and like a judge on the bench, he stared down at Mitchell as if ready to sentence him to hard time. "My guess, Jimmy, is that you made a bet with some boys down in Little Harlem that you could get a numb-nut desk sergeant to write a report that reads like a Hitchcock picture."

"*The Cop Who Don't Know Shit*," Cooper said, belching a laugh.

"So, Jimmy," Riley said, "you got anything else to say?"

"Now that I think it over, I must have dreamed the whole thing," Mitchell said, anxious to bolt.

"Smart boy," Detective Cooper said. "You start making wild allegations, some people might want to settle your hash."

Mitchell nodded, turned, and headed for the door, the men's laughter echoing behind him.

18
SLEEPING WITH HITLER

Chaplin Estate, Master Bedroom

The ritzy neighborhood of Summit Drive was as still as a painting on this breezy May night. The gates of the estates were closed, the only sounds coming from the grounds of Pickfair, where two of Fairbanks's dogs barked at a screech owl. All was quiet at Buster Keaton's Italian Villa and Harold Lloyd's Greenacres. In Chaplin's mansion, a light shone in a second floor window, the master bedroom.

Chaplin lay in the massive bed, leaning against the art-deco headboard, tufted green velvet set in a mahogany frame. Just as numerical equations flashed through Einstein's mind, dialogue zipped in and out of Chaplin's consciousness. For his new project, he was thinking about a scene where Hitler, or rather "Hynkel," and Goebbels, or rather "Garbitsch," discuss wiping out all brunettes in favor of blondes. The idea was to demonstrate the absurdity of prejudice and hate. The scene wasn't quite working, so he let it go and picked up a book from the nightstand.

Paulette Goddard, his wife of one year and co-star of *Modern Times*, sat at a vanity table applying night cream to her face.

He looked up, watched her reflection in the vanity mirror, and admired the brunette beauty eleven years his junior.

I love this woman!

Of course, he'd thought the same about his first two wives. He had vowed to be faithful to Paulette, but he was weak when it came to women. And it was just so damn easy to bed them if you were rich and famous and had a twinkle in your eye. And the twinkle was overkill, like a third coat of wax on his Rolls-Royce. Shortly after marrying Paulette, Chaplin amended his vow.

If I can't be faithful, at least I'll be discreet.

"Tennis with Harold and Mildred tomorrow?" Paulette asked.

"What!" He flinched, startled by her voice breaking the silence. For a brief second, he thought Paulette was asking if he wanted to play tennis with Mildred, his first wife. But that was also the name of Harold Lloyd's wife.

"Our court or theirs?" he asked.

"Riviera, followed by a late lunch."

"Fiddlesticks! I'm taking Albert to the ball game and then the German consulate."

"You and Albert. The Hopalong Cassidy and Windy Halliday of Beverly Hills."

"Yer dern tootin'!" Chaplin laughed, using a familiar line from the Westerns. "Do you think we'll need our six-shooters tomorrow night?"

"Unlikely. With bigwigs sponging free caviar, the Germans will put on their best face."

"Meaning a front as false as a saloon at a movie ranch?"

"Exactly." She noticed him watching her reflection in the mirror. "What, darling?"

"You're a peach. Say, have you heard back from Selznick?"

"Not directly, but everybody says it's between Vivien Leigh and me."

Chaplin put down his book. "Leigh? A Brit playing a Southern belle?"

She laughed. "Charlie, you're a Brit playing an American tramp."

"Excellent point. Fifteen love, sweetheart."

He opened his book and started reading again. She turned off the vanity lights, walked to the bed, and leaned over to read the cover.

"*Mein Kampf?* Are you going to bed with Hitler or with me?"

"I need to dig into the dark recesses of the Nazi mind. And this is a stew of delusions, paranoia, and hate seasoned with a God complex." He skimmed several pages, found what he was looking for, and said, "Listen to this, sweetheart. 'I act in accordance with the will of the Almighty Creator. By defending myself against the Jews, I am fighting for the work of the Lord.'"

"How grotesque."

She slipped into bed, taking her own book from the nightstand. *Gone with the Wind* by Margaret Mitchell, the bestselling novel of the past year.

"We need to stop Hitler before it's too late," Chaplin said.

"We?"

"I told Albert how I'm going to use my art against him."

"The satire about Hitler? I love you, Charlie…"

"I hear a 'but' coming."

"But when the curtain opens, your fans expect a comedy."

"Like gold in a Colorado mine," Chaplin said, "humor can be found in tiny crevices. The laughs come at the expense of Hitler. After I make him look ridiculous, I shift the tone and end the picture with a straightforward plea for peace and brotherhood."

She thought a moment before speaking. Chaplin could tell Paulette wasn't sold on the idea, and she was about to measure her words like a rookie bartender using a jigger to mix a martini. "This is a departure for you, Charlie."

"Right. Something important for once."

"Oh, please. The Tramp will live forever. The voice of the underdog, without an actual voice. A brilliant creation."

"Correction. Albert is brilliant. I am merely clever."

"All these years, and you still sell yourself short."

"Nothing in my prior work compares to this, sweetheart." He studied her a moment. "I get it now. You think it'll be a big, fat flop."

"I didn't say that. I don't know. It almost…"

"Yeah?"

Now, he knew, she would toss the jigger aside and just pour a waterfall from the gin bottle. "It almost doesn't sound like a motion picture," she said. "More like a lecture."

"Uh-huh."

"I'm sorry, Charlie. I should trust your judgment. My God, look at what you've accomplished."

"In floppy shoes and a fake mustache."

She took a breath and said, "Tell me more. Do you have a title?"

"I was thinking, *The Little Dictator*."

She shook her head. "Too close to your Little Tramp."

He laughed. "You're right! I married such a smart cookie. Thirty love, Paulette."

It was true that he loved smart women. But he also loved dim-witted, well-proportioned, acquiescent women, and if they tended to the younger side, well, them, too. It was a failing, he knew, his desire to be the first man in their lives, the one who molded them. He wished he could curb his voracious appetite for their warmth, for their curves, for the moist pleasures that lay beneath so many sheets on so many beds.

"Okay, sweetheart," Chaplin said. "Let's turn the title around. *The* Big *Dictator*."

She winced. "You're begging for bad reviews."

"How so?"

"The wags at *Variety* would call it *The Big Dick*."

"Ah. Another point for Paulette. Forty love. I'll keep working on it."

He picked up the book and continued reading. It took only a moment to find another vein in Hitler's motherlode. "Get a load of this, sweetheart. 'The receptive powers of the masses are feeble, so that all propaganda must be confined to a few bare essentials that are repeated until the very last individual has come to grasp with the idea.'"

"In other words," she said, "people are idiots."

"And can be controlled with lies," he added.

"How cynical and cold-blooded." She sighed. "And how sad for mankind."

Chaplin looked up from the book, cocked his head to one side, and gazed at her.

"I know that look," she said. "I first saw it when you auditioned me. You were deciding whether to cast me or bed me."

"Both, in your case. But what I'm thinking now is that you and Vivien Leigh look a lot alike."

"So I've heard tell."

"You're a better actress."

Paulette smiled and put on a deep Southern accent. "If Ah said Ah was madly in love with you, Rhett, Ah'd be lyin' and what's more, you'd know it."

He applauded and said, "If that's acting, the Academy will give you a little gold statue. If it's not, I'll throw myself off the top of City Hall."

"You won't get very far."

"Straight down is quite far."

"The shoulders of the building, the wedding cake design, would catch you. You've fallen farther in stunts."

"Foiled again. Game, set, match for Paulette."

19
AMERICA'S LITTLE DARLING AND THE LONE EAGLE

Konsulat von Deutschland, Rooftop Balcony

The Hakenkreuz flag, a black swastika on a white circle with a red background, snapped and cracked in the brisk nighttime breeze. The flag flew proudly on the rooftop balcony of the German consulate, where, just after midnight, Goebbels and Gyssling emerged from a stairwell. They had graduated from Scotch to champagne, and Gyssling carried a bottle of Dom Pérignon Brut, 1930 vintage, while Goebbels brought two crystal flutes. They walked to the edge of the balcony where an orange painter's scaffold ended at the rooftop.

Gyssling had expected the evening to have rough patches, but so far it had gone even worse than he could have predicted.

Dumping William Pelley in my lap? If he involves me in his deranged conspiracies, will diplomatic immunity keep me out of prison?

Why had Goebbels even journeyed so far from home? Just for the dedication of the new building? Not likely. His fascination with American paramilitary groups was an ominous omen.

Goebbels gestured toward the scaffold. "A shame the work was not completed prior to the reception."

"Quite a mess, Joseph. When the unions struck, it cost me a fortune to bribe the foremen."

Goebbels made a scoffing sound. "In Berlin, it was much cheaper to shoot the foremen and dissolve the unions."

Gyssling poured champagne, and they looked westward. A thin crescent moon hung over the ocean. "That small ribbon of light is the Santa Monica Pier," Gyssling said. "During the day, we have an excellent view of the beautiful beach and ocean."

"Ach Georg, your fondness for America is showing. I wonder if you see her weaknesses."

Below them, at treetop level, two black crows chased a pigeon, their *caws* sounding like battle cries. Gyssling decided to keep quiet and listen, hoping to avoid further missteps.

"The American economy still struggles," Goebbels continued. "Steel workers strike. Auto workers strike. Dust storms destroy livelihoods. The people are tired of Roosevelt."

Gyssling wondered what "people" Goebbels meant. Less than a year earlier, FDR had carried forty-six out of forty-eight states in his reelection. If he chose to run in 1940, he would be the favorite for an unprecedented third term.

Goebbels sipped his champagne and said, "Georg, who is the most popular person in America?"

"According to this new outfit called the Gallup Poll, it's Shirley Temple. America's Little Darling."

"Ach! You and your movies! I'm talking about someone who will be at our reception tomorrow."

Gyssling thought a moment, but Goebbels was impatient.

"The Lone Eagle!"

"But of course, Charles Lindbergh."

"And when you think of Lindbergh, what words spring to mind?" Goebbels asked.

"Young. Handsome. Heroic," Gyssling said.

Also, bland, vapid, uninformed.

"And Aryan!" Goebbels said. "As if we created him in the laboratory."

Agreed! Lindbergh seems stiff as a robot but with less humor.

"He's accepted Göring's invitation to visit Berlin and fly Willy Messerschmidt's newest fighter. Certain opportunities will be presented to him."

"Joseph, you're dancing around like teenagers doing the Lindy Hop. What's my role in all this?"

"First, you make Lindbergh a movie star…like Shirley Temple." On the street below, a police siren wailed.

"Next," Goebbels continued, "we make Lindbergh president. With you controlling messages from Hollywood and Pelley's Silver Shirts creating civil unrest, Americans will yearn for a strong, virile presence in the White House. A Midwestern man of the people. Not a cripple from high-society Jew York."

Jew York. Such a tiresome slur. And President Charles Lindbergh? Well, no more preposterous than Corporal Adolf Hitler, son of Alois Schicklgruber, becoming Führer.

"Does Lindbergh even want to be president?" Gyssling asked.

"He cannot decide. But he is adamantly opposed to America's involvement in another European war. We must convince him that only he can prevent such a catastrophe."

That might work if Lindbergh is a megalomaniac like you-know-who in Berlin.

"We also have certain subtle methods of persuasion that I cannot get into," Goebbels continued.

That usually means blackmail, but what do they have on Lucky Lindy? "So connecting the dots," Gyssling said, "the motive for taking over Hollywood is to install a friend in the White House."

Goebbels nodded. "And to have a powerful ally against the Soviets."

Whose idea is this? The alcoholic Himmler or the morphine addict Göring?

Overhead in the distance, an airplane flying south along the coast began a slow curl to the east over land. The last passenger flight of the night, a DC-3 from San Francisco to Grand Central Airport in Glendale, Gyssling figured. He momentarily wished he were airborne.

Where to? Anywhere!

Goebbels gestured over the railing toward the west. "This Santa Monica Pier you mentioned, Georg. What do you do there?"

Goebbels's question seemed untethered to their conversation, and Gyssling wondered what he was getting at. "I eat ice cream and ride the carousel like a child. The calliope music is quite rousing. Fanfare tunes mostly."

"John Philip Sousa marches?"

"Oh yes. All those trumpets and drums."

"So you tap your toes to 'Stars and Stripes Forever'?"

Ah, so there it was. A clumsy oaf, I stepped right into that trap.

Gyssling refilled their flutes again, buying time. "Joseph, what are you getting at?"

"Adolf asked me to judge if you had become Americanized."

That sent a shiver through Gyssling. It was as if Goebbels had said, "Adolf wonders if you've converted to Judaism." And Gyssling did not miss the reference to the Führer as "Adolf."

Letting me know just how close they are.

"Joseph! You know I love the Fatherland with all my heart."

"Yes, yes. But you also love the Hollywood life. The parties, the women...the carousel at the pier."

Gyssling drained his champagne, wishing it were still the Scotch. "What have I done to arouse the Führer's concern?"

"As you surely know, Adolf calls Charlie Chaplin a 'little Jewish acrobat...'"

"'As disgusting as he is tedious.' I know. I know. The Führer hates Chaplin and loves Mickey Mouse."

"And yet you invite Chaplin to our reception."

"The mouse had a prior engagement."

"Enough with your Hollywood wit! Is it true that Chaplin is planning a motion picture about the Führer?"

"A Hollywood rumor, Joseph. Studio chitchat. Nothing more."

"We have had eyes on Chaplin for some time, and we will step up those efforts."

"Surveillance?"

"For now. If more is required, our actions will be quick and discreet."

Mein Gott! Do these people—my people—know no limits?

"Then today," Goebbels continued, "I learn that Chaplin is bringing Einstein to the consulate." Ein-*shtein*. "Surely you know he's been declared an enemy of the state."

"Not the state of California," Gyssling said. "In Hollywood, Chaplin and Einstein are on what's called the 'A-list.'"

"Good for them," Goebbels said. "But they had better hope never to land on my list."

20
THE HAMMER AND THE ANVIL

May 5, 1937 - Hollywood Boulevard, Hollywood

The barbershop near the intersection of Hollywood and Vine had a stenciled window reading, HUBER ROSCH BARBIER-HAARSCHNITTE-25 CENTS.

William Dudley Pelley sat in the barber's chair, getting his two-bits haircut with his goatee trimmed at no extra charge. Two German American men sat in chairs, waiting their turns. One was reading the *Los Angeles Times,* and even in the mirror's reverse reflection, Pelley could read the front-page headline: LOOK UP, NEW YORKERS-HINDENBURG TO SOAR OVER MANHATTAN. The photo of the airship, swastika on its tail, took up half the page.

"Huber, what will the Americans think when they see the *Hindenburg* above the Empire State Building?" Pelley asked.

"That they're quite lucky." The barber, who had a chrome dome without a stitch of hair, waited while Pelley gave him a quizzical look, then added, "Lucky that it's not a Junkers Stutka dropping five hundred kilogram bombs."

Pelley laughed, and so did the two men waiting for their haircuts. It felt damn good, Pelley thought, to be among friends.

Fifteen minutes later, his face tingling from the spicy Pinaud Clubman cologne, Pelley emerged from the shop and hoofed it west on Hollywood Boulevard. A pleasant breeze danced among the buildings, pedestrians hurrying along, the street alive with honking horns and the ringing bells of the Red Cars, auto exhaust fumes mixing with the aroma of pork tamales from street vendors.

He glanced across the street at the Pantages Theatre, a cavernous hall for motion pictures and, until recently, vaudeville. The marquee advertised *A Star Is Born* with Fredric March and Janet Gaynor. Pelley despised March, the self-righteous son of a Presbyterian elder, who was one of the leaders of the Hollywood Anti-Nazi League, a bunch of hoity-toity Tinseltown types.

Pelley crossed Vine Street at a brisk pace, pedestrians in business garb crowding the busy intersection. With financial support from fascist sympathizers, Pelley's attire had improved in recent years. Today he fit right in with his three-piece suit of navy blue tweed, a white shirt with gold cuff links, and a burgundy silk tie. His cuffed trousers fell to the midway point of his reptile leather two-tone shoes, and his black felt homburg with a white ostrich feather was cocked at a jaunty angle.

This was his daily constitutional, and he enjoyed the exercise as well as observing the people hurrying about their quotidian tasks, oblivious as to what was coming.

The storm! The cataclysm!

He felt peppy, a hop in his step, swaggering along the sidewalk like a bantam rooster proud of its feathers. He had only one thing on his mind. He needed to hear from the Diekmann brothers that they were ready to snatch the weapons from the armory tonight. Meanwhile, he would be at the consulate, munching hors d'oeuvres with Joseph Goebbels and friends.

And wouldn't Goebbels be impressed? That blowhard Fritz Kuhn and his German American Bund never pulled off anything so audacious!

Exhilarated, Pelley felt primed for larger things. After tonight he would be an important figure in America's fascist future. He had envisioned it for years. Borders would be closed to all but northern Europeans of the right breeding. Jews and Negroes, the ones who didn't flee the country during the coming insurrection or die fighting against it, would be sequestered in their own fenced towns or shipped elsewhere. He wondered if the territory of Alaska might be the right place. The thought of Africans in Alaska made him smile, and not just because of the weather. As residents of the territory, they would never have congressmen or senators or any seat at the table of government. And why not send Jews to the same place?

Negroes, Jews, and Eskimos miscegenating in igloos. We could put their half-breed kinder in zoos!

He began humming "Horst-Wessel-Lied," the Nazi Party anthem. In his mind, he saw parades with drums and bugles and marching soldiers. So far, it had been a perfect day.

Crossing Cahuenga Boulevard, he slipped the silver flask from an inside pocket of his suit coat and, without breaking stride, took a long pull of Old Quaker whiskey. He crossed the street at Wilcox, quickening his step to avoid a trolley of the Pacific Electric Railway. To his right, in the hills, he could see the huge HOLLYWOODLAND sign advertising a real estate development. In his mind, he could see fifty-foot-high letters spelling out NAZILAND.

Between Cherokee and Las Palmas, he noticed a commotion in front of Musso and Frank Grill, the restaurant the Hollywood swells called home.

Now what's the rumpus?

Thirty yards closer, he saw exactly what it was.

A black Rolls-Royce Phantom II convertible, sleek and low-slung with a custom red pinstripe on the side...surrounded by a throng of people.

A throng of morons! Slobbering celebrity worshippers!

Sitting at the wheel of the open car was Charlie Chaplin, and next to him was Albert Einstein. He knew all about Chaplin. Married to a Jewess and his half-brother a Jew.

When he's asked, Chaplin never denies that he's a Jew, so put that in your menorah and light it.

As for Einstein, the most famous Jew in the world, why didn't he stick to his equations instead of spending all his time weeping about refugees and ranting about the wickedness of the Reich?

Pelley had seen them together six years earlier at the premiere of *City Lights*, the sappy fairy tale that earned Chaplin another million bucks or so. Pelley's distaste for the man in those days was partly jealousy, he would readily admit. But now there was something far more insidious at play.

The slanderous movie! The utter gall of Chaplin portraying the Führer, mocking his greatness, demeaning him with infantile humor.

Pelley carried a Luger under his suitcoat in a shoulder holster. He envisioned pulling the gun now, feeling its cool weight in his hand as he committed the most sensational double murder in history.

Hadn't the Führer said that each person is either the "hammer or the anvil," and if "men wish to live, they must kill others?"

Hitler would venerate me! So why not act now and be showered with hosannas tonight?

News of both his triumphs—the armory and the assassinations—would ripple across the consulate reception like secrets in the wind. He pictured the envious stares of men and the lustful looks of women.

Then his dreaminess stopped with a cold realization. His vivid imagination was both a blessing and a curse. It fueled his writing, which had won two O. Henry Awards and led to work in Hollywood, but it also lured him into fools' errands like his presidential campaign one year earlier where he won less than two thousand votes and was ridiculed by both commies and rival fascists. Killing Chaplin and Einstein in broad daylight on Hollywood Boulevard was a half-cocked plan. He was easily recognizable and on foot with no getaway vehicle. He needed to tame his imagination and slow down.

How long had Hitler planned the Night of the Long Knives?

Much like the Führer, Pelley would pull the strings of the assassinations but be nowhere near the scene of the crimes.

Now Pelley turned his attention back to the Rolls-Royce and the crowd of simpletons, the air thick with idol worship.

"How was lunch at Musso's, Mr. Chaplin?" asked a man in cowboy boots and denim trousers.

"Superb! Grenadine of beef for me, chicken pot pie for the professor," Chaplin answered. "And maybe an eensy-teeny martini for both of us."

The crowd laughed, and Pelley felt like retching.

"What's the secret of your comedy?" asked a woman in a plaid dress and seamed stockings.

"My pain may be the reason for somebody's laugh, but my laugh must never be the reason for somebody's pain," Chaplin said.

The people applauded, and Pelley glared at them for their infantile behavior.

The man in cowboy boots angled up to the Rolls. "Professor Einstein, how do you like America?"

"In a world of brutal dictators and helpless refugees, she is our best hope."

They applauded again, their brains mushy as oatmeal, Pelley thought, moving closer to the fancy car.

"Hey!" he shouted, and everyone turned to look. "What's the solution to America's Jewish problem?"

A low grumble ran through the throng of fans.

Einstein stroked his chin, smiled, and said, "*Nu*, the only problem I know is finding a decent matzoh ball soup."

Chaplin said, "The Jewish problem is that America has more than its share of ignoramuses. Petty, weak men who can only feel good about themselves by acting superior to others, and the only way they can do that is by prejudice and cruelty."

"And by dressing up like toy soldiers in a terrible German opera," Einstein chimed in.

The fans laughed and applauded, and Pelley scowled. Being laughed at was harder to take than a knee to the groin.

Chaplin gave the throng his movie-star smile. "Gotta go, folks. Heading to the Angels' game."

The crowd parted, and the Rolls pulled away from the curb.

Pelley grabbed his flask from inside his suit coat. His first drink of the day had been celebratory, but now the whiskey was fuel, gurgling on the way down, singeing his throat.

He coughed, smacked his lips, and said aloud, "Showy Jews will get theirs."

21
LET MY PEOPLE GO

Hollywood to South Los Angeles

The Rolls-Royce convertible turned from Hollywood Boulevard onto Highland Avenue, heading south toward the baseball stadium. Chaplin wore a bespoke, no-vent gray suit over a white shirt with long spear collars and a burgundy patterned tie. Einstein, who cared as much about his appearance as a woolly mammoth, wore ancient shaker knit blue and green cardigan over a brown shirt.

Chaplin explained that they were going to a Pacific Coast League game between the Los Angeles Angels and the San Diego Padres. "It's not the majors, but it's as close as we'll ever get on the West Coast."

"Majors, colonels, whatever. It's fine with me," Einstein said. He was happy to be in the open air, not sweating over theorems and mathematical constructs on his blackboard or worrying about Hahn and Strassmann working on nuclear fission.

Chaplin seemed enthused about sharing a slice of Americana, and Einstein decided to be a good sport, even if the game did not hold his interest. Something else was on his mind, the party at the German consulate. As long as they were going, why not do something useful? He would confront either Gyssling or Goebbels about the humanitarian crisis the Reich has caused.

"If you hate Jews so much, why make it so difficult to emigrate? Let my people go!"

Einstein wondered if he even had the courage to confront Nazi officials in their own building, essentially foreign territory. He knew there would be Schutzstaffel officers there, the SS, monsters in black leather. But surely his notoriety prevented them from dragging him to the basement in chains.

Or did it?

"Albert, do you know anything about baseball?" Chaplin asked, bringing him back to the moment.

"More than you might think. I have heard the expression 'As American as baseball and apple strudel.'"

"Close enough," Chaplin said.

"I have heard of Babe Ruth, Lou Gehrig, and a *lantzman* named Hank Greenberg."

"Great players. They can all hit the ball a mile."

"I seriously doubt that."

Chaplin let it pass and turned on the radio, which was tuned to a newscast, the announcer's voice stern: "FBI director J. Edgar Hoover told a congressional committee today that communist subversion is the number one threat to America."

"Only if your head's up your ass," Chaplin said.

"Shhh," Einstein said.

Hoover's voice came over the radio. "The Bureau has put the kibosh on outlaws of every stripe, but the Reds are more clever and insidious than Machine Gun Kelly and John Dillinger."

Chaplin turned off the radio, twisting the dial so hard it could have broken.

"Your J. Edgar Hoover held up my visa on grounds I had communist tendencies," Einstein said.

"In his pea brain," Chaplin said, "pacifists are communists. He's had me under surveillance for years as a Red…and a degenerate."

"This I must hear."

"For years, I've enjoyed sex with many different women, more than I can count."

"I see."

"You won't reduce that to an equation involving mass and energy, will you, Albert?"

Einstein shrugged. "Not unless you're *shtupping* at the speed of light."

As they headed south on Central Avenue, traffic thickened. It was a street of hotels, restaurants, grocery stores, blues clubs, and office buildings in the heart of African American Los Angeles. Well-dressed couples strolled the sidewalks, some pushing baby carriages. Music poured out of storefronts, Chaplin recognizing a jazzy piano number, Jelly Roll Morton's recording of "King Porter Stomp." A string of nightclubs caught their attention. The Apex Club, the Downbeat, the Flame, the Casablanca, and Club Alabam where the sign promised DIZZY GILLESPIE TONIGHT.

"This neighborhood looks like more fun than Beverly Hills," Einstein said.

"Way more, Albert. One night we'll come down for some jazz straight from Harlem."

Chaplin turned onto Forty-Second Street and drove three blocks to Wrigley Field, a smaller version of the Chicago ballpark. He pulled the Rolls-Royce into a parking spot in the V.I.P. Row, where "C. CHAPLIN" was painted on the curb.

Chaplin reached into the back seat and grabbed two baseball caps with blue bills and white crowns and "LA" embroidered in the front. He put one on Einstein's head, no easy task with all that white hair spilling out.

"What, are we going to synagogue?" Einstein asked in his familiar sing-song.

Chaplin put on the other cap, then opened the glove box and came out with two pairs of sunglasses with white plastic frames. He put on one pair and handed the other pair to Einstein.

"Why do we need these?" Einstein asked. "Are we handling phosphorus?"

"C'mon, be a sport, Albert."

Both men put on the sunglasses, exited the Rolls, and crossed the street to the stadium. They fell into step with hundreds of others, happily chattering on their way to a sunny afternoon of pure Americana.

Einstein watched the people a moment and said, "Charlie, do you ever stop to think how lucky we are that this big, beautiful country welcomed us, and beyond that, invited us to live in peace and prosperity?"

"Albert, my friend, I cherish that thought every day."

22
THE CHOIRBOY

Pacific Electric Railway, Hollywood Line

Pelley knew what would cheer him up. The Aryan Bookstore. The shelves would be stocked with his books and pamphlets, the adjacent German restaurant filled with like-minded people, some of whom might greet him by name as they enjoyed their schnitzel and beer. Fortuitous, because he had to be there anyway to receive the message from the Diekmanns, hopefully that the armory assault was on.

He hopped on an eastbound Red Car, handed the conductor a nickel, and looked for a place to sit. The trolley was crowded, the passengers a stew of races. Negroes. Mexicans. Chinese. A few white people and a man who could have been an Apache or just another Mexican.

Pelley spotted an empty space on a wooden bench next to a slim Negro man in a US naval uniform. Probably a mess attendant third class on one of the destroyers docked at the Long Beach port. No way Pelley would sit next to a colored swab jockey.

Pelley scowled as if his sauerkraut were too damn sour and squeezed between two middle-aged white women, who were not overjoyed at his presence. The trolley rang its bell, turned south onto Vermont Avenue, and smoothly eased south, passing

Sunset Boulevard, Santa Monica Boulevard, and Melrose Avenue, stopping here and there to discharge and pick up passengers.

At the Beverly Boulevard stop, a white man and Negro woman climbed aboard together. Late twenties, both in denim trousers, hers rolled up to midcalf as if she expected to wade through puddles. The man wore loafers that looked as if they hadn't been shined since the first caveman strapped leather hides to his feet. They sat down, so close together you couldn't slip a dollar bill between them.

Pelley studied the interracial couple for a long moment, maybe too long. He didn't know what his face showed, but whatever it was, the white man didn't like it.

"You got a problem, bub?"

"I'm not the one with the problem, sonny."

When the man didn't respond, Pelley smirked and said, "Did you know that coloreds are the prime carriers of venereal disease?"

"What!" The man balled his hands into fists.

"Scientific fact," Pelley said.

"How'd you like a knuckle sandwich, huh?"

"Our so-called melting pot of races, creeds, and religions will create a horde of mongrels who multiply like vermin."

The man started to stand, but the woman put a hand on his arm. "David, no! He's just an old rummy. I can smell the booze on him."

Pelley resented the world "old" coming from this impudent Negress. As for "rummy," he could hold his liquor like Harry James could hold a high note. Pelley got to his feet, wobbled once—the damn trolley jostling—and headed for the door.

"I'll walk," he said to the young couple. "Stinks in here."

☞ ☜

Pelley's spirits lifted as he approached the Aryan Bookstore on the ground floor of Alt Heidelberg. Less than eighteen hours earlier, he was huddled with his lieutenants in a private meeting room on the second floor, mapping out Operation Hollywood.

Where, other than the Reich, has there been such a glorious plan? Perhaps Torquemada's Spain in the fifteenth century.

Not that the evening had gone smoothly. There had been two intruders. A spy who looked like a Jew and a Negro—no mistaking that—had gotten past security. The spy had no identification papers, but he was working for a seat-of-the-pants outfit run by Leon Lewis, a lawyer who had been agitating, unsuccessfully, for the LAPD and the FBI to crack down on the Silver Shirts.

The spy was dead, and his remains would never be found, except by cows grazing in a pasture in the San Gabriel Mountains. The Negro had escaped, but it was doubtful he learned anything useful, and at the speed he was running, he might be in Mexicali by now.

Pelley looked into the front window of the Aryan Bookstore and stopped short.

What in Hades' name is this?

A workman was sweeping up broken glass, while two others prepared to replace a window. Knocked askew on the display shelf inside the window was a sign: BUY CHRISTIAN-BOYCOTT JEWS.

Pelley removed his feathered hat and walked inside, spotting a clerk he didn't recognize, a young man in a white shirt and black tie. Of medium height, he had broad shoulders and appeared fit. Pelley tabbed him to be eighteen or nineteen with short blond hair, pale blue eyes, and Nordic features. A clean-cut choirboy, the sparkling image of a Hitler Youth. Pelley gestured toward the broken window. "Jews or communists?"

"Is there a difference?" the young man replied.

"Smart lad!"

Pelley scanned the tables and shelves. The books and pamphlets were familiar to him: *The Roosevelt Red Record and Its Background, Protocols of the Learned Elders of Zion, Dupes of Judah,*

Mein Kampf in German and English, and the highly popular *The Jewish Question* by Henry Ford.

He noticed the young man staring intently at him. "What is it, son?"

"You're William Dudley Pelley!" Sounding awestruck.

Pelley saluted the young man with his homburg and bowed. "At your service…"

"Wendell, sir. Gustafsson. My buddies call me 'Gus.'"

"Gus it shall be."

"The manager said you'd be stopping by, and someone might call with a message."

"And did they?" Pelley asked, tamping down his excitement like a fireplace tender smothering hot coals.

"Yes, sir."

"Did you write down the message?"

"No, sir. I'm trained to remember things but never to write them down."

"Smart lad," Pelley said for the second time. "And…"

"A man called. Didn't leave his name. He said, 'The cow will be in the barn tonight.'"

Of course, the butchers, not the most imaginative of men, would make a bovine reference. If the Diekmanns worked for the Department of Sanitation, they probably would have said, "The shit will flow in the sewer tonight."

The brothers weren't exactly dumb clucks, but they weren't geniuses, either. Pelley believed they could handle what was simply a pickup and delivery like Consolidated Freightways did a thousand times a day.

"Good news, Gus. *Danke.*"

"*Gerne geschehen*, sir."

The young man grabbed a pamphlet. "We have all your writings about the International Jew. They sell like hotcakes."

"Music to my ears."

"Say, are you gonna run for president again?"

A touchy subject. Pelley seldom discussed his disastrous run the previous year as head of the Christian Party.

"The election's rigged, Gus. Does anyone believe that Roosevelt beat Landon by eleven million votes?"

"The Bund fellows say the same thing." He gestured toward the back of the bookstore. "They're in the biergarten most days, and they say the election was bunk!"

"Talkers!" Pelley said dismissively. "The Silver Shirts need men of action. But the Bund is right about one thing. Forget the ballot box, Gus." Figuring he would test the young man, he said, "The first essential for success is constant and regular employment of violence."

"*Mein Kampf,* volume one, chapter thirteen."

Pelley beamed. "You'll go far, Gus."

Pelley heard the door open, felt a swish of a breeze, and turned to see two young men in red berets saunter into the store. They were unshaven, shabbily dressed in dirty denim, and skinny as stiletto blades. The one closest to him wore a smile as stiff as a frozen frankfurter.

"What are you grinning at, shitheel?" Pelley said.

"My pal never seen a fascist close up, so I said, let's go to the Nazi bookstore 'cause that's where the chumps hang out, even if they can barely read."

"Lemme guess. You punks belong to the Communist League and sit around all day at Clifton's nursing one cup of coffee and planning your trip to Moscow."

"The Soviet Union is the future," the smiling commie said.

"You palookas think the red berets make you look like Trotsky," Pelley said, "but you know what? You look like a couple of Nancys over at Jimmy's Backyard on Cosmo Street." Gus laughed at that. Pelley noted that the lad had stepped alongside him so that both of them faced the two men. Gus's feet were spread to shoulder width, and one hand rested inside a trouser pocket. Pelley would bet dollars to doughnuts that Gus had a knife, probably a switchblade.

This kid has a bright future in the Silver Shirts.

"Aw, go back to Germany, why doncha?" the second commie said.

"Yeah, we don't want you crummy Krauts here," the smiler said.

Pelley reached inside his suit jacket and pulled a long-barreled Luger out of a shoulder holster. He calmly pointed the gun at the smiler. "You wanna say that again, you Bolshevik bastard?"

Nobody said anything until Pelley shouted, "Then scram!"

The two men scampered out of the store.

"Jiminy, that was something!" Gus said. "You were ready for trouble, Mr. Pelley."

"As were you, Gus. Is that a blade in your pocket?"

"Knuckle dusters." He pulled out a pair of brass knuckles that shined as if polished.

"Outstanding," Pelley said, slipping the Luger back into its holster.

"Do you think I could join your Silver Shirts and become a Ranger?"

Pelley smiled broadly. "You're just what we're looking for, Wendell Gustafsson. As the Führer said, 'He alone who owns the youth gains the future.'"

Pelley reached into a jacket pocket and pulled out the flask of Old Quaker. "Let's seal the deal, young man."

He offered the flask to Gus, who took a swig, swallowed, and coughed. Pelley then drained the flask in one gulp.

Something caught Pelley's eye. A pamphlet he hadn't seen before. He walked to the shelf and pulled it down. *Einstein's Jewish Relativity, the Science Fraud of the Century.*

That brought back the image of the Rolls-Royce with the actor and scientist on their way to the baseball game. A plan was forming, just as the whiskey roiled in Pelley's stomach. "Gus, do you have any experience with firearms?"

"I've shot my share of rats with a .22."

"Rats one day, rabbis the next," Pelley said.

That seemed to take Gus by surprise, and he was silent a moment. Pelley assessed the young man whose blue eyes looked past the broken window and into the street. He had an air of intelligence but not a poker face. He'd been taken aback by the suggestion of shooting a man.

Book knowledge is one thing, action quite another. Still, what potential he has!

"What I'm really good at, sir, is driving," Gus said. "I've raced at Hollywood Speedway."

"At your age?"

"Me and my pop restored a '31 Studebaker Roadster, and I drive the bejeesus out of it."

Pelley toyed with an idea for a moment. A way to test the lad. Get him out of the bookshelves and into the streets.

Yes, it might work, and what headlines there would be!

"Gus, where would that speedy Studebaker be right now?"

23
BALL IN PLAY

South Los Angeles, Wrigley Field

"I love that sound," said the man who mastered the silent picture. *The thrum of the crowd.*

Chaplin and Einstein listened to the low rumble of twenty-two thousand baseball fans. Fathers with sons, mothers with daughters, siblings, workplace friends, students playing hooky, retirees in seersucker suits, boaters shading their faces, tourists from the Midwest, all talking, cheering, shouting with their hot dogs and peanuts and beer, happy to be basking in the warmth of a fine spring afternoon.

They walked through the concourse toward the grandstand when a voice echoed from behind them. "Yo, Charlie!"

They turned and saw a dark-haired, handsome man in his thirties wearing a rust-colored double-breasted suit, wide at the shoulders, a matching tie with a diamond stick pin, a crisp white shirt, and black-and-white two-tone brogues.

"Hello, Ben," Chaplin said. "You're looking spiffy."

"Dress British, think Yiddish," Ben said with a New York accent.

Chaplin thought that no Brit he knew would wear the holstered revolver bulging from beneath Ben's suit coat.

"So you're full time in Los Angeles now, Ben?"

"You bet. I'm trying to get Lansky and Luciano out of Brooklyn, but they're allergic to sunshine."

"Ben Siegel, this is…"

"I know! Professor Einstein. Ay, Professor, you call me pronto if anybody in LA gives you trouble."

"You're what then, a professional troubleshooter?" Einstein asked.

"I ain't no amateur." Siegel rumbled a laugh. "Enjoy the game. I got five hundred clams on the Padres."

Siegel walked toward a buxom bottle blonde in a tight red dress, and Einstein said, "Nice fellow."

"As long as you don't call him 'Bugsy,'" Chaplin said.

They headed down the steps of the grandstand behind the first baseline. A slow buzz in the stands increased in volume as fans recognized them. Then a trickle of applause, which, within seconds, became thunderous.

"No wonder you like coming to the games," Einstein said.

Chaplin waved, pivoting to take in people to the right and left, above and below.

"Loosen up, Albert. They're cheering for you, too."

Einstein forced a smile and gave a little wave that knocked his ball cap askew.

"Hey, Charlie!" a man called out.

"What, more friends?" Einstein asked. "Did you buy them all tickets?"

They stopped at a box where a smiling man in his early thirties with a jutting jaw and hair slicked back was surrounded by three women who might have answered a casting call for one brunette, one blonde, and one redhead.

"Albert, this is Bob Hope, a dandy comedian," Chaplin said. "Bob…Albert Einstein."

"How do you do, Mr. Hope?"

"Say, Professor, I'm reading a book on anti-gravity, and I just can't put it down."

Puzzled, Einstein said, "I do not know such a book."

They continued down the steps and stopped at the front row of boxes adjacent to the field. It was scoreless in the top of the third inning with the San Diego Padres at bat. They took their seats as Ray Prim, a pitcher for the hometown Angels, faced Cedric Durst, a grizzled, gray-haired left fielder for the Padres. Prim worked the count to three-and-two, and Durst fouled off four consecutive pitches.

"Why is no one moving?" Einstein asked.

"The ball has to be put into play," Chaplin said.

"Tell me when that happens, please."

A slender Black man in a three-piece eggshell suit with notch lapels and a gold handkerchief in his breast pocket leaned into their box. A card reading PRESS stuck out of his hatband.

"Excuse me, gentlemen. I'm Jimmy Mitchell, reporter for the *Los Angeles Sentinel*."

"I read the *Sentinel*," Chaplin said.

"You read a Negro newspaper?" Mitchell looked surprised.

"To write Negro characters, I need to know about their lives."

Mitchell smiled with recognition. "In *Modern Times*, you had hard-working Negroes who weren't scared of that awful machine."

On the field, Prim struck out another batter, and Einstein said, "Still no ball in play."

Mitchell raised his left hand and showed Chaplin a gold ring with an engraved scales of justice, the logo of the National Association for the Advancement of Colored People. "My father attended an NAACP convention where you spoke."

Chaplin nodded, too modest to say he wrote annual checks to the group. "What can we do for you, Mr. Mitchell, and you'd better take a seat so you don't block the view."

Mitchell entered the box, sat in an empty chair, leaned close, and whispered, "There's something I need to tell both of you. Something both mysterious and dangerous."

"*Ya?*" Einstein looked at him quizzically.

⁂

Four men crouched in the press photographers' dugout behind home plate, just in front of the backstop. Three of the men aimed their cameras toward the field. But one, Klaus Spengler, who only yesterday had been perched in Douglas Fairbanks's tree like a sparrow awaiting a mate, looked elsewhere. He aimed his long lens down the first baseline into Chaplin's box.

In the crosshairs, he saw Chaplin and Einstein and a young Negro man with a press card in his hatband. He clicked several exposures and said aloud, "*Juden und Schwarzers.* Birds of a feather. But what mischief do you make for us?"

⁂

Jimmy Mitchell didn't know how much to say to the two famous men. If he told them that he witnessed a murder at Alt Heidelberg, they would think he was off his nut. But if he didn't tell them enough, would they be moved to action? Both men were known for their commitment to social justice, so surely they would be more willing to listen than Sergeant Riley and Detective Cooper had been.

On the field, on a three-and-one count, Prim missed the plate with a fastball, and the batter trotted to first with a base-on-balls.

"Still no ball in play," Einstein said, "but the man with the stick decided he would rather stand on that white sack than stay where he was."

"So what's the bee in your bonnet, Mr. Mitchell?" Chaplin asked.

"It's about Nazis, right here in Los Angeles," Mitchell said softly.

"I know they're bad eggs."

"Worse than you can imagine. What I witnessed last night, I mean."

"You seem like a nice young man. Why don't you—"

"It's a matter of life and death!"

Chaplin held up a hand to stop him, and Mitchell knew he'd gone too far too fast.

"Tell you what, we'll have lunch tomorrow," Chaplin said. "Talk about it then."

"But sir."

"Brown Derby at one o'clock."

Chaplin returned his attention to the game, and Mitchell left the box.

Walking up the steps to the concourse, the young reporter scanned the faces of the crowd. Happy faces, cheering fans, the people basking in the sunshine, oblivious to the dangers lurking under cover of darkness. Thinking of Cassandra, the prophet no one would believe, he wondered if humanity was, by nature, inclined to ignore doomsayers.

I must make myself heard!

Tomorrow, he told himself. Tomorrow, I will convince Chaplin that I have seen the evil within men's souls.

24

THE ROADSTER

Avalon Boulevard, South Los Angeles

On the street just outside the stadium, a 1931 souped-up Studebaker Roadster, a two-seat convertible the color of an egg yolk, drove past V.I.P. Row, its engine growling like a caged beast. The young driver, Wendell "Gus" Gustafsson, had a white silk scarf tossed casually around his neck.

Gus took a long look at the black Rolls-Royce Phantom. He glanced toward the stadium and estimated how many seconds it would take Chaplin and Einstein—his targets—to cross the street to the car. He already could hear the *thumps* of their bodies against the steel bumper, could see them sliced to ribbons by the vertical slats of the grill, body parts torn asunder, blood misting like steam from an overheated radiator.

Mr. Pelley, you're gonna be darn proud of me!

Gus made a rough calculation of the distance to the intersecting street beyond the stadium and, finally, his top speed if he floored it after turning the corner.

I'm damn good at this!

Hadn't he slid around a turn at eighty miles-per-hour at the speedway, cutting off old Barney Whitaker, who'd torn up his gears downshifting? Afterward, Whitaker, his face blackened from the

Studebaker's exhaust, yelled at him, "You think you're eggs in coffee, kid, but you're just a clusterfudge waiting to happen!"

Well, it hasn't happened yet.

As he drove past the stadium to the intersection, the starting line for his race to destiny, the rumble of the Studebaker's engine was a calming sound, like waves slapping the shore.

Gus let his mind replay the weighty moments of the day.

"Me and my pop restored a '31 Studebaker."

That's what he'd told Mr. Pelley.

As if I'm Andy Hardy and my pop is good old Judge Hardy.

But Judge Hardy never clobbered Andy with a ratchet wrench and never drunkenly pulled him out of the grease pit and screamed that he was a fucking moron who was probably the milkman's son. Gus could not help but compare his father, whose stained overalls reeked of sweat and grime, to Mr. Pelley, who dressed like a gentleman.

And carries a Luger in his suit the way most men carry Lucky Strikes!

What his mother saw in Harold Gustafsson was a mystery, though simple arithmetic showed that she gave birth to Gus five months after the marriage. Mom was a Lutheran who never went to church. Pop was an atheist whose political leaning, to the extent he had one, was anarchy. Free of the shackles of home-taught religion, Gus found something to believe in. He didn't become a clerk in the Aryan Bookstore because he was a fascist. He became a fascist because he worked there and read voraciously.

The Aryan Bookstore is my church, and Mein Kampf *is my bible.*

Nothing about fascism was murky. You never heard, "On the other hand..." Hitler's pronouncements were clear and certain and undoubtedly true. "The victor will never be asked if he told the truth."

I will be with the victors!

He remembered the day he told his mother he was a fascist. She seemed to awaken from a decade of slumber and screamed at his pop. "You're no father to him, so he wants Hitler to adopt him!"

Now, as Gus approached the intersection, he passed three uniformed LAPD officers walking toward the stadium. They seemed to admire the car but didn't pay much attention to him. Why should they? He was a young, neatly groomed white man who looked incapable of anything more nefarious than a college fraternity prank.

He glanced back at the trio of cops. Odd, he thought. A Negro woman and what looked to be a Mexican man and a Japanese man. He had seen maybe three Negro police officers in his entire life. Beaners and Japs? None that he could remember.

Do they send all the outcasts down here for traffic duty?

Mr. Pelley had written about the dangers of immigration, foreigners poisoning white Americans' bloodlines, echoing *Mein Kampf's* demand for racial purity. But words alone would achieve nothing.

"To reach our goals, Gus, we need to strike first and strike hard," Mr. Pelley told him earlier in the bookstore. "Today, you'll let the world know we mean business."

Damn right!

Gus had just one nagging thought, a niggling itch that he could not quite scratch.

Can I do it? Reading about political assassinations was one thing. Pulling the trigger—or flooring the accelerator—was something else.

25
ROYALTY ROW

Avalon Boulevard, South Los Angeles

Georgia Ann Robinson walked along the street adjacent to Wrigley Field, proud of the three gold chevrons on her sleeve and the silver badge over the left breast pocket of her navy-blue tunic. She had earned them.

Robinson was the first female Black officer on the Los Angeles Police Department. She had begun as a jail matron, was promoted to juvenile, then worked homicide in South Central— if the victims were people of color—and was now a sergeant.

As high as I'm likely to go.

Which was fine with her. She had blazed a trail for others, and, now in her fifties, was looked to by other officers—white, black, and brown—for advice. She had a strong jaw, piercing eyes, and projected an aura of calm, control, and intelligence.

This was not to say that the department was free of racial bias and even hatred. In her early days, crude messages had been scrawled on her locker. Some white officers still felt free to tell lewd racial jokes in her presence. But the path for trailblazers ran through a jungle of vipers and patches of quicksand, and she had learned how to stomp on snakes and stay on the path.

At a retirement party for a captain from Hollywood Division, after a couple of Old Foresters, Chief James "Two-Gun" Davis told Robinson she was a credit to her race.

As you are to yours, Chief.

She hadn't actually said that, because even had it been a compliment, it would not have been true. Chief Davis was a bigot with close ties to the Ku Klux Klan and ran a department whose corruption was a stain that bled through the fabric of the city, a den of thieves in blue.

Never invited to share the bribery and extortion spoils—not that she would have—Robinson was happy to walk a straight line her entire career.

Robinson was no longer spry enough to chase fugitives down alleys, so training traffic control officers was fine with her. This day, at the baseball game, she was in charge of two rookie patrolmen, Juan Escobar and Haruto Takahashi. They were good listeners, quick learners, eager to please, and they thought she was the cat's meow.

With the game in the late innings, it was time to get busy.

"Escobar, take Lot A. Takahashi, Lot B. Don't let anyone block the streets. I'll take Royalty Row."

Meaning the VIP section of reserved parking for celebrities, a row of shiny coupes, sedans, limousines, and touring cars.

"Hey, Sarge," Escobar said, "don't let any millionaires twist their ankles stepping off the curb."

Robinson laughed. She liked both men and thought they had bright futures. "I'm just glad Douglas Fairbanks isn't here, pie-eyed and swinging from lamp posts."

Escobar and Takahashi headed north on Avalon toward Santa Barbara Avenue. Robinson stayed put, scanning the area. She caught sight of a young man walking toward her, wearing rolled-up denim pants, a green checked ranch shirt with snap buttons and two chest pockets, and, oddly, a white scarf hanging loosely around his neck. His blond hair was trimmed and neatly parted, and he seemed to be whistling.

Earlier, she had seen him driving slowly along Avalon in a noisy, bright yellow Studebaker Roadster. She wondered where he had parked and thought he might be picking up someone from the ball game.

Robinson turned her attention to the stadium, where a few people were leaving early to beat the traffic. When she turned back, the young man was walking along Royalty Row. She watched him pass the empty spaces marked B. CROSBY, D. FAIRBANKS, AND S. TRACY. He passed the sporty Lincoln Roadster with its top down in Clark Gables's spot, gave a quick glance at the long, sleek Duesenberg limousine belonging to William Randolph Hearst, then stopped alongside Charlie Chaplin's Rolls-Royce.

He ran a finger along the bright red pinstripe on the side panel, and Robinson called out, "Young man, what are you doing?"

He turned, saw her, and started to say something but stopped. Then he smiled, but she knew that smile, which was really a smirk.

"Sorry, ma'am," He hit *ma'am* so that it sounded sarcastic. "Everything's jake. Just imagining myself behind the wheel of this swanky machine."

He raised his hands as if surrendering, then walked across the street toward the stadium. But his gait was elongated, she noticed, like a football official marking off a penalty. He knew she was watching him, *wanted* her to watch him, but why?

When he reached the curb, he turned back toward the Rolls-Royce and held up both hands, creating a rectangle with thumbs-to-index fingers, like a film director finger-framing a shot. Then he pivoted and looked at her through his hands.

"You oughta be in pictures, Sergeant."

He was observant, having taken notice of the stripes on her sleeve. Now he was making a show of whatever he was doing. She tried to size him up. A smart ass, to be sure, but that was hardly against the law.

He turned and started walking along the sidewalk toward Parking Lot A, and she returned her attention to the stadium. An elderly man approached her and said, "Where do I catch a bus to the Valley, Officer?"

"Other side of the stadium, sir."

She looked back toward the young man, but he was gone.

26
THE DECLARATION OF INDEPENDENCE

South Los Angeles, Wrigley Field

The Padres led the Angels 1–0 in the bottom of the eighth inning. An 18-year-old outfielder for the Padres—Ted Williams, by name—had hit a solo home run, a line drive over the right field fence that sounded like a thunderclap leaving his bat.

"How 'bout that skinny kid's swing!" Chaplin had said.

"And he doesn't look strong enough to lift a matzoh ball from the soup," Einstein replied. Other than the kid's home run, the ball game had less action than a spirited round of Parcheesi. Something had been troubling Einstein, so he just blurted it out. "Charlie, I think you were quite churlish with that young reporter."

"C'mon, Albert. I'm taking him to the Brown Derby tomorrow."

"He had something to tell us about the Nazis. You're making me go to the consulate tonight to learn whatever we can, and yet you shoo this fellow away."

"Whatever he's got, it can wait till tomorrow. And I'm sorry if I gave him the high hat."

"High hat. Low pants. I don't care, but I'd like to hear what he knows."

Having lost all interest in the baseball game, Einstein couldn't get Jimmy Mitchell out of his mind. The young man had seemed frightened. "It's a matter of life and death!" he'd said. Einstein's memories of Berlin under the Nazis were still fresh. Charlie hadn't seen the SS thugs up close. Did he share the false sense of security that seemed to be an American trait, even while the world was a powder keg about to explode?

"So, Albert, how do you like baseball?" Chaplin asked, unaware of his friend's ruminations.

"To be honest, it's like waiting for uranium 238 to decay."

A good straight man when he had to be, Chaplin asked, "How so?"

"A half-life of four-point-five billion years."

Chaplin smiled and said, "We don't have to stay till the end."

Einstein clopped his friend on the shoulder. "The best news I've heard since Newton got smacked by that apple."

"By the time we get home and put on our monkey suits," Chaplin said, "we'll need to hit the road straightaway for the consulate."

"Partying with Joseph Goebbels. Should I have a taster sample the hors d'oeuvres?"

Before they could get out of their seats, a gruff voice came from the aisle. "Hey, movie star!"

The man behind the voice leaned into the box, towering over Chaplin. A jagged scar ran from just below his ear and to the corner of his mouth, and his nose went east and west when it should have gone north and south. A small tattoo of an anchor was visible on his neck, just above his shirt collar. "My name's Skowron." He thrust a game program toward Chaplin. "Gimme an autograph for my boy."

Chaplin forced a smile. Most fans *asked* for autographs, rather than demanded them.

"Sure, Mr. Skowron. What's your son's name?"

"Adolf." Skowron smirked.

Chaplin shot him a look, noticed a folded newspaper under the man's arm. *Der Deutsche Beobachter*, published by the German American Bund.

"I seen you box," Skowron said.

"Uh-huh. *City Lights*."

"Looked fake."

"It was."

"I boxed Golden Gloves. For real. Till every week I had to fight a different coon, sweating all over me with their stink."

Chaplin grimaced and scribbled a few words on the game program, then signed his name.

Skowron grabbed the program and managed to read it without moving his lips.

"The hell's that mean? 'Adolf, study your history.'"

"Declaration of Independence, Mr. Skowron. 'All men are created equal.'"

Skowron scoffed, a sound that resembled a growling dog. "I don't need no lectures from the likes of you."

"Have a good day, Mr. Skowron."

The man stomped off, and Einstein asked, "What was that all about, Charlie?"

"The absurdity of hate."

❦

On their way out of the stadium, Einstein said he was hungry, so they walked through the concourse toward the concession stands.

"Yoo-hoo, Cholly!" came a woman's voice with a Brooklyn accent.

The men turned and saw a pretty blond woman of about forty waving a white handkerchief at them.

"She looks like a soldier surrendering," Einstein said.

"Marion Davies, Albert, and she surrendered to me a long time ago."

"*Oy*, not another one!"

"That big galoot with his back to us...that's William Randolph Hearst."

They walked toward Davies, who wore a formfitting dress in virginal white, topped by a white belted jacket, sheer silk stockings, spiky white strapped footwear, and a white pillbox hat.

"I'm getting a bratwurst," Einstein said, peeling off toward a concession stand. "Try to keep your pants on."

A moment later, Davies air-kissed Chaplin on both cheeks. "Cholly, Cholly, why don't you call me no more?"

"I heard that line in your last picture."

"I'm retired. Now it's just parties, one after another. San Simeon, it's like being in Timbuktu."

She drew a gold cigarette case from her white leather clutch purse, pulled out a smoke, and handed a lighter to Chaplin. He ignited her Lucky Strike, and she exhaled two plumes of smoke through her nostrils like a very pretty dragon.

She offered Chaplin a cig, and he shook his head. "No coffin nails for me, sugar." He studied her a moment. "What is it, Marion?"

"I'm as bored as a lifeguard in the desert."

Chaplin nodded toward Hearst, who was deep in conversation with a young man.

"Doesn't W.R. keep you busy, by which I mean on your back?"

"Aw, Willie's the worst lay I ever had. But to be honest, I kinda love the big lummox."

She moved closer to Chaplin, close enough to kiss, a wickedly reckless invitation with her longtime lover just paces away. No way he would anger Hearst, mainly because he loved the old tycoon's invitations to San Simeon, where he had bedded so many women, including, on occasion, his own wife.

27
THE WALKIE-TALKIE

Wrigley Field, Concourse

Twenty yards from where Chaplin was doing his best not to be seduced by Marion Davies, Skowron stood next to the beer stand, shadowed behind rows of empty kegs. A green canvas haversack was slung on his shoulder. Inside was a thirty-pound metal device Pelley had given him with a stern warning.

"This is brand new and top secret," Pelley said, boosting his own self-importance. "If you get pinched and the coppers grab it, we'll lose our friends at the armory, and there'll be hell to pay."

Fresh out of the box, it was an SCR-194 transceiver, developed by the Signal Corps for the infantry. Pelley told him that the device could transmit and receive voice messages over a distance of five miles. Skowron thought about all the trench runners he'd seen scampering like field mice at the Battle of Saint-Mihiel because there'd been no other way to deliver messages. So damn many of them dropped in their tracks by snipers.

"It's a helluva piece of equipment," Pelley said. "You can walk and talk at the same time, so they call it a walkie-talkie."

Skowron stepped farther back into the shadows and lifted the device out of the haversack. Pelley had told him to use 35.80 megacycles, so he twisted the dial until that frequency came up.

He screwed the telescoping antenna into its slot, turned the device on, and glanced back into the concourse. Einstein had disappeared into a crowd at a concession booth, and Chaplin was putting the rush on a blond woman who seemed familiar. An actress who looked a tad past her prime.

Skowron needed to talk to the kid in the Studebaker, give him the current status. He'd seen the car, a yellow two-door roadster, a real struggle buggy if you got a girl to take a ride up Mulholland Drive. Skowron's last regular gal was a hot tamale with obsidian hair named Maria Soto, which drove his old man crazy, that maybe being the point.

One night in East LA, they got jumped by a mixed crew of beaners and coloreds.

Hooray for the USA's melting pot.

Skowron decked three of them and ended up with two front teeth embedded in his knuckles, but one of the coloreds sliced his face with a straight razor. Bled like a son of a bitch, but the wound wasn't deep. Maria sat with him while he got sewn up in the ER, called him her *gran gringo valiente*, and rewarded him with her virginity. He'd toyed with the idea of settling down with her.

Dang fool that I was!

Without firing a warning shot, Maria chucked him into the trash like yesterday's newspaper and took up with a rich fellow named Harry something-or-other. Okay, maybe not rich, but his daddy owned a small clothing store on Olvera Street, and Harry worked there, a tape measure around his neck instead of a grappling hook on his belt. He had clean fingernails and a cherry-red Ford Cabriolet Roadster, and that was that. Skowron carried a torch for about a week, then said, screw her. He made decent enough money as a longshoreman, and most Saturday nights were spent with working girls in a San Pedro sporting house.

Now he pushed the button on the handset. "Alpha One to Beta One," he whispered, then released the button.

Nothing but static.

"Alpha One to Beta One," he tried again.

Still zip. He checked the dial. It was on 35.80 megacycles, just like Pelley said.

Alpha One. Beta One.

Pelley's instructions were to use code. Like he was Black Jack Pershing leading the infantry over the hill. Skowron knew that Pelley had never seen combat, had never even worn the uniform. What he did was prance around in his high leather boots and riding pants like some British duke. Not that it bothered Skowron. A leader had to spin bullshit into gold because the masses needed and expected it. He followed Pelley not out of respect for the man, but for his principles, which they shared. Skowron believed that hardworking, white Protestant men were sucking hind tit, screwed by Roosevelt's New Deal, standing in line behind Jews, Negroes, papists, and immigrants from countries a geography teacher couldn't find with a Collier's Atlas.

Skowron knew that Pelley considered him a big slab of meat, a punch-drunk pug, slow of wit but dangerous with his fists.

Well, half of that's true!

Pelley would be surprised to know that Skowron was a loyal reader of the *Los Angeles Examiner*, a Hearst paper that railed against unions, immigration, and communism. The *Examiner* took a wait-and-see attitude toward fascism in Italy and Germany and even published essays written by Adolf Hitler.

Skowron checked the frequency dial again. Right at 35.80 megacycles, where it belonged. Why wasn't the kid in the Studebaker answering?

Wait a second! Or was it 38.50 megacycles?

The yellow Studebaker, bright as a buttercup, was parked on Fortieth Place, just off Avalon Boulevard, waiting for the call that the targets were leaving the stadium. Gus turned the transceiver Mr. Pelley had given him to 38.50 megacycles and tried to reach Alpha One. Nothing.

He fiddled with the frequency dial until he heard a voice, scratchy with static. "Eight innings in the book, the Padres leading one nothing. And we'll be back with the final frame right after this word from Hamm's Beer, born in the land of the sky blue waters."

Radio station KRKD, carrying the baseball game. Where's the Silver Shirt radioman?

Gus felt sweat break out on his forehead. He didn't have a line of sight to the stadium and needed a signal when the targets headed for the Rolls. Where was Alpha One? He feared that Mr. Pelley wouldn't let him join the Silver Legion if this went kerflooey.

To settle his nerves, he did his final preparations. Gunned the engine and listened to its rumble, soothing as a mother's heartbeat to an infant. He pulled on his pigskin driving gloves, slipped a corduroy newsboy's cap on his head, and tied a loose knot in the white scarf around his neck.

He was ready. He was willing. He was able.

Just give me the word, and I'll hit the grind!

28
THE TOYS ARE STILL IN THE STORE

Wrigley Field, Concourse

William Randolph Hearst had not stood on a bathroom scale in twenty-five years. Once you've passed three hundred pounds—and that was far in the rearview mirror—what difference did it make? And just who had the moxie to tell him to lose weight? Not his doctors. Not his employees. Not his wife, Millicent. Well, maybe Marion, his mistress of two decades.

She'd say any damn thing that comes to her mind.

At seventy-four, Hearst was one of the richest and most powerful men in the world, and he enjoyed every dollar and every display of might. He owned newspapers, radio stations, movie studios, newsreel companies, real estate, and priceless works of art. He was on a first-name basis with presidents and dictators, kings and queens, sheiks and rajahs, industrialists and heiresses. And he never hesitated to tell them when they pissed on their own shoes.

Three years earlier, after a meeting in Berlin, he told friends that Adolf Hitler was a leader of destiny. He admired Hitler's nationalist views and ordered his newspaper editors to adopt a slogan of "America First."

Who, other than parlor pinkos and outright Bolsheviks, could argue with that?

Today, wearing a blue silk suit and red tie, with a white, stiff-collared shirt and a checked vest that strained to contain his belly, Hearst chatted with Jack Kennedy, one of Joe's boys, a handsome, albeit skinny lad, about to start his senior year at Harvard. After some pleasantries, Kennedy introduced Hearst to a pal, said cheerio, and followed a shapely brunette with a bouffant hairdo to the concession stand.

"Jack says it's your twenty-second birthday, Mr. Welsh," Hearst said to the newcomer.

"Yes, sir. We're painting the town tonight. And it's Welles. Orson Welles."

Hearst took the measure of the young man with wavy brown hair and a heavy jaw and was not impressed, particularly by his sporty brown plaid jacket with patch pockets and a patterned silk foulard puffing out of his open-collared white shirt.

"Are you at Harvard with Jack?"

"No, sir. I'm an actor."

"Aha. Will I see you on the silver screen?"

"That's a long shot, sir. But I'm on a new radio show called *The Shadow*, and I'm updating *Julius Caesar* for the stage."

"Updating? Shakespeare's not good enough for you?"

"I've rewritten the play as an allegory about fascism. It's set in modern-day Italy, and Caesar is basically Mussolini. I'm playing Brutus and also directing."

"A triple threat like Bronko Nagurski," Hearst said.

"Well, I don't know about that, sir."

"You want my advice, young man?" Hearst did not wait for a reply. "Pick one craft and stick to it. Spread yourself too thin, and you'll succeed at nothing."

Still in the shadows of the beer stand, the walkie-talkie hanging from a strap and growing heavy on his shoulder, Skowron wondered just how long all these swells would keep gabbing.

He saw a young man in a fancy jacket with a scarf stuffed into his shirt talking to an old mountain of a man he recognized from newsreels as William Randolph Hearst. The man had more money than God and if you believed Walter Winchell on the radio, Hearst might have thought he was just as divine. Skowron watched the young man walk away from Hearst in confident strides, maybe not impressed by rubbing shoulders with a gazillionaire. Then the old geezer approached Chaplin and the blond woman.

Skowron was startled to hear a scratchy voice on the transceiver.

"Alpha One, this is Beta One. Do you read me?" The male voice was young but sure of itself.

Skowron punched the button on the handset and said, "Beta One, this is Alpha One. The toys are still in the store."

Using the ridiculous code Pelley had given him. As if the FBI or Joe Stalin might be listening in.

"Alpha One. Stay on this frequency and update status as required."

"Beta One, roger that."

He returned his gaze to the targets. The "toys," as Pelley would have it, didn't seem in any hurry to leave.

❧ ☙

"Chap, good to see you!" Hearst said heartily. "Why don't you come up to San Simeon next weekend. Cary will be there, Greta, too. And Bette Davis and Joan Crawford, in case you want to see a catfight."

"Thanks, I might do that." Chaplin gestured toward Welles, who had caught up with Jack Kennedy and the shapely brunette at the concession stand.

"Say, W.R., were you imparting words of wisdom to that young man?"

Hearst coughed a laugh. "Not that he would listen. What's his name? Welsh. Just a dilettante. He'll never amount to a damn thing."

29
NEVER AGAIN

Avalon Boulevard, South Los Angeles

"The toys are leaving the store." Alpha One's voice conveyed just a hint of excitement.

"Roger that," Gus said.

With the top down, the gas tank full, wire wheels gleaming, and Gus in his goggles and racing gloves, the Studebaker Roadster was ready to go.

Raring to go!

The two-seater was called the "Bullet" by the racing crowd because of its aerodynamic design, and Gus intended to fire the gun. He depressed the clutch, hit the ignition, and the engine rumbled to life. He started slowly down Avalon toward the stadium, threading past the fans walking toward their cars.

He realized the distance to Chaplin's parked Rolls-Royce was a little farther than he had estimated, and now he sped up, the engine snarling. Outside Parking Lot A, the Mexican traffic cop he saw earlier looked toward the Studebaker and made a downward motion with both hands. "Hey, buddy, slow down!"

Gus clutched and shifted from second to third gear. He lay on the horn, and pedestrians crossing the street scattered. The Studebaker approached the entrance to Parking Lot B, the

Japanese cop standing in the street yelled, "What the hell, fella? Hit the brakes!"

His white scarf flapping in the breeze, Gus shot the cop his middle finger, the Studebaker racing past him with a foot to spare. "Knock your ass back to Tokyo," Gus yelled, not that his voice could be heard over the roar of eight cylinders pumping their hearts out.

Abreast of the stadium, he saw the colored sergeant standing astride the center line, her posture perfect, unafraid, holding up both her hands and blowing her whistle, as if that would stop him. The Studebaker passed so close to her, it brushed her blue tunic.

And the Studebaker roared on.

⚞ ⚟

Einstein was munching a hot dog, and Chaplin was talking about Hearst's parties as they stepped off the curb onto Avalon Avenue. The Rolls-Royce was catty-corner from them, maybe thirty-five feet across the street and another forty feet to the north.

They both heard a car horn wailing, the sound becoming both louder and more shrill, something Einstein knew to be the Doppler effect. Then a searing police whistle, possibly two whistles. They turned to look north along Avalon Boulevard and saw pedestrians scampering out of the street.

Gus hit the accelerator hard, the engine shrieking in third—the highest—gear. He was composed, smiling when he saw the frightened looks on the people diving to the curb, some falling to their knees and crawling. Ahead he saw the toys, Chaplin and Einstein, dead center in the street.

Chaplin grabbed Einstein by the elbow and pulled hard. "C'mon, Albert! Hurry."

Einstein dropped the hot dog but froze, his mind telling his legs to move, but the message taking a detour. He stared at the oncoming yellow convertible, the driver in goggles and a flowing scarf coming into focus.

Grinning! The driver is looking right at me, smiling crazily like a madman.

Einstein's knees buckled, and death was seconds away.

⌦ ⌫

In the long wait to hear from Alpha One, Gus had decided to give them a sporting chance. He would put the roadster into a power slide.

I wanna see the look in your eyes when my baby comes skidding at you, rubber burning, smoking hot! If you have the reflexes of a matador, there's a sliver of a chance you'll escape death. Otherwise, you're roadkill.

He'd done plenty of power slides at the speedway, professional maneuvers, thrilling to spectators. His next several actions took place in such quick succession as to seem simultaneous.

He smashed the brake pedal to the floor, shifting the weight of the car forward, unloading the rear tires, and reducing traction. He muscled the steering wheel hard left, and with the loss of rear traction, the back end of the car skidded right. He let up on the brakes, gave it gas, and counter-steered against the direction of the slide.

The roadster skidded hard, tires shrieking, one of the wire wheels flying off and bouncing down the street. Now the right side of the car was sliding directly at Chaplin and Einstein.

⌦ ⌫

Chaplin, the smaller man, but with wiry strength, grabbed Einstein's right wrist with two hands and, in one fluid motion, rotated his hips as if throwing the hammer in a track and field event and slung the older man onto the sidewalk. He turned back to see the yellow car on a collision course with him. There was no escape.

Chaplin leapt *toward* the sliding car, arms extended, kicking his legs over his head, and as his hands landed on the car's hood and with his bent elbows, he sprang upward, tucking his head, somersaulting forward, and landing upright on the pavement like an Olympic gymnast.

☞ ☜

Gus admired the stunt. He'd seen Chaplin leap off a building into a moving truck in *City Lights*, among other feats of derring-do. But wow...the closest he'd ever seen to anything like this was a clown at the rodeo jumping over a bull.

The Studebaker screamed to a stop, tires smoking. Gus engaged the clutch and gave it gas, so that the engine growled even louder. He looked toward the curb, where Einstein was sprawled on all fours, the famous scientist looking old and feeble and defeated. He could bounce the Roadster over the curb and mow down the old man, then throw it into reverse and plow into Chaplin. But he didn't.

Maybe striking fear of the Reich into them is even better than killing them, something that might have half the world in mourning.

That's what Gus would tell Mr. Pelley. This was just a spur-of-the-moment idea, not well thought out, not part of an overall plan, and from his reading, Gus knew that careful planning was a key to all fascist victories.

Gus noticed Einstein staring at him, his mouth agape, like he wondered what had just happened and why. Gus thought a two-word exclamation would be a sufficient explanation.

☞ ☜

Einstein locked eyes with the driver. Not that he could see the man's eyes behind the goggles that reflected the glare of the late-afternoon sun. Features obscured by the scarf, his cap pulled low on his forehead, the driver could have been a monster in human form. Now he was screaming over the noise of the engine.

"*Jü-dis-cher Par-a-sit!*"

The sun also struck the car's hood ornament. Not the Flying Lady, the symbol of Studebaker. That had been replaced by a chrome eagle clutching a swastika.

A nightmare. All of this, a nightmare come to life.

The driver yanked the steering wheel, and the Studebaker tore off past the stadium, heading south on Avalon and disappearing as it turned left on Vernon Boulevard.

❧ ☙

Chaplin squatted on his haunches like a catcher behind the plate and leaned close to Einstein, who sat on the curb, elbows on knees, head down.

"Albert, are you okay?"

"I'm…I'm…Charlie, I'm ashamed."

"What? No."

Watching his friend in distress, Chaplin felt guilty, responsible for bringing him here, making him a target of whatever evil or insanity had just befallen them.

Robinson hurried over and crouched down alongside the two men. "Professor Einstein, I'm Sergeant Georgia Robinson. Are you hurt, sir? Do you need an ambulance?"

"No, thank you, dear."

Einstein lifted his head and looked past both of them into the sky. "I…heard…the horn. Growing louder, more shrill."

He sounded shellshocked. Then he turned his gaze to Sergeant Robinson. "So, I knew the car was coming at me, but I felt powerless. Not in control of my own body."

"You're safe now, Professor."

"I was paralyzed by fear."

"It happens to lots of people," Robinson said. "We call it a 'deer in the headlamps.'"

"A Jew in the crosshairs," Einstein said, shaking his head.

"Albert, the driver shouted something at you, but I couldn't hear it," Chaplin said.

"*Jüdisher Parasit*," Einstein said. "It's from *Mein Kampf*. 'The Jewish parasite sucks the last drops of blood from the nation.' Something like that."

Patrolman Escobar, carrying the wire wheel that had spun off the Studebaker, approached them, and Takahashi was right behind.

"Mr. Chaplin. Professor," Robinson said, "I need to talk to my men, but I promise to be in touch as soon as we learn anything."

"Thank you again, dear," Einstein said, and Robinson nodded goodbye and joined the two patrolmen.

Chaplin helped Einstein to his feet and said, "We'll stay home tonight, eh, Albert? Maurice will make beef Wellington, and I'll break open a case of Château Lafite Rothschild 1928."

"*Nein! Nein!*"

Chaplin was startled by the volume of his friend's response, but maybe that meant he was coming out of his torpor.

"Charlie, we must go to the German consulate. Now, more than ever."

"Why?"

"To see what we're up against. What the world is up against."

"And then do what, Albert?"

Einstein stood, dusted off the seat of his pants, and said, matter-of-factly, "Whatever has to be done to stop the Nazis."

"The two of us?"

"Someone has to start, no?"

"Whatever you say, Albert. We'll put on our tuxes and go to the bastards' party. Then…?"

"We look them in the eye and show no fear," Einstein said. "Not now. Not ever. Never again."

30
STRAIGHT FROM THE CHIEF

Malibu and Wrigley Field

Just before sunset, the ocean was tinged orange, the shore break a frothy white. Gus held the Studebaker at a steady seventy miles per hour heading north on the Theodore Roosevelt Highway in Malibu. Exhilarated, his scarf flowing with the wind, he could feel the blood pumping through his veins as he hit the horn and passed slower vehicles on the narrow two-lane road.

He wondered if he would be in the newspapers tomorrow. Maybe someone took his photo in his goggles and cap and scarf, and wouldn't that be a pip? The Studebaker had a stolen license plate, so that wasn't a problem.

I'm untouchable!

He saw the blasted hole in Mugu Rock up ahead, a tiny tunnel for cars. He'd driven through it before at high speed, but he'd never done this…closed his eyes and screamed. Juiced with excitement, he drove blind through the tunneled rock and emerged on the other side perfectly centered in his lane.

What a day! Didja see the look on old Einstein's face?

Gus realized he would have to explain to Mr. Pelley why he hadn't run down the two men. It would be difficult because he wasn't quite sure. Using his superior reflexes and driving skills to scare the daylights out of them had seemed natural and even fun. But murder…well, it wasn't in his makeup. Surely Mr. Pelley would understand and could find important duties for a well-read, committed fascist who believed in the cause.

※ ※

Still at the scene, Sergeant Georgia Robinson scribbled notes on a pad while Escobar measured the Studebaker's skid marks, and Takahashi used a knife to scrape up burned rubber from the tires. Immediately after the incident, Escobar had raced to his patrol car and called in the description of the Studebaker and where it was last seen. But neither car nor driver had turned up.

Robinson sensed movement behind her. She turned to find Detective Carl Cooper approaching in that swagger he probably thought made him look like a cowboy instead of a potbellied, graying, bow-legged cop in a wrinkled brown suit and ancient porkpie hat that needed steaming and blocking. On a force riddled with corruption, Cooper had elevated bribery and kickbacks to a fine art. Seeing him made Robinson want to spit, so she did, hawked and spat on the pavement as he approached.

He wasn't wearing a bedsheet over his head, and he didn't greet her with a racial slur but still managed to make "Ay there, Sergeant" sound equal parts sarcasm and insult. His mouth was cemented into a perpetual smirk.

"What do you want, Cooper?" she said, skipping any false bonhomie.

"I heard on the squawk box there was a rumpus in the Thirteenth."

"And here you are, like a roach on a crumb."

Cooper turned to the two patrolmen. "Write any traffic tickets today, boys?"

"I'm surprised you have time for us," Robinson said, "with all the babysitting you do for the Nazis."

"Security for the German consulate," he corrected her. "All approved by Chief Davis."

In return for what, 20 percent of the cash?

She couldn't say that, of course, or Cooper would go running to James "Two-Gun" Davis, and she'd lose her stripes.

"We don't need you here, Cooper."

"You sure? 'Cause if stadium duty is too tough, you can go back to being a jail matron."

"What do you want, Detective?"

"My Red Squad is here to help."

"Really? Then ask your Nazi pals if they know anyone with a souped-up Studebaker and homicidal tendencies."

"Nah. This sounds smells like commies."

"The driver yelled an antisemitic slur…in German. That stinks like a Nazi."

"Could be a misdirection," he said.

"The hood ornament was an eagle clutching a swastika."

"Commies are tricky," Cooper said. "Get a plate number?"

"California 2X787. Likely stolen…maybe by those tricky commies."

"Where'd you write it down?"

"I didn't."

"When I was in patrol," Cooper said, "I'd write plate numbers on my arm." He gave her a smug grin. "Guess that wouldn't work with you."

Georgia Robinson shook her head, partly in sadness, partly in disbelief that she had to put up with this shit after all these years.

"Cooper, you know I outrank you, right?"

"On paper, maybe."

"And the Thirteenth is my precinct."

"Boyle Heights? All yours, Sergeant, right down to the last Jew, jigaboo, and wetback." He cackled with laughter. "Gotta go. Having drinks with the chief."

He turned to leave, and Georgia Robinson couldn't resist. "Hey, Detective. Don't tell the chief about that shiny new Packard you keep under a tarp. He might think you're shortchanging him."

Cooper wheeled around, his cheeks flushed. "You got some mouth on you, you…"

"You *what*, Detective?"

"Aw, nuts to you."

Something occurred to her, then, and she blurted it out. "Hold it, Cooper. You're spouting the department line, right? This was an attack from communists trying to frame the Nazis."

He shot her the shit-eating grin that he might have patented. "Well, look who's quick on the uptake. Two possibilities, Robinson. Either the Reds were behind it, or it was just an accident. Accelerator got stuck, happens all the time."

"That's baloney, and you know it."

"You're dog paddling in the ocean, Sergeant. Bigwigs are doing a ton of business with Germany, and the department is working hard to preserve those relationships."

"How, by covering up crimes?"

"No use jawing. This comes straight from the chief, so get off your high horse before someone knocks you off it."

"Just so we're clear," she said, "I'm shitcanned, and your Red Squad is handling the investigation."

He laughed so hard his paunch jiggled. "What investigation?"

He turned and walked away, and she called after him, "*Auf wiedersehen*, Cooper."

31

THE SCIENTIST, THE COMEDIAN, AND THE LADY COP

Chaplin Estate

The sun was just setting when Sergeant Georgia Robinson drove her Ford Model B up the steep incline of the driveway at 1085 Summit Drive and parked in front of the mansion.

There was room for twenty cars, but only one was there, Chaplin's Rolls-Royce Phantom, now with the top up. She had called ahead and was expected.

He probably thinks I'm on department business and will be shocked at what that louse Cooper told me.

She was still formulating her plan and wondered if Chaplin and Einstein would go along.

Will they trust me?

She had told Chaplin on the phone that her husband, Morgan, a building contractor by trade, was out of town at an NAACP convention, and would it be all right to bring her daughter, Melvia, along? Sure, it was fine. Getting out of her Ford, she looked up, taking in the two-story building of white stucco walls, recessed windows, balconies, and a red tile roof.

Georgia and twelve-year-old Melvia approached the imposing front door, fourteen feet high, made of oak with ornate carvings. Out of uniform, Georgia wore a below-the-knee wool skirt with a matching jacket, black pumps, and seamed stockings. Melvia was in a pleated navy-blue skirt with a white blouse and blue bow. Her shoes were black Mary Janes with frilly white socks.

"Spanish Colonial Revival," Melvia said as they paused at the door.

"What?"

"The architecture. My geography book has pictures. Red roofs, balconies, colorful tiles like the ones we're standing on, and big wooden doors that look like it's a castle. That's Spanish Colonial Revival Architecture."

Georgia was used to her daughter's habit of dropping esoteric nuggets of information into conversation. Melvia was, after all, a top student in the sixth grade at the Ninety-Ninth Street School. Instead of banging the wrought-iron knocker, Georgia rang the doorbell, which chimed with the playful melody of the Spanish folk song, "La Cucaracha."

Melvia giggled and sang, "*La cucaracha, la cucaracha, ya no puede caminar.*"

A uniformed butler answered the door and escorted mother and daughter through a corridor, past a dining room with a long, dark wooden table and place settings for more than a score of people, and into a library with hand-carved moldings, silk-upholstered chairs, and floor-to-ceiling bookshelves.

Chaplin and Einstein were bow-tied and waist-coated but hadn't yet slipped into their tuxedo jackets. Georgia introduced her daughter to the two men, who seemed delighted to meet her.

"Professor Einstein, I heard you answer schoolkids' questions in the mail," Melvia said.

"In emergencies," he answered. "Do you need help with your science class?"

"No, sir. I get all As and A-pluses."

"Don't brag on yourself, Melvia," her mother said.

"I'll bet you never got a wrong answer in school, Professor," Melvia said.

Einstein shrugged. "To tell you the truth, as a student, I was no Einstein."

The adults settled into the upholstered chairs, and Melvia explored the bookshelves.

Chaplin opened a bottle of Château Lafite Rothschild 1928 and let it breathe. "You were very kind to me today, Sergeant," Einstein said.

"Please call me Georgia. I'm off duty, and we're off the books."

"When I was in dire straits, Georgia, you treated me with such compassion."

Chaplin poured wine into three long-stemmed Lalique goblets with two capital *C*s etched on each bowl.

"*L'chaim!*" Einstein saluted them. They all sipped.

"Oh my," Georgia said. "I'm no expert, but this is like liquid velvet."

"My favorite Bordeaux," Chaplin said.

"If I celebrated Shabbos and could afford it, I would have this wine every Friday night," Einstein said.

As the adults drank, Melvia pulled a copy of *The Good Earth* by Pearl Buck from one of the bookshelves. She sat cross-legged on the floor and began reading.

Georgia Robinson told them everything she knew. The license plate came back stolen.

Police cars from the Thirteenth had mobilized but had not spotted the Studebaker. The identity of the driver was unknown.

"The department pulled me from the case," she said, and received, in return, astonished looks. "They're going to whitewash any Nazi involvement."

"In this country, such a thing?" Einstein was befuddled.

"Europe hasn't cornered the corruption market," Chaplin said. "Or fascism."

Einstein put down his wine and said, "So, Georgia, if I might ask, if you're off the case, why drive all this way to see us?"

"Because I'm not content to let this go. When a crime is committed in my precinct, I damn well do something about it, pardon my French."

"You won't get in trouble for doing this?" Einstein asked.

"It has to be on the QT."

She told them that some LAPD officers are members of fascist paramilitary groups, and Chief Davis doesn't give a hoot. Then she told them about Detective Cooper, who moonlighted for the German consulate.

"We're going to a reception at the consulate tonight," Chaplin said.

Her eyes lighting up, she said, "Mr. Chaplin, would you agree that you understand human nature?"

"I can tell when people are acting, which is to say, lying."

"And Professor Einstein speaks German," she said.

"I think I see where you're going with this," Chaplin said.

"Tonight, at the consulate, you can both look and listen," Robinson said. "Maybe someone will talk about what happened at the stadium. And this is a long shot, but it's possible the driver will be there. I got a good look at him before he put the goggles and cap on. Blond, clean cut, nice looking, no more than nineteen or twenty."

"Sounds like a Hitler Youth poster," Einstein said.

"He was in the street, taking these odd, long steps near your car. I didn't realize what he was doing, but now…"

"The little *pisher* was taking measurements!" Einstein said. "But why?"

"I think he wanted to know just when to hit the brakes based on his speed and where the two of you would cross the street to the car."

"I'd guess he was doing close to sixty miles per hour," Chaplin said.

"Roughly twenty-seven meters per second," Einstein calculated quickly, "yet he was skillful enough to stop one meter from the curb." Chaplin appeared puzzled.

"Skillful, Albert?"

"Don't you see? He wasn't trying to kill us! He believed the horn would drive us to the curb. He knew his car's braking ability and just where it would stop."

"A controlled skid," Chaplin said, catching on. "So…a race car or stunt driver like we use in the pictures."

All three of them sipped at the Bordeaux to think it over. Then Einstein said, "But why go to all that trouble just to frighten us?"

No answers were forthcoming, so more wine went down the hatch.

"I have an idea," Melvia piped up, putting down the book and joining them.

"Melvia, please don't bother the gentlemen," her mother said.

"It's quite all right," Chaplin said.

"What are you thinking, dear?" Einstein asked.

"Well, if he's a Hitler Youth, then maybe Adolf Hitler told him to kill you," she said. "But even though the boy is bad, he's not that bad. Not yet, anyway."

Chaplin and Einstein both smiled at her. "You are quite precocious," Einstein said.

"That's a fancy way of saying 'smart,' but Mama says to use regular words, or people will think I'm putting on airs."

Chaplin and Einstein exchanged knowing looks, and Robinson asked, "What? What is it?"

"Georgia, I suspect you have had to hide your intelligence on many occasions," Einstein said.

"So as not to make the dimwits at LAPD resent you even more than they already do," Chaplin chipped in.

Georgia Robinson realized that she liked both men. Not for their fame but for their intellect and kindness, for treating her as an equal, and for welcoming her and her daughter as if they were old friends. In all her years on the force, only one white officer had ever invited her into his home, and that had been for a well-intentioned but awkward dinner, his wife looking like she wanted to poison the meat loaf. There was nothing awkward here, just a common purpose and good fellowship.

"Mama," said Melvia, who was back at the bookshelves. "Are we going to have supper soon?"

"Blimey!" Chaplin said. "I'm a terrible host. What would you like for dinner?"

"We couldn't trouble you, Mr. Chaplin," Georgia said.

"Call me 'Charlie,' and it's no trouble. I'm not cooking." He turned to her daughter. "Melvia, what are your favorite foods?"

"Macaroni and cheese. Creamed chicken on biscuits. Beefsteak on my birthday," the girl replied.

Chaplin walked to a mahogany desk that sat in front of a stone fireplace big enough to park a car inside. He picked up a metal handset on an intercom that connected rooms of the mansion. "Maurice. You there? Pull a couple of Delmonicos from the Frigidaire. Biggest ones you've got. And fry up some potatoes. Did Betty bake today?"

After a moment, he turned to Melvia. "Lemon meringue or cherry pie?"

"Oh, I like them both," she said.

"Both pies. Big slices," he said into the handset. "And whatever ice cream is in the freezer."

Einstein drained his wine, smacked his lips and said, "Okay, Georgia. Charlie and I will be detectives tonight. If we learn anything, what do we do with the information?"

"You'll brief me. Off the books, we can work this together as a team."

"The scientist, the comedian, and the lady cop against the Nazis," Chaplin said. "I think we could make a helluva picture."

32
APPOINTMENT IN SAMARRA

Summit Drive, Beverly Hills

A Lucky Strike glowed barely a foot off the ground in the darkness, close to the hedge that surrounded the Chaplin estate. The cigarette dangled from the mouth of Ancel Eckart, the pudgy, sharpshooting Silver Shirt, who lay in the prone shooting position, his scoped 1903 Springfield on the ground next to him. It was his third Lucky of the night, and a fourth was propped behind his ear. When he finished each cigarette, he placed the butt in the cardboard box that housed his .30-06 cartridges.

"Leave nothing behind but two bodies," Pelley had told him.

They met earlier over pork chops, mashed potatoes, and corn bread at Clifton's Cafeteria downtown, greeting each other with "Eight-eight!" rather than "Heil Hitler!" Each number represented *H*, the eighth letter of the alphabet. Eckart thought the code was a little silly, like something the Hardy Boys would use to get into their secret clubhouse. But that was Pelley, a product of Hollywood, always with a flair for the dramatic.

Pelley told Eckart that Chaplin and Einstein would be going to the German consulate later that night. If he positioned himself alongside the driveway, hidden by the high hedge in the dark, he could get off two clean shots.

"They escaped their fate earlier today," Pelley said. "But tonight, they have an appointment in Samarra."

"Is that a town in the Valley?" Eckart asked.

"In Mesopotamia. It's a parable about Death stalking a man."

Having filched the *Saturday Evening Post* from mailboxes each week, Eckart was an avid reader of stories by F. Scott Fitzgerald, so he had a decent understanding of plot and theme. "What's the moral of the parable?" he asked.

"You cannot flee your fate, no matter how fast your horse. If your number's up, Death is inevitable."

"So I'm Death in this story."

"With a rifle and scope and a steady hand."

Now Eckart waited in the darkness, two thoughts crowding his mind.

When the hell are they going to leave? And can Death take time out to piss?

33
CIRCUMSTANTIAL EVIDENCE

Chaplin Mansion, Beverly Hills

Only two people were seated at the long mahogany dining table. Georgia Ann Robinson and her daughter, Melvia, sliced into Delmonico steaks so huge they hung over the sides of the gold-patterned China. A large bowl of fried potatoes sat next to a platter of jumbo asparagus, each spear the girth of a man's thumb, slathered in hollandaise. The pies, lemon meringue and cherry, were sliced and awaiting attention, and two dishes of Neapolitan ice cream—vanilla, chocolate, strawberry—rested in bowls floating on a tray of ice.

Chaplin and Einstein, decked out in their tuxedos, entered the dining room to say their good nights, and both smiled at the sight of their new friends enjoying dinner.

"I'm sorry if we made you late for the party," Georgia said.

"It's no party till we get there," Chaplin replied.

"Melvia," her mother said, "do you have something to say?"

"Thank you very much, Mr. Chaplin, for a splendid meal," she said, rather formally.

"You're very welcome, Melvia." He was used to bratty child actors at the studio, so it was a pleasure to have polite and precocious—*pardon me, smart*—Melvia Robinson in his home.

"Professor Einstein, I learned all about you when my class visited the Griffith Observatory right after it opened," Melvia said.

"A wonderful place for children," Einstein said.

"Melvia was so excited when she got home, I gave her an old pair of police binoculars to look at the stars," Georgia said.

Melvia popped a piece of steak into her mouth and said, "But it's so bright in the city, it's hard to see anything."

"I have a pretty good old telescope, a Watson, in a trunk at the house. Would you like it?"

"Would I ever! Can girls become astronomers?"

Einstein smiled. "Some of my best friends are girl astronomers." She regarded him suspiciously.

"Name one."

"Annie Jump Cannon developed the spectral classification of stars at Harvard."

"I'll bet the boys were mean to her."

"Aren't they always? Perhaps your mother will take you to the desert on a clear night, and with the Watson, you'll see stars in the Andromeda Galaxy."

"Then we'd be seeing what they looked like two million years ago," Melvia said, matter-of-factly. "The speed of light, you know."

"Oh, yes. I know," Einstein smiled.

Chaplin and Einstein were in the foyer on their way out when the doorbell chimed again with the tune of "La Cucaracha." Chaplin opened the door to find a Black man in his sixties with a bruised face. He wore dungarees and a plaid work shirt and clutched a soft cabbie hat in both hands, squeezing it into a ball of wool.

"I'm very sorry to disturb you, Mr. Chaplin." His face reflected equal parts nervousness and anguish. "My name's Henry Singleton. I'm the chief custodian at *B'nai Israel*."

"Yes, Mr. Singleton. I've seen you when I've spoken to the Men's Club." Chaplin was puzzled. "What can I do for you?"

"I know you donate money to the temple, even though you're not a member. So, I figured you'd want to know what happened last night."

"What is it, then?"

"I wonder if I could have a drink of water, sir. I rode the Red Car to the hotel station, then walked from there."

Chaplin knew he meant the trolley station in front of the Beverly Hills Hotel on Sunset Boulevard. From there, it was a one-mile walk uphill. "Of course! And perhaps a glass of Bordeaux?"

"I wouldn't say no."

"Then you'll tell me about the temple…and those bruises, too."

Chaplin and Einstein led the man into the dining room and introduced him to Georgia and Melvia Robinson. Singleton's eyes lit up when they landed on Georgia.

"I know you from the *Sentinel*," he said. "They had your picture way back when you became the first Negro officer."

"First *female* Negro officer," she said.

"And every time you got a promotion, they reported it."

"Plus, a swell story about Mama's Sojourner Truth Home for poor women," Melvia said. Georgia leveled her gaze at her daughter.

"Whoops," Melvia said. "Mr. Singleton, we don't brag on ourselves."

Chaplin opened a second bottle of the Château Lafite Rothschild, and Singleton sampled it.

"Oh my. My goodness. This is better than that sweet kosher wine at the temple."

"Motor oil is better than sweet kosher wine," Einstein said.

Fifteen minutes later, having told his story, Singleton was eating his own Delmonico and fried potatoes, drinking a second glass of Bordeaux, and eyeing what was left of the two pies.

Chaplin and Einstein were trying to make sense of the shocking information. Last night, criminals invaded the temple, pummeled Singleton, and vandalized the sanctuary. The destruction was enormous. The details of the damage brought tears to Einstein's eyes.

Chaplin wanted his personal physician to examine Singleton, who waved him off, saying he'd had worse than a couple of broken ribs and a few bruises.

"What's the name of the detective who's in charge of the investigation?" Georgia Robinson asked.

"That's the thing," Singleton said. "There ain't no detective."

He told them that Chief Davis personally visited Rabbi Geller in his study earlier that day. Singleton had been cleaning debris, taking it to the boiler room in the basement, as the rabbi instructed, so as not to shock congregation members who were filling the corridors, pacing and gabbing and feeling helpless.

"There's a heating vent in the basement that connects to the rabbi's study," Singleton said, somewhat sheepishly. "I heard most everything. The chief told the rabbi that young ruffians, juvenile delinquents, were the likely culprits. He said that publicizing the incident would only encourage more of them. The rabbi was mostly quiet. He's a good man, but…"

"But what, Mr. Singleton?" Chaplin asked.

"He's afraid to make waves. Sometimes I listen to the rabbi's sermons. He thinks that Jews are guests in this country and have to mind their manners, not make a fuss."

"So the LAPD is keeping the attack out of the papers?" Chaplin asked.

"Not just that. There's no police report, no investigation. It's like it didn't happen."

"Outrageous!" Chaplin said. "Just like the cover-up of the stadium attack."

"*Mein Gat!* It's like Berlin," Einstein exclaimed.

"Doing nothing is what encourages more violence," Robinson added.

"And I'm here to tell you the chief is full of feathers," Singleton said. "These were no young ruffians. They were grown men in their thirties and forties, wearing gray shirts with big letter *L*s on the chest."

"The Silver Shirts Nazi group," Chaplin said.

"As mean as the Klan," Singleton said, shaking his head. "What in the name of sweet Jesus fills men with such senseless hate?"

"Did you speak to the chief about what you witnessed?" Robinson asked.

"No, ma'am, but I told Rabbi Geller I could identify the man who beat on me. He had a face right out of a nightmare, a face you don't forget."

"How so?" she asked.

"Scars, like from a knife wound that wasn't stitched up right, and a squashed nose like a prizefighter."

That caught Chaplin's attention.

"Anything else, Mr. Singleton?"

"Small tattoo on the side of his neck. A boat anchor."

Chaplin slapped his hand on the dining table. "The man from the ball game! Said his name was Skowron and demanded an autograph for his son."

"Adolf," Einstein said, raising his bushy eyebrows.

"He named his son Adolf?" Robinson asked.

"It's doubtful any woman would have a child with this man," Chaplin said. "He was just bullying me."

"A monster," Einstein said.

Five minutes later, Singleton had devoured the rest of the pies, and Georgia said she would drive him home, which delighted Melvia, who had oodles of questions about the temple. Chaplin and Einstein accompanied the three of them to the front door. Georgia paused a moment and turned to Chaplin.

"I know what you're going to say," Chaplin said. "When we're at the consulate, find out everything we can about the temple desecration because it's linked to the attack at the stadium."

"Unless you believe in coincidences," she said.

"Only in the movies," Chaplin said, thinking of *It Happened One Night* when Claudette Colbert, the runaway heiress, hops on a bus, and there's Clark Gable, the down-and-out reporter in urgent need of a scoop.

"The Nazi thug was at the stadium and the temple," Georgia said, "circumstantial proof that the Silver Shirts were behind both attacks. They've gone from throwing birthday parties for Hitler to brutal violence." She lowered her voice to a whisper. "Be careful tonight."

Georgia reached out to shake Chaplin's hand. He took both her hands in his. Then Einstein clasped both his hands over theirs. They stood silently for a moment, a tower of six hands as one. Then Georgia said, "God be with you."

"And with you," Chaplin said.

"Ah-main," Einstein said, giving "amen" the Hebrew pronunciation.

34
TO BE IN THE SCHARFSCHÜTZENEINHEIT

Summit Drive, Beverly Hills

Ancel Eckart smoked three more Luckys and still lay in the prone position. He had gotten up to take a piss and he'd farted up a storm, the cafeteria pork chops not agreeing with him.

Forty-five minutes ago, he'd seen the damnedest thing. An old black Joe in work clothes and a cabbie hat walked up the street and looked through the giant wrought-iron gate at the driveway entrance to the Chaplin mansion. The gate was closed, but the metal pedestrian door alongside was unlocked, and the Negro opened it and headed up the steep driveway to the mansion. An hour before that, two Negroes—a woman and a girl—drove up to the house in a green Ford Model B sedan.

What's Chaplin doing? Holding a convention for the whadayacallit? The National Association of Coloreds?

Eckart peered through the scope mounted on his Springfield and twisted the focus knob for about the fiftieth time in the last two hours. He brought into sharp focus the two large metal *C*s that met at the closure of the wrought-iron gates.

This was his first mission for Pelley, and he damn sure was going to succeed. Eckart had joined the Silver Shirts figuring it was his patriotic duty. After all, an FBI agent was the one who suggested it.

You can't get any more red-white-and-blue than the FBI!

Eckart liked to tell people, especially single women who caught his fancy, that he was in law enforcement. It wasn't a total lie. He was a clerk in the US Postal Inspection Service office downtown. As every schoolboy knew, that agency traced its roots to Benjamin Franklin and was damn important in preventing mail thefts and frauds and everything else that can go wrong once you lick that three-cent stamp and mail your letter.

The FBI agent, a middle-aged man with a graying buzzcut and horn-rimmed eyeglasses, wore a baggy suit, and his bland, forgettable visage disappointed Eckart. He'd envisioned G-men as ruggedly handsome men whose moral character was engraved on their faces. Gary Cooper or Spencer Tracy, maybe. This agent, John something or other—he never said—handed Eckart a list of names whose mail he'd be checking. Some Hollywood stars and others in the industry whose names Eckart didn't recognize like writers, producers, directors, production workers.

"Hollywood's a suburb of Moscow," John told him, "and Boyle Heights is infested with Bolsheviks."

Eckart asked to see a warrant before giving John access to the mail, but the man laughed and opened his wrinkled suit coat to reveal his holstered handgun. "That's my warrant, son."

Eckart's superior gave the okay, and John made weekly visits to look at and sometimes open the mail addressed to people on the list. Eckart had never given much thought to politics but now he learned that Bolsheviks had the goal of confiscating private property and giving it to the new Communist States of America.

Well, that ain't gonna happen, Joe Stalin! Not with me and the feds on your ass.

He was not exactly sure how opening the mail of Edward G. Robinson, born Emanuel Goldenberg or Eddie Cantor, born Isidore Itzkowitz, was going to rescue the US of A, but if the FBI said to do it, by God, he'd do it!

"You're a patriot, Eckart," John had told him. "You oughta join the Silver Shirts."

***

An evening chill had settled over Beverly Hills, and Eckart wished he'd worn a coat. His shoulders had stiffened from propping up on his elbows in the prone shooting position. Then he heard an engine firing up.

Eckart focused yet again on the center of the two wrought-iron gates. The rumble of the car engine grew louder, and he saw the light from a car's headlamps spill out of the driveway.

Hey Chaplin and Einstein! Breathe your last, you dirty commies.

The gates slowly swung open, and a boxy Ford sedan nosed out.

Eckart's right index finger rested on the trigger, and despite the chill in the air, beads of sweat dripped from his forehead. The ornamental lights on the gate pillars illuminated the car, and through the scope, the crosshairs focused squarely on the side of a person's head.

The young Negro girl!

Eckart's hands shook, the rifle jiggling. Rattled, he threw open the Springfield's bolt and ejected the unfired round.

This was not what he had bargained for. He was a patriot whose goal was to rid the country of communists. Pelley had told him he had the right stuff to be a Silver Shirts Ranger.

"You have the patience, the skill, and the loyalty to crouch in a bale of hay for days to get off one kill shot," Pelley said. "You belong in an elite sniper unit, the *Scharfschützeneinheit.*"

But not to kill little girls, no matter their skin color.

Eckart lay there motionless while the Ford pulled onto the street. Moments later, when Chaplin's Rolls-Royce drove through the open gate onto Summit Drive and into the night, Eckart's hands were still shaking, his rifle on the ground.

35
THE YOUNGEST DIEKMANN

Long Beach Armory

Three men were squashed together in the rickety, rusted Ford Model TT panel truck, which was nosed against the chain-link fence that surrounded the Long Beach Armory. One night earlier, the truck had been in the same spot with William Pelley, giving instructions to Max and Kurt Diekmann. Tonight, Pelley was at a fancy German consulate shindig, and the Diekmanns were joined by kid brother Dieter. Sitting between his bigger, older brothers, Dieter could smell dried animal blood on their clothing, could feel their body heat.

I'm the pat of butter smooshed between two halves of a baked potato.

"You'll be in and out in minutes," Pelley had promised them, "with brand-spanking-new machine guns, rifles, ammo, and grenades."

Max and Kurt wore solid green wool shirts with DIEKMANN BROTHERS FINE WHOLESALE MEATS emblazoned in red thread above the left pocket. Kurt had hand-sewn large, red silk *L*s on each shirt, the symbol of the Silver Shirts. Dieter wore pleated cotton pants and a V-neck sweater over a white shirt and club tie, standard apparel for a college student.

Twenty minutes earlier, Max had used his old binoculars to watch the armory flag detail bring down the Stars and Stripes, just as they had done the night before. The last of the guardsmen's cars left the parking lot five minutes later.

"Jesus, Kurt, how long do we have to wait?" Max prodded.

"Did any officers ever order you to attack in daylight?" Kurt replied.

"This ain't daylight. This is…Hey, Dieter, what is it?"

"Twilight. Dusk. Gloaming."

Max laughed. "College boy's got three words when one will do." He struck a match, lighted a cigar, and turned to Kurt. "A dumb-ass lieutenant sure as shit ordered us to attack in daylight. Someone—don't know who—shot him in the back of his stupid skull." Max belched a laugh and exhaled a puff of cigar smoke through the open window.

"We wait for full darkness and then some," Kurt said.

"Ja, mein Kapitän," Max said, sarcasm dripping like fat from roasted pig knuckles.

He turned on the radio, twisted the dial through the static, and stopped when he heard a familiar male voice.

"Jews are constantly whining about their treatment in Germany. They don't tell you that those atheistic communist Jews Lenin and Trotsky killed twenty million Christians and stole forty billion dollars of Christian property in Russia."

"Give 'em hell, Father Coughlin!" Max shouted.

"Let's not worry about Germany," the radio priest continued. "Let's worry about America First. And let me tell you what's happening with the international bankers on Wall Street this very…"

Dieter turned off the radio. "Why listen to that hokum?"

"Father Coughlin gets eighty thousand letters a week," Max said, "a lot of 'em with money inside."

"God must be lousy at handling money if he needs more every week," Dieter said.

"Don't blaspheme!"

"All I'm saying, Father Coughlin's a demagogue for the untutored and unwashed."

"The hell you say, Dieter." He poked his younger brother in the shoulder. "I suds up every Saturday night, whether I need to or not."

Dieter loved his brothers. But let's face it, they're a pair of palookas.

Kurt and Max considered themselves Nazis without any knowledge of fascism's intellectual underpinnings. Dieter had read Schopenhauer, who believed that the driving force behind human behavior was *wille zur macht*, the "will to power." He had studied Nietzsche who pined for the *Übermensch*, a superman not bound by the rules of lesser mortals. Both philosophers rejected Judeo-Christian ideas of morality. Philosophically, Dieter considered himself a fascist, but that was as far as it went.

His older brothers' reading was limited to *Blondie*, *Li'l Abner*, and, of course, *The Katzenjammer Kids*. Born near Hamburg, Kurt, now thirty-seven, and Max, thirty-nine, were schooled in the trenches of Passchendaele and the Second Battle of the Marne. Born in Los Angeles, Dieter was twenty-one—obviously a surprise bundle of joy for his parents—and a junior at USC studying economics. He was the only one in the family who did not speak with a German accent.

While Dieter was lean and lithe with a shock of sandy hair and blue eyes, his brothers were dark-haired, mountainous men with foreheads like slabs of granite and shoulders like sandbags. They kept food on the table—literally—and paid Dieter's tuition. He knew he could never toil for hours in a thirty-five-degree walk-in cooler smelling of blood and entrails. He could not sling a side of beef from a meat hook to the butcher's block, much less cut through a cow's ribs with a handsaw.

What Dieter could do was argue endlessly in class. He loved debating pinkos, lefties, fellow travelers, and professors who were card-carrying commies. Coeds from wealthy Republican families found him a bit dangerous and therefore irresistible. Many perfumed nights ended in his apartment, their tight sweaters and torpedo bras discarded, Tony Martin on the phonograph warbling "When Did You Leave Heaven?"

He had no particular animus toward any race or religion, but his interpretation of history convinced him that democracy was a nifty experiment that had failed. The American economy was a wild herd of mustangs, dashing up mountains, crossing swollen waters, falling off cliffs. The economy must be controlled by a strong central government. Hitler realized this and revitalized the moribund German state. Of course, he did much more, not all of it admirable.

Dieter thought that the United States would turn to fascism without revolution or insurrection. It was an economic imperative. He did not approve of the Silver Shirts and their silly uniforms, looking like a troop of crazed Boy Scouts. And Kurt's and Max's predilections for violence disturbed and frightened him.

So why am I helping them heist crates of machine guns? To keep them safe.

It seemed paradoxical, he knew. But they really weren't good at this. He'd told them not to drive the truck with their names on the side.

Why not wear sandwich boards saying, "We're the Diekmanns, and we're stealing US Army property?"

But they said the mission would be a walk in the park. The weapons and ammo were waiting for them. No guards or soldiers on the premises. Fifteen minutes to load the truck, a mere ten-minute-drive back to their cold storage warehouse. They'd be home in time to listen to *The Jell-O Program* starring Jack Benny with the Phil Harris Orchestra.

Dieter admired his older brothers' confidence but not necessarily their skill at any task that did not involve dead animals.

He would protect them from their own mistakes. He had met the plan's architect, Pelley, a man whose self-importance bubbled to the surface like a percolating coffeepot.

Who, after all, would have the temerity to call himself the "American Hitler?"

Still, the plan did not have obvious weaknesses. Dieter hoped for a quick and flawless mission, and his brothers might be right. An hour from now, they should be listening to Jack Benny's jokes and the Phil Harris Orchestra playing "Boo Hoo."

36
THE LAST GULCH SALOON

Konsulat von Deutschland

The valet parker, a young German man in a white shirt and bow tie, took the keys to Chaplin's Rolls-Royce Phantom without whistling at it. The Rolls was just one of a parade of Cadillacs, Mercedes, and Duesenbergs. The male guests were in black tuxedos, the women in evening gowns of different hues, their necks dripping with diamonds and emeralds. Some women—poor things—wore necklaces of gold and silver, the heavy elements Einstein suspected were produced by the explosions of massive stars. Not that anyone had proven it.

Einstein craned his neck and looked up. Floating in the air thirty feet above the six-story building was…the *Hindenburg*!

Well, it looked like the German airship and was, in fact, a scale model forty feet long, tethered to the rooftop, peeking in and out of heavy fog.

An admirer of Carl Sandburg's poetry, Einstein recalled the line "The fog comes on little cat feet." This fog, called a "marine layer" hereabouts, must have come on an elephant's back, heavy sheets rolling across the sky like ghostly blankets. Three Klieg lights the size of Chevy sedans swept across the building and illuminated both the fog and the blimp.

Chaplin and Einstein walked through the open doors beneath the brass eagle clutching a swastika and passed through a foyer where several husky men in dark suits stood, legs spread, scrutinizing every guest. The men had swastika pins in one lapel and SS lightning bolts in the other. At a grand piano, a blond female pianist in a black cocktail dress played Beethoven's "Für Elise." No doubt, Einstein thought, it would be a night of Beethoven, Wagner, and Bruckner...Hitler's favorites. Felix Mendelssohn, not a chance.

As they approached the grand ballroom, Einstein thought that the winged collar on his bibbed tuxedo shirt was too tight.

No, that's not it. It feels like spiders are crawling up my neck!

He realized it was just a psychological response to being surrounded by Nazis. Maybe he would write his friend Sigmund Freud and ask if there was any particular significance to imagining eight-legged insects under his collar, as opposed to, say, dripping icicles.

They entered a mammoth ballroom, which buzzed with happy chatter in English and German. Interspersed with the tuxedoed and gowned guests were German military officers in dress uniforms. Six-foot-long *Hindenburg* balloons were wedged against the ceiling among the ornate chandeliers. Long tables were piled high with Beluga caviar and boatloads of shrimp, tidily arranged in rows like crustacean soldiers with bad posture. Tomatoes and carrots were trapped inside transparent hemispheres of aspic jelly, looking to Einstein as appetizing as bubbles of phlegm. A large wooden platter held a slab of pâté de foie gras that must have cost the lives of a flock of geese.

One table contained only two items. The centerpiece was an ice sculpture of the *Hindenburg*, and next to it sat a twelve-foot-long cake, which was, of course, a miniature of the airship with silver frosting and black swastikas on its tail.

"Why such a big *tzimmes* about a blimp?" Einstein asked.

"Marketing, Albert," Chaplin said. "The Nazis sell fascism the way Ballantine sells beer."

"I love cake, but I'm not eating a swastika."

"Marzipan filling, quite delicious!" boomed a voice from behind them.

They turned to find Georg Gyssling, six feet four and streamlined as a shark in a sleek bespoke tuxedo of shimmering black.

"Professor Einstein, it is a pleasure to make your acquaintance," the consul said, offering his hand.

Einstein warily shook hands. "How do you do, sir?"

"Relax, Albert," Chaplin said. "Georg is one of the good Nazis."

"Ach! Don't let Goebbels hear that," Gyssling said. "I could be cashiered. Or worse, sent to Moscow."

"We look forward to meeting Herr Goebbels," Chaplin said.

"Only if you promise to be on your best behavior, Charlie."

"I never make promises I can't keep, except to women, and then it's quite unintentional."

Gyssling's visage clouded. "Charlie, I heard what happened at the stadium today. Thank God you're both unharmed."

"Who told you about it, Georg?" Chaplin asked.

"A detective who's assigned to the consulate for security. You'd be surprised how much harassment we endure. Eggs tossed against windows, toilet paper wrapped around trees."

"Oh drat, those darned eggs," Chaplin said. "Any fatalities?"

"In any event, you survived the accident and look none the worse for wear."

"So, this detective told you it was an accident?" Einstein asked.

"Cooper. He's here tonight if you'd like to meet him. Apparently, a young man in a green Plymouth was showing off for the girls and drove quite recklessly."

"Yellow Studebaker," Chaplin corrected him, "and he was showing off for Hitler, Göring, and Goebbels."

"He screamed an antisemitic slur," Einstein explained. "And the car's hood ornament was an eagle clutching a swastika."

"It doesn't take Sam Spade," Chaplin said.

Gyssling's look hardened. "I hope you're not insinuating the Reich had anything to do with the unfortunate incident."

"Georg, you remind me of Chico Marx in *Duck Soup* when he says, 'Who ya gonna believe? Me? Or your own eyes?' You've been at this so long you're starting to believe your own hogwash."

"For the record, Charlie, I find the Marx Brothers' humor hopelessly broad. I prefer your finer touch."

"I imagine you also heard about the synagogue that was desecrated by Nazi thugs," Chaplin said.

"You're talking about B'nai Israel." Gyssling's expression took on a sadness, as if remembering a boyhood dog that had died. "A heinous act. If my hands weren't tied, I'd make a contribution for repairs."

"I'll be paying for everything, Georg."

"People are going to say you're Jewish, Charlie."

"I'd consider it a compliment. What does your Detective Cooper say about the temple?"

"Hooligans. Could be from the Valley. Could be from Fresno or Bakersfield. Very hard to track down."

The three men stood silently for a moment, engulfed in the babble of the partygoers, the *Hindenburg* ice sculpture melting drip by drip. Finally Chaplin said, "Georg, you spin bullshit like a weaver with a bobbin of yarn."

"And I consider that a compliment," Gyssling said with a rueful smile. He moved closer and lowered his voice. "These are dangerous times for anyone thought to be an enemy of the Reich, particularly those Hitler calls 'vermin.'"

"Go on, Georg."

"There are rumors you're planning a movie about Hitler. If true, this would displease people who—how shall I put this?—

have no limits. If they were carpenters, they would pound every nail to the board."

"Are you talking about homegrown, wannabe Nazis or the real deal from Berlin?"

"I honestly don't know, Charlie. I'm a figurehead, the maître d' at the front of the restaurant. I can't see what's happening in the kitchen."

"But you can smell what's cooking," Chaplin said.

Gyssling pursed his lips and seemed to consider just how much to say. "If this were a Hollywood Western, a kind soul would tell the hero, 'Whatever you do, stay out of the Last Gulch Saloon.' And the hero would, of course, swagger through the swinging doors, ready for a gunfight." He paused to let them imagine the scene. "But this isn't a movie."

"If you learn that any groups are planning violence, would you tell us?"

"You ask too much, Charlie. Despite my personal beliefs, I must follow orders."

"No matter what the orders call for?" Einstein asked.

Gyssling sighed and scanned the ballroom. "Sorry, but if you'll excuse me, I must make small talk with guests far less interesting." He started to walk away, then turned and said, "Stay out of the Last Gulch Saloon."

37
STAR SHELLS

Long Beach Armory

The armory was quiet. The three Diekmann brothers sat in the panel truck outside the fence, waiting.

"Not long now," Kurt said, without being asked.

It was a foggy night with no moon, no stars. Dark as a raven's wing, except for the occasional auto on an adjacent street, headlamps peeking through the fog. Max pulled a dented German military flashlight from the glove box and used it to illuminate the front page of a newspaper, *Der Deutsche Beobachter*. He tapped a finger on a photo of the *Hindenburg* under the headline "WELTGRÖßTES LUFTSCHIFF NACH USA GEBUNDEN."

With pride in his voice, Max translated, "World's largest airship bound for USA."

"German equipment is the best in the world," Kurt said.

"Nothing here compares," Max said, just as his old flashlight began to flicker.

"Ha! American torches are better," Dieter said.

"I've had this *taschenlampe* since the Second Battle of the Marne," Max said.

"Same underwear, too," Dieter jabbed him.

Max swatted his younger brother with the newspaper. "Still the pest, Dieter!"

"Enough talk," Kurt said, hitting the ignition. He put the truck into reverse and swung it around so that the double doors at the rear faced the fence.

"Grab the tools," he told his brothers.

※ ※

Bolt cutters sliced through the wire knuckles of the chain-link fence as if they were strands of spaghetti. A sledgehammer made quick work of the simple padlock on the loading dock's sliding metal door. Seven wooden crates, six feet long, three feet high, and three feet wide were neatly stacked, waiting for them, just as Pelley said they'd be. The stenciled printing read: PROPERTY OF THE UNITED STATES ARMY.

"Jesus, they look heavy," Dieter said.

Max, who could lift the rear end of the panel truck off the ground with two hands on the bumper, tried to heft a crate marked DANGER-LIVE MK2 GRENADES and let out a low whistle. "Sumbitch ain't a calf. It's a full-grown Hereford."

"Glad we brought you along, Dieter," Kurt said. "Now you can do something other than yap."

They figured a way that Dieter could slide the crates off the edge of the loading dock, and Kurt and Max would carry them across the asphalt driveway to the hole in the fence. But the crates were intended to be moved by pallet jacks, not two men, even ones who could put Two-Ton Tony Galento on his ass.

Halfway up the driveway with the first crate marked BROWNING AUTOMATIC RIFLES, Kurt's trick left knee gave way. He stumbled and the crate crashed to the asphalt, the top popping open, as the thirty-penny nails loosened. Kurt hopped around on his good leg, cursing, "*Scheisse! Scheisse Scheisse!*"

"Let's see what we got here," Max said, prying a loose board off the top of the crate. He shined his old flashlight inside and dug through the wood chips with the excitement of a kid on Christmas morning hoping for a Lionel train. After a moment, he came out holding a Browning Automatic. "I hate to admit it, but the Yanks make a helluva light machine gun."

He turned to Kurt. "How you doing, you gimpy *krüppel?*"

"Change of plans," Kurt said. "My bad knee's done. We gotta unload every crate and carry the stuff to the truck by hand."

"It'll take a lot longer," Dieter said.

"No choice, kid."

They found a crowbar just inside the sliding door and pried open each crate, starting with the Browning Automatics, then the crate marked DANGER-LIVE .30-06 AMMUNITION, and then the grenades.

Max reached into the ammo crate and came up with a grooved iron grenade in each hand. "Look at these pineapples." He pretended to throw one in the direction of a nearby street.

"Shake a leg, Max," Kurt said. "We gotta get going."

"Don't be a nervous Nellie. We got hours till those sacks of *scheisse* show up for reveille."

Dieter was just happy that Kurt hadn't inadvertently pulled the pin and dropped the grenade at their feet.

An hour later, they had placed nearly everything in piles in the driveway and finally came to the last crate marked STAR SHELLS.

"What the hell are these?" Dieter asked.

"Flares," Max said. "We can use them for night assaults." He reached into the crate, fished through layers of wood chips, and came out with a red tin box labeled RED STAR SIGNALS-DO NOT OPEN UNTIL CARTRIDGES REQUIRED.

Of course, he opened the box to show his brother the flare. "Small but handy," Max said. When the last tin boxes were added to the stack of weaponry, the machine guns, ammo, grenades, and flares were poking out of a knee-deep blanket of wood chips that had fallen from the crates.

"Where's my *taschenlampe*?" Max said. "I must have dropped it."

"Forget it," Kurt said. "Let's load up."

"Forget it? It's got my name on it!"

"Why's your name on a flashlight?"

"So Corporal Kleindienst wouldn't steal it!"

"Jesus, Max," Dieter chimed in.

"Just help me find it," Max said.

The three of them started kicking at the wood chips like kids in a pile of leaves. But it was dark, and all they accomplished was stirring up dust that obscured their vision even more.

"I can't see a thing." Dieter realized they needed Max's flashlight…to find his flashlight and wondered if that was a good example of irony he needed for a paper in his English course.

Max struck a match and bent over, brushing at the wood chips with a hand. No luck.

When the match burned down, he crushed the flame between a calloused thumb and finger. Then lighted another and kept looking.

The men froze at the sound of a wailing police siren. They each dropped face down into the wood chips. None of them noticed the lighted match that Max had dropped.

They stayed down for a half minute until the patrol car, its cherry light flashing, raced past the armory on the adjacent street, and the sound of the siren was lost in the night.

"Do you smell smoke?" Dieter asked.

38

OPERATION HOLLYWOOD

Konsulat von Deutschland, Ballroom

Chaplin and Einstein watched Gyssling glide across the ballroom with the grace of Fred Astaire, heading for United States Senator Ernest Lundeen from Minnesota, known to be a willing dance partner of the Reich.

"Are we getting in over our heads, Charlie?" Einstein asked.

"You're worried about what Gyssling said."

"He seemed sincerely concerned for our safety."

"Let's just stick with the plan and find Goebbels. We can always bail out like a batter who hits the dirt when a pitcher throws chin music."

"I have no idea what music has to do with baseball."

A server came by offering canapés with sour cream and caviar. Both men demurred.

Moments later, a second server, a young Black man in a red tunic over a white shirt, approached them with a tray of drinks. "Champagne, gentlemen?"

"Certainly." Chaplin reached for a flute just as the server swerved the tray toward him, and champagne sloshed on both of them.

"So sorry, sir." The server took a hand towel that rested on his shoulder and brushed off Chaplin's tuxedo jacket.

"I'm not really a waiter, Mr. Chaplin."

"Certainly not a good one," Chaplin said in a good-natured tone. "Wait a second. I know you. You're the reporter from the ball game."

"Yes, sir. Jimmy Mitchell."

"Night job, young man?" Einstein asked.

"Actually, I'm working undercover," Mitchell said.

"Like Robert Montgomery in *The Big House*?" Chaplin asked.

"What are you up to, Mr. Mitchell?" Einstein said.

"The police won't listen to me. But you two. You're famous and committed to justice. When you tell the authorities about it, they'll have to listen."

The naïveté of the young, Einstein thought. The police in this city, as he now understood from Georgia Robinson, were more adept at sweeping crimes under the rug than solving them.

As many rugs as the Arabian Nights.

"Tell the police about what, Mr. Mitchell?" Chaplin asked.

Mitchell looked left and right and nearly spilled more champagne. "Operation Hollywood," he whispered.

"Sounds like a Busby Berkeley musical," Chaplin said.

"Believe me, sir, the only music will be funeral dirges."

"A tad melodramatic, Mr. Mitchell."

"Only because you don't understand the gravity of the situation."

"Gravity is my business," Einstein said.

"What's all the hubbub?" Chaplin pressed the young man.

"I saw a man killed at Alt Heidelberg last night. I think he was spying on fascist groups."

Chaplin and Einstein exchanged startled looks.

"His dying words were 'Operation Hollywood,'" Mitchell continued.

"Meaning what?" Einstein asked.

"Putting that together with a tip we got at the *Sentinel*, it has something to do with *maschinengewehre*."

"Machine guns!" Einstein exclaimed.

"Have either of you heard of a man named William Dudley Pelley?" Mitchell said.

"The *Times* had a story," Chaplin said. "He founded the Silver Shirts. They sit around biergartens singing songs and blaming Jews for all their problems."

"Maybe that's how they started," Mitchell said, "but Pelley's turned them into a paramilitary force, a private army. He bragged about it at the rally last night."

"Aw, he's talking through his hat," Chaplin said. "This ain't Germany."

"Charlie, give the young man a chance," Einstein berated him. "Have you already forgotten what Gyssling said?" He turned to Mitchell. "Are these machine guns for the Silver Shirts?"

"That's the drift I got from eavesdropping on Pelley. I don't know how they're getting the guns or how they plan to use them, but I'd bet my last buffalo nickel they're not for parades at the fairgrounds."

"And Operation Hollywood…?" Einstein said.

"I figure that's the code name for the mission, the key to everything. It's the evidence I'm looking for."

"It might be what got that fellow killed last night," Chaplin said, a note of worry in his voice.

"Which means I'm on the right track." Mitchell made a slight gesture with his head. "Take a gander…three o'clock."

Both men looked in that direction. They recognized from newsreels, a short man with beady eyes and the narrow, elongated face of a ferret. Nazi propaganda chief Joseph Goebbels. He was speaking to a man in his late forties with a neatly trimmed gray goatee.

"That's Pelley with Goebbels," Mitchell said, "palsy-walsy fascist bastards."

"What do you suppose they're flapping their gums about?" Chaplin asked.

"My guess," Mitchell said, "Goebbels is saying how the Nazis are gonna carve up Europe like a Thanksgiving turkey, and Pelley's talking about insurrection here, starting with Operation Hollywood."

"Then we are staring into the heart of darkness," Einstein said.

"I've been trying to eavesdrop on them," Mitchell said, "but they shut their gobs when I get close. Now I'm gonna poke around the building and see what I can find."

"Poke around?" Chaplin said.

"Break into the consul's office, rifle the cabinets and drawers."

"That's far too dangerous, Mr. Mitchell," Einstein said.

"Albert's right. Lay your peepers over there." Chaplin nodded toward the entrance of the ballroom. "The twin Doberman Pinschers."

Two tall, lean men in black leather tunics belted at the waist flanked the door, heads on swivels, eyes sweeping the ballroom.

"What do you think, Albert?" Chaplin asked.

From this distance, Einstein couldn't make out the embroidered symbols on the collars, but he knew what they were from his days in Berlin. Double lightning bolts. "They're Schutzstaffel, SS."

"You should go home, Mr. Mitchell," Chaplin said.

He shook his head. "Got work to do. But I'll meet you for lunch tomorrow, Mr. Chaplin, just like you said. And I'll tell you everything I find out.

☙ ❧

Halfway across the ballroom, Klaus Spengler, the photographer from Douglas Fairbanks's tree and the baseball game, snapped photos of the partygoers with his Leica. Some prints would be mailed to guests as goodwill gestures, but many more—hundreds—would find their way into Foreign Office files. Attaching names to faces was also his job. Some names were easier than others. Charles

Lindbergh, Albert Einstein, and Charlie Chaplin, for example. Senator Ernest Lundeen and Congressman Hamilton Fish, too. Others required tedious work.

Something caught his trained eye. Looking through the telephoto lens, he spotted a Negro waiter speaking to Einstein and Chaplin. Nothing strange about that, except the conversation went on too long.

And the Negro looks familiar. How could that be?

It took only a moment. The man with the PRESS card in his hatband at the baseball game! Speaking to Chaplin and Einstein there...and here.

Either you're not a reporter or not a waiter.

Whichever it was, the Schutzstaffel would want to know. Spengler headed toward the two SS officers at the entrance of the ballroom, thinking next week he would ask for a raise.

39
PYROTECHNICS

Long Beach Armory

The Diekmann brothers were up to their knees in wood chips. Smoke thickened around them, and it was impossible to see the source of the fire. Seconds later, flames shot up, encircling them.

"*Verdammt!*" Kurt shouted.

They tried stomping out the fire, but its speed, fed by bone-dry kindling, shocked them. "Put it out!" Dieter yelled, as if it were an idea neither of his brothers had considered.

"Put it out!"

Max's shirttail caught on fire, and he yelped. He ripped off the shirt and tossed it to the ground. Kurt hobbled up the slope, through the fence opening to the truck, and grabbed a small red fire extinguisher. He liimped back and pulled the trigger. A thin stream of foam trickled out, like an old man piddling.

"*Scheisse!*" Kurt yelled.

Dodging the stacks of weapons and ammo they had unloaded from the crates, the men high-stepped out of the wood chips to keep from being incinerated.

"Kurt! Kurt!" Dieter's voice was laced with fear. He pointed to the flames engulfing a belt of .30-06 cartridges.

But that's not what exploded first.

The three brothers were jolted by a WHOOSH!

It wasn't a grenade. It wasn't a .30-06 cartridge. It was a star shell flare, blasting skyward, lighting the night with a red hue, before settling back toward the ground with a small parachute.

It's beautiful, Dieter thought.

So was the second one. And the third and fourth. But the next several didn't lift toward the heavens. They shot in all directions, helter-skelter, some sailing past the brothers, some flying toward the armory, others lighting up the adjacent street.

They would have grabbed some of the machine guns, except the .30-06 shells began exploding with the clamor of an infantry assault. They could take nothing.

"Let's get the hell out of here!" Dieter yelled.

His brothers didn't need convincing. They clambered up the incline, through the hole in the fence, and piled into the truck. Kurt gave it gas, but in a panic, he'd failed to adjust the choke, and the engine coughed, sputtered, and flooded.

Behind them in the armory driveway, grenades exploded, bullets punctured the night, and the flares' red glare—bursting in air—sent pyrotechnics high into the sky.

"Jesus, Kurt!" Max yelled. "The choke! Give it some air. You've flooded it."

Kurt froze, and Dieter said calmly, "Pump the gas pedal, Kurt. It'll drain the cylinders."

Kurt did as told, and after a long, perilous moment, the engine fired up. The rickety truck tore out of the bushes, the rear doors flapping open, as they'd forgotten to close them. As they raced along Stearns Street, three patrol cars, sirens screaming, passed them, going the other way.

40
OF MATZOH BALLS AND BOOM POLES

Konsulat von Deutschland, Ballroom

Pelley was just about to slurp down an oyster Rockefeller when he saw Chaplin and Einstein across the ballroom. His hand jerked involuntarily, and buttery breadcrumbs streaked across his mustache.

Hellfire! Had they escaped death twice in one day?

Skowron had told him what happened at the stadium. Gus was a helluva fine wheelman, Skowron said, but Chaplin pulled some movie trick, and the Studebaker had a near miss.

"Not a problem," Pelley said. "There's a backup plan." He had been unperturbed, temporary setbacks never shattering his optimism.

The backup plan was Eckart and a Springfield rifle at Chaplin's estate. What cock-up happened there, Pelley didn't know. The appointment in Samarra would be rescheduled. Perhaps he should have assigned the fearsome Skowron, all facial scars and unbridled anger, to the task. From his reports, the devastation of the temple had been a triumph. Now Pelley imagined Skowron with a Browning Automatic in his meaty hands. There was a fellow who could be trusted to complete a mission.

As for the two know-it-all geniuses showing up here, that was Gyssling's doing. How does Goebbels put up with a consul who practically farts "Yankee Doodle?" Thinking it over, there was an upside to seeing Chaplin and Einstein. He could speak to the two men from a position of superiority, knowing what they did not… that their fate had already been written.

He approached them from behind.

"Mr. Chaplin. Professor Einstein." The two men turned to face a man whose cologne had already announced his presence. "I'm William Dudley Pelley."

"We know who you are and what you stand for," Chaplin said, eyes drilling him.

"Now, now, I come in convivial fellowship." Pelley hung a smile on his face that was so tight, it might cause a toothache.

"I read a piece you wrote in a hateful little rag called *Liberation*," Chaplin said.

"My magazine, and it's quite highly regarded."

"In mental institutions, perhaps. The title was 'Who's Who in Hollywood? Find the Gentile.'"

Pelley snickered. "I've worked in pictures, and I know a matzoh ball from a boom pole. You must admit, Mr. Chaplin, that the tribes of Israel run Hollywood."

"Your point being?"

"Christian America is fed up with your immoral motion pictures."

"And yet they buy eighty million tickets each week."

"Because the masses are nitwits, especially the yahoos who find you entertaining." Pelley cocked his head, grinned slyly and said, "And just what twaddle are you planning for your next motion picture?"

"None of your Nazi-loving business."

"There are manifest whispers afloat that you plan a picture ridiculing the greatest man in the world."

"'Manifest whispers afloat?' No wonder you can't get screenwriting work," Chaplin said. "Assuming you can put an

English sentence together, what's the story with your Silver Legion of Simpletons?"

"Laugh if you must, but I will have two hundred thousand followers by Christmas."

"For what purpose?" Einstein asked.

Pelley did not blink. "To install a government that combines fascism with a theocracy and excludes Jews and Negroes. But we are as nonviolent as our Lord Jesus."

"Ach!" Einstein blurted out. "Now I recognize you. Earlier today, outside the restaurant, you asked about the so-called Jewish problem. So, enjoy the refreshments, Mr. Pelley. I hope you get heartburn that turns into an ulcer."

"Good night, gents," Pelley said. "And a word to the wise. Look both ways before crossing the street."

With that, Pelley turned and melted into the crowd.

"He wanted us to know it was him!" Einstein said, registering shock. "As open and unafraid as Brownshirts in the streets of Berlin."

"Bastard!" Chaplin said. "Let's find Goebbels and get this over with."

Working their way through the crowd, they neared a group of partygoers gathered around two middle-aged men who seemed to enjoy the sounds of their own voices.

"Those two meatheads are Senator Ernest Lundeen from Minnesota and Congressman Hamilton Fish of New York," Chaplin said. "They call themselves 'America Firsters' because it sounds better than 'American Fascists.'"

The men didn't notice Chaplin and Einstein approaching and kept talking.

"Ham, I've got no patience with our countrymen who catch a cold every time Hitler sneezes," Lundeen said.

"Hysteria, and it's gonna lead us to war and bankruptcy," Fish agreed.

"What we need is a return to a Christian, white America with adherence to our founding principles," Lundeen said.

"Like slavery?" Chaplin said, strolling past the men.

The two politicians whipped around, and Lundeen said, "Say, was that…?"

Einstein and Chaplin walked several more paces, scanning the crowd. "Do you see Mr. Mitchell?" Einstein asked.

Chaplin shrugged. "I assume the young fellow's trying to break into Gyssling's office, like he said."

"We should have stopped him."

"How?"

"I don't know, but I'm worried about him." Einstein turned toward the entrance to the ballroom. The two SS officers who had flanked the doors were gone.

"Charlie. The Doberman Pinschers! Where did they go?"

41
THE HUNT

Konsulat von Deutschland, Patio

All the servers were African Americans, all male, roughly between twenty-five and thirty-five years old, all dressed in black trousers, white shirts with black bow ties, and red tunics. Each man had a white hand towel neatly folded over his right shoulder. All of which made Klaus Spengler's job more difficult.

Like finding a single snowflake in a blizzard. Or more on point, a single piece of licorice in a coal bin.

He had lost sight of the Negro waiter or reporter or whatever he was. Now he was leading two, tall lean, grumpy SS officers onto the patio where the servers took their breaks. The officers had been reluctant to abandon their station at the entrance to the ballroom and took several minutes of precious time to find their superior to get permission. That had irritated Spengler, who had never served in the military and disdained all protocols and chains of command.

And isn't the proof that I'm mired in bureaucracy that the Negro has given us the slip?

The servers had been on their feet for hours. Now the ones on break took long drags on their Camels and Luckys and leaned against the scaffold, resting weary bones.

There! There he is!

Spengler saw his man from the side and pointed him out to one of the SS officers, who grabbed the fellow's shoulder and spun him around, his cigarette falling from his mouth.

"*Verdammt!*" Spengler spat. "Wrong man."

The officer turned to Spengler. *"Alle diese Neger sehen gleich aus,"* he said with disgust.

Ja, Spengler thought. *They all do look alike.*

42
THE DEPUTY OF DECEPTION

Konsulat von Deutschland, Ballroom

Chaplin and Einstein kept moving and neared three strolling violinists, their expressions as dark as thunderclouds as they played a Beethoven sonata. Goebbels appeared, stealthy as an apparition, at their side.

"Delighted to see such luminaries," he greeted them in an accent as thick as goulash.

"Personally delighted…or as Minister of Whatcha-ma-call-it?" Chaplin asked.

"Public Enlightenment," Goebbels said.

"Catchy. Better than Deputy of Deception. Or Envoy of Evil."

"Char-lie," Einstein said in a warning tone.

"Vicar of Vitriol?" Chaplin added, his eyes gleaming.

Goebbels's shoulders stiffened, and he pasted on a smile so cold it could put frost on the fine crystal.

"Enjoy the champagne, gentlemen. France's greatest…and only accomplishment."

"Before you toddle off to do more enlightening," Chaplin said, "I apologize for what I said, though mostly for laying a bigger egg than I did in a Montana music hall in 1911."

"Is there anything else, Mr. Chaplin?" Goebbels asked.

"Sure thing. Why is the Reich building armaments at such a furious pace?"

"What do you wish? That Germany simply lay down its arms?" Goebbels asked.

"No, sir. When Germany lays down its arms, it's always on the throats of its neighbors."

With the smile of a crocodile and a tone of delight, Goebbels said, "Tell that to the Cubans. Tell it to the Filipinos, the Chinese, and the banana republics the Americans have invaded, not to mention the Indians they have slaughtered for two hundred years."

"No one claims America is perfect," Chaplin said.

"And yet, when the Reich seeks to protect itself from enemies outside and within our borders, we are crucified."

"What do you know about what happened at the baseball stadium today?" Chaplin asked, trying to change the subject.

"I assume a baseball game."

"Cute. And the desecration of a temple on Wilshire Boulevard last night?"

"Is that a crime here?" Goebbels said with a toothless smile.

Einstein felt like smashing the German in the face. Instead, seeing no point in remaining silent, he said, "What can you tell us about Buchenwald?"

Goebbels's mouth twitched, perhaps not expecting the question. "Whatever rumors you have heard, Professor, rest assured we are building a most humane facility."

"Facility?" Einstein said. "You mean prison."

"We make no secret of the fact that we have many enemies of the state."

Enemies of the state.

Chaplin thought of his work-in-progress, the script parodying Adolf Hitler. He had hoped to use the consulate party for research, and meeting Goebbels had just proved fruitful. Bits of dialogue came to Chaplin for a scene with the oily, menacing Goebbels, or rather, Garbitsch, talking to Hitler, or rather, Hynkel.

GARBITSCH: *We had to jail a few dissenters, Your Excellency.*
HYNKEL: *How many?*
GARBITSCH: *Five thousand…a day.*
HYNKEL: *What do they dissent about?*
GARBITSCH: *The working hours, the cut in wages, chiefly the synthetic food, the quality of the sawdust in the bread.*
HYNKEL: *What more do they want? We feed them the finest lumber our mills can supply.*

"Let's count those enemies of the state, Herr Goebbels," Chaplin said. "Jews, Slavs, gypsies, communists, homosexuals." He plucked each finger of his right hand, from pinkie to thumb, then switched to the other hand. "Free thinkers, Freemasons, Jehovah's Witnesses, the disabled, and anyone who looks cross-eyed at a thug in a uniform. I've run out of fingers! As the Reich keeps adding people to hate, I'll have to take off my shoes."

Pointedly ignoring Chaplin, Goebbels said, "*Gute nacht*, Professor Einstein." He turned on his heel and started walking away.

"What about me, you Mouthpiece of Manure?" Chaplin called after him. "Don't I get 'good night, sweet dreams'?"

Goebbels looked back over his shoulder and said, "No wonder your audience prefers you to be silent, Mr. Chaplin."

Goebbels kept walking, and Einstein said, "Do you have anything to say for yourself, Charlie?"

"Yeah. I can't believe I let the little rat get the kick-out line."

43
THE DOGS

Konsulat von Deutschland, Corridor and Kitchen

In the corridor outside the ballroom, Jimmy Mitchell tried to appear like a hardworking server. He carried a tray of empty champagne flutes, but his real task was to find an elevator, zip to an upper floor, and search for the consul's office.

He thought over everything he knew, putting the pieces together from what he learned at Alt Heidelberg. It all started with the tip from Roscoe who had overheard German waiters talking about *der tag* and *maschinengewehre*. "The day" and "machine guns." Then, scampering from catwalk to stairwell, Mitchell heard Pelley say, "We have to strike quick," followed by one of his men saying, "Machine guns strike damn quick." Finally, the anonymous man, shot in the back, whispered, "Operation Hollywood."

I need to know the where, what, and when. Where are the weapons? What's the attack plan? And when it will occur?

Minutes earlier, Mitchell had seen Pelley and Goebbels in the ballroom speaking in hushed tones. If the Silver Shirts were in cahoots with the Reich, the evidence could well be in the consul's office.

Two-thirds of the way down the corridor, there was the elevator, with a husky SS officer in a black suit stationed by the door.

Dammit!

The man looked Mitchell up and down and said, "Kitchen's that way." Pointing and telling Mitchell to retrace his steps.

"Danke," Mitchell said and followed orders.

He came to an intersecting corridor and took it, finding a wide staircase with two SS officers standing guard.

Double dammit! How will I ever get to an upper floor?

They looked at him with mild interest. "Are you lost, *Afrikaner?*" one said.

"Kitchen?" Mitchell said, trying to look helpless.

"Didn't you come from there?" the other one asked, a hint of suspicion in his voice.

"So many corners, I got lost."

"Dummer Neger," the first man said, and they both laughed.

⊱ ⊰

Spengler, the photographer, and the twin Doberman Pinschers approached the elevator where the husky SS officer had shooed Mitchell away just moments earlier. They spoke quickly in German, and the officer at the elevator said, *"Küche."*

"The kitchen!" Spengler said to the two men. "We'll trap him there."

Spengler and the SS officers turned and retraced their steps, heading toward the kitchen.

⊱ ⊰

Jimmy Mitchell decided the empty tray he'd been carrying made him too conspicuous. He needed to load up flutes of champagne or platters of canapés. He stood in front of the half-size elevator that only ran between the ground floor and the basement kitchen. It took a few minutes, waiting for the servers in front of him to board and for the elevator to descend and return, and he made it with the second group.

He stepped out of the elevator into the kitchen, a brutally hot beehive of activity. Workers hustled and bustled and bumped into one another. The cacophony could burst eardrums, what with the clanging of pots, the shouts of workers, and mechanical groans and creaks that Mitchell couldn't identify. The place felt like a Turkish bath, the ovens steaming, spigots spraying, moisture condensing on everything and everyone.

Mitchell watched servers load canapés of biscuits overflowing with caviar and crème fraîche onto trays with the speed and skill of assembly line workers. The kitchen boss, an overweight, bald white man in a sweat-stained T-shirt with a bandanna around his neck barked orders and cursed the refrigerators, the ovens, the workers, the cramped quarters, and those "damn thirsty Krauts." When Mitchell came into his line of vision, he shouted, "Boy! Load up and get your black ass upstairs!"

Mitchell moved his tray to a stainless-steel counter, and an elderly white man filled twenty flutes with champagne, pouring two bottles at a time. Moving back toward the small elevator, Mitchell felt like a tightrope walker as he tried not to drop the tray or collide with other servers.

The Doberman Pinschers were dogs on the hunt, and they had the scent of the prey. Still, they could not know that the Black man they were tracking was a mere fifteen feet away, albeit straight down.

As Mitchell waited to board the elevator in the basement kitchen, Spengler and the pair of SS officers stood at the same elevator on the ground floor, Mitchell's destination. The trio had pushed their way to the front of the line of servers without so much as an "excuse me" or "*entschuldigung.*" The servers parted like sheep before wolves, and the officers stood impatiently at the door, repeatedly punching the red call button.

Forty-five seconds later, tired of the wait, Spengler said, "Let's take the fire stairs." The men pushed back through the servers, ducked down a corridor, and disappeared into a stairwell.

Ten seconds after that, Mitchell emerged from the elevator and headed back to the ballroom, unaware of his pursuers, and still unsure how he could get above the ground floor.

44
LUCKY LINDY

Konsulat von Deutschland, Ballroom

Chaplin and Einstein were walking around the fringe of the partygoers, debating what had happened and what to do next.

"I know you're upset with me for being rude to Goebbels," Chaplin said.

"Not for being rude. For pushing him away so quickly that we learned nothing," Einstein said.

"Do you think if I'd been nicer, Goebbels would have said, 'Oh, let me tell you all about Operation Hollywood?'"

Something caught Chaplin's eye. "Wait! There's Lindy. Let's talk to him."

Einstein looked toward the tall, lanky, handsome man surrounded by a half-dozen admirers. Charles Lindbergh, still famous and adored ten years after his transatlantic flight.

"Must we?" Einstein said. "Last time he spent twenty minutes extolling the virtues of eugenics."

"The Nazis love his lily-white ass. He may have heard something."

They approached Lindbergh, who was regaling a circle of devotees with his views on society, politics, world affairs, and other subjects on which he considered himself an expert.

"I'm not anti-Brit or anti-French or anti-Jew. I just don't want us to fight their battles," Lindbergh said.

"You're a true patriot, Colonel," said a heavyset man with a double chin that was propped up by the starched wing collars of his tuxedo shirt.

No, you're a dummkopf, Einstein thought.

"I'm for America first, that's all," Lindbergh said. "America first, last, and always."

"Our allies don't open the floodgates to the refuse of the world," said a woman in a fuchsia evening gown and diamond necklace. "Neither should we."

"There's no doubt that immigration dilutes our northern European blood," Lindbergh said with the authority of a geneticist.

Lindbergh spotted Chaplin and Einstein a few paces away, smiled shyly, excused himself, and long-legged it toward them. "Chap. Professor." He motioned back toward his fans. "You two probably get tired of all the doggone adulation."

"Never," Chaplin said.

"Not at all," Einstein agreed.

It took a moment for Lindbergh to realize they were putting him on. "You Jews are so darn funny," he said, chuckling.

"Charlie's not Jewish," Einstein said.

"Aw, c'mon. Charlie, everybody says you're a member of the tribe."

"Sadly, I do not have that good fortune."

Einstein cleared his throat and said, "Mr. Lindbergh, please tell us you're not going to Germany to accept a medal from the Nazis."

"Yeah, Slim," Chaplin said. "What gives? The Big Cheese Order of the German Beagle?"

"The Commander Cross of the German Eagle," Lindbergh corrected him. "It would be rude to turn down the honor."

"And we don't want to bruise little Adolf's feelings," Chaplin said. A server came by with champagne. All three men demurred.

"Mr. Lindbergh, when a man of your stature shows respect to those criminals, it emboldens them," Einstein said.

"Professor, I can't blame you Jews for looking out for your interests, but you could be making the situation worse for your own race," Lindbergh said.

Taken aback, Einstein was silent. Chaplin started to say something, but Einstein raised a hand to shush him. He wanted to hear just what was on the pilot-philosopher's mind.

"The danger is Jewish ownership of our motion pictures and our press," Lindbergh said. "If we wage war with Germany, it will go badly—I've seen their *Luftwaffe*—and then who do you think will be blamed?"

As the expected answer was obvious, neither man responded, and Lindbergh continued, "Just yesterday, I was talking to Henry Ford, and—"

"The biggest antisemite since Pharaoh!" Chaplin interrupted.

"Ford called my work 'Jewish propaganda,'" Einstein said.

"Henry can be rough around the edges, but he agrees with me that we must stay out of war at all costs," Lindbergh said.

"Especially the costs to his German factory," Chaplin said. "Slim, have you heard any scuttlebutt about the Silver Legion of America, the Silver Shirts?"

Lindbergh shrugged. "It's just one of those German American friendship societies, as far as I know."

"Any idea why they would want weapons?" Einstein asked.

"They probably had a twenty-one-gun salute on Hitler's birthday, but I doubt they're violent, if that's what you mean," Lindbergh said.

He seemed sincere, Einstein thought. Also, sincerely uninformed.

"Does 'Operation Hollywood' mean anything to you?" Chaplin asked.

"A Jewish plot to take over motion pictures?" Lindbergh said, grinning. "Wait! You already have."

"You goyim are *not* so darn funny," Einstein said. Lindbergh guffawed at that.

Einstein looked toward the ballroom entrance. The two Doberman Pinschers were back, now joined by four other men in black leather tunics, obviously also SS officers. The men spaced themselves out across the ballroom, roughly fifteen feet apart, and began moving in the same direction toward the opposite wall, scanning the faces of the servers. The officers looked like field workers who beat the ground with wooden poles to flush out quail. Concerned, Einstein surveyed the ballroom himself but did not catch sight of Jimmy Mitchell.

"Chap, you've been in this country more than twenty years," Lindbergh said. "Why the heck haven't you become a citizen?"

"One of Hoover's G-men asked me the same question, and I'll give you the same answer. Because I'm a citizen of the world."

Lindbergh looked perplexed. "Isn't that what communists say?"

"I wouldn't know, Slim. I deal mostly with filthy-rich capitalists."

"May I tell you two fellows a little secret?" Lindbergh asked.

"Our lips are sealed like Boris Karloff's in *The Mummy*." Chaplin ran a thumb and index finger like a zipper across his upper lip.

Lindbergh lowered his voice. "Herr Goebbels spoke to me privately. The Reich wants me to run for president."

"Of what?" Chaplin bit his tongue so that he wouldn't add, "The International Order of Odd Fellows."

"The United States, of course. Goebbels says that Roosevelt might run for a third term, and if he wins, he would send our boys off to war."

"But you have no political experience," Einstein said.

"Goebbels says that's my strong suit. That and my age. He thinks America is ready to jettison the old guard and head in a new direction."

Einstein did not miss the point: *Goebbels says. Goebbels thinks.*

"That new direction being toward Berlin," Einstein said, wondering how the pilot could be so naive.

"Toward world peace," Lindbergh said. "I'd also take a long look at the ownership of newspapers, radio, and the movies in order to restore America to its white, Christian values. No offense, Professor."

"Some taken," Einstein said, scanning the ballroom.

There he is!

Einstein spotted Mitchell near the long table with the dripping *Hindenburg* ice sculpture. He was holding a tray of drinks but wasn't offering any to the guests. Einstein fought the urge to signal the young man.

That would only draw attention to him.

The same with hurrying over to him. From this distance, it was difficult to tell, but Einstein thought the young man looked scared. Had he seen the SS officers sweeping the ballroom like bounty hunters searching for a runaway slave?

Lindbergh was momentarily distracted by an admirer, a fortyish man with a red carnation in his lapel, who asked for an autograph.

"Charlie, I fear Mr. Mitchell is in serious trouble," Einstein whispered.

But Chaplin was also distracted, his eyes affixed to a stunning woman with long blond tresses that fell in waves, covering one eye in the peekaboo style. Easily six feet tall, she wore a black silk dress with a plunging neckline and black velvet spiked heels that were sharp enough to pierce a man's heart.

"Yowza, Albert!" Chaplin said. "Get a load of the gams on this dish of strudel."

The woman approached them on long slender legs and said in a German accent, "The world's greatest scientist, greatest actor, and greatest hero. *Was für eine nacht!* What a night!"

"And the *nacht* is still young," Chaplin said, sounding naughty.

Chaplin was enthralled, but Einstein was troubled. He looked back toward the table where Mitchell had been, but he was gone. One of the SS officers passed nearby, his head on a swivel.

"Gents, this is Mitzi Kunz," Lindbergh said, "Herr Gyssling's secretary."

"Miss Kunz," Einstein said, bowing slightly but still looking around the ballroom. Chaplin, a world-champion flirt, shot the woman his movie-star smile.

"And just how is Herr Gyssling's dictation, Mitzi?"

"Some days, slow and steady." She cocked her head coquettishly. "Other days, it comes in spurts."

"You oughta write for the pictures," Chaplin said. "Except the Catholic Legion would ban every one."

Mitzi slinked close to Lindbergh and said, "Colonel, I haven't seen you since Berlin."

"And you shall again, *liebling*," Lindbergh promised.

"I have personally picked out a beautiful summer house for you and Anne in Wansee, just outside Berlin," she said.

"Why?" Chaplin asked. "Is hell fully booked?"

Looking deeply into each other's eyes as if agreeing to rent a room, Mitzi and Lindbergh ignored him.

"Every time I visit, I'm impressed by the vigor of the Aryan spirit," Lindbergh said. "It feels like *zuhaus*. Home."

"It makes me tingle to hear you say that." Mitzi slipped an arm around one of his. "Come talk to me. Just for a moment."

She guided Lindbergh a few paces, her curves fitting against him like a grease reservoir in an aircraft engine, and Chaplin let out a slow whistle. "Looks like Lindy is gonna get lucky tonight."

"Charlie, stop ogling the *maidel*," Einstein said.

"I thought I had a way with women, but I never made one 'tingle' just by talking."

"Charlie! Please. Mr. Mitchell needs our help."

45
THE CLIMB

Konsulat von Deutschland, The Scaffold

Einstein took a minute to tell Chaplin what he'd seen. "Don't be conspicuous but take a look at the SS officers spreading out across the ballroom."

Chaplin moved his eyes but kept his head still. "I see them, but where's Jimmy Mitchell?"

Einstein shrugged. "I don't know, but the good news is that the Nazi thugs don't, either."

"Only a matter of time."

Then Einstein saw him. "Don't look, Charlie, but Mr. Mitchell is heading toward the open doors to the patio."

"And the Nazis?" Chaplin kept his eyes on his friend.

"Spread out. Still in pursuit."

Searchlights swept across the building, cutting through the fog, and catching the *Hindenburg* balloon bobbing in the breeze. Most of the twenty or so servers on the patio either leaned on the scaffold or sat on the pavers, legs spread, elbows on knees, getting whatever rest they could before returning to the kitchen and ballroom.

Jimmy Mitchell looked up through the piping of the orange iron scaffold. Because of the fog, he couldn't see the rooftop, but he knew it was a six-story building. What he didn't know was the location of the consul's office. Unlike the Taft Building at Hollywood and Vine or practically any office building, there was no directory. The floor and room number of the consul's digs were apparently state secrets. If he found the office, he had lock picks to break in and use on any file cabinets.

Mitchell removed the hand towel from his shoulder and folded it over one of the crossbars. He started climbing, using the diagonal bracing for his footing and the vertical posts and crossbars to go hand over hand.

He quickly reached the second floor, where he stepped from a wood plank of the scaffold to a narrow ledge of the building. He tried to open a window. Locked. Then another. Locked.

Same thing along the face of the building. He resumed climbing and stopped at the third floor. A searchlight sweeping up from below caught the third-floor windows, and Mitchell flattened himself against the building. He felt like an escapee in a prison movie, except he wanted to break in.

When the searchlight passed, he tried more windows. Locked. He looked up and began climbing again.

❦

Chaplin moseyed from the ballroom onto the patio. If the SS had seen Mitchell with him earlier, there might be someone watching him. Once outside, he casually looked back. No one was following him. He circled the group of servers on break. No Jimmy Mitchell. He ducked under a crossbar of the scaffold. When you were only five feet five, it didn't take much ducking.

He noticed a hand towel draped over a bar and grabbed it. Moist. It might be the towel Mitchell used to wipe up the spilled champagne. A single breadcrumb on the trail. Chaplin feared for Mitchell. The young man's resolve and courage had touched something deep inside him. Mitchell wasn't just seeking a scoop for the *Sentinel*. He was devoted to rooting out a pernicious evil and had sought our help. What had he said?

That Albert and I are committed to justice. Sure. Albert talks about it, and I write checks to all the good causes. But Mitchell is putting his life on the line!

Chaplin considered the arithmetic. Machine guns plus fascists equals massacre. The code name 'Operation Hollywood' likely revealed the location of the attack. They didn't call the mission "Moon over Miami" or "Way Down Yonder in New Orleans."

The attack will be right here.

Chaplin looked up through the bars of the scaffold. He couldn't see anyone, but he knew Mitchell wanted to search the upper floors. He would find the young man and bring him back to Earth in one piece. He replayed what Mitchell had said.

"Break into the consul's office, rifle the cabinets and drawers."

Sounding as casual as if he'd said, "shop the Dollar Day sales on Broadway."

Oh, Jimmy! This building teems with S.S. thugs like rats in a hayloft.

Following Mitchell up the scaffold would be no problem. If Chaplin hadn't run off with a music hall company as a youth, he might have joined the circus as a trapeze artist. He rubbed his hands together, leapt up to the first crossbar, and began climbing with the agility of a cat burglar. For his size, he was remarkably strong. He thought of Laurel and Hardy, hauling that piano up the steps on Vendome Street in *The Music Box*. No matter that they pilfered the idea from *His Musical Career*, a Chaplin short, their physical comedy was first rate.

But life isn't a movie. And these Nazis aren't cardboard villains.

Chaplin noticed that his hands were sweaty, and it wasn't a warm evening.

So that's what fear feels like.
It wasn't the fear of falling. He could scamper up the iron bars blindfolded and perform somersaults on the planks without losing his pocket square. But just what would he find at the end of his climb?

⁂

Mitchell was at the fourth floor when he noticed a gauzy curtain blowing in and out of an open window. He stepped from the wood plank to the window ledge and peered inside. Pitch black. He crawled through the open window, dropping to the floor.

He pulled out a penlight, flicked it on. A bedroom, unlike any he had ever seen, but then, Mitchell had never been in a New Orleans bordello. The wallpaper and the bedspread were red velvet. Black-and-white photos of voluptuous nude women hung on the walls. A three-panel room divider was painted with sexual scenes: man-woman, woman-woman, man-man.

Mitchell's penlight stopped at a mirror on one wall, the reflection distorted.

What the hell is this?

He went up to the mirror, shined his penlight directly at it, and pressed his face to the glass. He was looking into the adjoining room. A two-way mirror for spectators.

And the Nazis say America is riddled with moral decay!

He went to the door, twisted the dead bolt, cautiously turned the doorknob, and peered down a long corridor. Thirty feet away, a uniformed maid was pushing a carpet sweeper, her back to him. Mitchell waited a moment until she turned a corner, then stepped into the corridor. He tried three other doors. All locked.

He headed into a stairwell and started climbing. A noise stopped him. Footsteps from below, their volume increasing with each second.

He picked up his pace, padding up the stairs, trying to make as little noise as possible. He paused at the fifth floor. The footsteps were louder, and voices echoed off the concrete block walls. Speaking German. Loud and angry and frightening.

46
WHERE THE BIG FIRES BURN

Konsulat von Deutschland, Fifth Floor

Mitchell exited the stairwell on the fifth floor. There was a door slightly ajar on the landing. He turned the knob. A utility closet with mops, brooms, and other cleaning supplies. He ducked in and carefully closed the door.

He could tell from the footsteps and the voices in the stairwell that the men were hurrying, heedless of the noise they made. Speaking German, they were likely SS, armed and dangerous. He felt like a rabbit, hiding in the underbrush, hoping the fox, in its haste, would dash past him.

The noises receded, meaning that the men had gone to the sixth floor, one flight above him. Also meaning that was likely the location of the consul's office. Sure, a suite with the best views. He could wait until the footsteps started moving down the stairwell. He opened the closet door a couple of inches and was startled by a telephone ringing.

                                                                                ⋈

Chaplin stopped at each floor on his climb up the scaffold, ducking against the building when a searchlight swept near him.

No sign of Jimmy Mitchell. No lights in any windows. Until the fifth floor.

Light spilled out of a double-hung window, the upper half open, the lower half closed. Chaplin stepped from the plank to the ledge that was barely eighteen inches wide and made his way to the lighted window. The only sound was the breeze rustling the trees below and faraway traffic…until a ringing telephone nearly caused him to fall.

Mitchell followed the sound of the ringing phone to a door in the corridor with light peeking out. He looked through the keyhole and had a partial view of a blond woman in a red gown. She picked up the phone, and he strained to hear the conversation.

Chaplin looked through the lower window and saw a woman sitting at a vanity table. She was about thirty-five and was wearing a snazzy red satin evening gown, her blond hair upswept from her neck in the elegant chignon style, a double strand of pearls around her neck, a telephone at her ear. The evening breeze whistled through the iron bars of the scaffold, and Chaplin strained to hear the woman's end of the conversation through the open upper window.

"*Frau Goebbels hier*," she said into the phone.

Magda Goebbels! Strong jawline, trim figure, makeup giving her a healthy glow, she was too damned attractive for that rodent of a husband. Who was it who said that beautiful women gathered where the big fires burn? Was attraction to power an aphrodisiac? Maybe Albert could ask his pal Sigmund Freud.

"*Natürlich kann man der* Operation Hollywood *zwei namen hinzufügen,*" Magda continued.

"Operation Hollywood!" Chaplin whispered while memorizing what she had said in German so he could repeat it to Einstein.

"Who are they?" She switched to English and fiddled with one of the pearls on her necklace. Then, after a moment, she trilled a laugh. "You think big!"

With the phone propped on one shoulder, Magda opened her vanity drawer and withdrew a single sheet of paper. She picked up a pencil and quickly wrote something.

Chaplin saw movement, a shadow in the light under the door to Magda's suite. Someone was on the other side of the door, listening. It could be an SS officer, but why? More likely it was Jimmy Mitchell, striding into the lion's den like Daniel of the Old Testament.

"*Und sie werden heute abend dreiundzwanzig maschinengewehre haben?*" Magda said into the phone.

"*Maschinengewehre,*" Chaplin said to himself. "Machine guns." Magda listened, then laughed once more.

"*Gute nacht. Heil Hitler,*" she said, and hung up the phone. She put the sheet of paper back in the drawer, took a key from a satin clutch purse that matched her gown, locked the drawer, then returned the key to her purse.

You're not just locking up your rouge and pancake, are you, Magda, you Nazi harridan?

She looked into the vanity mirror and must have liked what she saw, because she smiled broadly. Or maybe this was just practice for greeting guests she abhorred but whose positions demanded diplomatic courtesies.

Magda stood, turned, and looked straight through the lower window at Chaplin, who froze, waiting for the scream or, who knows, a Luger pulled from her girdle.

❧ ☙

In the corridor outside Magda Goebbels's suite, Mitchell heard the cables and pulleys of the elevator. The sounds grew louder, and he hurried back to the stairwell and reentered the utility closet. Seconds later, footsteps clamored in the stairwell, on their way down from the sixth floor. The elevator was a false alarm. And the footsteps were an excellent development, he thought. The sixth floor had been checked and cleared. He would wait a few minutes, and if all was quiet, up he would go.

※

Looking straight at Chaplin, Magda Goebbels puckered her lips. *She can't see me! She's looking at her reflection in the windowpane.*

Magda walked closer to the window. No more than a foot and a pane of glass separated them. Chaplin stuck his tongue out and wiggled his ears. No reaction.

He had a plan. When she left the suite for her fashionably late entrance to the party, he'd squeeze through the upper window and grab the paper in her vanity drawer. But then Magda closed the upper window and turned the lock. She went to the door, turned out the lights, and headed into the corridor.

Chaplin tried both windows, but they were locked tight.

※

At the end of the sixth-floor corridor, Mitchell spotted a set of double doors with a plaque: *Buto des Konsuls.*

The consul's office! Now we're cooking with gas.

The doors were locked, but he fished a lockpick from a pocket and went to work. Again, he heard the cables and pulleys of the elevator creaking. The elevator door was twenty feet down the corridor. He hurried, but his fingers felt stiff and uncoordinated. His cousin Roland, who had a habit of breaking and entering warehouses, had given him the lockpick and had shown him how to use it. But there had been no pressure breaking into his own apartment.

Now sweat dripped from his forehead onto his hands, which he dried on his pants. No more sounds came from the elevator.
Did it stop on this floor with the door to open in a second?
He couldn't tell and worked frantically.
Click. Click. Finally!
He opened the door and ducked inside.

47
HITLER IN THE DARK

Konsulat von Deutschland, Rooftop and Consul's Office

Chaplin resumed climbing the scaffold, finding only more darkened windows on the sixth floor. Those he tried were locked, so higher he went. At the rooftop balcony, he grabbed the railing and vaulted over it, landing gracefully.

A stiff breeze chilled the night air. He took in the view, the hillside homes to the north, discreetly lighted, peeking through the fog, the city office buildings to the east, and the vast darkness of the ocean to the west. At night the city was quiet and peaceful, he thought, just as he heard the wail of a police siren sounding like a woman's scream.

Jimmy Mitchell, where the hell are you? And where are those SS mugs who are looking for you?

If that had been Mitchell outside Magda Goebbels's door, where had he gone? Had he found the consul's office?

And where the hell is the office in this battleship of a building with its maze of intersecting corridors?

Buffeted by the wind, the giant *Hindenburg* balloon was barely twenty feet above Chaplin's head, tethered to the heavy metal housing of a huge exhaust fan. Illuminated by a sweeping searchlight, the balloon took on a greenish glow in the fog.

He kept repeating what he'd heard Magda Goebbels say in German so he could get Albert to translate.

"*Natürlich kann man der* Operation Hollywood *zwei…*" Something or other.

It would come back to him. He could recite from memory scripts and stage directions decades old.

Now what? He wasn't accomplishing anything on the roof. He was a man without a plan, an actor without a play. A heavy steel door on the roof led to the fire stairs. That would take him inside the building, so that's where he headed…to points unknown.

⁓⁓

Rather than turn on the lights in the consul's office, Mitchell used his penlight. The mahogany desk was polished and empty, except for an onyx desk set with a gold fountain pen, inkwell, and blotter. No papers. No inbox or outbox. It did not seem to be the kind of place where much paperwork was done.

The desk drawers were unlocked. Mostly empty, a few blank notepads, a box of consulate stationery and envelopes. One wall was lined with metal drawers, every one locked. He dug in a pocket for the pick and lost his grip on the penlight, which briefly illuminated the far wall.

What the hell?

Mitchell stumbled and slammed his knee against the desk, his heart feeling as if it banged against his ribs. Adolf Hitler was staring at him. The portrait must have been six feet high—taller than the man—and his eyes stared accusingly at Mitchell.

Who let the schwarzer *in?*

When his pulse returned to normal, Mitchell thought he would have to tell Luisa the story.

"You'll never guess who scared the bejesus out of me in the dark tonight!"

His fiancée had warned him not to come here tonight but quickly realized he was committed to the task. Luisa had helped with his research of the Friends of New Germany and its successor, the German American Bund, as well as the Silver Legion of America, better known as the Silver Shirts. A Negro man and a Mexican-American woman, they knew where they stood in the dark shadow of fascism.

He heard a noise in the corridor. Less of a noise than just a soft undefinable sound. Not the mechanical grind of the elevator. Not voices. Not heavy footsteps. The next sound was even softer. The knob on the office door began to turn with an almost inaudible squeak.

48
TO ME, YOU ARE BEAUTIFUL

Konsulat von Deutschland, Ballroom

In the ballroom, the decibel level seemed to have escalated as the blood alcohol of the partygoers increased. Einstein felt eyes on him. Not just the usual curious onlookers—"Is that wild-haired man you-know-who?"—but Schutzstaffel eyes. The SS. He hoped his face did not reveal the fear that boiled within him. He forced himself not to glance at the open door to the patio, the last place he had seen both Charlie and Jimmy Mitchell.

This is taking too long! Where are you two?

He walked toward a small stage where a swing band played the instrumental version of Benny Goodman's "Goody Goody." He tapped a toe to the beat, scanned the ballroom, and saw Goebbels in conversation with three SS officers in black leather. Were they closing in on Mitchell? On Charlie?

I need to create a distraction…but what?

The band's vocalist, a twentyish heartthrob who wore her platinum hair in a bobbed style favored by Jean Harlow, smiled at Einstein, who motioned her to step down from the stage.

"So pleased to meet you, Professor Einstein," she said when she reached him. "I'm Gracie Abbott."

"Gracie, dear," he said, "could you sing a song for me?"

She beamed. "I'd be honored."

"Do you know '*Bei Mir Bist Du Schön*'?"

"Of course! It's a big hit for the Andrews Sisters. I love the syncopated rhythms."

"Would you…?"

"I do it with a swing feel."

"Any way you feel is fine."

She beamed, gave Einstein a peck on the cheek, hopped onto the stage, and whispered something to the bandleader. In a moment, the band struck up the song with a brisk, energetic tempo, and Gracie began singing: "*Bei mir bist du schön, Please let me explain, Bei mir bist du schön*, Means you're grand."

Einstein felt movement behind him. It was Goebbels limping double time toward the stage, his face a mask of fury.

Gracie sang on: "*Bei mir bist du schön*, again, I explain, It means…"

Goebbels yanked the microphone from her. "Why are you singing a Yiddish song?"

Flustered, she stuttered, "I…I…I…don't know. It's a big hit."

Goebbels turned to the bandleader and said, "Take a break!" Einstein looked at Gracie and mouthed the words "I'm sorry."

She stepped from the stage, and Einstein said, "I hope I didn't get you into trouble."

"Aw, phooey on him. Say, do you know Yiddish?"

"But of course."

"What's it mean? *Bei mir bist du schön?*"

"'To me, you are beautiful.'"

"Aces!" She gave him a sly smile. "So, you must have known it was a Jewish song."

With a sheepish look, he said, "It's from a Yiddish operetta."

Gracie laughed, her face lighting up.

"What's so funny, dear?" he asked.

"I was just thinking. How strong can the Nazis be if they're scared of a Yiddish operetta?"

49
COME OUT, COME OUT, WHEREVER YOU ARE

Konsulat von Deutschland, Consul's Office and Goebbels's Suite

Jimmy Mitchell's penlight was off. The consul's office was dark. The knob turned slowly, and the door opened. A slice of light from the corridor spilled across the carpet.

Mitchell was curled into the fetal position in the knee well of the desk. If the intruder turned on the lights and came around the desk…well, it would be over.

The lights flicked on.

Oh, dear God. Why didn't I listen to you, Luisa? Or Chaplin and Einstein? Why am I such a damned fool?

He thought of his father, a caring and giving man, who began taking him to NAACP meetings when he was a boy of twelve. A proud union man, Coziah Mitchell still worked full time as a Pullman porter. He had promised to take Jimmy on the new Santa Fe Super Chief, which reached speeds of one hundred miles per hour and, even with all the stops, made the Los Angeles to Chicago run in a tidy forty hours. They might spot Clark Gable and Bette Davis playing gin rummy in the club lounge car and wouldn't that be an absolute pip? His mother, Beatrice, offered to pack food for them, but Coziah said the porters and conductors would be well fed by the dining car stewards.

Will I ever see my loving parents again?

A man's voice whispered, "Mr. Mitchell. Jimmy. Are you here?"

Chaplin!

Mitchell scrambled out from under the desk. "Holy moly! You scared the piss out of me, Mr. Chaplin. Whadaya doing?"

"Following you! And call me 'Charlie.' I feel like we're old friends."

"Sure thing, Charlie."

"I heard Frau Goebbels on the phone," Chaplin said. "Was that you outside her door?"

"Sure was, but I couldn't make out a word."

"I don't know who she was talking to, but she said, 'Operation Hollywood' and 'machine guns.'"

"I knew it!" Mitchell said. "It's not just Pelley and the loudmouths at the biergarten. It's the Reich."

"She wrote something on a piece of paper, then put it in her vanity drawer and left the suite."

"That could be the key to Operation Hollywood," Mitchell said.

"More likely than anything you'll find in here. I know consul Gyssling. Machine guns and violence are not his style."

"Then I've got to get into Magda Goebbels' suite."

Chaplin immediately regretted he'd told Mitchell what he'd seen. "Hold on a second, Jimmy. The building is crawling with SS. I didn't come up here to send you on a suicide mission."

"I made it this far."

"Please, Jimmy. The safest thing is for you to go back down the scaffold and get the hell out of here. Albert and I are working with an LAPD sergeant. We'll tell her everything we know and let her take over."

"I appreciate your concern about me, Charlie, but there's no time to waste. The world's not a safe place. My whole purpose for being is to do something about that."

Chaplin knew grit when he saw it—and commitment to ideals. He had friends who had joined the International Brigades to fight Franco's fascists. He admired them, but a couple came home in wooden boxes.

I admire your courage, Jimmy Mitchell, but I fear you're a leaf in a hurricane.

"Be careful, Jimmy," Chaplin said, realizing there was no stopping him.

Mitchell left, and Chaplin sat in Gyssling's deeply upholstered leather chair trying to figure out his next step. He couldn't risk taking the stairwell, so he would go back onto the roof and down the scaffold. Then he heard the elevator grind to a halt. He leapt from the chair and turned off the lights just as he heard the elevator door open, and a male voice said something in German that sounded angry, but didn't *Deutsch* always come out that way?

The Doberman Pinschers were, in fact, brothers, though not twins. Friedrich and Sebastian Koch each stood six feet three, and each was as lean as a knife blade and as mean as a snake. Both men had deep-set, dark eyes and the mottled complexions of speckled trout, heightening their resemblance. They had been goons with the Brownshirts and had eagerly changed uniforms to the SS after their leader, Ernst Röhm, was assassinated on Hitler's orders. Their bruising tactics and strict adherence to orders had elevated them to *untersturmführers*, second lieutenants.

While a psychiatrist might describe the men as incurable sadists, they considered themselves to be protectors of the state and all that the Führer held dear. With their dark hair greased straight back, their leather jackets cinched at the waist with brass swastika buckles, and their perpetual scowls, they often elicited confessions without breaking any kneecaps. That did not stop them, however, from inflicting pain for the general hell of it.

Now they stepped off the elevator on the sixth floor and headed straight for the double doors of the consul's office at the end of the corridor. Speaking in German, they debated whether the maid on the fourth floor could be trusted. She claimed to have seen a Black man dressed as a server, but everyone knew she kept a bottle of *schnapps* in her dustbin, and her veracity was questionable.

Sebastian reached for the doorknob, which surprisingly turned in his hand. "*Entsperrt!* It's unlocked," he said to his brother, drawing a Luger from inside his coat while Friedrich grabbed a heavy blackjack he enjoyed using in close quarters.

They entered the consul's office, turning on the lights. Adolf Hitler looked down at them with a grim expression. At first glance, the office appeared empty. Sebastian pulled the high-backed chair away from the desk and looked in the knee well. Nothing.

They debated whether the alcoholic maid could have left the door unlocked after cleaning the office. With nothing resolved, they left the office.

☞ ☜

Chaplin exhaled a long breath and gulped air. He hadn't realized he had failed to breathe for what…two minutes? It was certainly possible. His friend Harry Houdini claimed to be able to hold his breath for five minutes, though Harry was a legendary embroiderer of tales.

Chaplin was wedged into the recessed light cove that ran around the ceiling of the consul's office. If the Doberman Pinschers had looked up, they would not have seen him, but they might have caught sight of his silhouette on the ceiling, shadowed by the lights.

He waited another five minutes, then slung his legs over the cove and dropped to the floor.

☞ ☜

Mitchell had no trouble picking the lock on the door to the Goebbels' suite. Inside, he found two spacious bedrooms with canopy beds, dark wood armoires, and prints of sailing vessels on the walls. There was a modern bathroom with a clawfoot bathtub and a shower stall. The sitting room had a love seat covered in navy blue fabric and something much more important: the vanity with a large mirror surrounded by lights.

Mitchell went to work on the vanity drawer, which surprisingly caused him more problems than the door to the corridor. After several unsuccessful tries with the pick, he pushed the drawer in and pulled it out several times, each time with more force, rattling the contents inside. Then he stopped.

Was that a sound in the corridor?

He waited, listened. Nothing. Even new buildings had their own voices, he thought, their creaks and groans. He tried the drawer twice more, this time pushing down on its outer edge, then up sharply. The drawer's wooden track cracked, and while the lock never disengaged, the drawer slid open at an angle, nearly falling to the floor.

It took only seconds to find the single sheet of paper, and he immediately knew its significance.

"Jesús Cristo!" he said aloud, because that's what Luisa would say when he told her. He would put the drawer back as best he could so that Magda would not notice it had been tampered with. Still, he had a dilemma.

If I take the document, she'll discover it's gone, and they'll change their plans. We'll be ready for an attack that will never come and unprepared for one that does.

He had an idea, but it would take a minute or two. He listened for sounds from the corridor, heard nothing, and got to work.

※

If stealth were an Olympic sport, Sebastian and Friedrich Koch would be gold medalists. Once in Berlin, they tracked a trade unionist with communist leanings to a rundown apartment building whose floorboards creaked if you gave them a harsh look. The brothers removed their jackboots and padded in stockinged feet down the corridor, silent as cats on velvet paws. On the count of three—*eins, zwei, drei!*—they kicked open the man's door, Sebastian spraining an ankle, which only made him angrier. They caught the man painting a poster of Hitler's head on the body of a skunk. Twelve minutes later, with all ten fingers broken with pliers, the unionist's career as a political artist was over. And to compensate for his throbbing ankle, Sebastian extracted four of the commie's front teeth.

Tonight, they left their shoes on. The plush wool carpet in the consulate corridors—red, black, and white to match the Reich's flag—was new and cushioned all sounds. Still, like Trappist monks, they took vows of silence and did not utter a word as they walked the fifth-floor corridor, trying every doorknob.

※

The drawer replaced in its track and his task complete, Mitchell thought he heard something from the corridor. A metallic sound.
But so soft. Is he imagining it?
Seconds later, the same sound just a bit louder, and he realized someone was turning doorknobs in the corridor or trying to.
It's the sound of a locked doorknob, clickity-click, fighting against the torque.

He hadn't thrown the dead bolt when he came into the suite. Not that it would have done any good. Unlike the doors to the other rooms locked with a key from the outside, this knob would turn and whoever was outside, knowing the bolt was thrown, would knock and ask who was inside. He didn't think his Magda Goebbels impression would be convincing. An unlocked door was likely safer, he thought. Perhaps Magda neglected to lock it on her way out.

He looked toward the windows. Too small to climb out onto the scaffold. He heard a *clickity-click,* louder still. The room next door. He had no time.

☞ ☜

Finding the door unlocked, the Koch brothers entered the Goebbels' suite. They looked around. Both bedrooms empty. Bathroom empty. Sitting room empty.

"Now, where is *schwarzer* who climbs building like little monkey?" Sebastian called out in heavily accented English. He slapped the heavy blackjack into the palm of his hand, the lead buckshot crackling.

"*Komm raus, komm raus, wo immer du bist,*" Friedrich sing-songed. "Come out, come out, wherever you are."

The brothers retraced their steps, first in the smaller of the two bedrooms, looking through the closets and under the bed. Then the larger bedroom. The closet was empty. Under the bed, uncontrollably shaking, Jimmy Mitchell recited the Lord's Prayer as Friedrich dragged him out by the ankles.

50
BELLE OF THE NAZI BALL

Konsulat von Deutschland, Ballroom and Patio

Magda Goebbels floated into the ballroom, sleek as a sailboat, blond hair upswept, twisted, and pinned in back, with carefully designed strands falling across her forehead in front. Her floor-length red satin evening gown flowed behind her as if pushed by a sea breeze. The gown had an exposed back and was tied with a sash at the waist, emphasizing her curves. Adolf had once whispered to her that she cast an alluring shadow, but that was where the flirtation had ended. The Führer had been best man at her wedding to Joseph, and while the two men were fast friends, her relationship with Adolf—often speaking privately—was even closer. In private, the man exuded a hypnotic charm that eluded Joseph who, to be frank, had a fishy chill.

Now she greeted guests with whispered *hallos*, kisses on cheeks, smiles, nods, and waves, all without stopping and barely slowing down. She sought to radiate the glamour and sophistication of royalty, or at least, to be belle of the Nazi ball.

She found Senator Ernest Lundeen near the melting *Hindenburg* ice sculpture, holding a plate overflowing with raw oysters, sliced beefsteak, and various canapés.

"Frau Goebbels," he said between bites. "Love the grub."

"So pleased to see you enjoying yourself," Magda said.
You disgusting, repulsive, greedy glutton.
If he ate any more, she thought, he'd need one of the oxen from his Minnesota farm to carry him home.

"Senator, I so enjoyed your speech on the Führer's birthday," she said.

Lundeen slurped down an oyster. "Your husband is an excellent writer, Frau Goebbels."

"And your delivery is flawless."

She reached into her clutch purse and withdrew an envelope, thickened with hundred-dollar bills. Lundeen licked a tab of crème fraîche from a fingertip, grabbed the envelope, and slipped it inside his tuxedo jacket. He bowed, and a deviled ham canapé slid from his plate to the floor. "*Danke,* Frau Goebbels."

She forced a smile and moved on.

Now, where is Joseph?

Earlier tonight, she suggested that he settle the dispute between Consul Gyssling and the American, William Pelley. So as not to wound Joseph's manly pride, she always used the words "suggest" or "recommend." There was a second reason for the pillow-soft language. Joseph would not know whether the idea was merely one of her whims or whether it came from the Führer. Either way, her husband always did what was *suggested* or *recommended*.

She was speaking to a minor functionary from the Spanish consulate, a man with a flamboyant mustache, when the SS officer in charge of consulate security whispered in her ear. Afraid she had not heard him correctly, she asked, "My suite?"

The *hauptsturmführer* nodded. Appearing unruffled and taking care not to hurry, Magda followed the officer toward the door.

Georg Gyssling, Joseph Goebbels, and William Dudley Pelley stood in a tight circle on the patio, the buzz of the party reaching them through the open doors. The searchlights continued their endless sweeps, and the fog broke into puffs that drifted above the men like smoke from a campfire.

"You create chaos!" Gyssling pointed an accusing finger at Pelley.

"Which is my job!" Pelley replied.

"Job? You report to no one. You follow no orders."

"Perhaps you are not high enough on the chain of command to know my position," Pelley said. "And tell me, is that swastika in your lapel just a decoration, like a carnation on a banker?"

Gyssling threw up his hands. "Joseph, do you see what I'm dealing with? I wake up to learn that one of the city's largest synagogues has been vandalized, a worker injured. Then, today, Einstein and Chaplin are attacked at a baseball game."

"What does any of that have to do with me?" While Pelley's tone was one of innocence, his smirk seemed to be a confession, and a proud one at that. "But it is interesting that the consul would be upset if his Jew friends were killed."

"Stick to harassing little boys on their way home from Hebrew school," Gyssling said. "You're better at it."

"One morning you will wake up to discover precisely what I excel at," Pelley said.

"If you start killing Jews, you will only engender sympathy for them."

Pelley laughed. "Well, that would be novel, wouldn't it?" He turned to Goebbels. "I'm not sure that Herr Gyssling is fully devoted to the war."

Goebbels remained silent. Like a boxing referee, he let each man land his punches.

"We're at war?" Gyssling asked. "You'd think the Reichstag would have let me know, or at the very least, Göring would have dropped a note in the diplomatic pouch."

"The ultimate war for existence between Aryan mankind and international Jewry," Pelley said. "Is that too difficult for a diplomat to comprehend?"

"What you don't understand, is that diplomacy is subtle and delicate."

"As delicate as your manicured nails?"

"*Leck mich am arsch!*" Gyssling exploded, directing which body part Pelley should kiss.

"*Schweig!* Both of you." Goebbels, the referee, finally separated the boxers. He pulled three Partagás cigars from an inside pocket and handed out two of them.

"Light up, walk with me, and try to be civil."

51
FBI? COMMUNIST CELL? JEW GROUP?

Konsulat von Deutschland, Rooftop

Like most young men, Jimmy Mitchell had never seriously contemplated his own death. Never had he awakened fearing that this day would be his last. That he would never see another dawn, another sunset, another smile on Luisa's face, another hug from his mother or pat on the back from his father.

Now, legs akimbo, sprawled against the ventilation housing on the rooftop of the consulate, one clavicle broken, one kneecap shattered, his nose crushed and bleeding, he did not so much contemplate death as pray it galloped on a swift steed.

The excruciating pain and knowledge of the impending darkness combined to extinguish his fear. What seared his heart was the certainty that evil had triumphed, that he had been a fool, and that his life had been for naught.

Two Germans in leather jackets, their complexions so mottled as to resemble burn victims, hovered over him. One had asked the same question repeatedly and would not accept his answer.

"One last time," the man said in a thick accent. "FBI? Communist cell? Jew group?"

"The *Sentinel*," Mitchell said through swollen lips. "Just a reporter is all."

The second German stepped forward and twirled a leather-sheathed blackjack in front of Mitchell's face, the lead shot grinding with the cold bite of a knife scraping bone. Mitchell winced, and the German windmilled the blackjack into his collarbone, which cracked like a frozen branch underfoot. Mitchell screamed, the sound lost in the mechanical whir of the ventilation fan.

"What were you looking for?" the first German demanded.

"I told you," Mitchell whimpered. "Souvenirs. To sell. Ashtrays. Pens. Swastika pins."

The second German brought the blackjack slowly to Mitchell's temple, as if measuring the distance, then drew it back. Mitchell moaned, waiting for the blow.

"What were you talking to Einstein and Chaplin about?" the first German said.

"Whether caviar is kosher." Mitchell squeezed his eyes shut, anticipating the strike that would fracture his skull and end his consciousness.

"*Verdammt!*" the blackjack man said.

"Sebastian, stop!" came a woman's voice from the darkness.

Mitchell opened his eyes but through blood and tears could only make out the silhouette of a woman in a long dress.

"*Er ist nutzlos,*" she said. "He's useless."

"*Ja, Frau* Goebbels," Sebastian said.

"Accident or suicide," the woman said. "I don't care which."

52
WAKING THE SLEEPING GIANT

Konsulat von Deutschland, Flagstone Path

One question troubled Gyssling as the three men walked along the flagstone path that circled the consulate.

Does Goebbels favor Pelley over me?

Towering over the other men, Gyssling slowed his pace to allow the limping Goebbels and the diminutive Pelley to keep up.

Small landscape lights illuminated their way but were so dim he could barely make out the others' faces. As a trained diplomat, Gyssling excelled at reading expressions, discerning hidden agendas, chiseling apart truth from lies.

But not in the dark! Was it possible that Goebbels championed this egomaniac with delusions of grandeur? And if so, how can I undermine Pelley? How can I use his arrogance and recklessness to bring him down?

As they walked, maintaining the requested civility, Gyssling and Pelley puffed their Cuban cigars, which had the aroma of leather and the taste of coffee.

"Now that you two are finished squabbling like hens, let's iron out your lines of communication," Goebbels said, like the Berlin bureaucrat he was. "Georg, I must bring you up to date on what William told me earlier this evening."

Not a good sign if they've been speaking privately.

Gyssling exhaled a plume of smoke, wondering if the embassy in Havana had any openings. His Spanish was passable and strolling the Malecón with a *hermosa chica* seemed infinitely more pleasurable than tonight's company.

"Contrary to your statements, Georg," Goebbels began, "Mr. Pelley informs me that Chaplin is preparing a motion picture replete with calumny and character assassination against the Führer."

Feeling like a mountain climber who had just lost his footing, Gyssling turned to Pelley and said, "Do you have a copy of the script?"

"No, but one of my Silver Shirts works for Chaplin and was present at an audition."

"Hearsay, then?"

"It has the ring of truth, Georg," Goebbels said. "If I had any doubts, Chaplin's insolence tonight resolved them."

"I will look into it," Gyssling said, seeking a handhold on the sharp and jagged rocks.

"Too late!" Goebbels shot back. "Will no one rid me of this meddlesome actor?"

"I am your knight, Herr Goebbels," Pelley said.

Dear Heavens! Goebbels is playing Henry II and Pelley the assassin of the Archbishop of Canterbury, as if in a play at Deutsches Theater.

Feeling as if he were falling off the mountain, arms flailing, Gyssling nonetheless forced a smile, acknowledging their cleverness. In turn, Pelley grinned at him like the wolf who just leapt into the sheep pen.

"Now, let's turn to the larger picture," Goebbels said. "There are two schools of thought in Berlin. First, keep the Americans from assisting Britain and France with men and matériel, then eventually have them join us in the inevitable war against the Soviets."

"The prudent course," Gyssling said.

"The second school of thought," Goebbels said, "is to create bedlam and anarchy through assassinations of public officials. Split America into opposing factions and push the military into civil war."

"Chop off America's balls as a global power!" Pelley said, delighted.

"Insanity," Gyssling said.

"I am neutral on the subject," Goebbels said. "However, Magda leans toward violence as the surer course. And she does have Adolf's ear."

"The Führer calls my cousin the 'first lady of the Reich,'" Pelley said.

"Your *cousin!*" Gyssling blurted out. "You mean your wife's second cousin by marriage? I'm a closer relative to Charlemagne than you are to Magda."

Goebbels waved his cigar at Gyssling, the tip glowing in the night. "Enough! Georg, for the last time, be civil."

Pelley must have interpreted that as a cue to pound his chest like Tarzan calling to the apes. "I have military units training in Oregon as well as in the mountains not forty miles from here," he said in a boastful tone. "Within six months, they will have the fighting ability of the best *Wehrmacht* troops."

"To what end, other than waking the sleeping giant that is America?" Gyssling said.

"We begin with Operation Hollywood," Pelley said.

"What the hell is that?" Gyssling said.

"Something that Magda and William are planning," Goebbels said.

Something else I'm missing! It's Magda pulling the strings, and Joseph is her marionette.

"Have you secured weapons?" Goebbels asked, looking at Pelley.

"For Operation Hollywood, we'll be fine after tonight. But later, we will need far more."

Weapons! And what does that mean, "after tonight?"

"Arrangements will be made," Goebbels said cryptically.

"So, what is it, this Hollywood operation?" Gyssling asked, purposely mangling the name.

Goebbels said, "Georg, you are a charming diplomat and a dear friend." Gyssling could hear the "but" coming a kilometer away. "But it's better if we leave this to those who don't mind soiling their hands."

Bloodying their hands, you mean!

"Of course, Joseph. I have full confidence in your judgment," Gyssling said with the practiced sincerity of a serial prevaricator.

They had completed circumnavigating the building and were basked in the light streaming from the ballroom. All the better to see Pelley's victory smile crinkle his eyes. Gyssling was not a violent man, but at this moment he yearned to smash a rifle butt into Pelley's face, listen to the man's teeth plink on the flagstones like a handful of coins.

You're foolhardy, and you'll make a mistake, Pelley. When you do, I'll use all my resources against you, and Magda and Joseph won't be here to help you.

In fact, the couple would be leaving in two days for New Jersey to take the return flight of the *Hindenburg* to Frankfurt. By the time they were enjoying their baked halibut in a mousseline sauce, another dozen tasks would be on their mind.

William Dudley Pelley. As the Yanks would say, you have fucked with the wrong cowboy.

53
WHEN GRAVITY MEETS CONCRETE

Konsulat von Deutschland, Patio

Einstein last saw Jimmy Mitchell leaving the ballroom through the open doors to the patio. Shortly thereafter, Chaplin followed. Then the SS officers scurried about.

How long has it been? Thirty minutes? Forty-five? A lifetime?

He knew fear. He'd been bullied in the streets of Berlin, endured death threats, his office vandalized, his summer cottage ransacked, his beloved sailboat confiscated. This was different, a growing sense of dread that others would be harmed, and he was helpless to do anything about it.

But I will show no alarm, betray no trepidation.

Taking his time, feeling he was being watched, he walked onto the patio, pulled out his briar pipe, and stuffed a wad of sweet Turkish tobacco into the bowl. He was just lighting up when he heard a whisper behind him.

"Pssst. Albert."

Einstein turned to find Chaplin next to the scaffold, his bow tie undone, shirttail out, jacket wrinkled.

"Charlie! What happened to you?"

"I'm fine. Have you seen Jimmy?"

"No. I was hoping you'd found him."

"I did, but…"

A piercing, wailing, keening scream came from above, increased in volume and pitch like a whistling mortal round, and both men looked skyward in time to see something—moving too fast to tell what—plunging to earth. The scream died with a sickening *crunch*, a smashing of bones and tearing of flesh as a body hit the patio several feet beyond the scaffold.

Another scream, this one from one of the servers, closest to the body. Guests streamed out of the ballroom, ducked under the scaffold, and made horrified sounds. A female guest in a red chiffon gown gasped and fainted, her escort scooping her up before she hit the ground.

Chaplin and Einstein pushed their way past the guests toward the body but became trapped in the crowd. Chaplin, the smaller man, peered into the backs of taller men.

"Albert, is that…?"

"I can't see, Charlie." Einstein sidestepped two couples, then moved forward, edging close enough to see.

"*Got zol rachmen.* God have mercy."

"What is it, Albert?" Chaplin asked, his view still blocked.

"It's what happens when gravity meets concrete."

"Jimmy?"

"The body's face down. I can't tell for certain."

Two SS officers in black suits pushed roughly through the crowd, and one turned the body over. The blood-soaked face was flattened to the point of being concave and was barely recognizable as human. Another female guest went weak in the knees and pitched forward.

"The left hand," Einstein said. "He's wearing his NAACP ring." Chaplin let out an anguished cry.

A distraught Einstein said, "Why didn't he listen to us?"

"Albert, he listened to me! Oh God. It's my fault."

"What are you talking about?"

Sobbing, Chaplin told Einstein about the conversation in Gyssling's office and Mitchell's plan to break into Magda Goebbels's suite.

"I should have stopped him, Albert. Instead, I sent him into the belly of the beast."

A ring of SS officers surrounded the body, keeping guests back, not that any of them dared venture forward. Gyssling approached the circle with unhurried steps.

"Suicide?" Gyssling said to one of the officers.

"*Ja, Herr Gyssling,*" he replied. "Poor fellow."

Another SS officer crouched next to the body, pulled a wallet from the man's pants, and removed a driver's license.

The officer read aloud, "James A. Mitchell, 1180 East Forty-Forth Street. Apartment 205. Los Angeles."

Einstein saw Gyssling heading their way. "Charlie, tuck in your shirt and pull yourself together."

Gyssling looked at both men with what appeared to be sincere concern, but Einstein thought that diplomats were as accomplished actors as Hollywood stars.

"My sincere regrets, gentlemen, for this upsetting event," Gyssling said in the same tone one might use to apologize for a rain shower that ruined a picnic.

"Are the police on the way, Herr Gyssling?" Einstein asked.

"Technically, we are on foreign soil."

"You are exempt from the laws?" Einstein said, a note of anger in his voice.

"While the consulate doesn't have all the privileges of the embassy," Gyssling said, "Chief Davis lets us police ourselves. Nonetheless, I have called our liaison with the department."

Einstein's grief had quickly turned to rage, an unusual emotion that he did not know how to handle. He felt his body heating up, a river of lava in his veins. "So this can be swept under the rug, too?" he said, steel in his voice.

"I beg your pardon, Professor." Gyssling seemed shocked that the gentle genius spoke to him with such anger.

"I heard you suggest suicide," Einstein said. "Is that what you'll tell your liaison, as you call him?"

"I'm sorry you're upset, Professor." Gyssling turned to Chaplin, who had been uncharacteristically quiet. "What's wrong, Charlie?"

"Nothing, Georg."

"Your bow tie's crooked, and your hair's a mess. Have you been fiddling with a young lady in a dark corner?"

Chaplin ran a hand through his thick silver hair. "No fiddling tonight."

"And you've lost the top button of your jacket."

Chaplin's right hand shot to his jacket. The felt-covered buttons of his custom tux had two letter *C*s in gold thread, one inside the other, and yes, one was missing. "I'll have my tailor flogged," he said.

Einstein saw Goebbels coming out of the crowd, limping at a furious pace. Without preamble and in the tone of a prosecutor addressing a suspect, the propaganda chief said, "You two were seen talking to the Negro."

"That a crime in Reich-land?" Chaplin said, having regained his composure, if not his top button.

"What were you talking about?" A demand more than a question.

Before Chaplin could reply, Einstein said in an iron-willed tone, "The young man asked why the two of us would ever set foot in this den of iniquity, this breeding ground of hate, this malignant tumor of darkness and evil."

The left side of Goebbels's mouth twitched involuntarily like a hooked fish. Einstein smiled placidly.

Good, Herr Goebbels. Either you're angry or you're having a stroke.

"Oh, Professor," Goebbels said, "how I wish you were still in Germany."

"Ach, the Fatherland. Where your Führer's depravity is matched only by your own inhumanity."

The corner of Goebbels's mouth spasmed again, and his forced smile gave him the look of a palsied goblin. "And that you would say those words to me on the Kurfürstendamm on a beautiful spring day when my Luger has been freshly oiled."

Goebbels executed a crisp military pivot and limped away.

"Blimey! You rattled him." Chaplin clopped Einstein on the back.

Einstein was glad that Charlie seemed to have gotten his legs back under him. But he wondered if this was just a period of numbness, that the grief and guilt would come roaring back like the Rheingold train descending the Alps. He glanced toward the circle of SS officers and spotted Gyssling talking to a paunchy, middle-aged man in a wrinkled brown suit and stained porkpie hat. "That must be the consulate's so-called liaison."

"Good call, Albert. I'd cast him as a burned-out cop who drinks too much."

The man turned to the assembled crowd. "Anybody see or hear anything?"

"I heard a scream just before the body hit," a server of about thirty said.

Another server, a boyish-looking young man, stepped forward. "The body hit the ground in front of me. A second later, one of the shoes just missed me."

Einstein moved toward the young man. "Are you sure the body hit first?"

"Positive. I jumped back when it landed. Then I saw the shoe hit the ground."

"That's neither here nor there," the paunchy cop said. "The body's heavier, so it falls faster."

Ever the teacher, Einstein couldn't resist. "You misapprehend the physics of falling bodies, Officer…"

"*Detective* Carl Cooper. And I take it you're Einstein."

"Absent air resistance, every object, regardless of mass, accelerates at 9.8 meters per second squared," Einstein said.

"So what's that gotta do with the price of tea in China?"

"The man has a greater mass than a shoe, so the air resistance would be greater and the shoe would hit a split second first. Not a second later. A plausible explanation would be that a murderer threw the man off the roof and then tossed the shoe."

Cooper barked a mocking laugh. "Real life ain't like a la-bor-a-tory, Einstein. We got a suicide here. It ain't brain surgery."

"Certainly not," Einstein said. "It's Newtonian physics. Then there's the problem that the shoe is four meters from the body." Einstein picked up the shoe, noticed something, but kept quiet.

Chaplin saw a look cross Einstein's face but couldn't decipher it. He wouldn't ask, not with all the Nazis and their helpers around.

Are you making some genius calculation, Albert?

"Gravity causes objects to fall toward the center of the earth," Einstein said, as if delivering a lecture. "The shoe should be next to the body."

"Aw, jeez, sorry everything's not tied up with a pretty red bow," Cooper said, "but the guy's a jumper, pure and simple."

"Do jumpers scream on their way down?" Chaplin asked the question, not to get an answer but to distract Cooper from the body.

"Screams happen," Cooper said. "Not unusual at all."

On movie sets, Chaplin's extraordinary peripheral vision allowed him to look one way and see the movement of the actors and crew in other directions. Now, out of the corner of an eye, he saw Einstein pull something from inside the shoe and pocket it.

Good! The disheveled detective is looking directly at me.

"Seems more likely that two men slung him by the ankles and wrists," Chaplin said.

"Aw, I get it now. You think you're Jimmy Cagney in *G Men*. Infiltrating a criminal enterprise, huh?"

"I don't know." Chaplin looked side to side. "Is this a criminal enterprise?"

Cooper's look hardened. "You oughta stick to slapstick, Chaplin."

"You're overlooking one thing, Detective," Chaplin said. "The scaffold."

"What about it?"

"If I tried to jump off the top of City Hall, the wedding cake shoulders would catch me," Chaplin said, remembering his conversation one night earlier with Paulette. "Same thing here."

"I agree," Einstein said. "No way a man could clear the scaffold by jumping."

"You two big shots ever hear of Jesse Owens?" Cooper asked.

"A hero of mine for embarrassing Hitler at the Olympics," Chaplin said.

"Coloreds got springy legs like grasshoppers. Case closed." Cooper turned to the SS officers. "Now, clear the looky-loos out of here."

54
THE BIGGEST NAMES IN HOLLYWOOD

Malibu Pier, Malibu California

Chaplin had a place of refuge in times of trouble. Women trouble, studio trouble, and long ago, financial trouble. The place was the ocean. He did, after all, name his forty-four-foot ketch the *Panacea* after the Greek goddess of healing. But there would be no midnight cruise in these dark hours.

Chaplin and Einstein drove in near silence to Santa Monica, then up the Theodore Roosevelt Highway a short way to Malibu through a shroud of fog, heavy as a sodden wool blanket. Chaplin parked the Rolls-Royce at the foot of the Malibu Pier, a salty ocean breeze driving streams of fog over them, droplets of moisture splattering the windscreen. There was no moon, there were no stars, and the ocean was invisible through the marine layer, the world an artist's canvas painted solid gray. Waves slapped the pilings of the pier, spraying foam into the night.

The temperature had plummeted, and Chaplin hoped his method of working through his guilt and pain didn't result in Albert catching pneumonia. Somewhere, a foghorn sounded, the plaintive cry of a prehistoric bird.

"It's not your fault," Einstein said. "He knew the risks, but as with so many of the young, considered himself immortal."

"Exactly, Albert! And that's why it was my duty to protect him."

"Freud believes that guilt is a signal that the superego is trying to control the id."

"That's gobbledygook to me. Just tell me how to atone for my guilt."

"By achieving justice for Jimmy Mitchell. By finishing his work and saving others."

A car horn blared on the coast highway, one driver apparently unhappy with another's cautious speed.

"Okay, start by telling me what you grabbed from Jimmy's shoe."

"A single sheet of paper. I thought we'd look at it together."

"I assume it's the document from Magda Goebbels's vanity," Chaplin said without a glimmer of excitement. The importance of the document, which had seemed paramount hours earlier, had waned in the wake of Jimmy's death.

No writing could be worth the man's life.

Einstein pulled the sheet of paper from his pocket, and Chaplin flicked on a dashboard light.

"You read it, Albert. I'll listen."

"First, the handwriting is quite atrocious. At the top are three letters that look like 'J-A-M.'"

"James A. Mitchell," Chaplin said. "Bollocks! It's not Magda's. Jimmy wrote it."

"Hold on, Charlie. It seems to be a list of names and addresses, written very hurriedly, hence the scrawl." Einstein thought it over. "Jimmy didn't take the document, because that would have alerted Frau Goebbels. So, he *copied* the document! What a *kop* on his shoulders. Such a smart young man! And brave."

Chaplin felt yet another wave of guilt surge over him. "If he'd just grabbed Magda's document and run, maybe he would have gotten away. Oh, blast it!"

They sat silently for another moment, both thinking their private thoughts about the loss of Jimmy Mitchell. The only sound was the shore break crashing against unseen rocks.

"I don't have my cheaters, and I can't see in this light," Chaplin said. "Can you read me the list?"

Einstein squinted and read aloud, "'Louis B. Mayer, 6615 Franklin Avenue.'"

"Yeah, that's where Louie lives. What about it?"

"He's first on the list. Then, 'Samuel Goldwyn, 1200 Laurel Lane.'"

"Yeah, Mr. G's address. Go on."

"'Douglas Fairbanks, 1143 Summit Drive.'"

"Doug! My neighbor and pal for twenty years. Keep reading."

Einstein squinted and said, "The handwriting gets worse. 'Harold Lloyd, 1740 Green Acres Drive.'"

"Another friend! Right around the corner."

"Jack Warner, Al Jolson, Judge Henry Willis. All with addresses. There are more."

"What the hell is this, Albert?"

Einstein put the document on one knee and turned to his friend. "You said you heard Frau Goebbels on the phone say 'Operation Hollywood.' What else do you remember?"

Chaplin focused, conjured up the memory. "*Natürlich kann man der Operation Hollywood zwei namen hinzufügen.*"

Einstein translated. "'Of course you can add two names to Operation Hollywood.' That doesn't tell us much."

"In English, she asked, 'Who are they?' then said, 'You think big.' And finally, something else in German. Drat! I've lost it, Albert."

"Don't try too hard. Exhale. Relax. Let your mind wander. It's what I do in my thought experiments."

Chaplin followed instructions and blurted out, *"Und sie werden heute abend dreiundzwanzig."*

Puzzled, Einstein said, "And you will be twenty-three tonight."

"Something's missing," Chaplin said. "Wait! *Maschinengewehre haben.*"

"Oh my," Einstein said.

"What?"

"Magda seems to be repeating what she was just told, that the other person on the line will get twenty-three machine guns tonight."

A wave smacked the dune in front of the Rolls and showered the car with cold spray. "Twenty-three," Chaplin said. "Such an odd number. Why not twenty? Or two dozen? Or twenty-five?"

"Let's count the names," Einstein said, just as Chaplin said, "The names! How many?"

Einstein counted aloud in German, then said, "Twenty-three."

Chaplin let out a long, slow breath. "Twenty-three names, twenty-three machine guns. It's a hit list, the biggest names in Hollywood, one victim for each machine gun."

"Meaning they're to be killed simultaneously in different locations," Einstein said, "their homes, judging from the addresses."

"Mostly Jews. But the others…friends of Jews."

"Apparently a capital offense," Einstein said.

"The rest of the names, Albert. Can you read them?"

"With difficulty." He squinted some more. "'Fredric March. Paul Muni. B. P. Schulberg. Busby Berkeley.'" He stopped and slid his index finger down the list of names. *"Oy, gevalt."*

"What now?"

"The last two names, the ones they added tonight, are you and me."

"I'm last?"

"Bottom of the page."

"Outrageous," Chaplin said. "I should have top billing."

55
MY LITTLE SCHNUCKIPUTZI

Konsulat von Deutschland, Consul's Study and Bordello Room

It was just after 2:00 a.m., and Gyssling regretted hitting the bottle of Scotch after all that champagne. His stomach rose and fell as if he were on a raft tumbling over rapids on the Salzach River. His vision blurred, either from the alcohol or pure, fiery anger.

Magda Goebbels. You arrogant, reckless wench!

A murder on consulate property. Without approval of the Foreign Office. Could she have not waited until the guests had left?

Gyssling paced in front of the desk in his study. Magda and Joseph Goebbels sat in deep leather chairs, letting him vent.

"Frau Goebbels, you have exceeded your authority," Gyssling began.

"Have I now?" She sounded amused. She shook a cigarette from a gold case, leaned over, and let her husband flick the gold lighter Adolf had given him. Gyssling had the unmistakable impression that Magda was pissing in all four corners of his study, asserting that she was the dominant bitch and the two men were flea-bitten hounds.

"This is my consulate," Gyssling said. "I am responsible for everything that occurs within its walls…or on its roof."

"And you failed miserably at security."

"All my work is for naught if the Americans think we are barbarians."

"Joseph, please tell this clerk that one word to Adolf, and he will be cleaning toilets at the embassy in Kabul," Magda said.

She exhaled a plume of smoke, gracefully got to her feet, nodded toward the portrait of the Führer that loomed over them, said, "*Heil Hitler*," and left the study.

Gyssling remained standing with nothing left to say.

"I'm sorry, Georg," Goebbels said, "but you know how headstrong Magda is."

"The paperwork alone," Gyssling said, more to himself than to the propaganda chief. "Payoffs to the police and coroner and newspaper reporters. And frankly, with so many guests, I just don't know how to keep the lid on this."

"Oh, come now, Georg. Who's going to make a big fuss over one dead *schwarzer*?"

☞ ☜

Two floors below the consul's study, in a room decorated like a New Orleans bordello, Charles Lindbergh and Mitzi Kunz, both naked, were tangled in the sheets of the large bed as photos of voluptuous, nude women looked down at them from the walls. In the missionary position, Lindbergh pumped away with regular, mechanical strokes, not unlike the reliable pistons of the *Spirit of St. Louis*. Mitzi's moans could be mistaken for the epitome of ecstasy, but in truth, she was the greatest actress this side of Marlene Dietrich.

"Oh, oh, oh, my big, big, big pilot," Mitzi sighed in her thick accent.

"Ach, ach," Lindbergh grunted in the universal language of men with insufficient blood in their brains to form a coherent thought.

"Take me, take me now." She was quoting a *romanze* novel she'd recently read and realized that, strictly speaking, she should have given that order before Lindy entered her, not that he noticed the faulty timeline.

"We should have children. Beautiful blond children," he said, getting all domestic in the midst of lust.

"*Ja! Ja! Kinder.*" Mitzi rolled her eyes, not from an orgasm but from the certain belief that the pilot was a *dummkopf*, and she silently thanked the heavens for the excellent German diaphragms.

"Ach, ach. My little *schnuckiputzi*," Lindbergh grunted. "My little sweetie pie."

⋈

In the adjoining room, Klaus Spengler held his Leica to the two-way mirror and snapped photos. A new German Magnetophon tape recorder sat on a table, its reels spinning.

"My little *schnuckiputzi*," Spengler said aloud, giggling.

56
THE MOST DANGEROUS MAN IN AMERICA

Beverly Hills, Sunset Boulevard

Beverly Hills was a ghost town of palm trees shrouded in fog at 3:00 a.m. Chaplin nearly dozed off at the wheel as he drove home, Einstein snoring peacefully next to him.

Chaplin replayed the events and the emotions of the night. His paralyzing fear as he hid in the light alcove, his heart racing like a wildfire, his courage reduced to smoldering ashes. How close had he come to death? There were two SS officers searching the consul's office. He would wager they were the Doberman Pinschers from the ballroom and that they killed Jimmy.

The Rolls was on Sunset Boulevard in Beverly Hills, nearly home, with few cars on the road, when Einstein stirred, yawned, and said, "Sorry, Charlie. I must have dozed off."

"Not a problem. You're staying over tonight, my friend."

"What have you been thinking while I've been snoozing?"

"That we saw the face of evil tonight," Chaplin said.

"Indeed. Those SS thugs."

"Not who I'm thinking of."

"Goebbels, then. A soulless husk of a man."

"Rotten to the core," Chaplin said, "but too obvious. Cast him in a movie and you know in the first closeup that he's the villain.

I'm thinking of a face that disguises evil."

"Gyssling? He seems almost human."

Chaplin eased the Rolls into a turn from Sunset onto Benedict Canyon Drive. "The face that strikes fear in my heart is that of Charles Lindbergh."

"But, Charlie, he's so banal."

"The most dangerous man in America."

"How? The man has the intellectual velocity of a mollusk."

"A dozen years ago, a lot of Germans thought Hitler was a clown."

"Charlie, I don't see the parallel."

"You heard Lindbergh say that Goebbels wants him to run for president."

"I heard it, but it sounded far-fetched."

"Lindbergh goes on the radio, and millions of people take him seriously," Chaplin said. "He's Hitler's handmaiden, even if he doesn't know it."

"So he's the Nazis' *nützlichr idiot*," Einstein said.

"A useful idiot, sure. But what makes Lindbergh so dangerous is that he isn't evil. He simply fails to recognize evil in others. And where humanity is concerned, he has a total lack of empathy. But his celebrity is unmatched, even though his greatest accomplishment was staying awake overnight."

Einstein thought about it as Chaplin turned onto Summit Drive.

"Celebrity can't be quantified in a logical equation," Einstein said. "It's like bolts of lightning that strike random locations. The two pilots who flew together and crossed the Atlantic *before* Lindbergh…no one remembers their names."

"What I fear," Chaplin said, "is that the Nazis will use Lindbergh's celebrity to perpetuate their evil here."

"Then we must use ours against them," Einstein replied.

57

THE WHIPSY-DIPSY-DO

May 6, 1937 – Long Beach Armory

At 6:42 a.m., three fire trucks were stacked side by side when Detective Carl Cooper parked his Ford plain wrapper, eased out from behind the wheel, and surveyed the smoldering mess at the armory.

"Jumping Jesus Jehoshaphat!" he said, looking at a sooty crater four feet deep filled with Browning rifles twisted into pretzels, scorched wooden slats, and half-melted grenade casings. A blizzard of ashes churned in the morning breeze, the air tanged with the pungent scent of a forest fire.

Yesterday's shitstorm left him exhausted, his plate as full as a Shriner's tray at an all-you-can-eat diner. After watching the Negro's body loaded into the meat wagon with instructions that the autopsy was to be performed only by Dr. Carruthers of the coroner's office, Cooper left the consulate at 3:00 a.m. Then he visited Carruthers at home, waking him and his farting basset hound. He told the sawbones precisely what his conclusion would be—suicide—and sent him back to bed with a C-note.

This promised to be another shitty day. Cooper hadn't slept and wore the same wrinkled brown suit that had looked better yesterday morning. At least then it didn't carry the stink of formaldehyde, the coroner's daily cologne. At forty-seven, divorced twice, Cooper lived alone, thankfully with no rug rats to support. His buzz cut was graying, his paunch growing, and his mood worsening with the years.

He had been sitting at his kitchen table nursing a Hill Brook bourbon when Chief Davis called at 6:00 a.m. sharp, telling him to get his ass to the armory and pin this goat fuck on a commie cell before the army reached a different conclusion. The Reds were mostly nearsighted milquetoasts who sipped black tea and endlessly flapped their gums in a back corner of Clifton's Cafeteria. He would roust a few before the day was out.

Scanning the area, Cooper saw city firemen, arson inspectors, uniformed cops, plainclothes detectives, and a dozen National Guardsmen, plus the usual assortment of newspaper reporters with shiny pants bottoms. It would be easier to grow petunias out of asphalt than to plant evidence in this crowd.

He approached an LAPD photographer, a young man in dungarees, crouched in the soot, snapping photos. "Whadaya got?" Cooper asked.

"Tire track, check it out," the photographer said.

Cooper dropped to a catcher's position and saw a dime-size circle interrupting the tread. "Tire's been patched with a plug."

"Yep. This one and a million others in town."

Cooper moved on, came across Potter Stackhouse, a gray-haired sergeant he'd known from semi-pro baseball in his youth. "Whadaya got, Pots?"

"Damn little. No witnesses, and all the evidence blew sky-high."

"Any ideas?"

"Same ones you got, Whipsy." Stackhouse grinned, letting him know the chief had made more than one early-morning call.

"Nobody calls me Whipsy anymore," Cooper said.

"They would, if they'd seen you bat against that colored

beanpole back in the day." Anyone else, Cooper would clean his clock, but he could take the ribbing from an old pal.

No one could take away Cooper's moments of glory back at Santa Ana High School, where he'd captained the baseball team and broke every home run record. Might have had a professional career, but he couldn't hit a decent curveball. In a game against an all-Negro team, Cooper struck out four times, all on breaking pitches, including one the pitcher called his Whipsy-Dipsy-Do.

That one came soft and feathery as a white-winged dove, danced up, then down, a billiard ball dropping off the table. Cooper swung so hard that he fell face-first into the red dirt of the batter's box. The pitcher laughed. The crowd laughed. Cooper's teammates laughed. Dusting himself off, Cooper did not laugh.

"Cotton-picking grandson-of-a-slave made you eat dirt, Whipsy," Potter Stackhouse chided him that day.

Carl Cooper was not given to self-reflection, but he intuitively knew that he used his nightstick quicker and harder on the coloreds, which included Mexicans, Indians, Asians, and even Italians, and Greeks, if they looked at him cross-eyed.

Now, Cooper examined his soot-covered black oxfords, which looked as cruddy as the muck boots worn by the Okies he routinely dragged from their Hooverville shanties. He reached down to dust off his shoes, and something caught his eye. A scorched piece of fabric embroidered with a bright strip of red cloth about two inches wide, ending at a ninety-degree angle where it was burned beyond recognition…unless you recognized what it was.

A red *L*, the symbol of the Silver Legion of America. The Silver Shirts fascist paramilitary.

Gyssling had paid Cooper and a photographer to attend rallies of the Silver Shirts and the German American Bund.

"In this country," Gyssling had told him, "I worry more about our friends than our enemies."

Less than three weeks earlier, Cooper had attended a picnic in

Hindenburg Park, celebrating Hitler's birthday, with all the bozos singing songs, guzzling beer, and eating bratwurst. It resembled the parking lot outside the Coliseum prior to a USC game against UCLA, except football fans seldom wore lederhosen and swastika armbands.

To Cooper, the Silver Shirts' leader, William Pelley, in his riding breeches and high leather boots, resembled a character out of a Hollywood screwball comedy. It would hardly be a surprise if Pelley was behind the dumb-ass heist and employed a crew with all the competence of the Three Stooges.

And the information might be worth a couple hundred bucks to Gyssling.

Cooper grabbed the charred fabric, and his hand brushed something else.

Another piece of scorched cloth, apparently from the same shirt. The letters "m-a-n-n" were visible in black thread, then what appeared to be the start of a new word, "B-r."

Whatever the hell that meant—"mann Br"—he had no idea.

Cooper put both pieces of cloth in his pants pocket, looked around to make sure no one was watching, slipped a hand into a breast pocket of his suit coat, brought out two pamphlets, and dropped them. With his dusty oxford, he ground soot onto the pamphlets until only a small red corner was visible on one of them.

"Hey, Sarge!" he yelled at Potter Stackhouse. "Get a load of this!"

His old teammate took his time walking over, suppressing a grin. He'd lost his virginity at crime scenes so long ago, he couldn't remember when he first got bent.

"What'd you find, Whipsy?"

"Take a look."

Stackhouse grabbed both pamphlets, as firemen and patrolmen hurried over.

"Well, lookee here." He unfolded the pages, revealing a hammer and sickle inside.

"'Stand by the Soviet Union,'" he read aloud, then held up the bright red second pamphlet. "'Workers of the world unite. Communist Party of America.' Turning to Cooper, he said, "I guess the Red Squad will take over from here."

"Lickety-split," Cooper said.

58
HAPPY BIRTHDAY, HITLER

Konsulat von Deutschland, Consul's Study

Georg Gyssling was alone in his sixth-floor office, feeling downright exhilarated. After speaking to Detective Cooper on the phone, Gyssling tried not to celebrate, but excitement pounded in his ears like the crash of cymbals in "Also Sprach Zarathustra."

The Silver Shirts tried to knock over a US military armory! Pelley, you cocksure gasbag, I can nail you now!

Well, not quite yet.

Pelley was nowhere near the armory last night. He was at the consulate, exchanging whispered messages with Goebbels and establishing his alibi. Gyssling would have to track down Pelley's incompetent accomplices who nearly blew themselves up and left behind flaming articles of clothing.

A shirt with what appeared to be a partial name! It was almost like a business card.

Find those men, have Cooper sweat them, and they would name Pelley. Then Gyssling would present Goebbels with evidence of Pelley's stunning ineptitude. The propaganda chief would have no choice but to call off Operation Hollywood, whatever it was.

One thing for sure, it involved stolen firearms!

A second possibility came to mind.

What if Pelley's minions actually made off with some of the Browning Automatics?

The BARs were machine guns and possessing them was illegal under the National Firearms Act of 1934. Gyssling knew the law because the FBI adamantly refused to allow the SS to stock the consulate with MG 34s, the German light machine gun.

Ten years in prison! How does that sound, William Dudley Pelley?

The initial step was figuring out "mann Br." Lettering on a work shirt often spelled out the name of a business. The letters "m-a-n-n" formed a common suffix to German names. So, the name of a person followed by the business name sounded logical. He considered some common German surnames.

Baumann. Hartmann. Ehrmann. Beckmann. Dittmann. Hoffmann. Zimmermann. Neumann. Schumann. Too many possibilities. I'm going about this all wrong.

Cooper had mentioned seeing Pelley and a horde of his Silver Shirts at the picnic celebrating the Führer's forty-eighth birthday less than three weeks earlier. Of course! The detective had been there taking notes while Klaus Spengler shot photos. Gyssling's files had hundreds—perhaps thousands—of photos of rallies, meetings, picnics, and speeches covering the last five years. He always wanted to know who attended the events and what was said.

Not even God kept records as complete as the German bureaucracy.

Gyssling unlocked one of the drawers that lined the walls and pulled out several files. Cooper had taken notes on Pelley's speech, which included the usual diatribes: "We will rid America of Judeo-Communism."

Gyssling grabbed the file with Spengler's photographs. Frozen in time, the speakers in suits and fedoras looked sweaty and worked up, the casually dressed spectators fat and happy, many giving the bent-elbow *Hitlergruss* like wooden marionettes.

Get a dozen Germans together with a keg of beer, an oompah band, and someone to curse, and they'll form a committee with a director, a treasurer, and a recording secretary.

Looking at the photos, Gyssling could almost smell the grilling bratwurst, weisswurst, and knackwurst, could almost hear the snap and sizzle of the casings. He hated all wursts, not to mention sauerkraut and frankfurters, all of which he considered peasant food.

A separate file contained photographs of vehicles, most with license plates visible. Fords, Chevys, Packards, Hupmobiles, Cords, Auburns, DeSotos, and Hudsons. Another file was devoted to rows of trucks, vendors for the event. Breweries, bakeries, bands, rental companies that provided chairs and tables. And then…

Can it be this easy? This quick! Oh, this is meant to be! "mann Br"

A Ford panel truck emblazoned: Diekmann Brothers Fine Wholesale Meats.

Of course!

He knew the men. Or, more accurately, he had met them. They had been the purveyors of meat and poultry when Gyssling took over the consulate. He terminated the contract because of their price gouging and the meat, rather than "fine," was second rate. There had been some angry words exchanged when their last delivery was turned away.

Roughhewn men. Not particularly bright. The sort of men Pelley could inspire with his hateful rants.

A quick look at the telephone directory revealed an address in San Pedro. He took a Rand McNally street map from a drawer and located the business in the warehouse district near the harbor. Then he traced a finger across the map to the armory on Seventh Street in Long Beach, barely three miles away. Pelley probably thought he was a genius, planning such a short getaway. Then he chose amateurs, complete *dummkopfs*, to pull off a major crime.

Gyssling returned the files to the drawer and relocked it, noticing something where the top of the drawer met the wall. A button covered in black felt. He picked it up. Fine gold thread created the letter *C* inside a larger *C*. He remembered seeing Chaplin on the patio, looking unusually unkempt and missing the top button of his dinner jacket.

Oh, Charlie Chaplin, what have you done?

59
JAMES "TWO GUN" DAVIS

Los Angeles City Hall, LAPD Chief's Office

Sergeant Georgia Ann Robinson sat across from the police chief and next to a man she did not know. She said what she had come to say and now waited.

"Sergeant Robinson, let me see if I've got this straight," Chief James Davis said. "Just before he commits suicide, a mentally unstable Negro male breaks into the bedroom of a foreign dignitary. He apparently copies twenty-three names from a list he finds in a drawer. I say 'apparently' because there's no proof of it, just supposition. That document, which should have been turned over as evidence in the man's death, was purloined by Albert Einstein, of all people, a foreign national. His friend Charlie Chaplin, another foreign national and one with dubious allegiances, reaches the conclusion that the names on the list—some of Hollywood's top bananas—are to be murdered by machine guns in their homes. This fanciful plot is being orchestrated by the Third Reich and carried out by Americans who play dress-up soldiers and drink beer at Alt Heidelberg. How am I doing so far?"

"It's not the way I would characterize it, Chief," Georgia Robinson said softly but firmly.

"Now, nothing on this purloined list says anything about murder. It's not signed by Joseph Goebbels or anyone else for that matter. For all we know, it's an invitation list for the next champagne shindig at the German consulate."

"With due respect, Chief, that's really looking at this through blinders."

"Blinders, you say." He narrowed his eyes, and his face hardened.

Davis, who liked his nickname "Two Gun," was a double-chinned, stocky man of forty-eight with wavy gray hair and six gold stripes on the sleeves of his blue tunic. Robinson had been present when the chief told his officers to hold court in the street and bring criminals in dead, not alive. She had heard tales that he was on the payroll of a sizable portion of the city's six hundred brothels and eighteen hundred bookie joints and may have owned a slice of the slot machine business. He was also known to be chummy with the fascist groups, and today's meeting did nothing to dispel any of that.

"So, enlighten me, Sergeant," Davis said, his tone challenging.

"It wasn't a suicide. The victim was a reporter who'd gone undercover and discovered the murder plot called 'Operation Hollywood.'"

The chief glanced at the man next to him and raised his eyebrows. The man smiled. Gloria Robinson concentrated on not showing anger, a task she'd perfected long ago.

They're mocking me and having fun doing it!

Five minutes earlier, the man had introduced himself as "John."

"I didn't catch your last name," Robinson had said.

"I didn't drop it," the man replied.

Hardee-Har. Maybe you can go on the radio with George Burns and Gracie Allen.

"John's with the Bureau," Davis said, grabbing a Chesterfield from a silver case and igniting it with a lighter shaped like a hand grenade. "A special unit that keeps track of subversives and reports directly to Director Hoover. That right, John?"

"We read their mail, bug their telephone conversations, keep tabs on their sexual proclivities," the FBI agent said.

Apparently unconcerned if any of that is legal!

John wore a baggy charcoal suit, a white shirt, a gray tie, and horn-rimmed spectacles. He had a graying buzz cut and the bland face of an eighth-grade geography teacher. They were in Chief Davis's office downtown on the second floor of Los Angeles City Hall, a building of archways and beaux arts friezes and sculptures, its tower topped with a distinctive pyramid. Crossing the bullpen to the chief's office, Robinson's shoes had clacked loudly on the tile floor, not unlike the sound they made in a cellblock at the city jail.

Central Division, located in another building, had always seemed like a foreign country when she was the sole Black woman on the premises. There were a few more women of color in the department now, and the earlier requirements—a degree in nursing or education, married, between the ages of thirty and forty-four—had been relaxed. Still, today she had drawn stares.

Earlier, she had met Chaplin and Einstein for bacon, eggs, and endless free coffee at the Pantry, a café at Ninth and Francisco Streets. The two men looked shellshocked and sleepless as they told her of the horrifying events at the consulate. She tried to dissuade them from going to Jimmy Mitchell's apartment, their announced plan of the morning. The SS could be there, she told them. But they were undeterred.

They would continue, despite the risks. That's a trait they shared with her.

Only yesterday at Chaplin's home, she had expressed her admiration for their shared goals of combating evil.

And now we have an innocent young man brutally murdered. We have a plot to slaughter nearly two dozen people. We have Americans in cahoots with a foreign power that is evil to its core. If we don't do something about it, who will?

Returning her attention to Chief Davis and unwilling to give up, she said, "A man named William Dudley Pelley is behind the plot."

"We know Pelley and his Silver Shirts," John leapt in. "Like the chief said, they drink their share of beer, tell stories of the Fatherland, curse the Jews, and fall asleep at their tables."

"If we arrested everyone in LA who hates Jews, there'd be nobody left," Davis said.

"Except the Jews," John chimed in.

"Our biggest problem in LA ain't the fascists," Davis said, exhaling a trail of smoke. "We got the Red Menace in Hollywood, with their hearts in Moscow."

"And the Hebrew mobsters," John said. "La Cosa Nostra was bad enough, but with Murder, Inc., now we got the Kosher Nostra."

"Bugsy Siegel and Mickey Cohen," the chief said, "the worst racketeers this side of Brooklyn."

Meaning they won't pay you protection money.

"Back to the case at hand," the chief continued. "Just what would you have us do, Sergeant, based on this sheet of paper I hesitate to even call evidence?" The chief held the document with two fingertips, as if it might contain horse dung.

"First, notify everyone on the list that they're in danger. Most of them have the resources for private security, and if they don't, give them police protection."

Davis blew his cheeks out and said, "Whoa now! Tell Louis B. Mayer and Samuel Goldwyn that the Nazis are laying for them. Create panic. Make my department look foolish and me a nincompoop. No, ma'am."

"And put William Pelley under twenty-four-hour surveillance," she said, plowing ahead.

"No probable cause for pinning a tail on that donkey." He looked to John, who nodded his approval. "Now, I'm sorry to cut you short, Sergeant, but all hell's breaking loose with the commie attack on the armory down in Long Beach."

That stopped her. *Commie attack?*

"I hadn't heard," she said.

"Last night. Tried to make off with crates of Browning Automatics and whatnot."

"Machine guns! You're sure the perpetrators are communists?"

"My Red Squad says so."

Meaning Detective Carl Cooper, a guy as crooked as a corkscrew.

"That's your proof, sir! Of Operation Hollywood. It's fascists, not communists, who attacked the armory. Like I told you, Mr. Chaplin heard Magda Goebbels say, 'And you'll have twenty-three machine guns tonight.'"

"No, you said he eavesdropped on her through a window and heard something in German, which Albert Einstein later translated into that machine gun whoop-de-doo. Maybe Magda said bubble gum, and it was lost in translation." He guffawed and hacked a cough. "Sounds like Chaplin's writing a movie."

"A movie, sir?"

"You know, those mistaken identity pictures like the Marx Brothers do. A cop chases Groucho through a door, and Harpo comes out another door. Seems to me you're the cop waving your nightstick, just flailing away like a patsy."

"Looking for Chico," John said, grinning.

"Now, Georgia Ann," the chief said, "if I can get personal, your file is immaculate, and you're a credit to your race."

Oh, sweet Jesus. Does he forget how many times he's said that?

Robinson gritted her teeth so tightly she felt her jaw muscles flex. She had endured insults far worse, but dammit, this was so tiring.

"And you've been under a lot of pressure," he continued. "I know that Studebaker at the stadium damn near hit you yesterday. Had to be unnerving, eh?"

"I've been shot at, Chief, and attacked with a knife more than once."

"All the more reason to decompress once in a while. Everyone knows you pull extra hours for no overtime." He pulled a paper from a drawer. Even reading upside down, she could see it was a "Paid Leave" form, already filled out with her name. "Let's say thirty days with pay. Go to that Negro beach in Santa Monica. What's it called?"

"The Inkwell."

"Go to the Inkwell, drink some wine, have some fun." He stubbed out his Chesterfield in a brown glass ashtray. "But don't hang around with Chaplin and Einstein."

Davis shot a look at John, the quarterback handing off to his running back. "The Bureau believes they're both security risks," John said, "and you don't want to get caught up with their crowd."

What crowd is that? Actors? Scientists? Jews?

"Thank you both for your time," Robinson said in an even, respectful tone she had perfected through decades of climbing perilous trails on the treacherous terrain of the white power structure. She left the chief's office without another word.

60
SECOND-STORY MAN

Little Harlem, Los Angeles

Chaplin drove the Rolls-Royce, and Einstein sat alongside, each man thinking about the task ahead. Get into Jimmy Mitchell's apartment and find anything and everything—hopefully something!—about Operation Hollywood's blueprint for assassinating twenty-three people. With the convertible top down, they cruised through South Central, passing a church on Central Avenue where Black families, spruced up in fine garb, gathered on the sidewalk in a wedding party. The Rolls stopped at a red light in front of the Dunbar Hotel, where a sandwich board advertised that night's entertainment: SCATTIN' AT THE KIT CAT WITH DUKE ELLINGTON.

The radio was tuned to a newscast, the announcer's voice ebullient. "New York City is abuzz today, waiting for the *Hindenburg* to float over Midtown Manhattan. The observation deck of the Empire State Building will be jammed with tourists and New Yorkers alike as the great German airship will be almost close enough to touch."

Chaplin turned off the radio and said, "Albert, have you given any more thought to helping the Americans build a nuclear fission bomb?"

"Please, Charlie! I won't help blow up cities."

"Okay, but can you figure out how close the Germans are to lighting the fuse? C'mon, Albert. I know you're concerned the Nazis are going to beat us to the punch."

"Germany may be ahead, but there are some outstanding scientists fleeing Europe who are up to the task. Enrico Fermi, Leo Szilard, Neils Bohr. Others."

"You know all these guys, don't you?" Chaplin asked.

Einstein shrugged. "It's a small community."

"But you're the mayor, if you want to be."

Einstein bought time by taking his pipe from a pocket and tamping some Turkish tobacco into the bowl. He made no effort to light it.

"Charlie, who was the best baseball player at that game yesterday?"

"Ted Williams, the skinny kid who hit that rifle shot over the right-field fence."

"And how old, this skinny kid?"

"Eighteen. I told you yesterday."

"It was a rhetorical question. I was twenty-six when I published my theory of special relativity. Fermi is around thirty-five and Szilard, not yet forty. I met a young American physicist last week at the Athenaeum who is so brilliant he teaches at both Caltech and Berkeley. J. Robert Oppenheimer by name. He's thirty-three. An undergraduate at MIT recently sent me a letter asking some very incisive questions for a paper on cosmic rays. I believe he's nineteen, this fellow named Richard Feynman."

"Your point being?" Chaplin asked.

"Physics has become a young person's game, and I'm fifty-eight."

"Do you really believe the game has passed you by?" Chaplin said. "And don't answer. It's a rhetorical question."

The Rolls turned a corner, and Einstein said, "James A. Mitchell, 1180 East Forty-Fourth Street. Apartment 205," repeating the words of the SS officer who had pulled Jimmy's driver's license from his wallet.

The apartment building, like a thousand others in Los Angeles, was Mediterranean Revival with white stucco walls, a red clay tile roof, and an arched passageway that led into an interior courtyard paved with terra-cotta tiles. Bougainvillea vines bloomed with pink flowers along the sidewalk. Surrounded by neatly trimmed rosebushes, a wooden sign on the front lawn read, SOL Y SOMBRA DE MORENO. Hanging on hooks from the sign was a placard: NO VACANCY.

"Interesting name," Chaplin said. "'Moreno's Sun and Shadow.'"

The two men sat in the Rolls for a moment, studying the building. A Western Union messenger, a young Black man in a white shirt, black bow tie, and black felt hat, bicycled by, craning his neck for a longer look at the car or the men or both.

"Try to be inconspicuous," Chaplin said.

"Sure, Charlie. I feel as inconspicuous as a piglet at a Bar Mitzvah."

"I don't see any SS thugs hiding in the bougainvillea, so let's go."

They got out of the Rolls and walked through the passageway to the courtyard. The first-floor apartments had small concrete patios, while those on the second floor had balconies with wrought-iron railings.

"Here's 105," Chaplin said, "so that's 205, Jimmy's apartment, right above it. Look! The door to the balcony is cracked open."

"So?"

Chaplin pointed to the adjacent second-floor apartment at the corner of the building. "That's 204. I can climb up the downspout, pull myself onto that balcony, then leap to 205 like Doug Fairbanks in *The Thief of Baghdad*."

A skeptical Einstein said, "Or, we could walk up the stairs and knock on the front door. Perhaps a relative is there."

A deflated Chaplin reluctantly saw the wisdom of the suggestion. The two men took the stairs and found the door to 205 hanging open on bent hinges, the paint gouged by crowbar marks. They exchanged worried looks and cautiously entered.

Empty!

Not a table, chair, or lamp. Not a plate, fork, or spoon in the kitchen. The walls were ripped open, the floorboards pried loose.

"Whoever did this…" Einstein said.

"Was looking for something," Chaplin finished the thought.

"But did they find it?" Einstein said, throwing up his hands in puzzlement.

"Who are you two?" came a woman's voice from behind them.

They whirled around and saw a tall, slender woman of about twenty-five with a cinnamon complexion and dark hair. She wore Western denim jeans rolled up above her ankles, a wide leather belt with a brass buckle engraved with a bucking bronco, and a red plaid long-sleeve cotton shirt. Her eyes were puffy from crying.

"I'm…we're…friends…we were friends of Mr. Mitchell," Chaplin stuttered.

"No, you weren't." She lifted a Colt .45 revolver with both hands and pointed the barrel at Chaplin's chest. "Now, just what the hell are you looking for?"

61
THE MEAT LOCKER

Warehouse District, San Pedro, California

The air smelled of diesel fuel and dead sardines.

"Rolfe, please crank your window," Gyssling said to his chauffeur.

The Mercedes limousine turned onto a narrow street lined with industrial warehouses, citrus packers, transit sheds, lumber yards, a US Navy fuel depot, and a dozen sardine canneries, their acrid scents heavy in the air. Gyssling was on his way to meet Detective Cooper at the Diekmann Brothers butchery. From his one contentious meeting with the brothers, Gyssling knew they were tough, taciturn men. He counted on Cooper to convince them, by any means necessary to finger Pelley as the brains—loosely speaking—behind the armory heist.

Settling back in the passenger compartment of the limo, Gyssling turned on the radio from the mahogany-trimmed control panel.

"Disappointment in Manhattan today," the announcer said, sounding dismayed himself. "Thunderstorms have scuttled plans for the *Hindenburg* to fly over the city. Instead, the great German airship will head directly to Lakehurst, New Jersey, arriving just seventy-seven hours after leaving Frankfurt."

Gyssling was less concerned with the *Hindenburg*'s arrival than its departure the next day. Joseph and Magda Goebbels were booked on the return flight to Frankfurt. This evening, they would depart Los Angeles on the propaganda chief's Heinkel He 111, a two-engine aircraft that would require two stops for refueling to reach New York.

I must make my case against Pelley today.

Rolfe pulled the Mercedes to a stop in front of a two-story brick building, its ancient mortar bleeding, the bricks stained gray-black from a hundred years of belching smokestacks along the harbor. Somewhere nearby, a train whistle blew.

Gyssling did not wait for Rolfe to open the door. He exited and immediately heard a voice, "Back here!"

Gyssling entered a narrow alley, where Detective Cooper crouched behind the right rear tire of a Ford panel truck. "Look at this." He pointed to a plug in the right rear tire. "Matches the tread mark at the scene."

Gyssling took in the soot-coated truck, the blackened windows, the lettering on the side barely visible under the grime. It was as if the truck had been on the slopes when Mount Vesuvius destroyed Pompeii. "As if we needed any more proof," he said.

"Yeah, I've seen jalopies come through Oklahoma tornadoes looking spiffier."

Rolfe stayed with the Mercedes, and Gyssling and Cooper entered the building. A cluttered office with two desks just inside the front door was empty, so they made their way to a walk-in meat locker at the end of a long-bloodstained corridor.

As he opened the heavy steel door and stepped inside the locker, the stench of dead meat enveloped Gyssling like a poisonous fog. Skinned pigs and sides of beef hung on meat hooks.

Bundled in mackinaws and wearing blood-spattered aprons, Max and Kurt Diekmann butchered away. The burly Max hacked at a slab of beef with a heavy cleaver, while Kurt wielded a boning knife to separate meat from bones on an oak butcher's block. Max wore a red handkerchief over his nose and mouth, like a bank robber in a Western.

"Look who left his mansion to visit us common workingmen," Kurt said, wiping a splash of blood from his face with his sleeve. "Our meat wasn't good enough for him, but here he is."

Max pointed his cleaver at Cooper. "And this must be his hired help. I'll bet kidneys to sweetbreads he's the dirtiest cop on the force."

"Shut up, bozos!" Cooper ordered, "or I'll throw you in the clink with a dozen colored guys who won't like your accents."

Max removed the handkerchief from his face, revealing both cheeks as red as raw hamburger, obviously scorched from the fire at the armory.

"Jesus, if you two knuckleheads were any dumber, they'd have to water you twice a week," Cooper said.

With an index finger under his nose to ward off the smell, Gyssling said, "Who put you up to the armory heist?"

"Go pound sand," Max said. "You're not our Führer."

"Was it that lunatic William Pelley?" Gyssling demanded.

"Mr. Pelley is a great man," Kurt said. "He's going to hang Franklin Delano Rosen-*stein*, overthrow the US government, and install a fascist regime."

"Helluva day's work," Cooper said.

Max cleaved the side of beef with a swift and powerful swing. "Mr. Pelley's Silver Legion has a hundred thousand Rangers."

"In his alcoholic delirium," Gyssling said.

"Answer Herr Gyssling's question," Cooper ordered. "Who was behind the armory goat fuck?"

"We ain't snitches," Kurt said.

"It's time we fought back," Max said. "Christians have been persecuted since the days of Christ."

"There were no Christians in the days of Christ," Gyssling corrected him.

"We got nothing to say." Max pointed toward the door with his cleaver, blood dripping from the blade. "Now, scram, why doncha?"

Cooper reached into his suit coat, where a .38 revolver was holstered, and Max drew his arm back, cleaver poised. But Cooper came out with a pack of Lucky Strikes.

"I need something to get rid of the stink in here," he said, lighting up while keeping his eyes on Max. He slipped his right hand back into his suit coat and kept it there. "Try it, pal, and I'll put a hole in you, pound you into a patty, and serve you to my dogs as *wienerschnitzel*."

Without warning, Max swung the cleaver, and Cooper pulled his revolver. But the cleaver tore into a side of beef with a *ker-splat*, blood misting into the air.

For a moment, the only sound was the compressor churning and the fan whirring. Then Cooper holstered his .38 and said, "Now, you palookas listen up. I got you dead to rights." He pulled the scorched piece of Max's shirt from a pocket. "You left this at the scene of the crime. I could impound your truck as evidence right now, and when you're booked and photographed, your faces as red as a baboon's ass, you'll be indicted pronto. Or, if I'm feeling lazy, I might just turn you over to the feds. I'll get a commendation, and you'll do twenty years in Alcatraz for destruction of government property and attempted insurrection."

The brothers kept silent.

"But there's another way," Gyssling said. "Detective Cooper will write up a statement you'll sign saying you were following Pelley's orders when you hit the armory. This is an internal consulate matter, so I will not give the statement to law enforcement. As they might say in a Western, 'It's not your scalps I want.'"

"Do it Herr Gyssling's way, and we're square," Cooper said. "I'll pin the armory job on a couple of commies, and no one's the wiser."

The two brothers exchanged glances, their looks a silent sibling code. After a moment, Kurt said, "Two questions."

"Yeah?" Cooper asked.

"May I have a cigarette?"

"Sure. And…?"

"Do you have a pen and paper?"

Gyssling exhaled a long breath. It's going to be a very good day, he thought, while wondering if the Japanese laundry could remove the stench from his custom-tailored three-piece suit.

62

THE WAR ROOM

Sol y Sombra de Moreno, Forty-Fourth Street, Los Angeles

"You're not going to shoot me," Chaplin said, unafraid.

"How do you know?" the gun-toting young woman with cinnamon skin and puffy eyes replied.

"Because the barrel, cylinder, and frame of the Colt .45 Peacemaker are made of steel, and the grip is bronze. To keep it steady, you'd be holding it with two hands. What you've got is a prop gun for the motion pictures, probably made of Bakelite."

She lowered the gun and wiped a tear with her free hand. "You're not Germans?"

"No," Chaplin said.

"Yes and no," Einstein said. "I renounced my citizenship in thirty-three."

They were standing in the living room of what had been Jimmy Mitchell's apartment, now ransacked and bare. She studied them a moment. "You're Charlie Chaplin!"

"Guilty as charged."

"And you're…you can't be, Albert Einstein?"

Einstein shrugged. "And you are, Miss?"

She coughed, an unhealthy sound, congestion in her chest. "Luisa Moreno. Jimmy's fiancée."

"Oh my," Chaplin said. "I'm so sorry."

"Our deepest condolences," Einstein said. "We only met Jimmy yesterday. What an admirable young man."

"Why did you think we were Germans?" Chaplin asked.

"Before dawn, the police came by and told me that Jimmy had committed suicide, which is a lot of malarkey. I know where he went last night, and I can guess what happened."

Einstein started to say something, but Chaplin shushed him with a wave.

"The police told me to stay in my apartment, someone would come talk to me," Luisa continued, coughing and clearing her throat. "Not ten minutes later, two trucks pulled up. One looked like a moving van, but a tarp was hung over the side, so I couldn't see a name. Four or five men speaking German got out and tore Jimmy's apartment apart, while the cops kept people away.

"When they were done, the Germans came to my door. I didn't answer the knocking or the shouting, so they broke the lock and came in. Either the cops had already left, or they didn't care. The Germans went through every room, tore up all the closets, but they didn't take anything. In Jimmy's apartment, they were looking for his files. In my apartment, they were looking for me."

"But they didn't find you?" Chaplin asked.

"I was in the secret room where Jimmy worked. He called it his 'war room.'"

The men exchanged glances. Chaplin would get back to that, but now he asked, "You said there were two trucks?"

"The second one looked brand-new. An International with the cab over the engine and four rear wheels for heavy loads."

"That's some look you got at it," Einstein said, impressed.

"It's pretty distinctive. A shiny metallic color almost like chrome with smooth lines and curved corners, so it looks a bit like a toaster."

"A truck that looks like a toaster?" Einstein said, trying to picture it. "What's next, a boat like a refrigerator?"

"I never saw anyone get out of the International," she said. "It's like they were just observing what the Germans were doing."

"Something bosses might do," Einstein said.

Chaplin said, "Luisa, did Jimmy ever mention 'Operation Hollywood?'"

She shook her head. "I knew he was investigating American fascists, but he thought it would be dangerous if I knew too much. I did some research for him at the library, but that was it." Her eyes drifted, and it was obvious she was thinking of the man she had lost. "Now, why are you two here?"

The men took turns telling the tale, starting with the baseball game, then the consulate, Jimmy in waiter's attire, the climb up the scaffold, meeting in the consul's office, Jimmy breaking into Magda Goebbels's suite to get evidence, and, in hushed tones, his being thrown from the roof.

"I'm so dreadfully sorry we couldn't protect him," Chaplin said.

"I warned him not to go," Luisa said, "but he was so stubborn and so passionate about justice and democracy." She fought back more tears, coughed again, then said, "I love him and always will."

"Is there a chance," Chaplin asked gently, "that we could see the war room?"

"See it? You have to take it. When the Germans come back, they'll find it."

"The *momzers* are coming back?" Einstein said.

"They left me a note." She reached into her jeans pocket and brought out a slip of paper.

The scrawl was in English: "We will be back, *fräulein*."

Luisa led them down the stairs and around the side of the building to an unmarked, recessed door at the rear of the building. She unlocked a wrought-iron gate on the exterior of the door, and then two locks on the door itself. They entered Luisa's apartment through the rear door, walked along a corridor, passed a bathroom, and into a neat and tidy bedroom. Luisa approached a floor-to-ceiling bookcase and tugged at a book on the lowest shelf. The bookcase squeaked and opened slowly, revealing a door. She used another key to unlock it, and they entered a pitch-black room.

She switched on the light. A desk and chair sat in one corner of the windowless room. All four walls were covered with corkboard, which itself was covered with newspaper clippings in both English and German, Nazi pamphlets, and two pyramids of photos—Germans and Americans—connected by different colored threads. Hitler at the top of the German pyramid and American fascists atop their own groups. William Dudley Pelley, with a pipe in his mouth, crowned the Silver Legion of America pyramid, threads connecting him to photos of underlings below.

The wall of shame had like-minded racists atop diagrams of the German American Bund, the Ku Klux Klan, the Lode Star Legion, the Crusaders for Americanism, and the Black Legion. It nearly took Chaplin's breath away.

So many fascists within our borders! Do the American people have any idea?

Another group, the Christian Front, was labeled "in formation" and was topped by a photo of Father Charles Coughlin, the radio priest. A full-page ad taken in the *Los Angeles Times* by the American Nationalist Party implored gentiles to "prepare the way for an ultimate solution to the Jewish problem." The problem, it seemed, was this: "In Hollywood, international Jewry controls vice, dope, and gambling and provides young gentile girls to be raped."

So many push pins of different colors were stuck in a map of Los Angeles that if the map were a person, it would have bled to death. The pins corresponded to locations of fascist rallies and marches. Dozens of photos surrounded the map, many of well-scrubbed teenagers holding banners: AMERICA FIRST and FASCISM FOR AMERICA. Younger children in uniforms with swastika armbands were pictured at a Nazi summer camp in La Crescenta Park.

"The mother lode of fascism in the States," Chaplin said. "Right in our backyard."

"How can this be happening here?" Einstein said.

Half a dozen clipboards, thick with documents, hung from nails in the corkboard. One listed every cruise ship flying a German flag to have docked at the Ports of Los Angeles and Long Beach in the past year. Another was a list of German nationals who recently entered the ports and airports of California, as well as border crossings from Mexico.

Chaplin opened a desk drawer and found eight notebooks, Jimmy's daily journals, where he'd been, who he'd talked to, what had been said.

"It's going to take a week to go through all this," he said. "We'll take everything to my house."

"You'll need a truck," Luisa said.

"I have lots of trucks and lots of men. Do you have a phone?"

After Chaplin called his studio and arranged for a truck and four men, he sat with Einstein and Luisa at her kitchen table. She made tea, following Chaplin's instructions for "a good strong cuppa," and they sipped and talked.

"Jimmy's death won't be in vain," Chaplin said.

"Justice for Jimmy. That's our mission," Einstein said. "Thanks to his work, we have a chance to stop the American Nazis before they get started."

"How?" Luisa asked. "Jimmy said the LAPD is filled with Nazi sympathizers, and after today, I see he's right."

"The force has some good eggs," Chaplin said, "but not at the top. We have a sergeant who's helping us."

"One sergeant?" She sounded deflated. "What about the FBI?"

"Mr. Hoover thinks we're subversives," Einstein said.

"So what will you do? You're not detectives."

Einstein sipped his tea and said, "In a sense, I am. If you touch hot lead, you will get burned."

"A metaphor, Albert?" Chaplin asked.

"Not at all. I have ascertained that Miss Moreno met Mr. Mitchell at the *Sentinel*, where she is a Linotype operator."

"Jimmy told you that?" she asked.

"Not at all. You picked up a hot teapot without a glove or pad. That's when I noticed the calluses on your fingers, likely from handling hot lead slugs. Your cough probably comes from inhaling lead and tin fumes in the typesetting room. Several of Mr. Mitchell's notebooks are neither handwritten nor typed. They're printed in newspaper font, obviously from a letterpress, probably used by you at the *Sentinel* after hours."

"Impressive, Sherlock Einstein," she said.

"Albert is the brains of our operation, and I'm the brawn," Chaplin said.

She regarded Chaplin skeptically, as he wasn't much larger than the average jockey at Santa Anita.

"He's stronger than he looks," Einstein said.

Unwilling to leave Luisa alone, the two men waited until the studio crew arrived with the truck. As the crew carefully took apart the war room, Luisa packed a small suitcase.

"Where will you go?" Einstein asked.

"Friends in Mexicali. The doctor says the heat will be good for my lungs."

"Maybe replace that Bakelite revolver with a real one," Chaplin said.

"I'll be fine. I have seven male cousins there." She closed the suitcase and placed it on the floor. "The gun belongs to my uncle. Antonio Moreno."

"The star of *The Border Legion*?" Chaplin said. "That Antonio Moreno?"

"Do you know him?"

"I know everybody! That handsome devil is a fine actor."

"Sure. In silent pictures, when no one could hear his Spanish accent. In talkies, he just gets Pancho roles. It's a cruel business."

"But not all the people are cruel. Have Antonio call me. I'll have work for him. Good roles."

"Thank you, Mr. Chaplin."

"This place. *Sol y Sombra de Moreno*. He owns the building?"

"'Moreno's Sun and Shadow.' He thought it was a metaphor for his life in the industry."

"It's everybody's life, Luisa. Someday, it will be mine."

63
THE PACIFIST FASCIST

Clifton's Cafeteria, Downtown Los Angeles

On a mission to pin the armory heist on some local commies, Detective Carl Cooper hoofed it along Seventh Street, passing the Loew's theater where the marquee advertised *Strike Me Pink*, which he had already seen. Eddie Cantor played a meek young fellow, a real milksop, who had a crush on a brassy nightclub singer played by Ethel Merman. Cooper hated the picture, especially the timid male lead character.

Give me Cagney smashing Mae Clarke in the face with a grapefruit for giving him lip, that's what I wanna see.

Cooper turned onto Olive Street, stepping lively as a Red Car rang its bell and nearly flattened him. A sign on the corner read: US ROUTE 66 NOW EXTENDED TO THE SEA.

He entered Clifton's Cafeteria, a downtown eatery that looked like the background in Looney Tunes cartoons. It had a waterfall, a babbling brook, trees both alive and neon, a wishing well, and a sign inviting patrons to PAY WHAT YOU WISH. DINE FREE UNLESS DELIGHTED. The owner was a do-gooder, feeding the unemployed, welcoming the rich and the poor, cops and mobsters, regular Joes, a sea of white, black, brown, and yellow faces, a local League of Nations eating meat loaf and mashed potatoes. It was also the hangout for any number of commies, pinkos, and fellow travelers.

Cooper headed toward a back corner of the restaurant, where he spotted a long table of young people engaged in an animated discussion with gesturing hands and bobbing heads. He passed diners chowing down on fried chicken and Jell-O salads, then sidestepped a waitress carrying a tray with banana cream pie and red velvet cake. He stopped behind a pillar where he could observe the table of chatterboxes.

There were about a dozen men and women, mostly in their twenties, drinking coffee, munching doughnuts. Wannabe revolutionaries, most wore red berets or red scarves, as if their soiled dungarees, scuffed shoes, and unshaven faces weren't sufficient to advertise their Marxism.

Easy enough to pick a couple patsies to bust for the armory fiasco.

The lefties were arguing with two clean-shaven, neatly dressed young men. One was a blond kid of about eighteen wearing a corduroy newsboy's cap, a plaid cotton shirt buttoned to the neck, pressed khaki chinos, and brown oxfords. The other was a slim, sandy-haired fellow a couple years older in a blue denim shirt with two breast pockets, pleated trousers in a darker blue, and black-and-white saddle shoes.

"Communism is doomed to fail because the masses, by definition, cannot lead," said the older, denim-shirt guy.

The Red Brigade pounded the table and hissed.

"You're so wrong, Dieter," said a short-haired, pale woman in a red beret. "Fascism is doomed because of its basic inhumanity."

"Communism by its nature brings chaos," Dieter fired back. "I give you Lenin and Stalin."

"Authoritarians by their nature are evil," the woman replied. "I give you Mussolini and Hitler."

The clean-cut kid in the newsboy's cap spoke up. "Bolsheviks have committed far greater atrocities."

"Gus is right," Dieter said, Cooper now figuring that Gus and Dieter were outnumbered fascists. One of the commies, a young man with a pile of wavy dark hair, strummed a chord on a guitar. Cooper recognized him from a couple of busts for vagrancy and loitering. Woody Guthrie. No occupation, no permanent address, no musical talent Cooper could discern.

"Socialism is the only way to cure economic inequality," Guthrie said, the guitar chord still in the air.

Cooper stepped from behind the pillar and approached the table. "What's the rumpus?"

"An intellectual debate," one of the red beret men said.

"You wouldn't understand, Detective," Guthrie said.

"Lock up the pig's knuckles!" the young woman with short hair yelled in the direction of the kitchen. "The flatfoot's here."

"Class is over, kiddies." Cooper scanned the table and said, "Seeing a few new faces. I gotta tell Chief Davis the Bum Blockade at the border ain't working."

Guthrie strummed and sang in an Oklahoma twang:

"*Pretty Boy grabbed a log chain, And the deputy grabbed his gun, In the fight that followed, he laid that deputy down.*"

"Give it up, Guthrie," Cooper said. "You sound like a Model A that needs a brake job." He grabbed a chair, swung it around, and sat, straddling it. "So, where were you last night, anyway?"

"Ask your wife!" Guthrie shot back.

Cooper tugged at an earlobe and said, "How'd you like to spend the night in jail?"

"Depends," Guthrie said. "Chipped beef on toast again?"

A waitress came to the table with a coffeepot in each hand and set about refilling cups.

Fudging freeloaders, Cooper thought. When she was gone, he said, "You clowns might have heard. Some Reds tried to knock over the armory in Long Beach last night."

"These Bolsheviks wouldn't have the balls," Dieter said.

Cooper took a long look at Dieter and noticed that a name was sewn in black thread above the left breast pocket of his denim shirt: DIEKMANN BROTHERS FINE WHOLESALE MEATS.

Holy shit!

"Hey, smart guy," Cooper said. "Are you related to those dumb shit butchers?"

"Kurt and Max are my older brothers," Dieter said.

"So you're the runt of the litter."

"Not intellectually."

"Ain't saying much. Whadaya doing with these pinkos?"

"Teaching my young friend Gus how to deal with communists face-to-face."

"Other than kicking 'em in the nuts," Gus said.

"How long's this gonna take, Detective?" Guthrie asked.

"What's your hurry? Planning a one-way trip to Moscow?"

"Doncha know?" Guthrie strummed another chord on his guitar. "This land may be your land, but it's also my land."

"Bullshit! We don't need you Okies crapping in the middle of Broadway."

"Witness the tool of the corrupt police state," Guthrie said.

"Agree with you there," Dieter chimed in.

"Glad I could bring all you misfits together," Cooper said.

This was getting complicated, Cooper thought. The Diekmann kid would damn well know the commies didn't do the armory job. His idiot brothers might have already told him that they fessed up earlier in the meat locker. Cooper had no qualms about making false arrests, but he didn't like getting caught making false arrests. He needed time to think.

"I gotta take a piss," Cooper said, and headed for the men's room. He was about to open the door to the head when someone entered from the restaurant's rear door. Through the open doorway, Cooper spotted a yellow roadster in the parking space closest to the restaurant.

What do we have here?

His trousers half-unbuttoned, Cooper went outside and checked out a Studebaker with its top down, and yep, the hood ornament was an eagle clutching a swastika.

Son of a bitch! Most days, you step in mud up to your knees. But some days you just walk into a field of daisies.

There was no investigation of the stadium incident, so nothing to be gained at the department, Cooper knew. But Gyssling would love to know who tried to run down Chaplin and Einstein and, more important, who ordered it.

And when Gyssling wants something, there are a couple of C-notes in it for me.

He used a pocketknife to jimmy the glove box.

⊱⊰

Walking back into the restaurant, Cooper held up the Studebaker's registration card. "Which one of you bozos is Emil Gustafsson?" Looking at Gus, he continued. "I'm betting it's you, kid."

"Emil's my old man," Gus said. "Whazzit to ya?"

"C'mon, tough guy." Cooper grabbed him by the scruff of the neck and pulled him into the back corridor, the commies hissing like a pit of snakes and Dieter yelling, "You've got constitutional rights, Gus!"

Once they were away from the crowd, Cooper said, "Who got you to pull that stunt at the stadium?"

"Don't know shit about that."

"Dummy up if you want. I'll just take you downtown and sweat you."

"Do what you gotta do."

Cooper lowered his voice. "I got no beef with you fascists. You get that, right?"

"Cops are just thugs for hire. My Pop pays off two patrolmen every week just to keep his garage open."

"Cost of doing business,"

"I got a good idea of who's paying you today," Gus said, "but tomorrow...?"

Jesus, these friggin' kids today!

"Don't be a chump. The cop you almost hit, the colored lady, can ID you. You wanna do time? Cute fellow like you, you'll get passed around like a cherry Danish."

Gus studied the tops of his brown oxfords, his expression losing its arrogance. "If I have a criminal record, I won't get into USC."

"What! You wanna be a college man?"

"Like Dieter. He has a swell time jawing with the Bolshevik professors. Says I could make the grade."

"So why the hell did you try to kill two of the most famous men in the world?"

"I didn't! I mean, I thought about it. But in the end, I just wanted to scare them."

"Sorry, Gustafsson. I ain't buying what you're selling."

Gus chewed his lower lip and seemed to be thinking about how much to say. Cooper would wait the kid out. Suspects feel a deep psychological need to fill silences when their lawyers aren't there to order them to clam up.

After a moment, Gus said, "Sure, I was supposed to run them over. But we can protect the Aryan race without killing anyone. Like the Nuremberg Laws. Strip Jews of citizenship, restrict employment and marriage, and murder becomes unnecessary."

"Let's say I believe you're a pacifist fascist and want to cut you a break," Cooper said. "We're back to square one. Who put you up to it?"

"I ain't a squealer."

"Don't be a sap, kid. Don't you wanna watch Ambling Amby Schindler?"

"Who?"

"The USC quarterback. Come September, you could be in the Coliseum watching that sweet bastard play, or you could be staring through bars at Folsom. What's it gonna be?"

64
THE TWENTIETH CENTURY BELONGS TO THE REICH

Alt Heidelberg, South Alvarado Street

William Dudley Pelley was stewing. The armory heist had been a disaster. It was all over the radio, the only saving grace was that a police spokesman said communist agents were the prime suspects.

If he tallied up the hits, runs, and errors of the last few days, it was an ugly box score. Wendell "Gus" Gustafsson had failed to injure, much less exterminate, Chaplin and Einstein. Pinch-hitting, Ancel Eckart never took a swing, never got off a shot in Einstein's driveway. The Diekmann brothers were good Joes, but criminy, how they gummed up the works! Then there was Skowron, the only one who'd come through. The greatest job of sacking a synagogue since the Romans pillaged the temple of Jerusalem.

When the insurrection comes, when the flames burn, he will be by my side!

The thought brightened Pelley's mood as he walked along Alvarado Street downtown.

He sensed his day was about to improve when he heard the joyous sounds billowing out of the open doors of Alt Heidelberg, the friendliest place in town for German Americans. Songs, cheers, whoops, and hollers, induced by equal portions of beer and the excitement over the *Hindenburg*. The great airship was approaching Lakehurst, New Jersey, and Pelley hurried along so he could join his men and listen to the radio broadcast.

More than two hundred hardy patrons, nearly all men, were jammed into the biergarten, the smoke-filled air heavy with the tang of spilled beer and sizzling bratwursts. Young waitresses, mostly blondes—natural and bottle enhanced—scurried about, delivering steins of beer and replenishing bowls of sauerkraut on the long wooden tables. Their Alpine dirndl attire—tight-waisted bodices, low-cut, puffy-sleeved blouses, and knee-high white stockings—added to the Bavarian atmosphere the men cherished even if they'd never been farther east than San Bernardino.

At one end of the long mahogany bar, slick with beer suds, several men pressed their ears to a Philco console radio to hear over the roar of the *biertrinkers*. Periodic reports were coming in from New Jersey, and the listeners would shout the latest, their voices drowned out by drunken men singing the Horst-Wessel song in German.

"Mr. Pelley. Mr. Pelley."

He turned to find two tall, lean men in black wool suits, starched white shirts, and black ties. He recognized them as SS officers from the consulate. One handed him a purple velvet bag with a gold drawstring.

"With Herr Goebbels's compliments," he said in a German accent.

Pelley opened the bag and pulled out a bottle of Liebfraumilch 1929. "My favorite Riesling!" he said. "How thoughtful. And you are…?"

"Sebastian Koch," one SS officer said.

"Friedrich Koch," said the other. "Herr Goebbels sent us to help you."

"Help me what?"

Sebastian said, "For your Silver Shirts. Surveillance. Security. And…Friedrich, what do they call it in the American movies?"

"Freezers," Friedrich said.

Pelley was confused, and Sebastian said, "Not freezers. Ice. If you need someone iced, we are your men."

"Well, that's…grand," Pelley said. "But I'm not sure you really want to…"

"Herr Goebbels insists!" That stopped Pelley.

Goebbels wants his eyes and ears on me. And what Goebbels wants…

"Well, pleased to have you," Pelley said, forcing a smile. Friedrich scanned the crowd. "Your men?"

"Many of them," Pelley said.

"They drink a good game. Can they fight?"

"Some of them."

"We will be in touch." The brothers turned and disappeared into the throng.

Needing a drink stiffer than beer, Pelley pulled out his flask and took a long, hearty pull of rye whiskey.

No more foul-ups, Pelley vowed. With his relentless optimism, he believed this could be a positive development. He would impress Goebbels, who had momentous influence in Berlin. But that would have to wait. Today was the glory of the *Hindenburg*. He looked for the staircase to the mezzanine, where his officers awaited him.

Sitting behind his gleaming desk, Gyssling could not decide when to deliver the kill shot, when to reveal to Goebbels that Pelley was a blowhard, a hapless amateur who could not be trusted. Gyssling fidgeted in his chair and downed his Scotch quicker than he should have.

Why am I so nervous? I have Pelley dead to rights, as they say in the American crime movies.

Handwritten statements implicating Pelley in the stadium assault and the armory heist were neatly folded in a pocket of Gyssling's pin-striped suit, waiting to be unveiled. Detective Cooper had come through twice today, first with the Diekmann brothers, then delivering the bonus of the young Studebaker driver fingering Pelley for the stadium fiasco. Gyssling had peeled off three hundred-dollar bills, and the detective had grinned and said, "Mighty white of you, Herr Gyssling."

Gyssling did not particularly care for the expression, but Cooper probably thought he was currying favor, rather than disgust. Gyssling remembered what Chaplin had said to Einstein at the party.

"Georg is one of the good Nazis."

But he wondered: Is there such a thing?

Joseph and Magda Goebbels also sat in Gyssling's office, holding their own tumblers of Scotch. Each leaned toward the Telefunken console radio that took up a considerable amount of wall space.

"We're just minutes away from the *Hindenburg* docking at the Naval Air Station," the radio announcer said, his voice rising with excitement. "It will be quite a sight to behold, as the giant airship drops a mooring cable to the ground crew, which will secure it to the tall, slender mast and winch the lighter-than-air craft to the ground."

Goebbels sipped his Scotch and said, "I hope the lighting is right for the newsreel boys." Of course, that would be Goebbels's main concern. He had made certain that Universum-Film AG, the German newsreel company, was on hand, and he'd paid the way for British Pathé, Paramount, Movietone, Universal Newsreel, and News of the Day to film the event.

"Next week at this time, every movie theater in the world will be showing the might of German aviation," Goebbels had told everyone who would listen.

"Luxury travel has been revolutionized by this magnificent craft of the skies," the announcer said, "and not just because of the Rhine salmon, champagne, and caviar on the menu. One wonders how the United States has fallen so far behind Germany in airship development!"

Goebbels hoisted his glass and called out, "Because the Twentieth Century belongs to the Reich!"

⌘

Pelley climbed the stairs to the mezzanine of Alt Heidelberg, where a dozen Silver Legion of America officers waited. Serious men in business suits and ties, some with swastika armbands. The captains were company commanders of the Silver Shirts, leading five platoons of twenty-five men each. A few colonels were battalion commanders with five hundred men under their wings. A brigade commander led two thousand men. Every week, the number of Silver Shirts grew.

The triumph of the *Hindenburg*, proof of the might of the Reich, should be worth several hundred new recruits, Pelley thought. He shook hands and greeted each of his officers and looked over the railing at the patrons in the bar below. A sturdy group of workingmen. Most would be good soldiers. A cloud of cigar and cigarette smoke floated up from the bar and hung like a ghostly shroud over the mezzanine. One of his captains turned up the volume on an RCA Victor in the corner.

"This is Herbert Morrison of WLS Chicago, reporting from the Naval Air Station at Lakehurst, New Jersey," came the voice on the radio.

The captains, colonels, and brigade commanders hooted and hollered.

"Well, here it comes, ladies and gentlemen," Morrison said on the radio. "And what a great sight it is, a thrilling one, just a marvelous sight. It's coming down out of the sky, pointed directly toward us and toward the mooring mast. The mighty diesel motors just roared, the propellers biting into the air and throwing it back into a gale-like whirlpool."

Two waitresses, loaded down with trays of beer and pretzels, served Pelley's officers, ignoring a pinch here, a squeeze there.

"Now and then the propellers are caught in the rays of the sun," Morrison continued. "The sun is striking the windows of the observation deck on the eastward side and sparkling like glittering jewels on the background of black velvet."

"Fellow's a poet!" a Silver Shirts colonel enthused.

"The ship is riding majestically toward us like some great feather," Morrison said, "riding as though it was mighty proud of the place it's playing in the world's aviation. The ship is no doubt busting with activity. Orders are shouted to the crew, the passengers lining the windows looking down at the field ahead of them, getting their glimpse of the mooring mast."

Pelley wished he were there. Wouldn't he love being on the return trip to Frankfurt with Herr and Frau Goebbels? He imagined meeting Göring, Himmler, and Hess, and who knows, perhaps even the Führer himself. Well, someday.

☞ ☜

In the consul's office, Joseph Goebbels paced like an expectant father outside the delivery room. Magda's cheeks were flushed, either from the whiskey or something approaching sexual excitement.

"It's practically standing still now," Morrison said on the radio. "They've dropped ropes out of the nose of the ship, and it's been taken ahold of down on the field by a number of men."

Goebbels raised his tumbler of Scotch and said, "To the *Hindenburg* and Aryan supremacy!"

On the radio, Morrison said, "It's starting to rain again. The back motors of the ship are just holding it, just enough to keep it from…"

There was a pause. *Did they lose the broadcast?*

Morrison's voice returned, so loud as to hurt the eardrums. "IT BURST INTO FLAMES! It burst into flames! Get out of the way! Get out of the way!"

Magda and Joseph exchanged dumbfounded looks. Could this be real? Was it some trick?

Some cruel joke?

"Get this, Charlie! Get this, Charlie! It's burning, and it's crashing! It's crashing terrible! Oh my, get out of the way, please. It's burning, bursting into flames, and it's falling on the mooring mast, and this is terrible. This is one of the worst catastrophes in the world."

Gyssling looked at Magda, whose head was in her hands. Joseph fell back into his chair, dropping his Scotch, which splashed onto the carpet.

"And oh, it's burning," Morrison carried on, "four or five hundred feet into the sky. The smoke and the flames and now the frame is crashing to the ground, not quite to the mooring mast. Oh, the humanity!"

⁌ ⁍

Pelley gripped the railing of the mezzanine and looked down into the snake pit of humanity. The men were screaming, shouting, crying.

"Saboteurs!"

"Communists!"

"Jews!"

Pelley picked up the handset of a brass telephone, dialed zero for the operator, and said, "German consulate, Los Angeles."

After the switchboard directed the call to his study, Gyssling answered, then said to Goebbels, "It's for you, Joseph. William Pelley."

But he didn't immediately hand Goebbels the phone. Covering the mouthpiece with a hand, he said, "Joseph, I must talk to you about Pelley. I have proof that he was behind both the armory and the stadium debacles." He reached into his pocket for the handwritten statements.

"Not now, Georg!" Goebbels fired back. "Priorities, *Jesus Christus!*"

Gyssling handed Goebbels the phone and did the only thing he could do. Listen to one end of the conversation.

"*Ja. Ja.* I understand, William," Goebbels said. "You need twenty-three MG 34s. I can do better. How about two hundred?"

Gyssling kept his diplomat's poker face, even as a knot tightened his stomach.

Two hundred machine guns for this lunatic!

"And one hundred Mauser rifles and all the ammunition you need," Goebbels continued. "Don't worry. Hirohito can wait." A moment's pause, and then, "Stuttgart tomorrow. I cannot say more on the telephone."

Gyssling tried to make sense of what he was hearing.

Stuttgart? What does a city in southern Germany have to do with machine guns and rifles? And we're sending weapons to Japan? So much I don't know.

Goebbels hung up, and Gyssling tried again. "Joseph, please listen. Pelley is not reliable. He will do a great deal of harm."

"Do you realize the world just changed?" Goebbels said. "Pelley's a man of action, Georg, and you are not. And the Reich needs him to do a great deal of harm."

65
DEMOCRACY IS SO FRAGILE

May 7, 1937 - Chaplin Estate

It was the morning after the *Hindenburg* disaster, and while Chaplin and Einstein listened to news accounts the night before, their focus today was on Operation Hollywood. Sergeant Georgia Robinson joined them for one of Maurice's breakfasts: fresh-squeezed orange juice, hotcakes, corned beef hash with poached eggs, and several cups of coffee.

During the night, carpenters and set designers from United Artists, Chaplin's studio, reassembled Jimmy Mitchell's war room in the pool house. It was all there, the newspaper clippings, photographs, notebooks, maps, clipboards, journals, passport records, customs, ports, and airport records.

Somewhere in the documents, Einstein and Chaplin hoped, would be the clue to just where Pelley was getting and storing machine guns for Operation Hollywood.

Now Timothy Dozier, a private investigator who had worked both for Chaplin and his studio, was bent over his Photostat machine, which in a little over two minutes could produce a photograph of a one-page document. Dozier, who was given to white linen suits with matching lily-of-the-valley flowers in his lapel, believed in technology, and his business card boasted "Modern PI."

Copying the documents had been Georgia Robinson's idea. She had called a friend in the Denver office of the FBI, who in turn called the special agent in charge of the Los Angeles office, circumventing John No-Last-Name, LAPD Chief Davis's buddy. When Dozier had finished with the laborious task of copying a sample of the documents—it would take weeks to do them all—Robinson would take them to a meeting with the special agent in charge. He insisted that the meeting be off-site and off the books, both fine with Robinson.

It was just after noon when Chaplin and Einstein walked Robinson to her Ford sedan, which was parked in front of the mansion. Just as she exited the driveway with a valise of photographed documents in her trunk, a black Mercedes limousine pulled up the slope and stopped a few feet from the front steps.

Chaplin watched as the driver's door opened, and a uniformed chauffeur, a fit man with a thick neck, stepped out, his double-breasted tunic hanging open, revealing a Luger in a shoulder holster. Georg Gyssling did not wait for the chauffeur. He opened his own door, a cigarette dangling from a corner of his mouth.

Chaplin exchanged a glance with Einstein, then studied the chauffeur. "Georg, we're not going for a ride, if that's what you have in mind."

"Heavens, no!" He took a step, stumbled a bit, and turned to the chauffeur. "Rolfe, please take a walk, but don't frighten anyone."

Gyssling leaned against the front fender of the limo, two feet from one of the small, mounted Nazi flags. He exhaled a puff of smoke, tossed his cigarette butt, and ground it out with the toe of a polished black tasseled loafer. He wore pleated gray plaid trousers and a yellow piqué polo shirt. It was the first time Chaplin had seen the consul without a dark suit and tie.

"What's this about, Georg?" Chaplin asked.

"Life, liberty, and the pursuit of Pelley."

"Have you been drinking so early in the day, Herr Gyssling?" Einstein asked.

"Copious quantities," Gyssling admitted.

"Because of the *Hindenburg*?" Chaplin ventured.

"Only indirectly. It was the communists or the Jews, you know. Maybe even gypsies or dwarfs. Couldn't have been German engineering."

"Most likely, it was just a simple spark," Einstein said. "Hydrogen has low ignition energy and high flame speed, a deadly combination."

Gyssling gathered his thoughts a moment and said, "Pelley was behind the assault at the stadium."

"We know, Georg," Chaplin said. "He practically admitted it at the consulate."

"He's been trying to get his hands on a cache of machine guns."

"We know that, too."

"Taking into account the stadium assault," Gyssling said, "a fair inference would be that he plans to kill the two of you, plus many others."

"Herr Gyssling," Einstein said, "do you know when he's getting the weapons?"

"Today, Professor."

"How and where?" Chaplin pressed him.

"I don't know," Gyssling said, "but I have a clue that may help. Perhaps by working together, we can save lives and put Pelley in prison."

⋈

The three men sat at a banquette in the kitchen, Gyssling swilling coffee to sober up and nibbling coconut macaroons.

"Charlie, are we friends?" Gyssling asked.

Chaplin saw nothing to be gained from lying. "We enjoy bantering, chatting about motion pictures, music, and women, but no, we've never been friends, Georg."

That seemed to deflate the German, who leaned back, his chin sinking toward his chest.

"Goebbels doesn't trust me, and I could be recalled to Berlin at any time."

Never has the word "recalled" carried such ominous portent, Chaplin thought. "Friends or not, Georg, I would hate for you to be in peril," he said.

"The last twenty-four hours, I have been searching for a missing file," Gyssling said.

"What file is that?"

"If it had a label, it would read, "Georg Gyssling, Honor and Integrity.""

"Did you find it?" Einstein asked.

"I'm here, Professor, aren't I?"

"We're listening," Chaplin said.

"Democracy is so fragile," Gyssling said, seemingly out of nowhere. "Athens lasted what, two centuries before it fell to Sparta? Will American democracy last even that long?"

"Why wouldn't it?" Chaplin said. "Is Germany planning an attack?"

"Not directly. The United States can only be destroyed from within. Your Abraham Lincoln said as much. 'If destruction be our lot, we must ourselves be its author.'"

"And you're saying William Pelley is what, the perpetrator of another civil war?" Chaplin asked.

"One of many who are trying. If democracy is a shop of crystal figurines, Pelley and his cohorts are vandals with satchels of rocks."

"C'mon, Georg. You're talking in circles. Spill."

Gyssling picked up a coconut macaroon, studied it, put it back on the plate.

"Yesterday, just after the *Hindenburg* explosion, Joseph Goebbels spoke to Pelley by telephone. Goebbels told him he could have two hundred machine guns plus one hundred Mauser rifles and ammunition."

"Sodding hell!" Chaplin said. "Two hundred machine guns! We had heard twenty-three."

"Oy gevalt!" Einstein said.

"MG 34's from Germany," Gyssling said. "Goebbels told Pelley that 'Hirohito can wait,' as if the weapons were intended for Japan. And he said, 'Stuttgart tomorrow.'"

Calmer, Einstein said, "Herr Gyssling, how do you interpret it?"

"'Tomorrow' would be today. Other than that, I have no idea."

"Stuttgart," Einstein said, closing his eyes, imagining the city but seeing nothing to solve the mystery.

"Georg, what did you mean about putting Pelley in prison?" Chaplin asked.

"Ah, yes. It's a federal crime to possess machine guns. Get your authorities to apprehend Pelley with the weapons, and he'll do decades in prison."

"The authorities don't listen to us, Georg. Especially the FBI, but we have an LAPD sergeant who has a contact there, and we're hoping for the best."

"Hoping, are you?" Gyssling said.

"Why so dismissive?" Einstein asked.

"There's no time to depend on others. And why would you stop now?"

"What do you mean, 'stop?'" Chaplin asked.

Gyssling reached into a pocket and handed Chaplin his black felt tuxedo button.

"You left this in my office. Such a foolhardy act, Charlie, with the SS everywhere, but incredibly brave. The two of you, with your brains and your skills, just finish what you started. Whatever has to be done, do it yourselves."

"And you, Georg?" Chaplin asked.

Gyssling laughed ruefully. "I just committed treason. That's about as far as I can go."

66
STUTTGART

Chaplin Mansion, Pool House

The interior of the pool house was virtually identical to Jimmy Mitchell's war room.

Chaplin walked around the perimeter, scanning the documents on the wall, hoping for inspiration. "Where will they get the machine guns, and where will they keep them?" he said, as much to himself as to his friend. "And what the hell does Stuttgart have to do with it?"

Einstein was troubled, plagued by the fear that they would let Jimmy down, that Pelley and his rock-throwing vandals, to use Gyssling's imagery, would embark on a bloody rampage far worse than they had imagined.

Two hundred machine guns!

Chaplin was in constant motion, tearing through the documents, rifling files, scouring the clipboards and items pinned to the walls. Einstein stood, virtually motionless, other than sipping a cup of tea. He solved problems with quiet thought, and now considered just how the Reich would likely deliver the weapons to Pelley.

A large mass. And heavy. Not something you put in the trunk of a car. And where would the weapons be stored? In close proximity to where the Silver Shirts would train. Certainly not a city neighborhood or even populated areas of the nearby valleys.

"Charlie, where would you train a paramilitary?"

"In the mountains or canyons, which narrows it down to a few hundred thousand acres." A thought seemed to cross Chaplin's face, lighting up his eyes like a burst of sunlight.

"Hang on to your hat, Guv'nor!"

"I don't wear hats, Charlie."

Chaplin pulled a thick folder from a box his studio crew had packed at Jimmy Mitchell's apartment.

"The Murphy Ranch," Chaplin said. "A compound in Rustic Canyon. According to Jimmy's notes, the owners are Nazi sympathizers who've turned the property over to the Silver Shirts."

"Nazis have ranches here?" Einstein said. "Hitler's cowboys?"

Chaplin thumbed through architectural drawings and blueprints. "Plans call for a giant water tank, a diesel generator, bomb shelters, and a four-story mansion with a tower for God knows what."

"Keeping a watch or shooting intruders," Einstein guessed.

Chaplin pulled a map from the file and ran a finger across it. "Damn, this can't be the place. Even though it's in the mountains, that's the Palisades. There are houses out there, and you're not gonna train with machine guns where they can be heard or where hikers might stumble into your camp."

"Let's go back to Stuttgart," Einstein said.

"It could be a code. Maybe each letter corresponds to a word, but we don't have any way to decode it."

"Occam's Razor," Einstein said.

"Meaning?"

"Often, the simplest explanation is the correct one. Newton's elegant universal law of gravitation is an example. A code adds a layer of complexity that might not be necessary."

"Okay, I'll play that game. 'Stuttgart' might mean the weapons are being shipped from there. But to where?"

There was a knock at the pool house door, and without waiting for an invitation, Douglas Fairbanks walked in. He wore white linen trousers, rolled up at the ankles, and a beige turtleneck. His hair was parted in the middle, his mustache neatly trimmed, and despite the dissipation of alcohol and aging, his eyes still twinkled.

"How wags the world, gents?" he asked.

"More dangerous by the minute," Chaplin said. "How are you, Doug?"

"Sober as a judge. Not my divorce judge, but most of them." He nodded toward Einstein. "Good morning, Professor."

"Mr. Fairbanks," Einstein replied. "I was very sorry to learn of your divorce."

"Ah, marriage is like a beleaguered city," Fairbanks said theatrically. "Those that are out want to get in. Those that are in want to get out."

"That's very eloquent," Einstein said.

"It should be," Fairbanks said. "It's from *The Private Life of Don Juan*."

"We're really busy, Doug," Chaplin said.

Fairbanks scanned the walls. "The Nazi business? I got your message that I'm on some hit list. Professor, did you know my father was Jewish?"

"I did not."

"So, what's your play, fellows?" Fairbanks asked.

Chaplin summarized what they knew about Operation Hollywood and the machine guns, first thought to be twenty-three in number and now two hundred, with both assassinations and insurrection in the plans.

"Those Nazi knuckleheads!" Fairbanks said. "Right here in our country."

Fairbanks was sincere, Einstein thought, but he spoke with the diction and volume of a hammy stage actor delivering his lines to the third balcony.

Chaplin then told Fairbanks about the mysterious message, "Stuttgart tomorrow."

"I've been to Stuttgart," Fairbanks said.

"And…?" Chaplin said, hoping for some revelation.

"Mary and I toured Germany in twenty-nine to promote *The Taming of the Shrew*. If you think we argued in the picture, you should have been in our stateroom."

"Does anything stand out about Stuttgart that might help us?" Einstein asked. "I've racked my brain and have nothing."

Fairbanks shrugged. "Nice city. Friendly people. Excellent food. We were supposed to sail back to New York on the *Bremen*, but at the last minute they switched us to the *Hamburg*. Brand new. Helluva nice ship."

"Uh-huh," said Chaplin, who had returned his attention to Jimmy Mitchell's documents.

"I was hoping we could all have lunch at Riviera but can see you two are busy beavers," Fairbanks said, heading for the door. "Godspeed, gents."

Fairbanks was only gone a few seconds when Einstein said, "*Hamburg*! *Bremen*!"

"Yeah?" Chaplin said.

Einstein smacked himself on the head, "So simple! German cruise lines name their ships after cities. SS *Hamburg*. SS *Bremen*. SS *Potsdam*."

"Is there an SS *Stuttgart*?"

"I don't know. But yesterday Goebbels said 'Stuttgart tomorrow.'"

"The port schedules!" they said simultaneously.

It took a moment to find Mitchell's clipboard with the arrivals and departures of German ships. The most recent page was on top. Chaplin traced an index finger along the names and dates. Nothing. He turned to the second page, and there it was!

"Port of Los Angeles. SS *Stuttgart*, May seventh!" he shouted.

"Today!" Einstein said.

"Albert, look at this. It departs tomorrow for Honolulu and then to Tokyo."

"Goebbels said, 'Hirohito can wait.'"

"But we can't!" Chaplin said. "If it was on time, the *Stuttgart* docked two hours ago."

"What do we do, Charlie?"

"Just what Jimmy Mitchell would have done."

Einstein processed that and said softly, "What Jimmy did got him killed."

"Albert, you're the one who said the world is dangerous, not because of the people who are evil, but because of the people who don't do anything about it."

"Yes, yes, yes. And you've said that one either rises to an occasion or succumbs to it. But are we equipped for this? Shouldn't we call Sergeant Robinson and her FBI contact? They're meeting now."

"But off-site, and she didn't say where. Who knows how long it will take and where she'll go next."

"Let's think it through," Einstein said.

"Quickly, Albert!"

"Do you think we'll see weapons being off-loaded?"

"Doubtful. They'll be crated or bagged or hidden in other cargo."

"So our plan is what?" Einstein prodded him.

"I don't know! Some of my best scenes are extemporaneous. Let's just go!"

Einstein gave it another moment's thought and said, "We can't take the Rolls. It's too conspicuous."

"I have five other motor cars in the garage."

"Then let's rise to the occasion."

With that, they headed out the door.

67
BORN LEADERS

Port of Los Angeles, San Pedro Bay

William Dudley Pelley felt like saluting. It wasn't every day you saw that gorgeous flag flapping in the Southern California breeze. The background, a flaming red, the swastika, as black as a starless night.

The flag of the Reich.

This flag flew from the stern of the SS *Stuttgart*, one of the finest passenger vessels on the seas. Swimming pool, fine dining, even air-conditioning! Thirteen thousand tons of German high technology and advanced engineering. A symbol of Aryan supremacy that stirred his emotions as much as a pretty fräulein with large *brüste*.

The ship had docked a short time earlier, and he watched wealthy, well-dressed passengers tread gingerly down the ramp, but his gaze quickly turned to the longshoremen loading crates onto conveyor belts from the cargo hold.

His crates!

The machine guns and rifles would be in crates labeled NITROPHOSKA, a granular fertilizer manufactured by Farben.

As if I'm growing cabbage in the San Fernando Valley!

Inside the crates would be hefty bags that had been repackaged with fertilizer on top and firearms and ammunition below, everything sealed in burlap bags. Pelley had already dealt with the red tape, presenting his credentials and the signed document from Goebbels, diverting a portion of the cargo. He had given the head stevedore three hundred dollars to expedite the work. He had six sturdy men ready to load an International D-400 truck, a sparkling new cab-over-engine model with sufficient power to climb mountains. The truck belonged to a wealthy German American couple, owners of a farm and ranch in the San Gabriel Mountains, trustworthy fascists and Pelley's benefactors.

I learned my lesson with the devoted but dim-witted butchers and their pork wagon.

All he had to do now was clear Customs, and the weapons would be on the road to their new home. More weapons than he needed now, but Operation Hollywood would change that. Next week was the Jew holiday of Shavuot, perfect timing for the slaughter of Hollywood royalty, the spark that would ignite the conflagration.

Thousands will flock to my cause!

The publicity would be nationwide, and he envisioned opening paramilitary compounds across the country. He had visited the German American Bund's Camp Bergwald in New Jersey and Camp Siegfried on Long Island and came away impressed. Pelley hated to admit it, but the Bund was well ahead of his Silver Legion in men, matériel, and training. One year earlier, he had seethed with jealousy when Fritz Kuhn, the group's leader, and several fellow Bundsmen traveled to the Berlin Olympics and had their photos taken with the Führer.

The Bund wanted to move west, and he wanted to move east. That's why Operation Hollywood was so important. It would not just eliminate Chaplin and destroy his plans to humiliate the Führer with a slanderous motion picture. As precise as a surgeon's scalpel, the attack would kill twenty-three enemies in one day…a day that would live forever in history. The Bund would take notice! And so would the Führer.

He imagined Hitler asking Goebbels about the American who struck as quickly as a snake. Goebbels would reveal in hushed tones that Operation Hollywood was only the beginning. Hitler might ponder aloud, "Shouldn't Mr. Pelley be in charge of all clandestine activities in the States?"

His imagination on fire, Pelley could not keep himself from dreaming.

Hitler will see that I, too, am a born leader. We both inspire the masses to hitch up their boots and rain hell on our enemies.

As the Führer himself has said, "He who would live must fight. He who doesn't wish to fight in this world, where permanent struggle is the law of life, has not the right to exist."

68
THE PORT

Port of Los Angeles

The taxicab was painted bright yellow with black lettering on the doors, setting the price at twenty cents for the first quarter mile and a nickel for every quarter mile thereafter. A DeSoto Airstream with oversize tires and six air vents on its front fenders, the cab could carry seven hefty passengers in comfort, but there was only one, and he sat in the front seat next to the driver.

The driver had a neatly trimmed silver-streaked beard and wore a stained and scratched short leather jacket over a white shirt with a maroon tie that did not reach his belly button. A peaked cap with a stiff brim sat cockeyed on his head, and wire-rimmed eyeglasses were perched on his nose.

The beard was stuck to his face with spirit gum. The spectacles were clear glass. The outfit came from the wardrobe department at United Artists, the studio he co-owned.

The driver was, of course, Charlie Chaplin, and the passenger was Albert Einstein. The taxi came from Chaplin's garage. It was a gag prop, as he sometimes wore the outfit and drove the cab to pick up dinner guests. Now, it was Chaplin and Einstein's mode of transportation to the Port of Los Angeles and the SS *Stuttgart*.

Chaplin ignored the speed limits on the way to the port, which was about thirty-five miles due south of Beverly Hills. He knew the area, both from shooting scenes at the port and twice taking the SS *Honolulu* to Hawaii. Traffic was light on the straight shot down Sepulveda Boulevard, continuing on Arizona Avenue. He turned left on Center Street in Manhattan Beach and worked his way over to Normandie Avenue, turned right, and headed south through Torrance and Harbor City, straight into San Pedro. The last few blocks of the drive were through an industrial section of canneries and warehouses and finally a shabby section of bars, bordellos, and cafés frequented by sailors and longshoremen. Upon reaching the port, the change of scenery was immediate. Modern terminals, gleaming cruise ships at the docks, yachts anchored across San Pedro Bay.

With a squeal of brakes, Chaplin stopped the cab on a narrow strip of asphalt that ran down an incline from a passenger terminal to the docks. Quickly exiting the DeSoto, the two men could see the adjacent Port of Long Beach where a US Navy battleship and three destroyers were docked, big guns sealed with muzzle plugs. Peacetime mode. But Chaplin wondered, for how long?

On Terminal Island in the bay, scores of workers were building a dock for the Pan Am Clipper, the luxury flying boat that would soon be carrying passengers to Honolulu in a mere nineteen hours. Heading into port was the SS *Avalon*, one of the Great White Steamers that ferried passengers to and from Catalina Island each day.

Three cruise ships were docked in the berths below the incline. Chaplin and Einstein hurried in that direction, and there she was, moored at Berth Two, the SS *Stuttgart*, a sleek vessel more than five hundred feet long. The German flag, swastika and all, crackled in the sea breeze at her stern.

All the passengers had long since disembarked. A dozen cargo handlers and longshoremen were on the dock, loading crates labeled SUNKIST ORANGES onto conveyor belts that fed into an open cargo hatch.

They're loading cargo!

"Albert, we're too late! They would have unloaded cargo before hauling new freight into the hold. Blast it!"

"Relax, Charlie. Space is not filled with ether."

"What the hell does that mean?"

"Just that early assumptions can be wrong, even by great scientists." Einstein looked toward the longshoremen and spotted a lean man of about fifty in a corduroy jacket and a red cap who held a clipboard instead of a grappling hook.

"That fellow seems to be in charge," he said, gesturing. "Use your acting ability and find out what's what."

Chaplin pasted a concerned look on his face, hurried down the incline, and approached the man in the red cap. "Sir, sir! I'm here to pick up Mr. Pelley." He pointed toward his taxi. "Afraid I'm running behind schedule."

"Too late. He cleared out with his crew at least an hour ago."

Chaplin didn't have to use his acting ability to appear distressed.

"Oh, jumpin' Jesus. I'll be in big trouble with the dispatcher and even more with the owner."

The man looked sympathetic. "I'm a hatch boss, and I know the feeling when the bigwigs squeeze your balls." He looked toward the taxicab. "But I thought Mr. Pelley was taking the truck out of here with his crew."

"Oh, the truck." There was nothing to lose, so Chaplin, remembering what Luisa had said, took a stab at it. "His shiny new International."

"Yeah, with those curved corners, supposed to be aerodynamic, save on gas." *Air-ee-oh- dynamic.* "You ask me, that's just advertising."

"Maybe I can catch up with him. Did he say where he was going?"

"Didn't say, but his farm, I figure. The whole load was fertilizer." The hatch boss chuckled. "Must be a gentleman farmer. Fellow's quite a dandy in a three-piece suit and a feather in his homburg."

"His farm," Chaplin said, because he couldn't think of anything else. A sense of failure flooded his mind like a poisonous tide. He looked at one of the mooring ropes that lashed the *Stuttgart* to the iron bollards on the dock. In his agitated state, he imagined that the braided hemp was a giant noose tightened around his chest, gripping him so tightly that his ribs were about to splinter.

"Now that I think of it," the hatch boss said, "Customs has been damn busy with all the arrivals today."

"How's that?"

"Helluva thing. We're a port of entry for narcotics, counterfeit currency, even some exotic animals that Customs will seize. Slows down the process." He looked at his watch. "It's a long shot, but it's possible Mr. Pelley's still clearing Customs."

Chaplin raced up the incline to the taxicab, the hatch boss yelling, "Good luck, cabbie!"

69
LIFE HERE, DEATH THERE

Port of Los Angeles

Chaplin goosed the accelerator and swerved the taxi around several buildings, brakes shrieking as he slammed to a stop in the Customs House parking lot. Lots of cars, lots of trucks. No shiny new International cab-over-engine truck.

"Bloody hell! We must have missed them by minutes," Chaplin said.

"Or seconds," Einstein said. "If only your taxi could travel faster than the speed of light, we could go back in time and find them."

They sat in the taxi a moment, both men quiet, traveling not even one mile per hour, much less one hundred eighty-six thousand miles per second. Chaplin banged the steering wheel with an open hand. "I failed Jimmy at the consulate, and I failed everyone today."

"So are you going to stew in your own gravy, or can you try to do something?" Einstein said.

"Do what! What can we—"

"Charlie!" Einstein shielded his eyes with one hand and pointed with the other. "The side street! The glare!"

Chaplin squinted into the sun. It was difficult to see, but it appeared to be a truck glinting fiery daggers from its shiny chrome body.

It could be the International truck that shines like chrome.

Oh, Luisa, bless you!

Without a word, Chaplin engaged the clutch, shoved the floor shift into first, and burned rubber heading that way. The truck was motoring north on Harbor Boulevard, and the dazzling reflection of the sun left a trail like Hansel dropping breadcrumbs. And just as Luisa had told them, the International, with its curved metal edges, looked like a toaster on wheels. "We'll always keep at least one car in between us and the truck," Chaplin said, "and Pelley won't be the wiser."

"Where'd you learn that trick, *boychik?*"

"*You Only Live Once.* A box office dud with Henry Fonda as a death row inmate. Talk about miscasting!"

The truck turned right on Anaheim Boulevard, and they followed. "Charlie, maybe we should stop and call the police."

"We'll lose the truck, Albert. And just what do we say? A truck supposedly loaded with fertilizer actually has machine guns for the Nazis. Reach the wrong coppers, and they'll give 'em a police escort."

"Fertilizer, you said?"

"That's what the hatch boss told me."

"Hmm."

"Hmm, what?"

"Maybe nothing, maybe something. We'll see."

The International truck hung a left, and the DeSoto cab stayed two cars behind. After several minutes, they were on Long Beach Boulevard in the little burg of South Gate. The truck turned right onto Firestone Boulevard into the town of Downey. Another left to Whittier Boulevard, and after a series of turns, they emerged on San Gabriel Boulevard. There were no more turns for several miles in heavy traffic as they passed through Monterey Park, San Gabriel, and into Pasadena.

Chaplin loosened the death grip he'd had on the steering wheel. With each passing mile, the task seemed easier. Thankfully, back at the Customs House, Albert had looked up and caught sight of the truck without a second to spare.

Time! Life can turn in one second.

Now, driving due north, they passed through a forest of small oil derricks that lined the boulevard, endlessly pumping away, looking like steel worshippers genuflecting. In the distance were lettuce fields, brown-skinned men, women, and children bent low—stoop labor—weeding by hand.

Chaplin reached into a pants pocket and plucked out the tuxedo button Gyssling had returned. The events two nights earlier weighed on him like a yoke on an ox.

Life here, death there.

Time. Our friend one day, the Grim Reaper the next.

In Gyssling's office, had the SS thugs taken a few more seconds—seconds!—had they looked up, they would have seen the shadow of his body on the ceiling. How then would history—*time!*—have been changed? *I would have been taken to the roof, and Jimmy Mitchell would be alive.*

Einstein cleared his throat and said, "So, what exactly are we going to do when the shiny truck gets to its destination? They have machine guns and rifles, and we have what, your after-dinner jokes and my notions of gravity?"

"We stay out of sight, and when we know their destination, we get to a telephone and hope Georgia Robinson is out of her meeting with the FBI agent and reachable,"

Chaplin replied. "You like the plan, Albert?"

"I like the 'stay out of sight' part best."

"If Georgia made progress, great, bring on the feds."

"And if she didn't?"

"Then we're on our own, mate."

With a bus in between, they followed the truck into Pasadena.

"They've been heading due north," Chaplin said, "and I think I know their destination."

"*Nu?*"

"What do you see up ahead, Albert?"

"Mountains. Quite beautiful at sunset, which is rapidly approaching."

"The San Gabriels. That's where they're headed."

It took several turns to get through Pasadena and another turn to the north into the mountains on Route 2, the Angeles Crest Highway, a treacherous two-lane road still under construction, with blind curves and steep ditches just off its gravel shoulders. As the taxi climbed higher into the mountains, three cars behind the truck, the temperature plunged, and darkness arrived, not stealthily, but as suddenly as a switch being flipped. Chaplin turned on the headlamps. Thirty minutes later, they passed a sign that read ELEVATION 3,885 FEET.

Chaplin exhaled a visible breath and said, "We've come a long way from sea level."

Einstein pulled his cardigan sweater tight across his chest and made a *brr-rring* sound. "My *schmeckel* is frozen like a month-old knish at the bottom of the icebox."

Chaplin opened the heater valve and turned on the fan. The road narrowed, and the two cars that had been between the truck and the taxi disappeared down side roads. Chaplin slowed to put more distance between the two vehicles. Darkness enveloped them so completely that the canopy of trees overhanging the road was a black curtain that shielded the quarter moon and the background of stars. A half hour passed, and they came upon another sign: SAN GABRIEL PEAK 6,164 FEET.

"I've been here before," Einstein said. "Not here exactly, but close."

"How? When?"

"Edwin Hubble took me to Mount Wilson Observatory in a fancy Pierce-Arrow back in thirty-one. It's where he proved the universe is expanding."

"So, Albert, do you know your way around here?"

"In the dark, who knows anything? Trees, canyons, animals. We saw a bear."

They drove slowly through a series of hairpin turns, and when the road straightened, there were no lights ahead. No cars, no truck. Just another sign lighted by their headlamps: CAUTION –DEAD END– ROUTE 2 ENDS 1,000 FEET.

"What the hell!" Chaplin yelled. "Where's the truck?"

"They must have turned somewhere," Einstein said.

"Where? I didn't see a road."

Chaplin threw the floor shift into reverse and tried turning around, nearly putting the DeSoto into a ditch. It took three maneuvers, but he got the car heading slowly back down the mountain.

"Albert, look to the right, and I'll look left. It won't be a paved road. Maybe just an opening between trees, some weeds that are matted down."

Five minutes later, Einstein shouted, "There!"

Chaplin braked and eased the taxi onto a gravel path that disappeared into the blackness between rows of canyon oak trees.

"This has to be it," Chaplin said, driving slowly into the endless darkness. They were going slowly downhill. "Look for any lights. The truck. A house. A farm. A radio antenna. Anything."

"Can't see *bupkis*," Einstein said.

"Open the touring roof, and you'll get a better view."

Einstein cranked open the metal slide, stood on the seat, and poked his head out the opening. "*Gottenyu!* The wind is cold!"

Chaplin craned his neck and saw Einstein's wild hair flowing back over his shoulders like the mane of a galloping horse. Another few minutes passed, and they continued downhill, the gravel path curving to avoid ditches and fallen trees.

"Anything Albert?"

"I'm looking at Merak and Dubhe in the Big Dipper, and there's Polaris, which is due north. We're heading southwest, and the trees are thinning. I think there's a valley, flat land, ahead of us."

Another few minutes and Einstein said, "I'm making out shapes below us. Buildings, I think. You'd better turn off your headlamps, so we're not spotted."

Chaplin followed instructions, and soon they had descended far enough that the temperature began to rise. The night had been as silent as falling snow. Then, out of the darkness, a deeply pitched rumbling bellow, loud as a chainsaw, startled Chaplin, who hit the brakes hard. The DeSoto swerved off the path and over a fallen log, where it jolted to a stop.

"What the hell was that?" Chaplin said.

Einstein pointed toward a fenced pasture thirty yards away, where a herd of cattle stood motionless, their silhouettes visible in the moonlight.

"We're hunting Nazis with machine guns, and a cow frightened you," Einstein said.

Chaplin engaged the clutch, shifted into reverse, eased up on the clutch and gave it gas.

The rear wheels spun, but the taxi didn't move. He tried first gear and reverse again, rocking the DeSoto until it shot forward over the log, and from the undercarriage came a loud *cra-ack*.

"And that," Einstein said, "was not a cow."

Chaplin gave it gas, but the taxi didn't roll so much as thump along, the sound of metal scraping the ground. They got out, and Chaplin used a flashlight from the glove box to look under the taxi. "The front axle is broken."

"So you *schlepped* me into a forest, and now we're stranded?" Einstein said.

"Not a forest, mate." Chaplin gestured to an area beyond the fenced pasture. With their eyes accustomed to the darkness, several rows of light poles were visible in the distance. The poles encircled a farmhouse, several outbuildings that looked like horse stables, and a large barn with an attached silo. Nearby were two tractors, a plow, a wagon, and various farm and ranch equipment. Parked haphazardly were about twenty cars, and on an inclined ramp to the barn was the International truck they had followed from the port. "We're stranded on a Nazi ranch."

70
THE DAIRY FARM

Kirchoff Dairy Farm

"Stay in the shadows of the tree line," Chaplin said. "Keep your head down, and don't make any unnecessary sounds." He licked an index finger and held it up. "Bollocks! We're walking downwind. If they have guard dogs, they'll sound the alarm before we get close."

"And you learned all this how, Charlie?"

"From the Arapaho."

"On a reservation?"

"In *The Covered Wagon*, a damn good silent picture."

They had walked less than fifty yards along the trees when they heard someone much less stealthy than the Paramount Pictures Arapaho.

"Schmidt! Told you I heard an engine!" came a man's voice from the darkness. Chaplin and Einstein froze, not even taking a step for fear of snapping a twig.

"*Hä?* A taxi way up here, Cranston?" said a second voice, this one with a German accent. "Look how it's cockeyed. It's wrecked."

"Bonnet's still warm," Schmidt said.

"Whoever was in it would have started walking back to the road," Cranston said. "C'mon!"

There was a metallic *clack-clack*, the unmistakable sound of a shotgun racking. And then another.

Chaplin and Einstein stayed silent until the men's voices faded, and the only sound was a light breeze rippling through pine trees.

"This way," Chaplin whispered. They came out of the tree line, heading down the incline toward the farmhouse.

"Are you planning to knock on the door and ask if anyone called a taxi?" Einstein asked.

Chaplin studied the array of vehicles near the buildings below them. "Someone would have left his keys in a car. We try them all till we find one. There has to be a second road into the ranch, something on the far side of the buildings. Then back to plan A. We get to a phone and call Georgia."

Einstein did not have a better idea, so they began walking, hunched over, keeping their heads below the top rail of the pasture fence, as they descended toward the buildings and vehicles. They were alert for movement, for shadows that would come to life as men with guns. But nothing moved, not even a cow. They passed a rusted metal sign nailed to the pasture fence: KIRCHOFF DAIRY FARM-TRESPASSERS WILL BE SHOT.

They neared the end of the fenced pasture when Chaplin said, "Do you smell rotten eggs?"

"Cow farts," Einstein said. "Methane gas seasoned with cow poop."

They were one hundred yards from the barn when a voice commanded, "Halt! Who goes there?"

Both men froze. In the darkness, they made out the silhouette of a short, pudgy man pointing a rifle at them. The glare from one of the pole lights reflected off his spectacles.

"*Verpiss dich!*" Chaplin fired back, sounding annoyed. "I'm taking a piss, so relax, soldier."

"*Zu viel bier.* Too much beer," Einstein added, staying put in the darkness.

"Password!" the rifleman demanded.

"Heil Hitler!" Chaplin said.

"That ain't it," the man said.

Chaplin scratched his phony beard and said, "That was it yesterday."

"Yesterday ain't today," the man said with perfect logic but a slight loss of confidence.

"I'm *Leutnant* Bierwagen. What's your name, *Soldat*?" Chaplin demanded, using the German word for "soldier."

The man saluted and said, "Eckart, sir."

"Eckart! What are you even doing here! Schmidt and Cranston just found a car at the top of the pasture. They're looking for spies."

"Jumpin' Jesus!" Eckart said, heading up the slope toward the taxicab at an awkward trot.

Chaplin and Einstein had not taken five steps toward the parked cars when a deep bass *oompah*—louder than a cow's bellow—sounded across the property. They turned to see a tuba player in front of the farmhouse. Honking great breaths into the mouthpiece, the man wore *lederhosen* and suspenders, a red waistcoat, and a Bavarian hat with a feather stuck in the band. In a semicircle around him were five similarly dressed musicians. A trumpet, a trombone, a clarinet, an accordion, and a drum rounded out the oompah band, which played a lively polka.

The band was between the men and the cars, so that escape route was cut off.

"Should we run?" Einstein said.

"No! They've seen us, but at this distance, they don't know who we are. Wave to them."

"Wave?"

"Be friendly."

Einstein waved, as instructed. Chaplin spread his arms and smoothly moved both hands in tempo with the music, like an orchestra conductor. The drummer signaled his appreciation with a drumstick salute.

"Now, slowly move toward the barn," Chaplin said. "Under the overhang."

Einstein immediately saw what Chaplin meant. The red wooden barn had a stone foundation and matching wall underneath an overhang that was in complete shadow. As they casually walked that way, the door to the farmhouse opened, and men spilled out, nearly all holding something. Einstein felt a shiver of fear, but after a moment realized they held beer steins, not guns. The men gathered around the band and sang raucously in German.

A few seconds later, Chaplin and Einstein pressed up against the dark side of the barn, hidden from view. "Any ideas?" Chaplin said.

"There should be a door on this wall."

"The doors are on the end of the barn," Chaplin said, gesturing toward the earthen ramp where the International truck was parked. "The rear of the truck faces the double doors. That's gotta be where they off-loaded the weapons and ammo."

"It's a German barn," Einstein said.

"What's that even mean?"

"The stone foundation and banked construction. The gabled roof. The forebay above us, what you called an overhang. The attached silo. It's a German barn, and it will have a small door in the wall we're leaning against. We just have to find it in the dark."

Chaplin gave him a look that seemed to ask, *How the hell do you know this?*

"Hermann Weyl, a brilliant mathematician, had a farm near Göttingen. We used to go there to think. And to milk cows."

They ran their hands along the wall, picking up a few splinters but not finding a door.

The sound of whistling stopped them cold. Once again, they pressed their backs against the wall. Twenty yards away, a heavyset man in a mackinaw walked toward the earthen ramp. He was whistling the popular Irving Berlin song, "Cheek to Cheek."

"Bizarre," Einstein whispered.

"Surreal," Chaplin whispered back.

The man's face was illuminated by one of the pole lights. A jagged scar ran from just below his ear to the corner of his mouth, and his nose was bent. Chaplin recognized him and remembered he'd given them his name.

Skowron! The thug from the baseball game who wanted an autograph for his son Adolf. The man described by Henry Singleton as the leader of the vandals who desecrated the temple.

Skowron passed their position without looking toward the barn. "How do we do it?" Chaplin said softly.

"Do what, Charlie?"

"Kill him."

Einstein felt the same rage but still believed himself incapable of taking another man's life. Not to mention that Skowron had a much better chance of killing them than the other way around.

"Just hold that idea, Charlie," Einstein said. "I'm working on a thought experiment."

Skowron stopped at the earthen ramp, pulled a flashlight from the pocket of his mackinaw, and aimed it into a tangle of vines that covered the earthen ramp, reached into the twining shrubs, opened a hidden door, and stepped inside.

"What in the world…?" Chaplin said.

A moment later, Skowron came out carrying a keg of beer without even straining. He held the keg in one hand as he closed the door with the other. Then he walked back toward the farmhouse, lugging the keg.

"A beer cellar?" Chaplin asked.

"A storm shelter. Or bomb shelter. Or bunker," Einstein said. "Whatever you call it, a safe place for the farm family. Or for us."

"Why for us?"

"Do you smell the wheat? In the silo."

Chaplin sniffed and said, "I smell something dusty. Makes me want to sneeze."

"And you said the machine guns are hidden in bags of fertilizer."

"So I was told," Chaplin said.

"German fertilizer contains ammonium nitrate, and grains produce dust. Both are flammable. Together, you're talking about a bomb."

"Are you saying what I think you're saying?" Chaplin said.

"We need a safe place, Charlie, because we're going to blow up the barn and everything in it."

71
A TINDERBOX IN SEARCH OF A FLAME

The Barn

As soon as they found the forebay door and entered the barn, Einstein took control. Using Chaplin's flashlight, he quickly found dozens of fifty-kilo bags of fertilizer stacked near the silo.

"Nitrophoska," he said, reading the label. "Perfect. As I thought, ammonium nitrate is the source of the nitrogen. Quite a wonderful explosive."

"You're starting to sound like a mad scientist," Chaplin said.

"Oh, but I am. When I was a boy in Munich, I was fascinated by a massive grain silo explosion in Hamelin. Several men were killed. That was an accident, an inadvertent spark. We are going to light a fuse, quite literally."

Chaplin looked at his friend, the pacifist, the man who had flatly rejected his plea to help build a nuclear fission bomb.

The world is shifting under our feet, tectonic plates colliding, creating landscapes that would have been unrecognizable only moments earlier.

Einstein examined one of the stacks of fertilizer bags. The bag on top was torn open, the granular fertilizer spilling out. Inside, a burlap bag had been sliced open. Two MG 34 machine guns were inside, but there was room for one more.

"Of course, they'd want to try one of the guns," Einstein said. "My guess is that tomorrow, everybody singing the polka tonight will get a machine gun or a rifle to take home. That's why we have to do this now."

Einstein surveyed the interior, which was larger than his friend's German barn but contained similar equipment. Hand-operated milking machines, milking stools for the workers, cooling tanks for storage, dozens of cans for transport, wooden crates for storing produce, and two ancient corn shellers with hand cranks. Larger farm equipment, too, a manure spreader, a hay baler, and an old, rusted Fordson tractor. Tools and implements hung on the barn walls or were strewn about. Pitchforks, shovels, wheelbarrows, hoes, sickles, scythes, and various chains, ropes, and pulleys. Twenty feet above the floor was an open hayloft with a pulley and rope hoist to lift and lower bales. And, of course, the interior silo.

Einstein walked to the silo, threw the bolt on the bottom hatch, and opened the door a few inches. A thin trickle of wheat spilled out, accompanied by a sour smell. "The wheat's fermented into silage. Deliciously flammable."

He sounded as delighted as if he'd just discovered another dozen moons of Jupiter.

He knelt down, slipped a hand inside the door, and tapped the inside wall with a finger. "Masonry exterior, tempered-glass interior. Excellent for our purposes."

Chaplin didn't ask precisely what those purposes were.

Quiet, genius at work.

Einstein's gaze moved to a wooden post that was hung with three kerosene lamps.

"Charlie, grab a few of those rags in that wheelbarrow and soak them in kerosene," he instructed.

"Rip the rags into strips. Take off your shoelaces, tie them together, and put them inside the rags, which you'll wrap tightly lengthwise, and that'll be our fuse."

"Will do, Guvnor," Chaplin said.

The balance of power had shifted between the two men. From the moment they left for the port, Chaplin had been in charge, but he was happy now to let Einstein take over.

They could hear the oompah band outside, which had begun a spirited rendition of "Beer Barrel Polka," the Silver Shirts enthusiastically singing along:

"Roll out the barrel,
"We'll have a barrel of fun."

While Chaplin worked with the rags, Einstein took in the rest of the interior, then closed his eyes. Knowing how his friend's mind worked, Chaplin figured Einstein was picturing a diagram of all the equipment and machinery and the distances between them. His mind would figure out what would happen first, second, and third and how much time each step would take. And, Chaplin hoped, how to keep them alive through each step.

A thought experiment in real time with life-and-death consequences.

Einstein pointed to a large wooden structure propped four feet off the barn floor by concrete pillars. "That's a corn crib with perhaps five hundred kilos of corn still in their husks. It's built up to keep out the rodents, and for our purposes, the open space underneath the bin is the perfect place to start the fire because we'll have a sufficient oxygen flow."

"Corn is flammable?" Chaplin said.

"My goodness, yes. The husks are dry leaves, the corn silk is kindling, and the kernels are filled with starch. Starch plus dust plus ammonium nitrate, ka-boom! We're in a tinderbox in search of a flame." He seemed to think something over for a moment. "There's just one problem."

"We have to get into the bunker before the barn blows to kingdom come," Chaplin said.

"Well, there is that. But we also need to blow the dome off the top of the silo."

"Because…?"

"First, if the dome holds, there'll be an explosive force directed back toward the floor of the silo, not unlike a breech explosion in an artillery cannon. It could create a crater big enough to envelop the entire barn, including us in the bunker."

"Yikes! What else?"

"Second, we want to blow the dome open to turn the silo into a torch with flames visible all the way down to Pasadena."

"A Roman candle to bring the coppers."

"Police. Firemen. Highway Patrol. FBI."

Chaplin's nose twitched, and he sneezed. The combination of wheat, corn, and dust was playing havoc with his sinuses. "So how do we blow the lid off the silo?" he asked.

"See the ladder rungs leading to the top?"

"Sure."

"You'll climb up there and take care of the bucket elevator." Einstein pointed to a machine with small buckets attached to a chain that ran from the floor to a hatch near the top of the silo, where a pulley system returned the buckets to the floor. "The elevator will carry buckets of fertilizer to the top hatch, and you'll make sure they're poured on top of the silage."

"Where it'll cause a second explosion. Brilliant!"

"I'll tell Robert Goddard you said so. He's been tinkering with multistage rockets with multiple combustion chambers."

Einstein spent a minute or two outlining the sequence of fiery events. They would spread a path of Nitrophoska from under the corn crib to the silo. At the bottom hatch, they would build a pile of fertilizer perhaps four feet deep. The kerosene-soaked rag fuse would light the fertilizer under the corn crib, and the flames would race to the hatch, where the first explosion would rocket up through the silo. The second explosion near the top would blow the dome off and ignite the torch that, at this elevation, should be visible halfway to the heavens.

"It sounds like a Rube Goldberg contraption," Chaplin said.

"I don't know this Mr. Goldberg."

Einstein grabbed a scythe from the wall and began slicing holes in the Nitrophoska bags.

Chaplin used a shovel to spread a path of fertilizer from beneath the corn crib to the bottom of the silo and, for no apparent reason, burst out laughing.

"What is it, Charlie?" Einstein asked.

"The other day, you said you were a theoretical physicist who couldn't even make an omelet."

"So?"

"Watching you now, I think you could make a nuclear fission bomb if you wanted to."

"Which I don't!"

Just then they heard machine gun fire from outside the barn. Startled, they both hurried to the wall closest to the sound. Peering through crevices in the wood slats, they saw roughly fifty Silver Shirts guzzling beer around a bonfire. A few paces away, a semicircle of men—perhaps two dozen—looked on as two men dressed identically in black appeared to be addressing them. One held a machine gun.

"The Doberman Pinschers from the consulate!" Chaplin said.

"I see them," Einstein said. "They may come for the rest of the guns at any moment.

"Let's hurry."

72
THE GOLDEN CROWN

The Bonfire

Sebastian and Friedrich Koch, each wearing black wool cable-knit turtlenecks and black trousers, demonstrated how to use the MG 34 machine gun. Sebastian rested the stock of the gun on his right hip as Pelley and his handpicked twenty-three-member "firing squad" looked on and listened. Pelley's concerns about the Koch brothers had lessened. Sure, they were here to spy for Goebbels, but the Silver Shirts had taken to them. Probably a little hero worship, he thought.

Flesh-and-blood Nazis! SS officers with machine guns!

It was as if Lou Gehrig stopped by to hit fungoes and chat with the men.

Rather than resenting Goebbels, Pelley was grateful. The propaganda chief had come through with the promised weapons.

Operation Hollywood is back on!

"The *Maschinengewehr* 34 is the newest and best light machine gun in the world," Friedrich Koch said to the group.

Aiming in the direction of a strand of pine trees, Sebastian let loose a volley of thirty or so rounds with a three-second trigger pull. The firing squad whistled and hooted, anxious to get their hands on the sleek and beautiful weapons.

The bonfire seeming to inflame the scars on his face, Skowron stepped out of the group and approached Pelley. "I've got a souvenir for you, sir." He opened a canvas rucksack and handed over what looked like a small gold crown, something a child king or queen might wear.

"Whoa, that's heavy," Pelley said, hefting it.

The light of the bonfire revealed three glowing domes of golden leaves, inlaid with precious stones and strung with delicate gold chains. The dome on top resembled a miniature medieval helmet with a sharp spire at its peak.

Skowron said, "If you're wondering what it is…"

"Oh, I know what it is!" Pelley said. "It's the crown atop the Good Book of the Jews, what they call their Torah. You pinched it from the temple."

"I bet it would bring a pretty penny if you wanted to sell it."

"Never, Skowron. We keep it. Not for myself. For the Silver Legion, as a memento of our holy crusade."

An idea came to him. Why not collect artifacts from our enemies?

What treasures might be found in the homes of Samuel Goldwyn, Charlie Chaplin, and all the other targets of Operation Hollywood? He envisioned a museum of their bounty—perhaps with his name carved on the pediment—a place that would last centuries. After all, the *Führer* promised that the Reich would last one thousand years.

He clopped Skowron on the shoulder. "Good work, my friend. Come with me."

The two men walked toward the bonfire, where two dozen Silver Shirts were pleasantly plastered. Pelley found a stick four feet long, jammed it into the ground, and placed the crown on top, where it sparkled in the reflection of the flames. Pelley was about to give the men a short speech about the glory of their crusade, but just then, the oompah band struck up *"Ein Prosit,"* a drinking song. The Silver Shirts sang along, toasting each other with raised beer steins.

Pelley decided to wait to give his pep talk. He left the crown on its stick in front of the bonfire, looking like a totem to be worshipped by an ancient tribe.

73
THE BUCKET ELEVATOR

The Barn

When they finished laying the path of Nitrophoska, Chaplin and Einstein began the backbreaking work of carrying fertilizer bags to the foot of the silo. A weary Chaplin then climbed the silo's iron rungs to the platform where the buckets would approach the top hatch. He shined his flashlight into the opening, saw the silage a few feet below, and sneezed again.

Einstein found the switch for the elevator and turned on the power. It made a *clackety-clank* sound as it started up, and the racket only grew louder as the lowest buckets began scooping up the fertilizer. Einstein used a shovel to re-stock the pile of fertilizer, so each bucket had material to pick up. He wasn't concerned about the machine's noise because the oompah band was playing a number heavy on the drums, and the general commotion around the bonfire kept up a steady pulse of noise.

His mind drifted a moment because something was bothering him. Charlie's constant pestering about a nuclear fission bomb. If there was one thing Einstein knew for certain, it was that he would never be involved in such a project.

When we get out of here—if we get out of here—I will tell Charlie to please never mention it again.

74
OF GENIUS AND STUPIDITY

The Yard and Barn

If Sebastian Koch were a deep thinker, which he most assuredly was not, he might have considered the next moment as revealing some pattern in the universe, some interconnectivity of disparate events. Or, what down-to-earth people call a coincidence. But Sebastian was only thinking about unbuttoning his fly and taking a piss against the barn's forebay wall. It was seconds later—in midstream—that the oompah band stopped playing to take a break and simultaneously, almost magically, the decibel level of the revelers dropped as if a radio had been switched off, and Sebastian heard a *clackety-clank* coming from inside the barn.

He finished his business, buttoned up, grabbed the MG 34 that was leaning against the wall, and headed for the door to see just what was going on inside the barn.

◈

Chaplin saw it happen from the ladder near the top of the silo. He had finished loading the fertilizer from the bucket elevator into the top hatch, and Einstein had turned off the power, but it was too late. One of the Doberman Pinschers from the consulate stood in front of the corn crib, machine gun resting against his hip, an ammo belt of fifty rounds hanging from the feed tray. He stood twenty feet from Einstein and slowly raised the barrel of the machine gun to chest height.

"What the hell is going on here!" Sebastian Koch demanded in a German accent.

"*Guten Abend, Herr Offizier.*" Einstein kept his voice calm, even though his knees trembled like leaves in a storm. "My name is Albert Einstein."

"I know who you are. The Jew everybody says is a genius."

"In my experience, when everybody says the same thing, they are usually wrong."

"So you are not a genius?"

Einstein shrugged. "Who am I to say? All I know is that the difference between genius and stupidity is that genius has its limits."

"I saw you talking to the little *schwarzer* who climbed up the consulate slowly and came down much faster." Koch grinned slyly, a spine-chilling look.

Thirty feet above them, Chaplin heard the conversation, realized the German was Jimmy's killer and wished to all that was unholy that he had a gun. He moved slowly down the rungs, careful not to bang a shoe against the side of the silo.

Don't look up, Albert! If you look up, so will the SS thug, and I will be dead.

Koch raised the machine gun from his hip, now holding it in both hands in firing position, still pointed at Einstein's chest.

Climbing down the ladder, Chaplin felt a tickle in his nose and was about to sneeze. He pinched both nostrils, clamped his free hand over his mouth, and nearly fell. The sneeze was silent. Then he leapt from the ladder into the loft, landing on all fours like a cat, the sound cushioned by the hay three feet deep.

"Tell you what," Koch said. "Prove you are a genius, and I'll kill you quick and painless. Otherwise, I will see how many rounds it takes to amputate all your limbs and how long it takes for you to bleed to death." Koch threw the cocking bolt of the machine gun and chambered a round.

"No, no, no! Look what you're standing in!" Einstein said. "Ammonium nitrate. Behind you is a corn crib, dry as tinder. If your bullets don't blow us up, the hot ejected cartridges surely will."

Koch saw that he was standing in several inches of fertilizer. "Is this some Bolshevik trick?"

"More like a chemistry trick," Einstein said.

Koch craned his neck and looked at the corn crib that rose above him. He took another moment scanning the barn and, for the first time, noticed the four-foot-deep pile of fertilizer in front of the floor silo hatch.

"Saboteur! Just like the *Hindenburg*. But not with Sebastian Koch on watch!" An idea appeared on his face as clearly as the sun emerging from clouds. Still holding the heavy gun in one hand, he bent over and pulled a knife from a leather sheath inside his boot. It was a hunting knife with a shiny eight-inch blade and a deer-antler handle.

"Knife makes no fire," he said.

In the loft, Chaplin quickly attached the hook at the end of the hoist rope to the baling wire at the top of a bale of hay. He grabbed the other end of the rope, which ran over a pulley, and yanked it down, testing the weight of the bale.

This could work!

He pictured Johnny Weissmuller as Tarzan, swinging through vines, and Doug Fairbanks as Zorro, riding a rope from balcony to rooftop.

I can do this!

Koch brandished the hunting knife and said, "What will happen now, genius Jew?"

"'If you prick us, do we not bleed?'" Einstein said.

"*Was ist das?*"

"Shakespeare, Herr Koch."

With the rope wrapped around both hands, Chaplin took a running start and launched off the edge of the loft. He kept his legs straight in front of him, intending to kick Koch in the skull.

Except the rope was too short.

Koch sensed movement above his head and looked up to see Chaplin sail over him, both feet crashing into the slatted door of the corn crib. What Koch could not see was the wooden latch on the door splinter. The door flew open under the weight of the corn inside.

Hundreds of pounds of corn tumbled out, a Niagara Falls of husks and cobs enveloped in clouds of dust. The corn pummeled Koch's head and shoulders. His neck snapped downward, his knees buckled, and he pitched forward, the avalanche stopping just short of Einstein's feet. Koch dropped the knife from one hand and the MG 34 from the other, but not before involuntarily pulling the trigger and firing a burst of six rounds.

Einstein watched the spent cartridges eject from the MG 34 and tried to follow their trajectory into the mound of corn that buried Koch, who had disappeared like a sailor swept overboard in a storm.

I lied! Without experimentation, I could not know if the spent cartridges would ignite anything. Maybe they are not hot enough.

But then…the first spark! And then a second! Just tiny flickers of orange deep in the pile of corn but still above the fertilizer on the barn floor.

For how long…? Was it mere seconds before the conflagration engulfed them?

"Charlie!"

After bouncing off the corn crib and losing both his laceless shoes, Chaplin held on to the rope long enough to swing halfway to the silo, where he let go and tumbled to the floor.

The sparks were now a small flame, glowing, spreading, racing toward the fertilizer piled in front of the silo hatch.

"Charlie, run! The bunker!"

William Dudley Pelley used a flaming twig from the edge of the bonfire to light his cigar.

A whiskey man, he did not partake of the barrels of beer being consumed by his men. He had already downed a flask of Old Quaker, his belly warm, his brain happily fuzzy. It was a night for celebrating. He heard what sounded like a burst of gunfire. Sebastian Koch, no doubt, playing with the MG 34. Farther away this time, judging by the muffled sound.

He thought he saw something beneath the barn overhang, two figures moving, but it was dark there, and through the smoke of the bonfire and the buzz in his head, well, he wasn't sure. He puffed his cigar, a Cuban Partagás Goebbels had given him.

What a perfect day! With so many more to follow.

Pelley noticed Friedrich Koch and Skowron chatting amiably near the bonfire. He walked over to join them. "Where's your brother?" he asked Friedrich.

Chaplin and Einstein pushed through the door beneath the earthen ramp and plunged into the total darkness of the bunker. Chaplin felt along the wall of concrete blocks and wood planks and found a switch, which he flicked, turning on a single overhead bulb. A low-ceilinged triangular room no more than fifteen feet long. Sandbags and beer kegs on the floor, two cots, two chairs, a sink and a toilet, and a ventilation pipe. An interior steel door was heavy enough that it took both of them to close it and throw the bolt.

A kerosene lamp hung on one wall, a bag of fireplace matches alongside. "Light the lamp, Charlie," Einstein said. "We'll probably lose electricity."

Chaplin did it and asked, "Any other precautions?"

"Let's cover our ears."

"When?"

"Now, Charlie." They sat in the two straight-back chairs, hunched over, and covered their ears.

Seven seconds later, a thunderclap knocked them off the chairs and onto the floor. The concussion wave shook the bunker and toppled several sandbags. Dirt drizzled down from the ceiling, and the roof beams sagged and groaned like an aging peddler hauling a bag of iron pots.

"Stay on the floor, Charlie. The second one, the top of the silo…"

The second thunderclap erupted like a volcano rending a mountain apart. Again, the bunker shook, and their ears rang like the bells of Notre Dame. They heard the crashes and clunks of objects—rocks, timbers, detritus—hitting the bunker's steel door, the exterior wooden door apparently obliterated.

Several minutes passed, or was it just seconds? As if in general relativity's strong gravitational field, time seemed to have slowed down.

"Should we get out of here?" Chaplin asked.

"Let's take a peek," Einstein said.

Chaplin tried to slide the bolt on the steel door, but it wouldn't budge.

"The concussion wave." Einstein pointed to the lower half of the door, which was bent inward.

"What do we do, Albert?"

Dazed, Einstein shook his head. "I'm sorry, Charlie."

"What? You must have an idea, a plan."

"I underestimated the force of the blasts, particularly the second one. I thought this was the safest place. But it might well be our coffin."

75
THE FLYING SAUCER

The Yard

Less than one minute before Chaplin and Einstein had dashed to the bunker, Friedrich Koch was telling Skowron that when he visits Berlin, he must take photos of Neptune Fountain in the Schlossplatz, the Palace Square. Pelley joined them and said they would all have a grand time together in Germany.

At that moment, the barn exploded, splintering like a child's balsa wood toy stomped on by an elephant. The fireball, a blazing sun come to Earth, rolled across the yard, flames spitting in every direction.

The thunderous din—a hundred jackhammers battering concrete—burst both of Pelley's eardrums, and the concussion wave picked him up and tossed him ass-over-elbows until he tumbled to a stop against the trunk of a fir tree.

The wave knocked Friedrich Koch into the bonfire, where his clothes burst into flames, and his face blazed red, then purple, then black within seconds. Perhaps he screamed—no matter—no one could hear him.

Skowron, the heaviest of the three men, braced against the concussion wave and kept his feet. He never saw the Torah crown fly at him like a piece of shrapnel, its helmet spire impaling him just below the Adam's apple, the golden leaves ripping flesh and cartilage and blood vessels until the top half of the crown disappeared into his neck. He stumbled backward, hands clawing at the crown, dislodging it, and both his carotid arteries exploded, spraying blood in two parabolic arcs, not unlike the water spouting from the Neptune Fountain that he would never see.

Shards of burning wood rocketed across the yard, tearing at the meat of men's bodies, breaking their bones, and setting fire to their clothing. Every window in the nearby farmhouse exploded, and the house itself moved a foot off its foundation.

Sprawled on the ground, his bushy eyebrows singed, his suit coat blackened and smoking, Pelley curled into the fetal position, hands over his head, as debris—hot as molten lead—rained from the sky. Seconds after the first blast, the silo blew its dome with the roar of a freight train through a living room. Pelley watched in disbelief as the dome, spinning like a flying saucer in a Buck Rogers comic strip, soared over the farmhouse, clipping its chimney before disappearing in the vicinity of an alfalfa field.

A solid wall of blue and orange flames burst from the open silo and reached a hundred feet into the night sky. Hypnotized by the sight, Pelley saw the flames leap higher as the seconds ticked away and wondered if he was dreaming. Or dead.

Someone tugged at his shoulder and said something, but Pelley couldn't hear a word. He recognized the man, Eckart, who pointed toward the parked cars in the distance. But Pelley thought he was fine right here.

I might take a nap for a while.

Eckart shook him harder, got no response, then picked him up in a fireman's carry and staggered toward the cars.

Good man, Eckart. Stronger than he looks. And he'll have the moxie to handle the MG 34.

The guns! The ammo!

It was just starting to sink in.

76
HAMS IN THE SMOKEHOUSE

May 8, 1937 - The Bunker

In the early-morning hours, after painfully pulling off his beard, Chaplin dozed on one of the cots, which amazed Einstein, who was too worked up, too worried, to sleep. Certainly, the day and night had been exhausting, but just how did Charlie manage to relax when they were trapped?

Einstein had been right that they would lose electricity, so he kept a kerosene lamp burning. But that was worrisome, too. Kerosene gave off carbon monoxide and sulfur dioxide, so Einstein checked every few minutes to make sure the ventilation pipe had not been clogged by debris.

It was not yet dawn when he heard the sirens. Fire trucks and police cars, he was sure. He shook Chaplin awake, and they waited as the sirens grew louder, and then the growls of engines grew nearer. And, finally, the shouts of men outside, the sounds reaching them through the ventilation pipe.

They each tried yelling, but their voices could not be heard. They took turns slamming a chair into the steel door. Surely someone would walk close enough to hear them, Einstein thought, fighting a sense of panic.

Will our bones be discovered when a bulldozer razes the property?

More than two hours had passed when they heard a shout. "Hey, Captain! Look at this. I think it's a door."

Chaplin picked up a chair and banged it against the door with renewed vigor as Einstein yelled through the ventilation pipe, "We're in here!"

※ ※

Captain John Jacoby of the California Highway Patrol was in charge. He was a clean-shaven, broad-shouldered man of about fifty with a gut just starting to peek over his belt. In his command tent, he made sure that his two rescued celebrities had hot coffee and cold sandwiches. An assortment of county sheriff's deputies and firemen from several departments poked in and out of the tent, hoping to take a gander at the movie star and scientist. An assistant chief from the Pasadena Fire Department announced that two cows had given birth to calves prematurely at the moment of the explosion.

Sergeant Georgia Robinson was there, even though the farm was out of her jurisdiction. She hugged each of her two friends and said, "Thank God you're alive, you crazy swashbucklers. I was worried sick, and Melvia couldn't sleep when I told her you were missing."

They murmured their thanks for coming to their rescue. As Einstein had hoped, the silo's flaming torch had alerted police and fire departments far and wide. There had been some difficulty finding a route through the woods to the farm, especially for the larger trucks.

"We got a call from a Professor Charles Richter at Caltech," Captain Jacoby said. "Do you know him, Dr. Einstein?"

"Of course. Our offices are on the same floor."

"He said his seismograph registered a two-point-nine here last night. Any idea what that means?"

"If an earthquake is like an orgasm, that's not a very impressive one, but still, the earth moved," Einstein said.

The captain cleared his throat, somewhat embarrassed, while Georgia Robinson stifled a smile.

Chaplin and Einstein took turns telling their story, starting with Jimmy Mitchell's murder at the consulate, their discovery of Operation Hollywood, the weapons on the ship, the pursuit through the mountains, and their building a bomb. A look crossed Captain Jacoby's face that Chaplin missed but Einstein did not. It was just a slight raising of the eyebrows and furrowing of the forehead.

"Hold it right there, gents," Jacoby said. He cleared the tent of everyone other than the two men and Georgia Robinson. "Are you thinking what I'm thinking, Sergeant Robinson?"

"Charlie, Albert," she said in the tone of a kind schoolmarm with rambunctious students. "I believe what Captain Jacoby is saying is that you might want to speak to lawyers before you say anything else."

"Have we done anything wrong?" Einstein asked.

"Other than protecting this country from violent insurrection," Chaplin added.

"We've got a building blown to smithereens and six corpses, maybe seven," Jacoby said. "The coroner hasn't had time to fit all the body parts together. I don't have a count of the wounded, at least three dozen in hospitals down the mountain. So, yes, an ambitious district attorney might look at you two as a ticket to Sacramento, seeing as you just admitted to arson and multiple homicides."

"Oh my." Einstein appeared troubled, his words halting. "I never intended…to kill…I am a committed pacifist. My only goal was to destroy the weapons, and obviously I failed to accurately determine the scope of the destruction. Which is the problem with bombs, as I've been saying all my life."

"No second-guessing, Albert," Chaplin said. "We did what seemed right at the time."

Captain Jacoby scratched his chin with a knuckle and said, "Sergeant Robinson tells me that the two of you are kind and gentle souls. Now, if I hadn't known her since the day she was sworn in, I might think she was smoking reefer. But her word is gold. Which leaves us in need of an alternative narrative. Georgia, any thoughts?"

"Accidental silo explosions happen quite frequently, often without explanation," Robinson said.

"True enough," the captain said. "There was that grain elevator in Omaha back in nineteen. Five dead, if I recall correctly."

"Which pales in comparison to Kansas City," Robinson said. "What was that, forty or so dead?"

Chaplin knew a script when he heard one, and Einstein recognized the teamwork between the two cops. Their friend Sergeant Robinson and Captain Jacoby, apparently a new friend, were tossing them a life preserver.

"Spontaneous combustion," Einstein said.

"Terrible accident," Chaplin said.

"That's what I figure," Captain Jacoby said." He leaned forward and spoke softly. "I fought the Hun in the Great War, and I'd bet a double sawbuck we'll be at it again. If we don't stop the Nazis, who will? But you two gotta stay on your side of the road. Understood?"

"Yes, sir," they said simultaneously.

"Now, you put a dent in the fender of the local fascists. But that's all it was. And back in Germany, planes and artillery are rolling out of their factories while Washington's playing canasta. So, I understand why you took matters into your own hands, but it's only a matter of time before our government appreciates the threat and does something about it."

They thanked the captain, and Georgia Robinson said she'd be driving them to Beverly Hills. "Do you mind if we keep the windows open?" she asked.

"No, why?" Chaplin said.

"Because the two of you smell like hams left in the smokehouse too long."

77
FRIENDS

May 14, 1937 – Chaplin Estate

One week after the "horrific farm accident," to quote the *Los Angeles Times*, life had returned to its routine. Einstein was back lecturing to eager physics students at Caltech, and Chaplin was working on his screenplay about Adolf Hitler, or rather, Adenoid Hynkel. The newspaper reported that drifting sparks from a nearby bonfire apparently caused the silo explosion. A men's social club that rented the farm for a wingding seemed to be responsible. Neither Chaplin nor Einstein was mentioned.

Today, Chaplin would drive crosstown to pick up twelve-year-old Melvia Robinson and then head north to Caltech in Pasadena. He had received two phone calls that morning. First, Georgia Robinson called to tell him that William Pelley, minus eyebrows and with bandaged hands and a scorched face, was holding rallies at Alt Heidelberg, recruiting new members for his Silver Legion. The FBI was attempting to infiltrate the group with the aid of a band of Great War veterans, some Jewish, some gentile. LAPD Chief Davis had reluctantly assigned Robinson as liaison to the FBI task force, as she had requested. "Sooner or later, we'll nab Pelley, Charlie," she said. "I promise you that."

Georg Gyssling had also called, saying he was thankful that both Chaplin and Einstein survived their harrowing night.

"What's that crackling sound?" Chaplin asked.

"Ah, that. My personal papers seem to have fallen into the fireplace."

"What's happening, Georg?"

"I've been recalled to Berlin."

Chaplin squeezed his eyes shut, his stomach tightening into a knot. "Will you be all right?"

"The Gestapo wants to interrogate me as to why I failed to file timely reports about American military installations on the West Coast."

"I didn't know your duties included spying."

"Apparently I had misplaced the communiqués. All forty of them."

"Georg, I must apologize to you for something I said last week. You are my friend, and I will always remember you as a man who did the honorable thing, even when it was the harder path."

"Oh, please, Charlie, too soon for eulogies! I am not as accomplished an actor as you, but I am well equipped to spin tales in an interrogation room." He lowered his voice to a whisper. "Do you have a title for the picture you are working on?"

"The Great Dictator."

"Perfect, Charlie! You are the master of irony. And I intend to be around to enjoy it."

78
SCIENCE FOR HUMANITY

Pasadena, California, Caltech Campus

Einstein was scheduled to lecture to a graduate-level physics class, a task he usually enjoyed, but today his heart was heavy with the ghosts of his guilt.

Never did I think I would build a bomb. Never did I think I would be responsible for men's deaths.

Chaplin had spent the week trying to cheer him up but to no avail. Now, holding a battered briefcase and wearing baggy pants and a cardigan sweater that had seen better days, Einstein waited at the entrance to the Norman Bridge Laboratory of Physics. He caught sight of Chaplin with Melvia Robinson, who ran to him. "Professor, I saw the rings of Saturn with the telescope you gave me!"

"Excellent, my dear," Einstein said. "Perhaps we can look at Europa and Io together one night."

"The moons of Jupiter that Galileo saw! Hot diggity!"

"I hope you don't get in trouble for playing hockey today."

"*Hooky*, Professor. And my teacher's almost as excited as I am."

Einstein smiled for the first time in a week. He turned to Chaplin and said, "Thank you for bringing Melvia. There are things I want you both to hear."

"So, I shouldn't take a nap when you start doing equations?" Chaplin asked.

"No numbers today, Charlie."

The building, which housed labs, offices, and classrooms, was Mediterranean Revival with beige stucco walls and arched windows. Walking down the corridor, their shoes clacking on the tile, Melvia said, "This is the most beautiful schoolhouse I've ever seen."

"My fondest hope is that, in a few years, you will tread these floors on your way to class," Einstein said.

⊱⊰

Seventeen graduate students sat at one-arm wooden desks. Another dozen or so stood at the rear of the small classroom, as they usually did for Einstein's lectures. The male students wore jackets and ties or, in some cases, crewneck sweaters and ties. The female students all wore dresses. Pencils were poised over composition notebooks or leather-bound journals. Melvia and Chaplin sat in straight-back chairs near the door.

"We have been talking about Otto Hahn and Fritz Strassmann and their attempts to create nuclear fission at their laboratory in Berlin," Einstein began. "I am told that they are close to achieving success." He turned to the blackboard, where an equation was still scrawled in chalk from their last class. "But no equations today."

$$^{238}_{92}U + n \rightarrow\ ^{239}_{92}U\ (40\ seconds) \rightarrow\ ^{239}_{93}ekaRe\ (16\ minutes) \rightarrow$$

He erased the board with vigorous strokes.

"Some say that nuclear power will produce electricity, that it will propel ships on the seas, that nuclear medicine will cure cancer, that splitting the atom will be a panacea for mankind. And some say that my special relativity gets the credit for these fantastic events in our future.

"But I wonder if 'blame' might be a better word than 'credit.' I wonder if my work might be the original sin of a new age of terror. For electricity and medicine are not the purposes behind Germany's quest for nuclear fission. The Reich is attempting to create bombs of unimaginable cruelty. Some of you have asked me, as have some very good friends, why don't I help the Americans build such a bomb? When facing such evil, isn't that the prudent course?"

He glanced at Melvia, who watched with rapt attention. Next to her, Chaplin nodded.

Einstein continued, "I am a pacifist. Even before the Nazis came to power, even before the Great War, I opposed German militarism, racism, nationalism, and the use of violence in foreign policy." He gave a sad smile. "As you can see, I was not very successful."

Some of the students took notes, even though they must have known that the lecture would not be followed by an exam. Others simply listened intently. All had competed for a seat in the class, and many would likely tell their grandchildren of the experience.

"Now, I will admit to a change of position. Once the Nazis came to power, I no longer considered myself an absolute pacifist. To fight against a vicious aggressor does not violate my principles. But to build such an inhumane bomb, that is a bridge too far, at least for today.

"Tomorrow, I cannot say. I have learned both in science and in life not to use the word 'never.' That is enough about me. You students will be on this earth long after I am gone. I urge you to use your intelligence and skills for the good of all. Use science to cure the sick and feed the hungry and raise up the poor. If you work with nuclear power, let it be atoms for peace and science for humanity. It is with these thoughts that I bid you good day."

The students erupted in applause. Melvia and Chaplin leapt to their feet and cheered.

Thirty minutes later, over lunch on campus at the Athenaeum, between bites of her creamed chicken in a pastry shell, Melvia peppered the men with questions. "Is it hard being an actor, Mr. Chaplin?"

"Not if you are an exceptional liar."

"Professor, if I went to Caltech, would I still be the smartest person in class?"

"It's not important to be the smartest," Einstein said. "What's important is to have passionate curiosity about everything you don't know."

She thought that over and took a piece of celery stuffed with Roquefort from the relish tray. "I am curious about atoms for peace and science for humanity," she said, sounding mature far beyond her years, "and I want to learn everything there is to know."

79
VERY TRULY YOURS, ALBERT EINSTEIN

July 30, 1939 – Einstein Cottage, Peconic Long Island

Two years and two months after delivering his Science for Humanity lecture, Einstein was sitting on a hardback chair on the screened porch of his rented summer cottage, wearing beach sandals and knee-length shorts. He puffed his long-stem pipe and watched Leo Szilard and Edward Teller get out of a Plymouth sedan and head his way. Einstein knew why the two Hungarian-born physicists had driven from Manhattan to this village across the bay from the Hamptons.

They want me to do something I never thought I would do.

Szilard conceived of a nuclear chain reaction six years earlier, and to his consternation—and Einstein's—the German scientists Otto Hahn and Fritz Strassmann achieved it just seven months ago. Bombarding uranium with neutrons, they unlocked the secrets of splitting the atom.

Szilard and Teller had one mission in mind: to awaken the sleepy United States government to the urgent need for a robust research program into nuclear fission and the development of a new kind of bomb. To command attention, Szilard wanted the help of the most famous scientist in the world, sixty-year-old Albert Einstein.

Szilard was forty-one and had been conducting nuclear research at Columbia University. Teller, only thirty-one, a physics professor at George Washington University, was visiting Einstein for the first time.

Einstein served the men tea and cookies, and they debated their course of action. They knew their task was unorthodox, and they had only one shot at persuasion. They would write a letter to be signed by Einstein, and the recipient would be President Franklin Delano Roosevelt.

Einstein's change of heart did not come without doubts and second thoughts. *Make that a hundred second thoughts!* Where could you safely build such a weapon? Not in Szilard's lab at Columbia or Enrico Fermi's at the University of Chicago or at Berkeley, where those brilliant young physicists Ernest Lawrence and J. Robert Oppenheimer toiled.

"I worry about safety considerations," Einstein told the younger physicists. "Consequences would be devastating in the event of a *Schnellschuss*."

Szilard chuckled at Einstein's use of the slang term for "premature ejaculation."

"I imagine an entire laboratory town would be constructed hundreds of miles from any city," Teller said.

Einstein tried to consider the many variables. Who could even determine the power of this mythical bomb's explosion? The temperature at the bomb site? What would be the size of the fireball and resulting firestorm and the impact of a concussion wave? Just how widespread would the damage be? And let's not forget about radiation, the cause of death of his friend Marie Curie. How much radioactivity would be unleashed?

No equations can answer the questions because we don't know the variables, much less the numerals.

"It speaks well of you, Albert," Szilard said, "that you have changed your thinking with the times."

"Ah, the times! As bad as they are, the future looks even more dire," Einstein said. Like so many others, Einstein was horrified by events in Europe.

In the last two years, Germany annexed Austria and invaded Czechoslovakia, a prime source of uranium. Orchestrated by Joseph Goebbels, the SS, the SA paramilitary, and the Hitler Youth brutally executed Kristallnacht, the Night of the Broken Glass, a *pogrom* that destroyed Jewish homes, businesses, and synagogues, killed scores, and incarcerated thousands. Rumblings across the ocean were that Germany was about to launch a widespread war on its neighbors.

"If I needed any more reason to change my views," Einstein said, "the Germans are already advancing toward a nuclear bomb at Kaiser Wilhelm."

"If FDR approves the program, would you be willing to take part?" Teller asked, the young man speaking up for the first time.

"I don't think you will need me, and J. Edgar Hoover would throw a fit," Einstein said.

"But with your connections..." Teller said.

Szilard cut him off. "Edward, what Albert is saying is that he would rather not. We will respect his wishes."

Einstein exhaled a puff of tobacco smoke and nodded.

They drank their tea and decided what should be in the letter and what should be omitted. The word "bomb" should be there, of course, but perhaps not in the first paragraph, they agreed.

"Leo, I would be pleased if you would draft the letter for my signature," Einstein said as the day grew late.

Removing myself a half step from advocating this bomb of unfathomable power. And yet my name is affixed to this moment for all eternity.

"I understand, Albert. It will be in your hands within three days."

As the visitors rose to leave for the drive back to the city, Teller said, somewhat formally, "Professor Einstein, I only escaped Europe because of your Relief Association. I am very grateful that I have the chance to thank you personally."

Einstein beamed. "That, undoubtedly, is the best news I shall hear today."

⊱ ⊰

The two-page typewritten letter was dated August 2, 1939, and given to Alexander Sachs, an economist and friend of the president. He intended to hand-deliver the letter to FDR and read it aloud to him. Then the world intervened. The gathering storm in Europe exploded on September 1, with Germany's invasion of Poland. Two days later, Great Britain and France declared war on Germany. FDR was not taking meetings unrelated to the fast-paced movements of troops and shifting alliances.

Finally, on October 11, Sachs fulfilled his mission. In the Oval Office, he read aloud the letter to the president The scientific terms were clear, concise, and understandable.

"It may be possible to set up a nuclear chain reaction in a large mass of uranium, by which vast amounts of power and large quantities of new radium-like elements would be generated," Sachs said in even tones. "Now it appears almost certain that this could be achieved in the immediate future."

The language about a bomb was cautious, perhaps even understated, which may have added to its power.

"This new phenomenon would also lead to the construction of bombs, and it is conceivable—though much less certain—that extremely powerful bombs of this type may thus be constructed," he continued. "A single bomb of this type, carried by boat and exploded in a port, might very well destroy the whole port together with some of the surrounding territory."

Sachs looked up and took in Roosevelt's grim expression. "Mr. President, the letter is signed, 'Very truly yours, Albert Einstein.'"

Roosevelt cleared his throat, turned to an aide and said, simply and directly, "This requires action."

80
THE GREAT DICTATOR

October 14, 1940 – New York City, Astor Theatre

Einstein half expected Chaplin to be driving the taxi that would pick him up in front of the Waldorf-Astoria Hotel, but no… Charlie was in the back seat. "Give me a second," he told the driver.

Chaplin leapt from the car and gave his old friend a hug. "Three years! How did we let the time go by?"

"I think of you all the time, Charlie. Sometimes, at the Institute, I'll be racking my brain about unified field theory, and when you come to mind, I'll just break out in laughter."

"I hope that holds true tonight, but only in the funny parts."

The men, both in suits and ties, slipped into the taxi for the short drive to the Astor Theatre in Times Square. So much had happened, Einstein thought, since Chaplin told him about his plans for a mistaken identity comedy that would ridicule Hitler.

When in human history had so many horrific armed conflicts ignited in so many places over such a short time?

Although Einstein had been cocooned at the Institute for Advanced Study at Princeton, he stayed current on the appalling state of multinational wars. Japan invaded China. Italy invaded Albania and Ethiopia. After Germany invaded Poland from the west, the Soviet Union invaded from the east, attacked Finland, and occupied the Baltic States. As if all that were not enough, Germany invaded France, Belgium, the Netherlands, and Luxembourg and for the past three months had been engaged in barbaric bombing raids on London. The Reich forced Jews into slave labor in Poland and began what it called "population transfers" of Jews.

When he wasn't brooding over the state of the world, Einstein sometimes thought of that endless night when a few ejected cartridges from a German machine gun sparked tiny fires that led, within moments, to a titanic conflagration. The Highway Patrol captain had been right. Their actions changed little. Fascist groups across the country continued to grow. A German American Bund rally at Madison Square Garden, complete with swastikas and "Heil Hitlers," drew twenty thousand followers. On behalf of the America First Committee, Charles Lindbergh made speeches preaching isolation and blaming FDR, the British, and Jews for advocating war with Germany.

And just what was the United States government doing? The "action" that President Roosevelt had promised was in slow motion, Einstein thought. The government granted Columbia University six thousand dollars for Szilard and Enrico Fermi's work, and the physicists succeeded in creating nuclear fission. But building an atomic bomb would take years and unfathomably vast sums of money.

Tonight, Einstein vowed not to let the problems of the world interfere with his reunion with Chaplin and the motion picture they would watch together. They alighted from the taxi in front of the Astor Theatre on Broadway where the marquee read CHARLIE CHAPLIN—THE GREAT DICTATOR.

No Klieg lights, no throngs of fans. That would be tomorrow at both the Astor and the nearby Capitol Theatre, a two-screen premiere. Tonight was the press screening with dozens of journalists spread out in the middle of the theater, some with penlights so they could take notes as the film ran. The two friends sat in the last row, Chaplin clearly nervous, both about Einstein's reaction and that of the *New York Times*.

The laughs came early, the humor at times broad and at times subtle. In military uniform and mustache, Chaplin indeed looked like Hitler, as Douglas Fairbanks had told him years earlier. His character, Adenoid Hynkel, was both ludicrous and terrifying. Rather than the Führer of Germany, he was the Phooey of Tomania. The comedic actor Jack Oakie portrayed a bloated Benzino Napaloni, the Dictator of Bacteria, obviously intended as Benito Mussolini. Einstein thought that the British actor Henry Daniell could have been even more rodent-like in his portrayal of Garbitsch, the Goebbels character.

In a pivotal scene, Garbitsch tells Hynkel that, "Within two years, the world will be under your thumb."

Hynkel picks up a globe of the world, which is actually a balloon.

"My world," he says gloriously. He spins the globe, smacks it toward the ceiling, and kicks it gracefully in a silent ballet that ends with him holding it in both arms until it explodes in his face.

Yes, the symbolism!

"Brilliant," Einstein whispered to Chaplin. "Wait for the end," Chaplin said.

In the film's final moments, Chaplin's forlorn Jewish barber is mistaken for Hynkel and vice versa. In the dictator's uniform, the barber addresses the people. Looking directly into the camera, Chaplin steps out of character and becomes everyman, his eyes warm and pleading.

"Life can be free and beautiful, but we have lost the way," he says. "Hate has goose-stepped us into misery and bloodshed. Dictators free themselves, but they enslave the people. Now let us fight to free the world, to do away with national barriers—to do away with greed, with hate and intolerance. Let us fight for a world of reason, a world where science and progress will lead to all men's happiness. In the name of democracy, let us all unite!"

The monologue went on for nearly five minutes. Einstein was transfixed, but Chaplin squirmed in his seat, clearly afraid that this unorthodox ending would land on the critics' plates like a stale bagel.

The lights came up, and the critics turned off their penlights, closed their spiral notebooks, and made their way up the aisle. "If they look at me, it's a good sign. If they look away, the picture will lay an egg, and my career is in the crapper," Chaplin said.

"It's a wonderful picture, and I loved every moment of it," Einstein said.

None of the critics met Chaplin's gaze, and he groaned. Most talked among themselves or were silent. The straggler was a handsome man of about thirty-five in a herringbone jacket, white shirt, and dark tie. "Bosley Crowther of the *Times*," Chaplin whispered. "A Princeton man who considers himself a film scholar, whatever that is. He hands out compliments as if they're gold doubloons."

Crowther gave a friendly nod as he approached, and Chaplin, unable to contain himself, blurted out, "I have this sinking feeling that you hated my speech."

"To my taste, a bit maudlin, not to mention quite long," Crowther said.

Chaplin squeezed his eyes shut. He steeled himself for a horrendous review and wondered if he would ever see a dollar of the $1.5 million of his own money he sank into the picture. "And I suppose, Mr. Crowther, you will use the word 'maudlin' in your review."

"Near the end. It's a minor point."

"And the beginning of the review?"

"Come, now, Mr. Chaplin. You'll have to spend your nickel like everyone else."

Crowther took two more steps, then stopped. "Oh, blast it. Your first picture in four years and a rather unconventional one, plus the first time you've talked on the screen. No wonder you're nervous."

Crowther looked left and right as if to see if anyone was watching, then opened his notepad and read aloud. "*The Great Dictator* is a truly superb accomplishment by a truly great artist—and from my point of view—perhaps the most significant film ever produced." He smiled and continued up the aisle.

Chaplin let out a long breath and said, "So, Albert, I guess my career isn't over."

Einstein laughed. "My dear friend, this film will outlive us both."

Chaplin gave him a quizzical look.

"Fifty years from now, one hundred years from now, people will watch and learn from it. So hard for you to see, Charlie, but your art is immortal."

81
PROFESSOR MELVIA ROBINSON

December 15, 1953 - Philadelphia, Pennsylvania,
Horn & Hardart Automat

Snow flurries swirled on Chestnut Street. Taxis honked their horns. City buses squealed and whooshed as drivers hit the air brakes. A police siren wailed, and pedestrians clutched their coats around their necks against the wind.

Inside the Horn & Hardart Automat, it was warm, and the large dining area bustled with the chatter of customers and the clatter of plates. It was a mixed crowd of well-dressed downtown business workers, construction laborers, students, Main Line residents who took the train to the city, ladies who lunch, and out-of-town visitors.

Melvia Robinson insisted on paying for lunch, and she had a purse filled with coins to prove it. Now twenty-eight, Melvia was a tall, willowy woman with a degree in chemistry from Berkeley and a master's in physics from MIT, where her studies concentrated on both thermodynamics and general relativity. She wore a navy skirt suit with a white bow-tie, silk blouse, seamed stockings, and navy pumps. She could be taken for a lawyer or an aide to the mayor. But she was an assistant professor on the tenure track at Lincoln University, the nation's first degree-granting historically Black institution of higher learning.

She put two quarters and two dimes into the slot, the window opened, and she took a plate of stewed chicken on a biscuit with spinach to her guest. "Thank you, dear," Albert Einstein said. He waited for Melvia to return to the table with her breaded veal cutlet in a tomato sauce with macaroni, seventy-five cents, roll and butter included.

Einstein, now seventy-four, carefully forked his chicken so as not to slop sauce onto his mustache. He had dressed in his best pin-striped charcoal suit for the day, but he had lost weight and appeared shrunken to Melvia. She also noticed he had missed an area of whiskers under his chin. But he still had a twinkle in his eye, and her affection for him had only grown over the years. She knew that Chaplin, along with his wife, Oona, and their children, were in the process of moving to an estate on Lake Geneva in Switzerland. He had chosen exile rather than fight the federal government's efforts to ban his reentry to the country after a European trip.

"Have you heard from Mr. Chaplin?" Melvia asked.

"He seems happy enough. But if Charlie is an 'undesirable' in this country, what have we come to? We defeated fascism only to live with a paranoid fear of communism."

"So hard to believe, but the Red Scare has made us afraid of our neighbors," Melvia said.

Einstein was cutting into his chicken when he said, "Do you think I made a mistake back in thirty-nine?"

"The letter you wrote to FDR?"

"Leo Szilard wrote it, but I signed it, so I am culpable, to be sure."

"Once Hahn and Strassmann split the atom, you had no choice. If the world's most famous pacifist advocates a nuclear program, how could FDR refuse?"

"But I never imagined Hiroshima or Nagasaki. Now we are in a race with the Soviet Union for the biggest bombs. Where will this end?"

They ate in silence for a few moments, and then Einstein said, "I am very proud of you, Melvia. I hope you know that."

"I thought you might be disappointed that I didn't become an astronomer or a theoretical physicist."

"What? And look for a four-leaf clover all your life? You affect the lives of real people every day. Young people. Our future. Now, what do you want for dessert? I will share the warm mince pie with you if you don't tell my doctors."

82
THE BIG CHILL

Lincoln University, Chester County, Pennsylvania

Ninety minutes after finishing coffee and dessert, Einstein sat in the back row of a classroom on the Lincoln University campus and watched Melvia Robinson lecture to her physics students. There were about two dozen sophomores and juniors in the class, all Black, a few more men than women, and they studiously scribbled notes as Melvia spoke.

"The entropy of a system always increases over time," she said. "Even the universe is not immune to the second law of thermodynamics. It, too, becomes more disordered and random with time."

On a smaller scale, and in a different context, it sounds just like our world, Einstein thought.

"Entropy also tells us that, as the universe continues to expand and cool, all stars will eventually burn out, all matter will be evenly distributed, and there will be no more transfers of energy from one form to another."

One student, a young woman in a blue and orange Lincoln sweater, raised her hand. "Professor Robinson, are you saying that entropy predicts the end of the universe?"

"It does, in what is sometimes called the 'Big Chill,'" Melvia said. She smiled. "But you'll all have your degrees long before that happens, some trillions or even quadrillions of years from now."

The students chuckled, and Melvia continued, keeping her lecture on point.

Einstein smiled contentedly as he listened. Despite the troubles of the time, something about this day gave him hope. He was proud that he could call himself an American, having taken the oath thirteen years earlier. Proud of dear Melvia Robinson, for what a woman she had become! He remembered her all those years ago, sitting cross-legged on the floor of Chaplin's library, reading whatever caught her fancy. He remembered, too, the day Melvia sat in his classroom at Caltech, attentively listening, their positions reversed now, and tears came to his eyes.

Young people! Maybe there is hope for this world!

After the class, the students gathered around Einstein and peppered him with questions about gravity, time travel, and whether it was true that he had been less than a stellar student. His answer was the same as it had been to Melvia sixteen years earlier, and several times in between. "As a student, I was no Einstein."

The students laughed. One had a Kodak Brownie camera, and the students took turns posing with the famed scientist. Later, Melvia accompanied Einstein to the auditorium, where he gave a lecture to the faculty about his hope for nuclear disarmament.

"I was heartened one week ago to listen to President Eisenhower at the United Nations speaking about the need to curb the arms race and devote nuclear power to peaceful endeavors," he began. "The president said, and I quote, that 'the miraculous inventiveness of man shall not be dedicated to death but consecrated to life.'"

Einstein turned toward the faculty members and mused, "Maybe it takes a general who has seen the horrors of war to advise his countrymen to beat their swords into plowshares."

Cracking a smile, he continued, "Now I'm sorry I voted for Adlai Stevenson."

When he concluded, the audience gave Einstein a standing ovation. Melvia invited him to join her and some friends, saying they were going to paint the town, as much as that was possible in tiny Oxford, Pennsylvania. He hugged her and said, "I have a greater chance of riding a wild mustang than any town painting."

83
HOME

Princeton, New Jersey

It was nearly midnight when Einstein stepped off the Pennsylvania Railroad train at Princeton Junction. He had liked trains for as long as he could remember, especially in those distant days of thought experiments, when he conjured two bolts of lightning striking a moving train and the different perceptions of observers in different locations. But he was tired this night, and the jostling train irritated his stomach. He had been diagnosed with an abdominal aorta aneurysm that would almost certainly kill him, if a city bus didn't run over him first.

"You're living on borrowed time," his doctor had told him while puffing on a Chesterfield.

"Aren't we all?" Einstein replied.

He would continue scribbling equations he hoped would create a theoretical framework to describe all the fundamental forces of nature in a single, unified manner. But he doubted he would live long enough to master that monumental task.

His thoughts returned to President Eisenhower. In April 1945, as Supreme Allied Commander, he accompanied the 89th Infantry into one of Buchenwald's death camps. Witnessing the carnage, Eisenhower cabled Washington and insisted that military aircraft be provided for government officials and journalists to see firsthand the evidence of the horrific crimes against humanity. That way, he told fellow generals, future generations could not dismiss what he had seen as propaganda.

Perhaps Eisenhower was just the man to lead this "unhappy country," Chaplin's term for the state of the USA. Einstein was more optimistic than his exiled friend. He believed that this big, crazy, wonderful country—the country that had welcomed both the striving young Brit and the fleeing Jewish scientist—might dabble in political extremism but would always return to a peaceful equilibrium.

A taxi drove him from the train station to the intersection of Alexander and Mercer Streets in Princeton. It was a three-block walk to his house, and he wanted to stretch his legs. He wore an ancient wool topcoat over his suit and a white scarf around his neck. A whistling wind stung his face with snowflakes. He wore no hat, and his wild hair was soon soaked, so he wrapped the scarf around his head. He did not mind the falling snow or the night chill, for it reminded him of his great fortune at having a warm bed, a full stomach, and a lifetime of work he loved and friends and family he cherished.

The wonder of it all!

How had this bored patent clerk unlocked the secrets of the universe...or at least some of them?

As the snow accumulated, the branches of the maple trees sparkled like diamonds in the glow of the streetlights. Climbing the steps to the porch of his modest two-story house, Einstein allowed his mind to drift to that night long ago at the premiere of Chaplin's *City Lights*.

The selflessness and sacrifices of the Tramp took on a new meaning. Surely, he knew that the beautiful girl, once her eyesight was restored, would not return his love. Yet he endured every hardship, suffered every indignity, to help her.

Was the Tramp a metaphor for America? Hardly beloved, but rising up to do what was right, what no one else would do, time and again.

To save the world!

As the president said just a week earlier, America's goal was to bring peace, happiness, and well-being to all souls. With that heartwarming thought, Einstein unlocked his front door, turned on the lights, and decided that hot tea—a good strong cuppa, the way Chaplin liked it—might be the perfect end to a glorious day.

AFTERWORD

Charlie Chaplin spent the last twenty-five years of his life at his estate in Corsier-sur-Vevey, Switzerland. The US government had banned him from reentering the country from England in 1952 on trumped-up morals charges and claims he was a communist sympathizer. Although his lawyers expressed confidence that they could prevail, Chaplin chose exile rather than a court battle. In his autobiography, Chaplin wrote that his friend Einstein, an "incurable sentimentalist," cried at the final scene of *City Lights*, as described in Chapter 1 of this novel. Chaplin's 1943 marriage to Oona O'Neill, mother of eight of his eleven children and thirty-five years his junior, lasted thirty-four years, until his death in 1977 at age eighty-eight.

Albert Einstein never discovered a unified theory ("theory of everything") that could explain all the fundamental forces of nature and all the particles of the universe. Neither has anyone else. The International Relief Association, which he founded in 1933, is still engaged in global humanitarian aid under the name International Rescue Committee. Einstein died in Princeton, New Jersey, in 1955 at age seventy-six. In tribute, President Dwight Eisenhower said, "No man was more modest in the possession of the power that

AFTERWORD

is knowledge or more sure that power without wisdom is deadly."

Georgia Ann Robinson was, as portrayed, the first Black female LAPD officer. She founded the Sojourner Truth Home, a women's shelter, and was active with the NAACP. Attacked by a prisoner while on duty, she was seriously injured and lost her eyesight, leading to her retirement. She died in 1961 in Los Angeles at age eighty-two.

Melvia Robinson, her daughter, is a fictional character.

William Dudley Pelley was, as portrayed, the founder of the Silver Legion of America fascist paramilitary group. While much of the dialogue attributed to him is supported by the historical record, many of his actions in the novel are fictional. As portrayed, he had been a Hollywood screenwriter with more than a dozen credits. When he was on trial for sedition and fomenting insurrection within the US military during World War II, his lawyer accidentally referred to him as "Mr. Hitler." Pelley was convicted and served eight years in prison. He died in Indiana in 1965 at age seventy-five.

Georg Gyssling was, as portrayed, Germany's consul in Los Angeles in the 1930s and was brutally efficient at censoring Hollywood films for German distribution. A complicated figure, he also befriended Albert Einstein and adored Charlie Chaplin's films, including *The Great Dictator*, which ridiculed Hitler, whom Gyssling despised. He also secretly funneled information about domestic fascist groups and classified German activities to American authorities. He died in Spain in 1965 at age seventy-one.

Charles Lindbergh considered himself to be neither antisemitic nor a Nazi sympathizer. Yet his public statements and conduct called both into question. (His dialogue in the German consulate party scene is taken largely from his speeches). At the invitation of the Reich, he made several trips to Germany in the run-up to World War II, inspecting aircraft factories, meeting with government officials, and otherwise keeping busy. (He fathered

AFTERWORD

at least three out-of-wedlock children on visits after the war). Lindbergh died in Kipahulu, Hawaii, in 1974 at seventy-two.

Jimmy Mitchell, the courageous reporter, is a fictional character, although the *Los Angeles Sentinel*, an African American newspaper founded in 1933, is real and still in business.

Luisa Moreno, Mitchell's fiancée, is likewise a fictional character, although Antonio Moreno, her uncle in the novel, was indeed a silent movie star in the 1920s.

Douglas Fairbanks was, as portrayed, one of Chaplin's closest friends and a neighbor on Summit Drive in Beverly Hills. Excellent athletes, Fairbanks and Chaplin frequently played tennis. A legendary partier and reveler, Fairbanks died at fifty-six in Santa Monica, California in 1939.

Joseph Mankiewicz was, as portrayed, the twenty-eight-year-old producer of *Three Comrades*, the film slashed to ribbons by Georg Gyssling. Also as portrayed, **F. Scott Fitzgerald** adapted Erich Maria Remarque's novel for the screen but was rewritten by Mankiewicz and others. In back-to-back years (1950–1951), Mankiewicz won Oscars as best director and best adapted screenplay for *A Letter to Three Wives* and *All About Eve*. He died in Bedford, New York, in 1993 at eighty-three.

Magda and Joseph Goebbels were loyal Nazis to the end. The end being May 1, 1945, when Magda, age forty-three, poisoned their six children with cyanide, and she and Joseph, age forty-seven, committed suicide in the Chancellery garden in Berlin. In a letter to her adult son Harald, a POW of the Allies, she wrote: "The world that comes after the Führer and national socialism is not any longer worth living in and therefore I took the children with me."

James "Two Gun" Davis was, as portrayed, LAPD Chief in the 1930s and was widely regarded to be corrupt to the core, accepting payoffs from brothels and gambling operations of organized crime. He formed a "Red Squad" to hunt communists and used its powers against union members on strike. Stationed at the Nevada and

AFTERWORD

Arizona borders, his "Bum Brigade" forcibly turned back "Okies" and other transients who attempted to enter California. Davis also sanctioned violence against political reformers. He died in Helena, Montana in 1949 at age sixty.

Senator Ernest Lundeen of Minnesota, who appears in one gluttonous scene at the Nazi consulate, was, as portrayed, on the payroll of the Reich. He accepted bribes from a Nazi spy who also wrote speeches for him. Lundeen died at age sixty-two in the mysterious crash of a commercial airliner in 1940. Also on board and killed were two FBI employees and a federal prosecutor.

Operation Hollywood: The plot by American fascist groups in the 1930s to kill Jews and overthrow the US government has been documented in several nonfiction books. One of the real-life heroes was Leon L. Lewis, a courageous Los Angeles lawyer and a founder of the Anti-Defamation League, who ran an undercover operation to expose the plots.

"This daring group of men and women uncovered a series of Nazi plots to kill the city's Jews and to sabotage the nation's military installations. Plans existed for hanging twenty Hollywood actors and power figures, including Al Jolson, Eddie Cantor, Charlie Chaplin, Louis B. Mayer, and Samuel Goldwyn; for driving through Boyle Heights and machine-gunning as many Jewish residents as possible; for fumigating Jewish homes with cyanide; and for blowing up defense installations and seizing munitions from National Guard armories on the day the Nazis planned to launch their American putsch." —Ross, Steven J., *Hitler in Los Angeles: How Jews Foiled Nazi Plots Against Hollywood and America,* New York: Bloomsbury, 2017.

ACKNOWLEDGEMENTS

For years, my wife, Marcia Silvers, has graciously allowed me to pilfer transcripts and briefs from her criminal cases—she's a lawyer, not a defendant—for my Jake Lassiter series of legal thrillers. This time, she insisted I come up with my own plot, and, surprisingly enough, it turned out well...with some help from my friends.

My thanks to the legendary Hollywood producer Gerald W. Abrams and the crackerjack wordsmiths Jacqueline Winspear, Ed Zuckerman, and Lee Goldberg for their encouragement and insightful editorial insights.

Over the past thirty-five years, I've worked with many publishers, but my best experience has been with the sharp and savvy women of Amphorae Publishing Group: Lisa Miller, Kristina Makansi, Laura Robinson, and Stacey Walker. I'm also indebted to cover designer Asya Blue and the uber-talented video production team of Meagan Adele Lopez and Sophie Lamont of The Lady Who Productions, along with motion graphics guru Lizzy Platt. Thanks as well to foreign rights agent Whitney Lee.

Wiley Saichek, my longtime publicity wizard, and marketing dynamo Carol Fitzgerald deserve credit for bringing this book to your attention. Thanks also to Bob Marshall, Kristen Weber, and Penina Lopez for their keen early reads and to Daniel Harmon at Brilliance Audio.

Additional advice came from Wendy Levine-Sachs, Carmen Finestra, Lauren Dunlap, Steven Booth, and of course, Marcia Silvers, who valiantly read several drafts. Special mention goes to Michael Levine who lent his baritone to the video trailer and to Stuart Grossman for his unflagging encouragement. Finally, without the indefatigable efforts of ace agent Kimberley Cameron, to whom the book is dedicated, none of this would have been possible.

ABOUT THE AUTHOR

The author of twenty-four novels, Paul Levine won the John D. MacDonald Fiction Award and has been nominated for the Edgar, Macavity, International Thriller, Shamus, and James Thurber prizes. The international bestseller, *To Speak for the Dead*, which introduced readers to linebacker-turned-lawyer Jake Lassiter, was named one of the top mysteries of the year by the *Los Angeles Times*. His novel, *Bum Rap*, reached #1 on Amazon's bestseller list. He also writes the critically acclaimed *Solomon vs. Lord* series of legal capers. *Midnight Burning* marks the first of his Einstein-Chaplin series. A former trial lawyer, he also wrote twenty episodes of the CBS military drama JAG and co-created the Supreme Court drama *First Monday* starring James Garner and Joe Mantegna. He is a member of Penn State's Society of Distinguished Alumni and graduated, with honors, from the University of Miami School of Law. He lives in Santa Barbara, CA. Visit his website at https://www.paul-levine.com or follow him on Facebook at facebook.com/PaulLevineAuthorPage/ and on X: @Jake_Lassiter.